# A
# Single
# Captive
# Spark

# ALSO BY EMBERLY ASH

## Secrets of the Faerie Crown

*Crown of Earth and Sky*

*Throne of Air and Darkness*

*Court of Vines and Vipers*

*Queen of Blood and Vengeance*

## The Covenants of Velora

*The Frost Witch*

*The Halfling Prince*

# A
# Single
# Captive
# Spark

EMBERLY
ASH

47N⬤RTH

Published by 47North, Seattle

www.apub.com

Amazon, the Amazon logo, and 47North are trademarks of Amazon.com, Inc., or its affiliates.

EU product safety contact:
Amazon Media EU S. à r.l.
38, avenue John F. Kennedy, L-1855 Luxembourg
amazonpublishing-gpsr@amazon.com

ISBN-13: 9781662537370 (paperback)
ISBN-13: 9781662537387 (digital)

Cover design by Shasti O'Leary Soudant
Cover image: © Alvin Huang, © fotograzia, © Remigiusz Gora / Getty

Printed in the United States of America

*To the newly awakened.*
*May we never be fooled again.*

# Chapter 1

## Fionna

*Irska has been alone for as long as I can remember. And my father before me and his father before him. When magic fell, the rest of Eerin abandoned us. Left us to the humans and their bloody ways. Can you believe the humans were refugees in the beginning? They came across the sea "looking for farmable land," they said. They'd come from war and sought a peaceful life. A lie, all of it. Oh, they started off peaceful enough. First, they took the land no one else wanted. Then, when the bad years came, they used their gold to buy the land the rest of us couldn't afford to keep. And suddenly, they owned it all—we were the refugees. Beggars in our own land. My father, his father before him. We were the ones who decided not to take it anymore. We made the Rebels into what they are today. We made the first fireballs. We were the ones who decided to punish them. Not just the nobles up in their castle. All the humans. All of them are responsible. They all deserve to die.*

*—Baris Beacom, Síofran Rebel Army*

For as long as I can remember, I've been called lucky.

Lucky that I was taken to the castle after my parents' gruesome death, rather than relegated to one of the orphanages on the outskirts of Irska.

Lucky that the young princess took a liking to me, selecting me from among a crowd of pitiful human children, newly orphaned and lodged in the castle for mere days as a show of goodwill by the Irskan nobles. I was lucky that the young princess's parents denied her nothing, even at the age of six.

Lucky, lucky, lucky.

But I did not feel lucky as I stood knee deep in horse manure and rotting leaves.

The master gardener might call it fertilizer, but I called it what it was—shit. I was climbing through shit, trampling plants with every step, knowing that every single crunch underfoot was one less cup of frostbloom tea. The gardener was married to the tea master.

Crushed plants. Angry gardener. No frostbloom tea.

The next week would be torturous without it to calm the ever-present beast of anxiety in my chest.

But not as torturous as today would be if I didn't return with one of the precious golden apples. On this particular day, the needs of the moment outweighed the discomforts of the morrow. Our survival depended on my ability to constantly calculate those two odds against each other.

I paused to assess my progress. I'd made it through the protective ring of roses the master gardener had transplanted a few days ago—his latest attempt to secure the king's coveted golden apples. But if I could get through the briars with only a handful of scrapes to show for it, so could whoever—or whatever—had been stealing the apples for the last fortnight. The court was obsessed with the mystery of the disappearing apples, both abovestairs and below. Maybe it was the gossip that had inspired Princess Aurelle to ask for one. Not from her father, who would have surely denied the request, but from me. An expendable servant.

The maids in the laundry whispered that it was a bad omen. The golden apples were one of the last vestiges of magic in Irska, and the only kind we humans could access. One apple, and the eater was granted one hour of elemental power. Pitiful, compared to the sort of powers attributed to the Síofran by the history books. That's what I would have thought, if I'd bothered to think about those rumors at all.

Whoever was stealing the golden apples must have been mustering a force to overthrow the king. The changeling rebels, surely. Though which group, the whispers never said. Síofran Rebel Army or Síofran Liberation Corps, it made no difference to me. If they overthrew the king, our protection would disappear.

Perhaps I should stop by the kitchen, speak with the master gardener, find a way to tell him gently that the protections he'd planted were ineffectual, help him safeguard the apples and thereby the king—

*Not. My. Problem.*

We had survived for ten years by keeping our heads down, not meddling above our station. But Princess Aurelle was my problem, and if I disappointed her, my luck would run out. Quickly.

Because it wasn't luck that had kept us alive for the past decade. Luck was a privilege not afforded to lowborn servants. One careful choice, one belabored calculation after another. But let them call it *luck*, if it kept them from looking too closely. Existing on the fringes was the best way to survive.

I ignored the stinging in my calves and focused on the trunk of the tree. The thorns of the roses were sharper than average, bred by the master gardener over decades to be so, but a little blood was inconsequential. Even the tears to the edge of my fine silk skirt didn't really matter. Aurelle would cast off another soon, and I'd alter it for my more generous figure. I'd need two gowns, realistically. Aurelle was as slight as her mother.

Gods above . . . *Dresses?* I needed to focus on those golden fecking apples.

I'd made it through the protective ring of bushes and the thick manure that supplied them. Another step, and my feet would tangle in the roots of the tree. Another defense, this one belonging to the tree itself. If I even skimmed the bark with the sole of my shoe, one of those roots would rise up and twist around my ankle. My thigh. Pull me down and hold me prone in the muck until some castle guard found me and dragged me before the king.

Would Aurelle defend me? Explain that she had been the one to wake in the night craving a precious golden apple?

Only if I was lucky.

The lowest branches were only two feet above my head, but there was no way they would bear my weight. I cursed myself for the second serving of creamed potatoes I'd eaten at supper the night before. And the fried peaches with candied nuts the night before that.

Food, at least, was plentiful in the castle, and I had a weakness for it. Unlike the princess, who always sat across from me at mealtimes, I understood what it meant to be hungry.

My foot tapped soundlessly—and entirely against my will—in the thick shit mixture. Once, twice . . . or had I tapped it more times than that before noticing? Fecking hell. Before I could stop myself, I was starting again. One tap. Two taps. Three taps. Always three taps. Then I forced my foot to stillness. The thrum of my heart in my chest eased, just a fraction. Just enough to focus.

If I grabbed the lowest branch, it would snap and I'd crash to the ground, only to be ensnared in the roots of the tree. The first branch that would bear my weight was at least another foot higher. If I jumped and missed, my fate would be the same. Bad options, all.

My foot twitched against the ground. I held it firmly in place. I did not have time for more anxiety-induced compulsions. Aurelle would emerge from her bedroom soon, expecting a sliced golden apple to break her fast.

Sliced . . . The knife.

There was a small knife in my belt. I'd carried it with me since my parents' death. Not a family heirloom, nor anything special, really. There had been no heirlooms to recover. Fireballs destroyed everything in their wake, leaving no bodies to be used as trophies.

For the briefest second, I imagined driving the knife into the tree trunk and using it to swing myself up to the safety of sturdier branches.

A crisp laugh cold enough to compete with the frostbitten air fell from my lips. Those sorts of maneuvers were the purview of the Peace Guard, not orphaned servant women.

But if the knife was my only asset, I'd use it. I tapped my foot as I considered—three times—then drove the small knife into the trunk with all the considerable weight of my body behind it. Not high up, to use as a handhold, but low—just above the threat of those roots. A foothold.

In the distance, still far away and outside the orchard, voices sliced through the early-morning fog. I did not have time to test the knife to see if it would hold my weight. I'd considered my options, made a calculation, and now I had to trust in it. My methodology had kept us alive for a decade. I would not fail today.

I stepped up onto the knife, careful to avoid the roots, and reached. I let one hand skim the lowest branch, just enough to give me balance as I reached for the safety of the sturdier one above it. The voices were closer now, probably Peace Guards patrolling the castle grounds. While I knew many of them by name, and most of them by sight, I did not fancy a conversation. Who knew whether Aurelle actually had leave from her father to eat the golden apples. There was no telling if this was a spontaneous request or one she'd been working up to for years. And if she did not have permission, I knew who the scapegoat would be.

Ten years. I'd kept us alive. I would not be felled by the whims of a spoiled princess.

I got my hand around the branch, my palm now singing a stinging chorus with the cuts on my calves, and pushed off the dagger with all my strength. I caught a branch beside the first. Crunching my abdominal muscles tight, cursing my love of cheese biscuits, I scrambled up the trunk. It wasn't graceful, but I managed to wedge my foot into the apex where a large branch shot off from the trunk. Each movement more ungainly than the last, I began to climb.

Even in the dark of a predawn winter morning, the treetop was thick with leaves. Magical fecking tree. The leaves scraped against my skin, leaving behind red scratches that would garner attention once I returned to the castle proper. But at least they provided cover. The Peace Guards would not see me, no matter how close they came. Which meant I could focus on my task—an apple.

Whatever or whoever was stealing golden apples from the king's orchard, they had not stripped this tree. My breath scissored in and out, bitter cold slicing my throat with each inhale. When I finally let myself pause, my back wedged against the trunk, branches bracing my legs and arms, I saw them. Four perfect golden apples.

They might have been ornaments, crafted from metal rather than pale flesh. My royal-adjacent education told me that inside, they looked no different from any other apple. It was only the peel that gleamed that bright, ornamental gold. But one had to eat every bit—flesh, peel, and seeds—in order to reap the magical gift within. What elemental power did Aurelle intend to wield? Probably something stupid, like ice. Ice in winter. She'd use it to build fanciful sculptures in the garden or fashion herself a crown more ornate than the ones her father let her wear.

Nothing useful. How many fires could she light in the peace villages with a magical flame that would spare the poor an hour of wasted fuel? How many crops could she raise from the winter garden to feed those same hungry souls?

Such considerations would never enter Aurelle's mind. And maybe I was just as bad as she, because they didn't enter mine, either.

For a second, I let myself imagine it. Sinking my teeth into the soft flesh, upper and lower jaws coming together against the resistance of perfectly ripe fruit. The flavor was rumored to be richer than any cream, sweeter than any cake. I'd eat every bite, even the bitter core. And with the elemental magic promised? I would use the wind to lighten our footsteps. To make us faster than any Peace Guard or Síofran Rebel. I would get us out of Irska, use the wind to fill the sails of a ship, to carry us across the sea to the mainland, where humans and changelings did not have to coexist.

But I'd need more than one apple to make it happen. And just stealing one—fetching, not stealing—was already making my head spin.

I never let myself get caught in daydreams. There was never the time.

It must have been the cold beginning to get to me. Or the exertion from climbing. I was not used to it. The princess was demanding, but usually only in the emotionally taxing sort of way, rather than the physical sense. The cold certainly did not help the stinging cuts along my calves.

I needed to get out of the tree and back into the relative safety of the castle. A quick survey allowed me to pinpoint one golden apple glinting a mere two feet above my head, but a tangle of thick branches blocked an easy grasp. Another, at the end of the branch where I'd stretched my left leg, was the better option. Farther, but the way was largely clear and the branch thick enough that I could shimmy my entire body along it.

My cloak caught halfway along the branch. *Clear* was relative. There were still sharp little branches protruding from the larger one, and they tugged at the thick velvet. I pushed on, knowing the cloak was rubbish now anyway. But then I couldn't move, not another inch.

The thicker threads of embroidery in the front of the wide, decorative collar were tangled around a little branch. I tugged again, reached out for the apple, but I was still too far away. Tear the cloak or snap the branch; it should have been an inconsequential decision. My cloak, face, and legs were already in a sorry state. What was one more tear? I started to heave myself forward, gritting my teeth hard in expectation of the rip of fabric and string.

But my next breath froze within me, ice colder than Irska's frigid winter surging through my veins.

I was no longer alone.

"It's too fecking cold to be out here," the youngest Irskan prince groused. The whiny one. I knew his voice almost as well as his twin's. When they'd been small, they rarely parted. Prince Trinar cultivated adoration. Once Aurelle's attention had begun to linger on his friends, he stopped spending time with his twin sister.

Three quick exhales, muffled as they filled a set of clasped hands. "There is no record of any beast that feeds on golden apples." Odinar. The quiet one. He preferred the library to the training courtyard.

"This is Peace Guard business," Trinar whined. Even at sixteen years, he was still a child. Like his sister. But Trinar did not merit my concern. If there were two princes in the orchard, then the third . . .

"Gripe as you will. I will enjoy peeling away the traitor's flesh."

Prince Vainar. I pressed my eyes closed, tighter and tighter, until my face was so tense that the creases burned.

He'd had a fascination with flesh since childhood. It had begun with slicing the serving girls for fun, to see how much skin he'd have to cut away before the blood began to gush. After adolescence, his predilections had turned sexual. For many years, I'd escaped his notice, no more than a cipher in his younger sister's household. But once I'd fully blossomed into womanhood, his eyes found me.

My thighs clenched together involuntarily, instinctually.

Aurelle hated Vainar. She did not want her playthings to be scarred. But if he found me out here, without her protection . . .

*You are safe. You are safe. You are safe.*

*Calm as a lake. Strong as a tree. I bend but don't break.*

I needed frostbloom tea. The chanting would hold the monster in my chest at bay temporarily, but not forever. It would overwhelm me. When it did, I must be back in the castle. Tucked away where no one could see my weakness.

*You are safe. You are safe. You are safe.*

Gradually, the rushing in my head cleared enough to make out the princes' voices once more.

". . . as Father commands. If the Peace Guards were capable, they'd have the traitor in chains already," Vainar said.

I knew if I opened my eyes, if I looked down, I'd see the glint of his dagger, always in his palm, always ready.

So I kept them closed.

Trinar's voice floated up through the foliage. "It has to be a change-ling. Those Rebel Army bastards—"

"Have not had access to their magic for three hundred years." Vainar snorted. His disdain for the fairer sex extended to his younger brother, it seemed. Or maybe it was just for all living beings.

Odinar's voice was softer, but I was still able to make out his words. "It could be a rogue Defender, trying to get an edge on the Rebels or Libs."

A decent guess. The Irskan Defense Force may work outside of official Irskan law, but they were rarely punished for it. Maybe one of them had gambled that even if they were caught stealing a golden apple, the king would look the other way.

The princes' argument was muffled. I did not need to hear it. Irskan Defense Force, Síofran Rebel Army, Síofran Liberation Corps. The internal conflicts of Irska were not my problem. Get the apple, get back to the castle. Stay alive long enough to save the coin needed to buy us passage away from this cursed place.

Trinar huffed his breath again. "You've inspected the bloody orchard. Can we go inside now?"

Metal sang. Odinar cried something unintelligible. Snow and ice crunched. Trinar yelped as he fell into the rosebush.

My eyes popped open. I wasn't overly fond of Trinar, but Aurelle would be upset if he were injured, and she was less predictable when upset. But I couldn't see well enough through the tangle of tree branches to tell what was happening.

But I could see the city.

It was just light enough to see the winding roads of Irska sprawled out below the castle. A low fog snaked between the buildings, indiscriminate between the human and changeling neighborhoods. Peace villages, they were called, officially. But there was nothing peaceful about Irska. Violence and poverty were close conspirators, and the changelings' obsession with the former had driven them into the throes of the latter.

They did not call themselves changelings. Instead, they claimed a derivation of the goddess who'd first gifted them magic—the Síofran.

I had not seen any of it for myself. After the explosion that killed my parents, and my extraction to the castle, I'd never ventured into Irska again. Never needed, never wanted, never dared.

The sounds of the princes squabbling below faded away, replaced by memory.

*My sister's squalls, so much noise from such an impossibly small body. My parents' laughter, proclamations of her good health. Celebration. As if they did not already struggle to fill our bellies. As if they would not be dead in a fortnight.*

I closed my eyes again.

*Here and now. That is all that matters.* Survive one moment and then the next. String enough of them together and you have an hour. A year. Then a decade.

I dared not tap my foot against the branch. But within the safe confines of my shoes, my toes tapped against the soft soles. One time, two times, three. My heartbeat slowed fractionally, the anxiety loosening its hold.

The voices of the princes were fading. Whatever their plan to catch the intruder stealing the king's golden apples, it did not involve lingering beneath my tree.

When all sounds had faded, I opened my eyes, wrenched my cloak free of the claws of the branch, and began to move. It would be fully light soon, and slipping back into the castle would become impossible. Inch by agonizing inch, I dragged myself along the thick branch. Ignoring the slight cracking sound it made as I moved. Refusing to acknowledge that it was thinning out faster than I'd estimated. Another foot and I'd have the fecking apple.

I reached out to the next branch over to more evenly distribute my weight. But just as my arm stretched, moving across the empty space, the world began to shift. Just for a second, the world spun. I was up too high. My body was moving uncontrollably. I was reaching for the next branch, reaching for the apple—not reaching.

Falling.

Crashing through branches and leaves, my arm raked down the trunk, flaying open my flesh. My ankle caught in the crook of two branches, slowing my fall just long enough for my body to pass it, wrench it free, and send tendrils of white-hot pain up my calf.

I landed outside the ring of roots. Just beyond their threatening reach. I earned more scrapes from the rose thorns. Yet as I pushed up onto my hands, I found my body more or less whole. Aching, but whole. A miracle. A blessing from the gods. But the real blessing was what I'd managed to grab on my way down.

There, no sign of bruising where my fingertips dug into the glimmering skin, was one perfect golden apple.

Maybe I was exactly what they said—lucky.

# Chapter 2

## Fionna

*The changelings are nurtured on violence from the cradle, so our own training begins early. Many of us were given to the Peace Guard as toddlers. Second sons, mostly. It is considered an act of faith to the Crown for nobles to give up their spares for the protection of Irska. It's not so bad. The barracks are on the castle grounds, so I can still see my family. I grew up in those barracks, learned discipline. But it's the recruits who come in when they're older who are the most dangerous. Teenagers, orphaned by the changelings. For me, the guards like me, punishing the changelings is as mundane as porridge. But for the older ones, it is different. They enjoy the killing.*

*—Aengus Hennigar, Peace Guard*

Every step toward the castle was torture. My ankle cried out as it bore my weight, but I did not let the limp show. No weakness. Even alone on the snowy grounds, early as it was, I knew there were eyes upon me. There always were.

I entered the castle through the Mountain Gate, the most direct path to Princess Aurelle's quarters and the one she always used when walking or riding on the grounds. Nothing unusual about the princess's companion entering the castle from an early-morning walk.

Hopefully, whatever eyes watched me were too far away to discern just how sorry the state of my cloak was.

Through the Mountain Gate's small courtyard, into the welcoming heat of the inner bailey. I hung my ruined cloak on a peg with the other miscellaneous winter gear left behind by Peace Guards, knights, other servants. I'd come back for it later.

I checked my appearance as best I could without a mirror, smoothing my hands over my hair and gown. My fingers snagged on the belt at my waist, on the little knife now safely back in its sheath. I dragged one fingernail across the leather-wrapped hilt, letting the familiar texture soothe me.

Each step into the castle brought more sound, more light, more scents. The fortress had been slumbering when I ventured out, but now it was fully awake.

"The queen awoke in a fit again. They'll try to hide it from the king, mark me . . ."

". . . another fireball, just last evening. A dozen dead, they say."

"Get out of my way, you fecking beast!"

I sidestepped the dog, scrambling away from the booted toe swinging in its direction. But I was not as agile as the beast, and suddenly I was face-to-face with the man who'd done the swinging.

"Well met, my lady." Garen bowed low, a wide sweep that took up the entire passageway and sent several servants scuttling out of his way.

The smile on my face wasn't entirely forced; I'd once held affection for Garen. Before he'd become a Peace Guard and started kicking dogs. He was an orphan of changeling brutality, like me. But he'd been older—a teenager—when he found his way into service in the castle by way of an aunt in the laundry. A sweet boy arrived, but the years had made him a hard man. Something closer to a cruel one. Cruelty was a prerequisite for joining the Peace Guard.

Yet no matter how many times I tried to gently reinforce the distance between us, Garen always seemed to find me.

Give a man your virginity and he'll think he's entitled to your heart. No matter how many men warm your bed in the years to follow.

"Good morning to you, Guard Garen." I smiled, dipping my chin. "I see the Peace Guard has made you no less gallant."

If he caught the sarcasm, he didn't show it on his rough-hewn but handsome face.

"You'll always be a lady to me," he said, rising.

Which implied I'd been one at some point. But that was wrong, too. I was a servant. I'd always been a servant. The odds were, despite my endless efforts, that I always would be.

*No. Someday we will be free.*

Why was I wasting time making idle talk with Garen? A dismissal sprang to my lips, I stepped forward, and—

The torchlit lines of the corridor blurred around me. I blinked rapidly, trying to clear the fog, but it didn't help. The stone walls moved in a sinuous dance all around me.

I reached out a hand to steady myself. Garen took the motion for invitation. Stepped closer. But I was too dizzy to step away without falling. Fecking hell, was he going to try to kiss me right there in the corridor, with servants and guards all around—

"Fionna!" A shoulder-height black mass rocketed beneath Garen's outstretched arm and straight into my chest. If I hadn't been holding the wall already, I'd have fallen flat on my ass.

*Treasa.* The second half of the "us" that occupied my every calculation.

By the time I managed to peel her off me, Garen had retreated several feet, his blue-and-white cloak thrown back over his shoulders to avoid the thick layer of black that coated my sister's skin.

Saved by a soot-covered imp.

"Where have you been all morning? I lit the fire in your room, and your maid said you'd left in the middle of the night to get warm milk from the kitchens, but when I went there, no one had seen you, and then I had to go tend the fires in the east tower and—"

"Here I am," I interrupted. If I let her go on, I would never make it to Aurelle in time. Garen was already backing away. Wiser than I gave him credit for, maybe.

The world had stopped spinning. I had to eat something. The too-hot tea I'd slurped down in the predawn dark was not enough to sustain me, especially after this morning's exertions. The golden apple weighed heavily in my pocket.

But if there was any reason to delay, even if only a few seconds, it stood before me now.

"Have you eaten yet this morning?" I asked my younger sister, smoothing back a wavy black lock that had escaped over her forehead. My finger came away covered in soot. Treasa was a firestoker. Not the most auspicious of posts for a servant, but I'd maneuvered carefully to obtain it for her. Her duties were done by midmorning, and then she could attend lessons in the afternoon. She'd need to be able to read and write for the future I had planned for us, free of Irska and its bloody conflict.

Treasa made a face. "Have you?" she countered.

I was tempted to pull the golden apple from my pocket. But the fewer people who knew about how the princess had obtained her trophy, the better.

"I am going to breakfast with Princess Aurelle this very moment," I said. With one hand on a sooty shoulder, I eased my sister to the side. "Go eat before you tend any more fires."

"Cook gave me a yeast bun with ham this morning when I went in looking for you," Treasa admitted with a toothy smile. Despite the slight gap between her two front teeth, she was a beautiful girl. Young woman, really. She'd be thirteen this year.

"Off with you, then," I said, pushing a bit harder. "I shall find you when the princess takes her afternoon nap."

Treasa made a face—she would certainly have preferred if I did not check up on her lessons—but the crinkling quickly gave way to a smile. She followed the direction of my push, toward the kitchens, and left me alone.

Alone, but surrounded by a constant bustle of servants. I wiped the soot on the inside of my sleeve and continued on. At the end of the hall, the corridor split. Up the stairwell would take me to the main arteries of the castle, where Irskan nobles and royalty mingled. Down, to the servants' realm.

In the beginning, I'd hesitated. But a decade later, my steps were sure. Up I went.

I walked a strange line between servant and lady. As Aurelle's companion, I dined with the princess, attended balls, had received an excellent education. I might not own the lively black mare I rode when Aurelle wanted to go out on the grounds, but no one else rode him, either.

But everything I did was at the princess's pleasure. If she stopped bestowing her old gowns upon me, I'd have to spend my meager salary on silk or risk looking unworthy of standing at her side. If she woke in the night desiring a golden apple from the king's forbidden orchard, I could not question her too sharply. Though, as my ankle throbbed and the cuts along my legs and arms started to burn more insistently, I regretted not putting up more of an argument to her wild midnight request.

At least now that I'd entered the avenues of the castle occupied by the Irskan nobles, the cruel stone stairs were covered with a thick burgundy carpet. Up, up, up I climbed, holding back a wince with each step. Halfway up the second stairwell, I had to grab the balustrade for support as my head swam again. The pain was getting to me, merging with hunger and the beast of anxiety in my chest, beating against the restraints I tried to keep him in with every passing minute. Aurelle was surely awake. Maybe even at breakfast already.

*Keep. Going.*

Imagining Treasa's soot-covered face got me up the final flight of stairs. Someday that face would always be clean, lifted to the sun. Soon

I would have enough money to buy passage out of Irska and never look back. But only if I delivered that golden apple.

Evie was exiting the princess's suite as I arrived. She quirked an eyebrow, lowering her voice as she passed, arms laden with several dresses. Presumably for mending. "Your sister was looking for you," she whispered, darting a glance back over her shoulder to the still-closing doors.

Aurelle was already at breakfast, then.

Treasa's characterization of Evie as "my maid" was generous. We both attended Princess Aurelle, and we shared a room connected to hers. Sometimes, Evie helped me dress. Most of the time, we were coconspirators in surviving the princess's whims.

"She found me," I said, moving out of Evie's way. "All is well." As long as I got that golden apple to Aurelle.

I could see the questions lingering in Evie's face, but her arms were full and I could not dally. I nodded to the guards posted on each side of the princess's suite—regular castle guards, not Peace Guards—only to come up short as I nearly collided with a stout woman fleeing the rooms.

She clutched a half-drunk—or half-spilled—cup of tea to her bosom. But it was the look on her face that stilled my steps. Princess Aurelle's governess was as stoic as they came. If she was rattled—

"What happened to your face?"

I cringed. The branches had done more damage than I'd realized. Garen and Evie had been too polite to comment, Treasa too preoccupied with being almost-thirteen to notice.

I dug into my pocket at last. "The princess made a late-night request."

Bela blinked at the golden apple in my outstretched palm. From either side of the doors came two twin inhales—sharp, surprised. The guards did not comment. Bela did.

She pinched the bridge of her nose, exhaling a long sigh. "Sometimes I think that child is a changeling."

I huffed a soft chuckle—unlike me. Delirium again.

"Treason with your morning tea, Bela?" Though Aurelle would take more offense to the former insult—she was resolute that she was not a child, even though at sixteen she'd never set foot outside the castle grounds—the latter was enough for the Peace Guard to throw the old woman into the dungeons.

Flustered Bela might be, but not a fool. As she spoke, she nudged me back through the doors, into the princess's receiving room.

"Aye, well, if you've any care for me at all, don't leave me alone with her before I've had my morning cup," Bela said, sipping from her half-emptied teacup. Through the next set of doors, I could hear the clink of dishes. Breakfast was underway.

"I'd much rather have spent my morning wrapped up in blankets, sipping my tea, and listening to Aurelle complain," I replied, "than nearly falling to my death for a stupid apple."

I did not bother to restow said apple.

"Now who is speaking treason?" Bela lifted a brow as she settled into a wingback chair in the corner of the receiving room. Wherever she'd been escaping to when I arrived, she'd changed her mind. Probably because I was now here to take the brunt of Aurelle's complaints.

"I already drank my tea." I stilled the compulsion to wink. Winking? What was wrong with me? My stomach growled, and my head spun in time, the apple in my hand suddenly looking dangerously appealing.

I did not spare Bela another word. I pushed through the doors into the dining room, steeling myself for the reaction . . .

"You have it! Oh, you darling girl!" Aurelle squealed. She jumped to her feet, clapping her hands with all the excitement of a toddler. "Was it difficult to obtain? Your face looks a mess."

The words spilled out of her, a string of wildly interconnected thoughts that she neither expected nor wanted an actual response to. But I answered anyway. "My legs took the brunt of it, Your Highness."

Aurelle was uninterested.

"Quick, quick! Let's have it!" She shoved aside the egg-and-potato pie in front of her, nearly sending it off the table. A serving maid rushed forward, just catching the plate.

A new plate appeared before Aurelle could get another word out. I passed the apple off, a knife appeared, and the serving girl cut the fruit quickly, despite the nonstop fluttering of Aurelle's hands.

I waited only for her first bite before lowering myself into my customary chair across the round table.

Aurelle cleared her throat delicately. "The firestoker was looking for you."

I was focused on the spread of food. The spinning in my head was becoming difficult to ignore.

I selected a thick slice of bacon and a cheese scone, devouring the first and nibbling the second.

"My sister," I responded, keeping my words carefully flat. I did not offer Treasa's name. If Aurelle did not know it, all the better. I'd chosen a position for Treasa that kept her away from the auspices of any particular noble or royal. I could not help the position I'd been forced into. But anonymity protected Treasa.

Aurelle had already forgotten the inconsequential urchin who minded the fire in the mornings. She turned over a slice of apple in her hand, lifting it to the morning light now streaming through the windows.

"How extraordinary. It looks just like any other apple." She devoured another slice. And another.

I finished my scone. Sipped another cup of tea. Realized that the manure I'd crawled through had made it through my cloak and onto my gown. I needed to excuse myself to change. When Aurelle finished, she'd go into her dressing room to change out of her nightclothes. That would be my opportunity. With the apple gone and fresh clothing, all I needed was a salve from the infirmary for my cuts, and then all evidence of my morning excursion would be erased.

Except the apple was not gone.

The core remained.

I stilled the working of my jaw, a telltale sign of annoyance. A headache was forming between my eyes. I kept my hand flat on the table instead of reaching up to massage away the ache.

"You must eat the entire thing," I said with forced mildness.

Aurelle clucked her tongue. Then sighed dramatically. "That *is* how it works," she admitted. And then, a second later, "Honey!"

I blinked. "Honey?"

"Yes, honey! For the bitterness of the core." She clapped her hands again, pleased at her own cleverness. I did not let my eyes roll. I did cast them toward the serving maid positioned at the wall.

She jumped to attention. "Right away, Your Highness."

Aurelle's hands stilled. "No, Fionna will fetch it, won't you, dear? Fresh, from the hives. I like it fresh."

Fresh honey. Honey lasted centuries. That was its primary attraction as a food source. The hives were on the other side of the golden apple orchard where I'd spent my morning. My ankle throbbed at the thought.

"Of course," I said, because there was nothing else to say.

I stuffed another scone into my pocket to avoid throwing it at Aurelle's head. I left before she could level another ridiculous request at me. After this, I would go to my room and sleep. The headache was fully and truly in bloom now. That was the real reason for my spinning head—it had to be. Because even with food in my stomach, I had to pause at the door, gripping the doorknob while the world continued to move around me against my will.

I made it through the door. Bela was gone. Out the final set of doors and back to the ornate curved staircase. I would go to the kitchens first. If I was as lucky as everyone said, maybe the cook would have fresh honeycomb there. The tea master sometimes infused it with different herbs for use in the infirmary. I could beg a bit for Aurelle. So long as the master gardener had not yet discovered what I'd done to his roses. If he had, I'd need to be clever and persuasive. Not lucky.

One flight down.

*Why are the stairs moving like that—*

My feet tumbled out from under me. I grasped for the balustrade, my fingernails scraping across the stone, breaking. But it slowed me just enough to land on my bottom, not my face.

The ache in my head was inseparable now from the spinning. Not just spinning—the walls and floor undulated around me. A sensuous dance, slow but constant, clear enough for me to make out reality, but distorted to the point of danger.

Widowsbloom.

I'd felt this before—once, when the tea master had been away from the castle and I'd tried to make the frostbloom tea that calmed my anxiety on my own.

Frostbloom tea was singularly unique, made from the leaves of a frostberry crossed with a widowsbloom. The hybrid they created transformed the deadly qualities of the widowsbloom into something less dangerous. The delicate frostberries tempered the hallucinogenic, debilitating poisons of the widowsbloom into a mild sedative. Most people would only drink frostbloom after the death of a loved one or the birth of a child. For me, it made my daily existence bearable.

And now . . . it had betrayed me.

No, I'd betrayed myself. Or had it been Aurelle? Was it her fault for asking, or mine for allowing her ridiculous request? The cuts on my legs and arms burned. I knew where the widowsbloom had come from.

The roses that encircled the magical orchard . . . not mere roses. Hybrids.

Meant to protect the king's famed golden apples. To incapacitate the intruder until the guards could apprehend them. My tolerance to the widowsbloom, after years of drinking the frostbloom tea, must have delayed the effects.

Tendrils of curling fire snaked through the winding pathways of my veins until I felt the aching pain with each beat of my heart.

The infirmary was too far.

The kitchens. If I made it there, the tea master would realize what had happened. He was married to the gardener, after all.

I just had to make it.

I could not collapse there on the stairs.

Then everyone would know I'd gone to the orchard. I'd stolen one of the king's precious apples. Aurelle would not defend me. I'd always known the answer to that stupid fecking wondering.

*Get up.*

My muscles refused to move.

*Get up, get up, GET UP!*

Still nothing.

*Treasa. You can do this for Treasa.*

I pulled myself upright. The stairs moved. So did the balustrade. I pressed my eyes shut. I could do this by feel. I'd taken these stairs thousands of times. I knew exactly how long my footsteps needed to be. If I just kept hold of the balustrade, I would not fall.

One step. Another.

I heard voices. Ignored them. Kept going.

Three more steps. I nearly fell again, my eyes flying open by instinct. Wrong. That was so much worse. But before I slammed them shut again, I saw movement.

Not the walls or the stairs, but people. Faces I did not recognize. Impossible. I knew everyone in the castle . . . The widowsbloom had addled my mind . . .

Hands closed around my wrists. More at my waist. How many hands did this person have? A man—the scent was distinctly male. For one second, I saw swimming green and gold before my eyes, just as something was shoved over my head.

Then I saw only darkness.

# Chapter 3

## Helio

*The women in my family have always been martyrs to the cause. My mother served time as a teenager in the Irskan Penal Colony. She and my aunts are the reason they had to open up the women's division. The humans have no imagination. They think their women are weak. Síofran know our women are strong. The most blessed of Síofra herself. Women make the best warriors because the humans always underestimate us. Growing up, we looked up to them. My aunt lived in the flat above us. She never recovered from the beatings they gave her in the Colony. Walked with a limp. Hands trembled. I fed her supper every day. It was my honor. I wanted to grow up and serve my people, just like her.*

—*Chena Moloon, Síofran Rebel Army*

Black hair, dark eyes. Average height. Always richly dressed. Apartments in the west tower of the castle, near the Mountain Gate.

It had cost us months of research and the life of two operatives to glean even those scant details.

Servants who worked directly with the royals did not leave the castle. The Irskan nobles were barred from describing the princess or her brothers on pain of death. They hardly left the castle themselves.

For more than twenty years, the King of Irska had kept his children in seclusion for just this reason—to avoid their being used as pawns in the never-ending war of hellfire between the Síofran and humans.

But we'd done it. We'd kidnapped the Irskan princess.

Holy fecking hell.

If we wanted to live to see the sunset, we needed to get her far away from the castle. Which was going to be a hell of a lot harder now that she was unconscious. A knife pressed to her back would have been much more effective than the valerianroot-soaked hood. She may have fought us some, but at least she would have walked out of her own power.

Heath dropped her legs when we reached the ground floor.

I did not bother to tell him to be careful with the Irskan princess. I did not much care how many bruises she had. As long as she was alive.

Heath cleared the room. Mendara appeared from around the corner, indicating that the path ahead was clear of guards and other threats. I hefted the princess over my shoulder and ran.

We eschewed the servants' corridors. Common sense told us this was their busiest time of day. There was less cover in the plush hallways frequented by the Irskan nobles, but at the moment, most of them were still abed. Hate rolled up inside me . . . How easy it would be to sneak into their quarters and slaughter them in their beds. They slept in safety, while in the city below the children of Síofra died every day. The castle was the one place that neither the Rebels nor the Corps had ever been able to touch.

*Someday, we will make them pay.* The familiar chorus echoed in my head.

Except someday was today. And the princess over my shoulder would suffer for every terrible thing her father and her human ancestors had done.

—◠◡◠—

The back door of the tavern opened on Mendara's third knock.

"Clear?" Heath barked, one step behind me.

"Only Síofran inside," the slight blond woman who'd opened the door confirmed. She backed into the darkened hallway, pressing against the wall so we could pass. The only light was the low glow of the fireball she held at the ready. "But best not to be seen," she added, eyes never pausing in their constant sweep.

Mendara led the way up a narrow flight of stairs. I had to angle my body to avoid smashing the princess's head on the rough stone wall. Maybe if I did, she would wake up and haul her own heavy ass.

Another door closed behind Mendara. This time, she remained outside of it, dagger in hand. The light in this room wasn't much better, but I could see the outline of the princess's face clearer as I dropped her on the dirty bed in the corner. She had a broad, round face made more interesting by high cheekbones and long black lashes that matched her hair. She was objectively beautiful. My stomach curled in distaste.

Heath took up a position just inside the door, weapon at the ready, nose twitching. But it was the small blonde, still gripping her fireball, who came to stand beside me.

"She smells like shit," Karine said.

Because she was covered in it from the midcalf down. A detail that had been impossible to miss with her slung over my shoulder for the last twenty minutes. "I hadn't noticed."

Karine took a step closer to the bed, though she made no move to touch the princess. "Is this really the time for humor?"

She should have known better. There was not a humorous bone in my cursed body. "Apparently it is the time for stupid, useless observations."

Karine hissed through her teeth. "We need to change her clothes. That scent will follow her and give us away."

"Do people expect a princess to smell like shit?" Heath weighed in from the door.

This conversation was a waste of time. Our third would arrive any minute, and we needed to be ready.

"Change her clothes," I ordered Karine. "We'll dump some liquor on her and pass her off as an unconscious drunk. It won't be hard in this place."

Karine's nose wrinkled at the suggestion, but she took a step closer, gingerly reaching for the laces holding the princess's silk gown in place. I turned for the trunk across the room, under the window. The tavern owner's son was an inducted Rebel. Over the last week, Rebels had been dropping off clothes of various sizes, all in the Síofran style. Few knew the reason; they only did as they were told. This operation had been as compartmentalized as we could keep it. Even the tavern owner did not know who we were bringing to the bedroom he'd offered to the cause. I opened the trunk, rifling through to find clothing that would fit the princess's generous frame.

"Fecking hell, Helio. What did you do to her?"

A second, and I was across the room again. Karine had drawn up the princess's skirt to remove her stockings—only to find them torn to shreds.

"She's covered in scratches," Karine breathed, leaning in for a closer look. Apparently her earlier revulsion had resolved itself in service of practicality.

"I did not do anything to her." Other than put a bag over her head, render her unconscious, and kidnap her from the only home she'd ever known.

The scratches on her legs were grotesque. Deep, they'd leaked blood that turned nearly black as it dried. They must have been painful— would be still, when she woke again.

I felt nothing.

No sympathy. No revulsion. Not even satisfaction.

The princess was nothing more than a tool—like the fireball that Karine had stowed away in her pocket or the long blade strapped across my own back.

"Should we call for a healer?" Karine looked over her shoulder to Heath, still standing silent at the door.

"We do not have time." Our third would be here any moment.

I noted the way Karine bit the inside of her cheek, holding back whatever flippant response came to her tongue. Her words were still sharp as she said, "If she dies, we'll have a much bigger problem."

"Only if the king finds out." The possibilities turned over in my mind. She'd be less trouble to us dead. We could still cut off pieces of her and send them to the king. Then eventually, dump her body at the castle gates. Or better yet, a different piece of her body at each gate.

Karine's fingers twitched. Probably for the fireball in her pocket. She'd had a temper since we were children. But she would not waste the valuable—and devastatingly destructive—weapon on me.

Instead, she stripped away what remained of the princess's stockings, cut the laces of her gown with her knife, and started to peel away the rest of her clothing, leaving only her shift in place.

"We have to clean those cuts or they'll get infected," she said without looking up at me.

"Later."

Karine flinched but did not speak. I watched, waiting for consent. Acquiescence. I was her superior. She'd sworn upon induction to follow the dictums of her superiors within the Síofran Rebel Army without question. Just like every other operative did.

She tossed the silk gown and stockings into the fire burning in the hearth.

She took the fresh clothing from my hands, her eyes lined with defiance. But her mouth said, "Fine."

That was all I needed. I did not care whether Karine disagreed with me. She'd follow orders, and that was all that mattered in this moment. I'd argue with her later, I was certain. She was the closest thing I had to a sister, and she thought that entitled her to question me. But only outside of the chain of Rebel command.

Three sharp knocks echoed through the small bedroom.

Weapons flew to hand immediately. Even with Mendara standing guard outside, safety was never assured. Always an illusion. I'd subverted that very illusion dozens of times myself.

But when the door opened, a familiar hulking shape stepped in. He was the opposite of his sister in every physical way. Brown hair, wide and tall. What Link did share was Karine's big mouth.

"Why does a princess smell so bad?" Link went so far as to cover his nose and mouth.

Karine finished wiping up the princess's legs and arms with a damp cloth—removing the gown had revealed similar cuts along her forearms—and tossed that into the fire as well.

"Maybe she was in the stables this morning. We know she likes to ride," Karine said, moving on to redressing.

"Enjoying a ride and mucking a stall are different things," Link said from behind his hand. He stepped forward, helping his sister position the princess's body, slipping a new, homespun wool dress over her head, then thicker stockings and a cloak.

I provided the liquor from my own flask.

Done.

Link reached for the princess, but I shouldered him aside. This was too important. I needed to have her in my arms, under my control. This time, I swung one arm under her legs and the other beneath her neck. The way you'd carry a drunken friend or lover, rather than a captive.

"She's not what I expected," Link observed as Karine finished putting the room to rights—or rather, wrongs. Like the poorly cared for residence of an aging Síofran bachelor. "Have you seen Queen Mya? She would fall over in a strong wind. This one is . . ."

"Sturdy," Karine finished for him.

*Soft,* my mind corrected. Fecking hell.

It had been months since I'd been with a woman, and my traitorous body knew it. Holding her like this had fooled my body into thinking that she was something other than what she was—a tool. A beautiful one, yes. But evil. Just like the rest of the humans. And most especially the Irskan royal family.

She was an instrument of revenge.

The heat inside me shifted instantly to a different kind of desire. It would be so easy to end her, here and now. I would not need a blade or a fireball. I'd enjoy choking the life out of her with my own two hands. Marring the fresh, creamy skin with dark bruises.

Karine interrupted my fantasies. "We're ready."

Heath opened the door; Mendara appeared just long enough to give a nod—the way was clear—and then disappeared back in the direction of the alley door. Heath would stay behind in the bedroom in case we'd been followed or detected, to ensure our trail ended here.

Link took the lead down the stairs, Karine falling in behind me. When we emerged into the tavern's public room, Karine hung back. So early in the morning, there were only a handful of patrons. A few were still in their seats, where they'd passed out the night before. Only two sat at the bar top, hunched over ale. They kept their eyes down. The type of people who patronized taverns before breakfast were generally uninterested in conversation.

Link made a show of tripping over a chair leg, laughing rancorously, and then nearly collapsing sideways. I gave the grunt I normally would have suppressed, letting my annoyance show, playing the part of the aggravated friend escorting two drunkards back to their beds after a long night of drinking.

Another method of covering our trail. Four cloaked figures had entered the tavern through the alley, faces hidden. Two tall, two middling height. Now one drunken, hulking man left, his friend carrying their sotted-beyond-consciousness third. Any impression we left was erased a minute or so later, when Karine emerged from the tavern's kitchen.

She'd let down her golden hair and loosened her bodice. Prostitute by night, kitchen maid by day, or merely a disillusioned Síofran young woman who'd spent her evening trying to forget her tragic past—it did not matter. She was the one who would be remembered.

Link and I staggered along the street, no more than a pair of drunks who could not walk straight, stumbling through the fog, eager for our beds. The streets were still blessedly empty, but we kept up the performance. Someone was always watching, waiting to pass along information. There were too many competing interests in Irska, even within the relative safety of the Síofran peace villages, to truly relax.

Karine rejoined us several minutes later, fireball once again in hand.

"No commotion," she reported.

At the next corner, we ducked into an alley, our steps straightening.

I adjusted my hold on the woman in my arms, refusing to look too long at her face. The less I thought of her as a person, the easier it would be to kill her when the time inevitably came.

"Good. Let's get the princess to her cell."

# Chapter 4

## FIONNA

*In those days, the fireballs were a fact of life. It was as normal as making porridge for breakfast. The market, the alehouses, the bridges. They were all good targets. Were we scared we might get caught up in it? Sure. But mostly we were proud. And if we were in the wrong place when the fireball exploded? Well, that wasn't our fault. That death was at the hands of the humans. We only had to set off the fireballs because of what they did to us first. But the castle, that was always the goal. The Irskan nobles did not care about the humans who died on the streets of Irska. Oh, they'd send out their Peace Guards, hunt us down, try to infiltrate us. But no change happened, nothing substantive. Not ever. That is why we decided to bring the fight to them. To prove that even behind their thick walls, sitting high up on the hill, they weren't safe from us.*

*—Nieve Zoric, Síofran Rebel Army*

The first voice I heard was my own. A low moan that echoed through my aching head, even quiet as it was. The fog of widowsbloom still clung to the edges of my mind, turning the entire world black as I opened my eyes.

The world didn't seem to be moving anymore. But it had descended into darkness. Maybe the master gardener had introduced a third plant into the rose-and-widowsbloom hybrid. Maybe the tea master would know what his spouse was up to and how to counteract it. The kitchen was closer than the infirmary anyway. I just had to stand up again and haul myself down the stairs.

Except I couldn't.

I couldn't stand up.

I wasn't on the stairs. And the black around me was taking shape as my eyes adjusted to the darkness. I was not in the castle.

My heart leaped into my throat, the beast in my chest roaring to life. Tingling—it began in my fingertips, spread through my arms, along my legs, and all the way to my toes. My stomach flipped inside me, again and again. Violent. I was going to retch.

I wasn't in the castle.

The images came back to me in flashes.

Something tight closing around my wrists, holding me in place. Hands. Hard and cruel and unyielding. Then darkness over my head, the rough texture of cheap fabric against my cheeks.

A snatch of voices, and then my head was swimming again.

I tried to breathe, but air refused to stay in my lungs. In and out, in and out, faster than I could sustain. But I couldn't stop it. I'd completely lost control of myself; the anxiety in my chest held sway, attacking again and again.

*Calm as a lake. Strong as a tree. I bend but don't break.*

It did not help.

*You are safe. You are safe—*

No, that was not true. Safety had always been a thin illusion, but even that had been stripped away entirely.

*Calm as a lake. Strong as a tree. I bend but don't break.*

My eyes started to burn.

It wasn't fecking working.

I would tap my foot. Three times. A breath, repeat the verse, and then three times again. That would calm me. That would force the beast back into its cage, slow my heart and my breath.

One—

I couldn't tap my foot. My legs were bound. Not my legs, my ankles. My foot twitched against the restraints.

My lower lip began to shake, my eyes burning. I could not cry. If I started, I would not stop. This time I forced the words out, a broken whisper. "Calm . . . Ca . . . Calm as a lake . . ." The sound of my own voice made it worse.

The tears were coming.

No, no, no. I couldn't cry. I had to transform the fear into something sharper. To anger. But I just *couldn't*.

I threw my head back and cried out, wrenching my wrists and my ankles, rocking my whole body against the restraints, letting the burning of the ropes against my skin fuel my rage. My injured ankle screamed, but my mind and body were too out of sync for it to impact my consciousness.

"Struggling will only pull the knots tighter."

My heart stopped. So did my screams. And my struggles.

That voice would have stopped me anytime, anywhere, no matter the hysteria. I'd known more than my share of cruelty. My parents were murdered by a changeling firebomb. In the castle, I'd been lashed by other female servants jealous of the privileges of my position. Men had shown me their brutality more than once. One in particular.

But that voice . . . It was not like any I'd heard before.

The cruelty was endemic to the notes. It etched every vowel. It was there in the cadence of the syllables. The sound of it slipped over the exposed nape of my neck, lifting the curls that had come free in the struggle . . . Which struggle? In the apple tree, when I'd been taken, just seconds before when I'd screamed and thrashed? When was immaterial. Trivial. Nothing, compared to my next realization.

He stood right behind me.

"Be a good girl, and I won't hurt you, Princess."

*Yet.*

The unspoken threat was there as clearly as the words he'd said aloud.

And yet he offered no further guidance on what it meant to behave.

The hammering of my heart inside my chest changed. Less violent, but still rapid. The panic receded as some primal survival instinct took charge. A decade trapped in service in the castle had given me something, it seemed. A chance.

My captor stood behind me, breathing. Each inhale was even, measured, followed by an equally precise exhale. I counted each one. In between, I tried to take stock of my surroundings as best I could without moving a single muscle in my body.

The walls I could see formed three sides of an approximately square room. On my left, in the periphery of my vision, was a singular door. From what I could tell, I was nearly centered in the room, as was the fireplace on the wall directly in front of me. It wasn't lit. The only light came from a brazier set into the wall beside the door.

There was no way to tell the time of day, not a single window to bleed in daylight. I'd been taken in the morning, while the princess was still at breakfast. How long would Aurelle wait for her fresh honey before she sent someone looking for me? Would she forget she'd sent me at all? Give up, choke down the rest of the apple, and be too distracted by the magic it gave her to think of me at all?

Treasa.

She'd miss me first, when I did not appear in the afternoon to check on her lessons.

Or maybe she'd take it as a reprieve, toss them aside, and go play with the other children in the cellars.

A cellar.

That's where I was, surely. Most changelings were poor. They would build their residences and businesses with windows by necessity, to maximize the light and minimize the money they need spend on firewood. The absence of windows meant I had to be in a cellar.

Of course, I'd been taken by changelings. There was no one else. In Irska, only the changeling rebel groups would exact violence on a human.

But not changelings—I could not call them that. Not if I wanted to live to see daylight again. My anxiety begrudgingly yielded to my mind, allowing me to think through the fog.

They called themselves the children of Síofra.

Síofran.

Rebel Army or the Liberation Corps?

The Rebels were more organized, the Corps more violent. Either was entirely capable of orchestrating an abduction. Both had.

I knew one thing for certain—those they abducted were never seen again.

"You are trembling, Princess."

I pressed my eyes closed by reflex. Princess. My lady. I was neither. But I understood the mocking in his tone. To the Síofran, anyone who served the royal family or the Irskan nobles was guilty of all their crimes. As if the ones the Síofran orchestrated did not count. As if my parents' deaths did not count.

"It is understandable to be afraid, though not entirely useful. Fear will not save you."

No, it would not.

But neither would words. Both sides killed informers.

My ankle still throbbed. The cuts on my arms and legs from those cursed widowsbloom roses still burned. Every limb was restrained. Even if I got myself free, I would not be able to outrun them. It could not be this man, alone, who held me prisoner.

I had not even laid eyes upon him, and I knew he would be formidable. More than I could overcome.

But he had not taken me alone. I'd felt more than one set of hands on me in the castle. This was not a single changeling man's deranged plot, then. It was a full-fledged Síofran abduction. Which meant there were other conspirators.

Hot breath skittered across my neck. My muscles tightened, my face scrunching tight in anticipation of my captor's next words . . .

The door sprang open.

It creaked on ancient hinges, loud and ungainly. Metal—the door was made of metal. How, why . . . To hold a prisoner. What hope would I have had against a wooden door, let alone a metal one? And especially, tied to a chair.

But maybe the door was to keep rescuers out, as much as to keep me in.

Rescuers.

The taken were never rescued.

Two newcomers entered the room. A blond woman I would have described as dainty, were it not for the weapons strapped all over her body—a bow and arrow slung over her shoulder, several daggers in a bandolier across her chest, and a roughly rounded black sphere in her hand emitting an undulating glow not unlike an ember in a fireplace. At her side was the largest man I'd ever seen. What sort of changeling was he? There were classes, I remembered from my history books. Within those, dozens of varieties with various abilities. I had never paid much attention to the history of Irska. I'd never planned on dying here.

The woman wore a stern frown. Her companion, despite the fact that we were in a dark cellar, was smiling. My stomach dropped several inches within my body. The smile was worse.

No, the most terrifying was the undisturbed silence from the man behind me. His words had been torture, cold and soulless. But the lack of them heightened the tension. Especially when the two newcomers looked past me straight to him.

"She'll be no use to us if you scare her shitless," the woman said. She was not afraid of the male at my shoulder. At least, not enough to hold her tongue.

"You're scarier than he is," the smiling one countered, rolling his huge shoulders. He nudged the woman's shoulder. She rolled her eyes.

There was an easy familiarity between them. Lovers, maybe. Or siblings. At the very least, good friends.

I almost snorted aloud—changelings, having friends. How could such heartless beings even begin to have such a normal relationship?

But then I'd almost laughed. While strapped to a chair, faced with my own torture and death.

Fecking hell.

The mind did strange things to protect itself. But it was better than the beast of anxiety rising up within me and causing an incapacitating attack. I'd struggled with it for as long as I could remember, even before my parents' deaths. It had always been there, a constant companion even when the rest of my life spun out of control. Of course, it would not desert me now.

I blinked, trying to refocus on what was happening around me. What the changelings—Síofran—were saying. But they weren't saying anything. They were watching me. Waiting.

I sank my teeth into my lower lip.

The blonde tilted her head to the side. "I thought she'd be begging for her life by now."

"Maybe she figures that if we haven't killed her yet, we aren't going to," her companion said, smile still intact. "At least not right away." He winked.

There was something to that reasoning. They'd infiltrated the castle. They could have killed me there on the stairs, or dragged and staged my body to be found somewhere more consequential. Instead, they'd gone to the trouble of kidnapping me. Which implied some larger purpose to my life—for the time being.

The third said nothing.

Still, the heat of him lingered behind me. As effective a threat as any words.

A shiver snaked down my spine, contracting my muscles involuntarily and causing my limbs to tug at the restraints.

"Cold, Princess?"

The trace of his words over my skin sent another shiver racking through me.

"We can't have that," the female said, lifting her free hand. She snapped her fingers.

The fire roared to life.

I flinched back, nearly upending the chair, crashing into something. Him. It had to be him. But he didn't touch me. Did not make a sound. All of a sudden, I was righted, the four legs of the chair back on the floor and a fire roaring in the hearth that seconds before had been black and cold.

How could that . . . *magic*.

My gods. I'd never seen it. Truly, I thought it was nothing more than a legend. Síofran did not work in the castle. I'd never even set eyes on one, except from afar, when I'd looked out the castle windows and seen the throngs of people on the streets of Irska. But at that distance, there was no way to distinguish human from changeling. There were no physical, apparent differences between us. Only where we lived and how we dressed.

I'd been *taught* magic was a myth. Every human knew that the only magic left in Irska lay in the king's precious golden apples, and those were rarely gifted outside the royal family. In ten years, I'd never seen one used. If I hadn't been kidnapped, maybe . . .

But there was the proof before my eyes.

A fire, conjured from nothing.

It couldn't be. Magic had been gone for hundreds of years, extinguished after the war. Historians speculated on why it had disappeared. Perhaps Síofra had withdrawn her favor from the changelings. Maybe with human dominance established, the magic in the changelings' veins had petered out like an untended flame. The king's golden apples were all that remained of magic, and whatever recipe the changelings used to create the fireballs.

Except there was no other explanation.

*This cannot be true. I cannot be here. This is a dream. A nightmare. Magic is gone.*

"Your wounds have been tended," the blonde said, gesturing to my legs. I could not see them to judge for myself, nor my arms. The cuts still burned slightly, but less than they had when I'd awoken a few moments before. Perhaps they'd applied a salve of some kind. The female walked to the fire she'd started, leaning back against the mantel. "Care to tell us how you got them?"

My teeth sank deeper into the inside of my lower lip.

The woman glanced behind me—a quick dart of her eyes—then back to the unassuming but huge male at her side. But it was not he who spoke.

"Tell us how you were injured."

*Tell me why you kidnapped me.*

He was not as close, but his words felt the same.

I would not answer.

Keeping my mouth closed was my best chance of . . . survival? Immediate survival, at least. If I started giving them information immediately, they would have no incentive to keep me alive. They were also less likely to torture me.

My mind whirred with calculations, the mental gymnastics a distraction from the anxiety that lingered in my clenched fists.

"Why were you covered in muck?"

*Because I made a stupid mistake. You'd never have taken me if not for the widowsbloom.*

It took me a second to realize he'd spoken in past tense, and the implications. My head jerked down, my eyes leaving the two Síofran by the fireplace whom I'd been watching so carefully and instead surveying my own body. They'd changed my clothing. The silk gown I'd worn as I'd trudged through manure to retrieve Aurelle's precious golden apple had been replaced by a dark-blue woolen dress. From the fabric peeking above the bodice, it appeared I still wore my own shift. I recognized the decorative edges; Treasa had embroidered it for me as a birthday gift, a year past.

Treasa. My heart strained. What would she do when she realized I was missing? Would she be able to find the money I'd been squirreling away for the past decade? It was enough to buy her passage out of Irska, though not yet enough for both of us.

It was the worst of my miscalculations. I should have sent her ahead. I'd agonized over that choice, but had been unwilling to part with her.

And now I might cost her everything.

Never mind the cost to myself.

The door opened again. A fourth rebel entered. This one made no attempt to hide his disgust as he came to stand between the two Síofran already in front of me. His upper lip, shadowed with a thick beard that covered the lower half of his face, curled upward at the mere sight of me. The others did not remark on his appearance or spare him a glance; they'd been expecting him.

"She's not talking." The woman sighed. She had that strange glowing orb in her hand again. Her fingers caressed it like a pet.

A smile turned the corners of the bearded man's sneer. Then he moved.

It happened so fast I wasn't sure what happened at all.

The aftermath told me.

The angry male growled, twisting his arm away. Above my head, another arm had shot out, grabbing his wrist, stopping his fist mere inches from my face.

He growled again, bracing one hand on the back of the chair, to the side of my head, to use as leverage to pull his arm free.

But the hand that held him did not release. I watched as the fingers tightened, knuckles turning white, fingertips digging deep into the toned arm muscle of my attacker.

"Let me go," he demanded, gone still now.

He'd stopped fighting, at least physically. Inside my chest, my heartbeat picked up speed. I knew this type of male. Among the humans, they usually became Peace Guards. There was hatred in his dark eyes, and it was not reserved for me. It flowed across the space over my head, straight toward the male behind me.

"Touch her without my permission, and I will kill you."

I could see the desire to argue in the male's face. But whatever he saw over my shoulder, it held back any physical retaliation. When he tugged on his arm again, the male behind me released it.

The bearded man laughed. Cold. Humorless. "She is a prisoner. We interrogate prisoners. Have you suddenly gone soft, Helio?"

Helio.

A name.

The male behind me made an inhuman sound. If I'd had any doubt that he was a changeling, that moment dispelled it. It was not quite a growl. That word missed the nuance. It was a sound from another world. From the gods themselves. From Síofra, the mother of the changelings.

And it was all threat.

Heat flooded the room. Not from the fire, but from the male behind me. Helio. As if his anger manifested itself physically. That was impossible. The widowsbloom must still have lingered in my veins, however faintly.

The man's laugh faded, but his sneering smile remained. He left through the creaking metal door. The oppressive heat did not cool.

"She is a prisoner," the female said quietly.

"We are not human trash. We do not hit women."

*Because you imagine we are weaker? Untie me, and let's find out.*

I had no formal weapons training. But I'd taught myself the basics of self-defense, even if those had been useless when they took me. Fecking widowsbloom. I could use that to my advantage later, though. Wait until they relaxed their guard, untied me for some reason. I had to relieve myself eventually, or they'd have a real mess. They wouldn't expect me to know how to fight back. I would choose my moment carefully. Instinct told me I'd never defeat the male at my back. But

I could wait for him to leave. Watch. Figure out which of my captors was the weakest.

Until then, I had to keep my mouth shut.

"Account for your injuries."

I said nothing.

Two hands landed on either side of my head, on the back of the chair. The wood groaned beneath his grasp. I'd seen the power of those hands not a minute before, closed around the other male's arm, threatening to rip the other man apart.

Panic flooded through me, but I did not speak. Could not speak. Not if I ever wanted to get back to Treasa.

The wood splintered. The next words were spoken in a whisper, just beneath my ear, the heat of his breath caressing the tender spots of my neck like a lover.

"No rescue is coming. She will burn this place to the ground with her fireball rather than let them find you. Even if all of us are still in it."

My eyes flew to the blond woman, now standing up straight. That glowing black-and-red orb was a fireball. The most destructive of the weapons in the changelings' arsenal. Small ones could destroy a carriage. The larger ones could bring down a building in an explosion of fire and brimstone that destroyed everything and everyone in the vicinity. Like the one that had killed my parents.

My entire body started to shake.

Helio's exhale slid along the nape of my neck as he straightened, still out of my view.

"How does a princess end up injured and covered in manure within her own castle walls?"

A princess?

This had to be a joke. He was trying to disorient me. He could not possibly think . . .

"I am growing impatient, Princess."

*Princess.* He'd been calling me *Princess* since the moment I opened my eyes. I'd thought it a mockery of my presumed status. It would be easy to mistake me for an Irskan noble, given my clothing and where I'd been walking in the castle.

But no . . . he thought I was *the* princess. They thought they'd kidnapped Princess Aurelle.

*No, no, no.* This was worse. So much worse. When they found out I was nothing, nobody, they would surely kill me. I was useless to them as a hostage. No one but Treasa would even notice I was missing, let alone care enough to pay a ransom or mount a rescue.

Or maybe they would release me.

I suppressed another unhinged, uncharacteristic laugh.

They could not release me. I knew one of their names. But maybe they would not guard me as closely once they realized I was not the princess. Gods, it was too many calculations. I needed a moment to figure out the way forward, to consider all the options, as I always did.

But I did not get a moment.

Footsteps echoed through the room. For the first time, I heard him move. Three steps, to come around the chair. He stepped out of the shadows.

A monster.

Until that moment, some sliver inside me had believed what everyone said about luck. My careful decisions kept us on the right path, but luck helped us along.

That belief died right then and there. Luck would not save me now.

My mouth fell open. And from it, five words. Five words that would surely mean my death. "I am not Princess Aurelle."

# Chapter 5

## HELIO

*Magic is our greatest secret. Keeping it is the only thing the Libs and Rebels ever agreed on. It is the first lesson that Síofran children learn, before walking or talking or even their own names. It's why we keep the young children inside, even in the peace villages. The humans think it's because we can't feed them, because we are starving. Some of us are. But really it's self-preservation. If the humans ever realized that the whispers were true, that the small magics remained . . . the Irskan king would burn the city to the ground.*

*—Jozef Corrigan, Síofran Liberation Corps*

Lying human filth.

I'd spent my entire life fighting them, but my stomach still curled with hate at the audacity of the human princess. It had taken us years to infiltrate the castle perched on the hill above the city. Countless Rebels had died for the information that led us through the gates and into the heart of the human fortress. It was a plan that was good only once.

The humans were selfish and ruthless, but they were not stupid. Eventually, they would figure out how we had gotten in, and they'd shore up their defenses. Even now, they were likely realizing their princess was gone.

I needed to move through the city, check the pulse of the peace villages to see whether news had already begun to spread or the humans would suppress it.

But not yet.

"The first words out of her mouth are a lie. Fecking humans," Karine cursed.

The fireball in her hand glowed brighter for several heartbeats, then banked. The magic used to create it was self-contained, but it responded to the surge in her emotions. Even without access to her full power, she stood close enough to her brother for their unity to make the dormant magic in her veins sing.

And that was all it would do. If enough of us gathered together, we could muster small magics. Lighting a fire. Raising the temperature in the room with my anger. After the humans' treachery, that was all that remained of the mighty power that my parents had died to pass down to me.

I had more control than most . . . and more vestigial power than any.

I notched the temperature of the room higher. A bead of sweat slid down her temple, following the rounded curve of her jaw before sliding down to her pale throat.

She was beautiful, even in the homespun clothing Karine had changed her into. Her regal clothing had been in poor condition, courtesy of whatever had caused those nasty, leaking cuts on her legs. Princess Aurelle was known for her mercurial nature; it was one of the few details about her that had escaped the castle over the last decade. What childish human schemes had she been up to before we took her?

I took one step closer. I'd seen her lips trembling before. Now I could count the little grooves in the bottom one. Even as the tremble turned into a wobbling shake.

I knew the impact I had on people, even my own kind. It was another weapon in the arsenal gifted to me by Síofra herself.

I crouched down, bringing my eyes level with hers. "Princess—"

"I am not the princess," she insisted, mastering that quivering mouth long enough to infuse her words with anger.

Link flinched in time with the hiss from between Karine's teeth. No one in the Síofran Rebel Army had dared to interrupt me in a decade.

It was naive of them to be surprised. She was not a Peace Guard or a rogue member of the Irska Defense Force. This was the Irskan princess. She'd known only comfort and privilege. She'd never seen the aftermath of a fireball or witnessed a Peace Guard raid.

If she'd even seen a child of Síofra at all, it had been a corpse strung up from the castle walls.

But she would learn, and I would be the one to teach her. Even as the heat in the pit of my stomach rose to match the temperature in the room.

Her eyes burned with a tumultuous mixture of fear and hate. One fueled the other, as it usually did for the humans.

So fecking beautiful, with those black curls swirling around her shoulders, clinging to her neck from my heat. She was like a widows-bloom, the dark spiraled flower with poison-coated petals.

But all flowers died once plucked.

I straightened, giving her the illusion of retreat. Karine and her brother were still frozen at my back, the thick heat of the air undisturbed.

I folded my arms across my chest. Karine held the fireball to center herself. I needed nothing so tangible. I had righteous hate. "You are not Princess Aurelle, but you wore her clothes, exited her chambers, and fit her description."

The princess's mouth fell open in a delicate little moue of surprise, but she schooled the expression almost as quickly as it came. She was well trained. So was I.

I took one step, then another, slowly circling her chair. She did not twist her head to keep me in her gaze. Foolish, to expose such a pretty neck to a predator. Or wise, to accept her place as prey.

Her breathing shifted as I moved behind her, her ample chest moving up and down quicker than before. Panic was natural, princess or not.

*Princess or not.*

The Firebird inside me screeched.

She'd seeded doubt. I sorted through my observations quickly. The scrapes. The regal defiance to the tilt of her head. Her rounded curves, so different from the Irskan queen. Her appearance on the stairs that led from the royal suite in the west tower. Confirmation or confusion.

She had to be the princess.

"The only way to help yourself is to answer me," I breathed. I watched the words skitter over the nape of her neck, lifting the lightest of her rampant curls.

She snapped her shoulders back against the chair, a stubborn refusal to react to my breath on her neck.

"They kill informers," she said. I could not see her face, but I did not need to, to know she was letting nothing show. The words were even, the outline of her jaw barely moved.

There was no need to specify the "they." All sides killed informers, and none of them released captives. Princess or not, she was smart enough to realize the danger of her situation.

It had been hours since we'd absconded from the castle. Soon we would know what tack the Irskan nobles would take—sound the bells of betrayal, alerting all Irska to the treachery of a stolen princess, or stoic silence and refusal to admit they'd been bested by the children of Síofra once again. Their moves would require counters of our own, as they had for the last three hundred years.

But the higher-ups in my chain of command would decide those moves. My task was in this room, with the recalcitrant human princess.

*If she is a princess at all.*

I stepped forward, completing the circle and meeting her turbulent dark eyes with my own. She did not flinch this time, but her pupils dilated. I knew what I looked like. I'd long since become immune to the reaction of weakling humans and fair maidens.

I crossed my arms over my chest. "Whether you talk or not, you are considered an informer simply by being in this room. The only mercy that remains to you will come at my hands."

I felt every beat of my heart as she held my gaze. She could stare me down all she liked; it did not change the reality, which was exactly as I'd laid it out. This woman was at my mercy, and I was known for having none.

Whether she saw that fact in my eyes or was simply unable to bear the disgust, she finally jerked her head away, pressing her eyes closed.

"I am not the princess," she said again. She'd averted her eyes, but her voice remained strong and steady. Insistent.

Karine made a sound of disgust in her throat, identical to the one she'd made in childhood whenever she was displeased. Adulthood had made it a harbinger of something more lethal.

I braced myself for the fight. She was as dangerous as Heath in her own way. I would not need to forcibly prevent her from harming the captive princess. Yet she bore scars just like the rest of us.

But for once, she did not follow up on her scoff. "We have other places to be," Karine said, tucking the fireball into her pocket.

Link shifted beside her. "Right, we are supposed to meet Kinley—"

"Shut your brother's mouth, or I will shut it for him," I said without looking at either of them. I kept my attention fixed on our captive, trying to deduce whether she'd caught the scrap of information Link had carelessly offered to her. Her eyes were still pressed closed.

Karine moved for the heavy door, pausing at my side to rake her eyes over the woman tied to the chair. She did not say anything; she did not need to. We'd grown up side by side in the fight against the humans, both orphans of the cause. I knew a part of her would always resent me for the status I'd attained, for the superior rank that granted me the right to give her orders. Just like I also knew that she would always, ultimately, follow them.

She left with her brother through the heavy metal door, leaving me alone with the captive princess.

As I watched, she pressed her eyes closed tighter. Princess or no, she was a quick learner. She recognized true danger—and what a lack of witnesses might mean.

"If you are not Princess Aurelle, then who are you?"

Her eyes popped open, moving to me in time with her chin. Our informants had said only that her eyes were dark. But even in the low firelight of the basement where we'd stashed her, I could see the absurdity of such a simple word. Tiny flecks of amber dotted the near-black irises, their slight shimmer the only way to differentiate between the ring of color and the pupil at the center. The sparse light should have darkened them completely, but instead the reds and oranges of the fire at my back brightened the amber to a burnished gold. Or maybe it was some internal fire that did the trick.

"I am no one," she said. This time, her mouth moved, her chin bobbed, her throat slid. She had the ability to keep her emotions bottled, but it was not easy or natural for her. Which made it easier to exploit. They were tiny details that most would have missed. She was working very hard not to let her fear take control. But the reason I'd succeeded so thoroughly at the role carved out for me was my ability to see what others tried to hide.

"It is better to tell me the truth now." *Before I have to extract it from you by more brutal methods.*

The unspoken words hung in the thick air between us. Her throat slid again. Clever girl. She understood exactly what I did not say.

Torture was a requirement of my position within the Síofran Rebel Army. Those with weak stomachs did not rise high in the ranks, no matter what class of Síofran power slept in their veins.

But for once, the desire to maim did not rise within me along with the heat. I wanted to peel this young woman back layer by layer. Instinct told me that violence would not be the way to do it. Those same instincts that had me entertaining the impossible.

My instincts had yet to lead me astray. She held her shoulders straight as I stepped into her space, but when I reached over her shoulder to untie the bounds on her hands, she flinched violently, nearly upending the chair.

I caught it easily, the four legs hitting the stone floor with enough force that the impact jarred through both of us. My forearm brushed against the exposed column of her throat, heat searing up my arm. But it was nothing compared to the rage that built in my stomach, pounding up through my chest and spreading across my shoulders to the thick muscles built to support what was not there.

Her eyes had been wide before, but now they seemed to take up the entire upper half of her face. They sparkled—not with excitement, but with fear.

Fear I could use. Fear that would help me set my people free.

But the contrast was too sharp to dismiss. It should have been an opening, a weakness for me to exploit. Instead, anger solidified in my stomach. Raw and undeserved, but there nonetheless.

She'd held on to control, masking her fear and choosing her words with purpose. Until she thought I was about to strike her.

I wanted her to be afraid, I told myself. Of *me*. Not of whoever had come before. Her violent flinch spoke multitudes, but it did not tell me everything.

The effort was gargantuan, control only truly made possible by the fact that Karine and Link had gone. The magic we'd bolstered together, the three of us unified in the Síofran cause, was dwindling now that I was alone with the human woman.

*Human. Fecking. Princess.*

But who would dare?

I needed the answer more than my next breath, and I couldn't afford to stop and analyze why.

I eased myself away from her, the place where my skin had touched hers still tingling. "Who hurt you, Princess?"

She only released her breath when I was fully clear. Her lower lip began to tremble again, but she clenched her jaw together to force it still. "You were the one who put a hood over my head and dragged me out of the castle." The fear lingered in her eyes even as she bit out the words.

That was not what I meant, and we both knew it.

She flexed her hands. She probably thought I could not see it, as they were bound behind her. She did not realize how closely attuned I was to every line of her body. Attention to detail was key to learning a captive's weaknesses so I could exploit them later.

She wanted to live. That was the reason she was so determined to keep her mouth shut. But I'd already told her the reality of the situation. Silence would not save her now. She only had to be smart enough to realize it.

Despite the fear that glistened in her dark eyes, they narrowed. Clever girl. "I did this to myself," she insisted.

Impatience was rising to keep company with the rage. If I pushed her too hard, too fast, she'd retreat entirely within herself. But I could not help myself. I had to know.

My body moved without conscious thought, my legs bending until I was crouched before her once more, not towering above, but eye to eye. This time, she did not flinch away from my mismatched gaze. "Not the scratches."

I felt her inhale. But she kept her mouth closed.

*Stop pushing.*

My instincts ignored the logical demands of my mind. "I made it clear to my subordinates that I would not allow anyone to harm you. But you still flinched away from me."

My victory reflected back in her sharpening eyes, in the control that slipped her bounds. "You told him that he could not touch me without your permission. All that tells me is that you want to do the touching yourself."

She sank her teeth into her thick bottom lip. She knew exactly how that sounded.

The desire that rolled through my gut took second place to the anger, now a flame as visceral as the one that blazed in the hearth.

It should have dwindled to cinders by now, but I could still hear the crackling of a vibrant blaze.

I pressed my forearm into her knee, leveraging myself closer to her. She hissed through her teeth, but she could not retreat. Not bound by arm and leg to the chair.

"Who"—I shifted my weight forward, leaning until my face was mere inches from hers—"hurt you?" Question and demand.

More than three decades of harsh life in Irska had taught me not to have expectations or hope. But I wanted an answer, and she opened her beautiful mouth and gave me one.

"Vainar."

The Firebird screeched, my tether to my mortal form held in place by the lost magic of my kind. My shoulders ached, begging to take their true form. From my earliest memories, I'd felt the creature within me. But never before had it revolted like this, demanding and driving to burst from the binds that discord had built.

I was on my feet without remembering rising. Her eyes had been wide before, now they seemed to swallow up all the light, impossible dark pools that glowed as I rose to my full height above her.

"There have been rumors about the prince," my voice said, not entirely my own.

"Not rumors." Her chin jutted out in defiance, even as her pale skin flushed from the heat that emanated off my body.

I could not move a muscle for fear that the little control I still had would slip. But neither could I keep in the fury. "There will be no mercy for the prince. He will beg. With every slice of skin that I remove, every bone that I crush, he will beg. Maybe not in the beginning, proud as he is rumored to be. But I will enjoy dismantling him, joint by joint. I will crush each finger, the tiny bones, one by one until they are nothing more than shards. I will burn his flesh until it melts away and those shards are nothing more than ash. When I come for him, there will be no escape. No mercy. Prince Vainar will never touch you or any other woman again."

My breath scissored in and out of my chest as I waited for her revulsion.

If half the rumors were true, it still was not sufficient punishment for the king's middle son. It had never bothered me. Why would human atrocities committed against other humans even garner my attention? But then she'd flinched away from me.

There was no explanation for it—not my reaction, nor hers.

She nodded, her halo of dark curls bobbing with the motion, the soft skin below her chin wobbling slightly. Her eyes glistened, unshed tears coating the dark orbs. But she did not let them fall. I would not have thought less of her if she had.

As the rage cleared from my chest and shoulders, a singular thought remained.

She was not Princess Aurelle.

The Irskan king was many things, but even the humans would not allow their princess to be tortured by her elder brother or subject to his perverse sexual attentions. They'd gone to extreme lengths to protect her from the children of Síofra, concealing every detail about her on pain of death. She was an important bargaining chip and bastion of legitimacy. When she came of age, trading her away to a kingdom across the water would cement human supremacy and rule in Irska.

"Do you believe me now?" she asked. She'd managed to regain control of whatever emotions I'd stirred with my outburst, as well as her face.

"Who are you?" I asked again, crossing my arms over my chest and forcing my fists to relax their tense hold.

She debated telling me, the war in her eyes clear even though the rest of her features remained unmoved. Her eyes were my way to read her. I noted the information for future interrogations.

But she wasn't the princess, which meant that every plan I'd had, every step, had to be reassessed . . .

"I am Princess Aurelle's companion," she said, her voice a few octaves higher than before. "A servant."

My mind moved quickly, through the chain of command I reported up to and the course of action I'd been ordered to take over the next several hours and days. I needed to take the pulse of the city, maybe interrogate a Peace Guard or two, before deciding what to do next. The castle would react differently to a missing servant than a missing princess, but perhaps not initially.

"Let me go," she said, interrupting my thoughts. "I do not know anything meaningful. If you release me now, I can explain away my absence. They will never know I was taken by the changelings—children of Síofra. I am just a servant."

How long had she been working on that argument? Probably since opening her eyes and realizing where she was.

I did not do either of us the disservice of considering her proposal. "If you want to live, you will keep that information to yourself."

She recoiled, processing my words. "You want me to lie. Lying is worse. Lying will get me killed."

As if she had not just proposed lying to the humans in the castle. What little patience I had was quickly evaporating. "If they figure out you are a worthless hostage, they will kill you."

They—my superiors. The other members of my cell. Any of the unaffiliated but righteously angry Síofran that waited in the peace villages.

She exhaled slowly, her leg twitching. "Why haven't you killed me?"

*Because I'm not ready to admit to my chain of command how deeply I fecked up.* "A princess is a valuable hostage."

I turned away so she would not be able to dissect the expression on my own face. Servants were observant, whether by nature or necessity. As captor and captive, we'd be spending a lot of time together. It would allow me to understand her nuances, but I could not give away mine.

"I can be a valuable hostage."

It was a damn good thing I was facing away from her. Even so, I felt my head snap up to attention. I hadn't expected her to speak again. She was a blasted servant, if a somewhat mouthy one.

It took another moment for the force of her words to take hold.

I turned back to face her. "Have you given up negotiating for your release?"

Her mouth tightened, but only for a second. She had her retort ready. "I have been in service in the castle for a decade as a companion to Princess Aurelle. I may not fetch a ransom, but I have a wealth of information."

The fear was not gone, but she'd mastered it enough to plan a strategy for herself. *Interesting.*

"And you think that information is valuable in this war?" I pressed. I wanted to see what she'd say next, where she would take the stilted conversation.

She paused, her lips moving over unspoken words, then she exhaled again. "The war is over. You lost."

"We all lost the day the humans enslaved my people." I waved a hand and the fire behind me died. "If you believe anything else, then you are just another human who cannot see beyond their own selfish pulse. But I will make sure I get every piece of information out of you before I hand you over to my superiors. I will make you count, princess or not."

The threat echoed with the same veracity as the promises I'd made about Vainar. But just like before, she did not turn away.

Her leg tensed, the toe of her shoe moving up and down in a familiar rhythmic pattern. Familiar . . . She had done it before, more than once in the hour I'd had her in the basement. A nervous tic, maybe something I could use to my benefit. She was right about one thing. I would not allow Vainar, nor anyone else, to touch her, because now she belonged to me.

Now I had to determine what the feck I was going to do with her.

I tossed a cloak over her shoulders before I left, the temperature in the basement already dropping. It was only when I emerged onto the street above that I realized the lingering irony.

We were bonded by a secret that could be deadly to us both, and I did not even know her real name.

# Chapter 6

## FIONNA

*No one alive remembers Irska before the peace walls. Growing up, they were as much a part of the landscape as the water in the bay or the hills in the distance beyond the city. At least, that's what I thought as a child. But as I got older, I saw them for what they truly were—the walls of a prison. Meant not to keep us safe or even separate. They were to keep us in. We did not live in peace villages. But we certainly died in them.*

*—Aiofe Nowak, Síofran Rebel Army*

I slept upright in a hard wooden chair. It was not the first time. Aurelle had subjected me to all sorts of indignities over the past decade. Honestly, climbing through brambles and being cut up by poisoned widowsbloom rose thorns was not even in the top five most painful and humbling experiences I'd lived through at her behest.

But I'd never slept with arms and legs bound. Still, mental exhaustion was as real as physical, and my body was about to lose the battle to stay conscious.

They'd taken me in the morning, but I had no idea how long I had been unconscious. My stomach growled. Not exactly a reliable marker of time, given the fact that I was used to three rich, filling meals a day.

There were no windows in the basement to mark the time, and neither Helio nor any of his three companions returned.

Helio—my tormentor. The leader of the changelings who'd kidnapped me, but surely not the leader of all the changelings. Did they even have a leader? They were fractured, I knew that much. But other than knowing the names of the major factions, I had never bothered to learn about the internal workings or conflicts between them. My sole focus had been Treasa.

My heart twisted in my chest, the demands of exhaustion fully eclipsed.

I was already a dead woman. It did not matter whether they believed me or not, whether I kept the secret of my identity or not—at least, not insofar as my own survival was concerned. The changelings would kill me because that was what they did.

The taken were never seen again. It was an axiom I remembered from childhood, before my parents died.

In some ways, knowing that I was going to die made things easier. For years, every calculation had accounted for my survival as key to Treasa's—only by staying alive could I adequately protect her. But now that my death was a foregone eventuality, my calculations were simplified.

I did not care about the humans. I did not care about the changelings. Maybe if my parents had lived longer, I would have grown up with some bias. A decade on, it was a moot point. The only calculation that mattered now was how to get my sister to safety.

But I was too tired to think clearly. I'd tapped my foot so many times that the muscles in my calf ached. Still, the beast of anxiety inside me demanded I keep going. Three taps, and then I could sleep. Except maybe if I tapped three more times, then Treasa would be safe tonight. Was it even night? I could not risk it. I tapped three times.

My eyes drifted closed.

Sleep had always been slow to come for me, but this was worse. Every time it came near, the weight of my own head lolling to the side snapped me back awake. My mind began to conjure images, half dreams that blurred the line between the reality of the dark basement and my imagination.

Helio's words echoed in my mind.

*I will enjoy dismantling him, joint by joint.* I would enjoy watching.

*I will burn his flesh until it melts away and those shards are nothing more than ash.* I'd mark the destruction of every finger, the ones that had curled around the blade as it cut into my skin.

In my half-sleeping haze of exhaustion, I could picture Helio's cruel face, his mismatched eyes, one blue and one green, narrowed in brutal focus, the scar that curved around his right eye crinkling as they narrowed. I saw his wide shoulders, his muscles bunching as he leaned down to sever one of Vainar's fingers. His dark-burgundy hair fell forward to skim his jaw as he drew another scream from the prince.

Fantasy or dream . . . either way . . .

It did not disgust me. My stomach did not turn. What did that mean about me? Was I really any better than the Rebels who'd captured me?

*Tap, tap, tap.*

I was still awake. Fantasy, then.

Rough wool rubbed against my cheek. The weight of my own head was too much, the exhaustion was going to win.

Winning did not matter—it never had. Survival. That was always the goal. I would not survive. But my sister would.

Treasa. I would save Treasa . . .

—⁘—

A melodic, steady beat filled the air, filled my ears. My body rotated on the spot, searching for the source of the sound. A bodhran, maybe, though I'd only ever seen one in the royal museum, a wing of the castle that Aurelle had only visited when forced to by her tutors.

But the street was empty, every window sealed, the entire scene cast in shades of gray. Gray was normal in Irska, positioned on the Isle of

Eerin, nestled into a cold northern sea. But this gray felt different . . . like seeing the world through slightly shaded glass.

Seeing a world that I did not recognize, yet I knew . . . this was Irska.

How could I dream of a place I'd never seen?

I swallowed, disrupting the steady beat. Realization. The sound was not a drum but my own heartbeat. I was in my body, seeing the dream through my own eyes. Yet it felt strange, different in a way that I could not quite quantify. Like a garment that is just a little too small or a sentence whose wording needed finessing.

I reached out to steady myself, and suddenly the world spun. A new one reappeared, this one just as new and yet eerily familiar. My hand clung to the stone—

What stone?

I stumbled as my head fell back, trying to take in the enormity of the wall rising above me. I'd never seen the peace walls as anything other than snakes slithering through the city in the distance. But what else could it be, this expanse of concrete that towered above my head?

They divided the city into human and changeling peace villages, so named because they protected both sides from the endemic conflict of Irska.

But there was nothing peaceful about this street.

It was as empty as the one that had come before. But where the windows had been closed, these hung open on broken hinges. Half the street had been wiped away entirely, the wreckage of a changeling fireball left behind in its wake. Rubble littered the street, and wood smoldered, as if the explosion had only just occurred, but then where were all the people . . .

My feet carried me back, away from the wreckage. But the peace wall was there, hemming me in. My hands flattened against it, fingernails digging into the hard concrete . . .

I blinked and the street filled with people.

Where the wreckage had been a two-story wood and stone edifice rose up.

People moved through the street, individual voices lost to the clatter of a crowd. Even with the wreckage gone, the street still wore the ravages of war. Rubble on the ground—old rubble, from past attacks. The shutters still hung from the windows in disrepair, though now a woman leaned out overhead to string up laundry, and from the other side of the street, a baby cried.

A trio of women manned a stall next door to the not-destroyed wood and stone building. They were dressed in tattered clothing little better than rags, like everyone else on the street. But that was not what caught my eye.

As I watched, an elderly man approached. He drew something out of his cloak. It took me several heartbeats to understand that it was two halves of a broken stoneware jug. He held them out to the women, one in each hand.

Words passed between them that I could not hear. Then the three women joined hands.

I blinked again, not believing what I saw.

The two pieces of broken stoneware were gone, and in their place a singular, rounded jug. The elderly man nodded. The women unclasped their hold on one another. Coin passed from hand to hand.

Magic, like I'd seen in the basement.

How . . . was it not an anomaly? Was the magic I'd witnessed . . . It couldn't be . . . the norm?

Magic had been extinct in Irska for hundreds of years. Yet there it was, right before my eyes.

Even more startling was the realization that the people moving all around me were not human at all . . . They were changelings. The differences were subtle—the style of plait their women preferred. The colors and design of their clothing, emphasizing layers that could conveniently hide weapons. It was a changeling peace village . . . but why would the changelings firebomb their own kind?

Two young men appeared from the alley to my right, one shoving the other. I tried to move out of the way, but I wasn't fast enough—

They passed through me. Straight through me.

A dream, I remembered. None of this was real. A dream. A bad dream. *None of this is real.*

# Chapter 7

## FIONNA

*No one dreams of becoming a Defender. We aren't like those changeling scum who raise their children for violence from the cradle. Humans fight because we have to. They are the ones who created the fireballs and started targeting civilians. They lost the war, but they couldn't leave it there. What choice did we humans have but to retaliate? That is why I fight every day. I couldn't join the Peace Guard, they only take men. But the Defenders will take anyone. I have a wife and daughter. I fight for them. If I die for them, then they'll remember me in their prayers.*

*—Enna Dutko, Irska Defense Force*

The door opened on soundless, oiled hinges, but the shift in the air was enough to wake me from my fitful slumber. I knew it was him even before I turned to look. Maybe it was the magic that drew my gaze with unspeakable demand. Or maybe it was a sense of self-preservation seeded so deep within me that I could not hope to recognize it consciously.

The cloak fell from my shoulders as I turned, determined to take in as many details as I could despite the darkness. I'd been in and out of sleep for the last hour, and my eyes had had plenty of time to adapt to the lack of light. The details of the basement were as ingrained as those of my tiny shared bedroom in the castle. Focusing on physical details was the only thing keeping the anxiety in my chest under control. I'd faced it down my entire life, and I would not lose to it now. The changelings had robbed me of the little control I'd had. I would not let my anxiety have the rest.

I did not allow myself to dwell on my nightmares or to interrogate the fact that they were not of my captor, but of Irska itself.

Blue-gray light leaked in around Helio's hulking form in the doorway. Daylight, not candlelight. I blinked, trying to force my eyes to adjust to the change. Before I could, the bounds on my wrists were cut and something forced into my hand.

I must have blinked at the roll stuffed with cheese and meat for longer than I realized.

"Eat," Helio ordered.

My traitorous stomach growled.

"How do I know it is not poisoned?" I flinched at the sound of my own voice, gravelly from disuse.

For now, Helio wanted the rest of the Rebels to believe I was Princess Aurelle. Because it served his purpose, not mine. But I could exploit that for as long as those coincided. It was a dangerous calculation—the most dangerous of any I'd made over the past decade.

The toe of my shoe lifted from the ground, determined to tap. I was powerless to stop it, as always. But after the third tap, the weight in my chest eased just a fraction. Just enough.

I could do this. Not for myself, but for Treasa.

Hers was the face that kept coming back to me between the strange, lucid nightmares I couldn't quite parse. She'd been my motivation for ten years, and just because my circumstances had changed, that had not.

My captors had left me alone for several hours, and the time I hadn't spent sleeping or fighting my panic I'd used to plot. If Helio was determined to keep my real identity a secret, then he was also limited in his ability to research my background. He'd mustered enough resources to infiltrate the castle, so he clearly had valuable contacts. But they'd failed him when it came to kidnapping the right person. So they were not entirely reliable. I had to exploit that. The trick would be to give him information without revealing too much about myself and endangering my sister.

"Because we don't bother with slow deaths unless you're conscious for them," Helio said, crossing his arms over his chest.

The scent of the roll made my treacherous stomach growl again. But I pretended not to hear it. "Not all poisons cause unconsciousness."

One dark-red brow lifted toward his hairline. "Is an education in poisons usual for royal servants?"

*No. But it is when you spend an inordinate amount of time convincing the tea master to brew special teas to combat your anxiety.*

Not that I would be arming him with any additional information about me. I'd done my best to hide my compulsions, and the anxiety could be attributed to my current circumstances. He did not need to know that it was something I'd lived with my entire life.

I chose my words carefully. "I benefited from growing up at the princess's side."

He stalked a step closer, his looming presence even more intimidating with the light behind him, darkening his features. "You are going to have to give me more than that if you want to prove your worth."

"Ask me a question." This time, the roughness of the words was not caused by disuse.

Something flickered in his eyes, both of them. It looked different in each. It might be amusement. He enjoyed playing with his captives.

"I might learn more from watching you throw out tidbits you think are without value," he said, confirming my observation with a single sentence.

"Maybe I'd be better off not speaking at all." I was dead. No matter what happened, what I said, I was dead. It might even be better for Treasa if I died sooner, before the Rebels could connect me with Treasa.

He crouched down, bringing our gazes level. Another tactic, I told myself, this one to try and lessen the perceived power discrepancy between us. How often had I made sure to lower myself to a curtsy before making a request of Princess Aurelle or another superior? Helio would have to try harder than that to deceive me. It seemed the games of servant and master were not so different from captive and captor.

But when his eyes flickered this time, it was not with amusement, cruel or otherwise. Whatever it was that caused his eyes to narrow, obscuring the gold within the green and brightening the icy blue, I was not quite able to discern its meaning.

"You're not ceding the battlefield already, are you?" he challenged, his words no more than a whisper.

They were words he said for me alone, to goad me, to prevent me from descending into despair. Not for my own sake, but for his. A despondent captive was less helpful than one that was spitting mad.

"Feck you," I hissed.

He straightened, all pretense dissolving. "I don't consort with human filth. Now eat."

Rage boiled me from the inside out. I wanted to live . . . if only so I could fecking kill him. No matter that it was a physical impossibility.

I lifted the roll to my mouth and took a defiant bite, holding his gaze as I chewed and swallowed.

His jaw ticked, but his mouth hardly moved as he spoke. "Good girl."

I shivered despite the heavy weight of the cloak and the heat flushing over my skin.

"We're wasting time feeding the inmate," a sharp voice cut in, puncturing the tension in the cellar. She appeared in the doorway Helio had vacated only moments before. He'd left the door open, I realized. "I suppose even vermin need food and water to stay alive."

Her blond hair was braided back in the same Síofran style, but her clothing was different. At least a day had passed, and in that day, she'd felt secure enough to return to a place of residence and engage in normal routines, like changing into fresh clothes. I tucked that information away, unsure what it might mean for me, while trying to ignore the threat in her words.

Helio had said no one would touch me. No one except him. I should not have found that as comforting as I did. Especially given the way he was staring at me.

His mismatched eyes were even more stark in the daylight, the blue and green distinctly different. Either color would have been remarkable—the pale icy blue, the green striated with gold—but together they were otherworldly. He was a child of Síofra. No one could look at him without knowing he'd been touched by a goddess.

The intensity of his gaze forced my own down. I rolled my wrists in a circle, the limited freedom dangerously heady. But I did as I was told and lifted the roll to take a bite. Helio watched as I chewed, swallowed, and went back for another.

The woman made a sound of disgust.

"Karine, go secure the alley," Helio ordered in the same tone he'd commanded me to eat.

I slid my gaze her way without moving my head, trying to watch her reaction without drawing any more of her notice. She opened her mouth, closed it, and turned away to follow orders without another word.

I committed her name to memory—not that I was likely to forget the murderous gleam in her eyes. Helio had not let her name slip. He'd given it to me as an offering, a little bit of information that worked on two levels. More information would give me a false sense of security. More information also shrank the already nonexistent possibility that I would survive my captivity.

"She hates me," I said, letting the half-eaten roll drop with my hand into my lap. My legs were still bound.

"We all hate you," Helio said without looking at me. He did not bother to light the fire or any of the torches set into the wall, moving behind me instead. With my arms unbound, I had more range of motion than before. I could see the crates and burlap bags stacked along the wall behind me. Apparently my basement had other uses beyond just as a prison cell.

That quashed any lingering hunger, despite the half-eaten roll still in my hand. "All humans, or me in particular?"

Helio settled a pack over his shoulders, another in his hand, before turning to me. "Yes."

I swallowed down the anxiety that rose in answer to his single word. The statement of a fact I already knew should not have unsettled me so much. But my anxiety did not give a single feck about logic.

Footsteps sounded from the stairs that led out of the basement. Voices, too. But before I could try to make out any words, Helio dropped the second pack and knelt before me.

"What are you . . ." The ropes that bound my legs snapped free.

I shot to my feet without conscious thought, freedom a demand I could not refuse. I ignored my ankle's protest at the sudden movement. They were truly going to release me. My captor had realized I was worthless and . . .

Iron manacles snapped around my wrists.

I dropped the remains of my roll on the floor.

Helio towered above me. I was average height for a woman, but he was unnaturally tall. *Unnatural*, that was the only word to describe him. There was no other word for those unsettling eyes and the cruel light in them.

He enjoyed watching the hope die upon my face. He was glad to be the one who murdered it.

Anger rose up in my chest, subduing the anxiety and flooding my senses with interminable heat. But Helio spoke before I could lose my temper.

"We are moving to another safe house. If you want to live to your next meal, you will keep quiet and not cause any fuss."

The heat remained, but the edge of my anger dulled instantly.

He threatened *my* life. Which confirmed that Helio did not know about Treasa, which meant the rest of the Rebels did not, either. If they had, they would have leveraged her against me to ensure good behavior. For now, she was safe.

And I was still a dead woman.

I bit down hard on my tongue to keep in the words that threatened to spill out of me. Helio lifted one dark-red eyebrow, as if waiting. The corner of his mouth curled, the closest thing to a smile I'd seen on his face. It lacked all warmth, all humor. A smirk of malice. The face of a monster.

I'd spent my entire life with a monster living inside me. I would not be scared of this man.

Footsteps sounded louder on the stairs. The pack on the ground shifted, sliding to lean against my shin. It had to be for the Rebel descending the stairs, the rest of my escort, probably Karine, the woman who'd as soon gut me as see me to supposed safety.

I jerked my gaze away from Helio, wiping all expression from my face, determined to deprive him of any perceived advantage that a window into my feelings might give. But I was powerless to keep my mouth closed as the woman stepped into the room.

Not Síofran. Not a Rebel.

A human—one I knew.

Sima braced one hand against the wall to mediate her surprise. I would rather have died on the spot than reached for Helio to steady me.

It could not be. I must still be sleeping, still dreaming those strange nightmares. The taken never returned, and the dead always remained so.

Except I was also fairly certain they did not speak.

"Fionna?"

# Chapter 8

## FIONNA

*We've all lost friends to the other side. Family, too. It's impossible not to when a conflict goes on this long and runs this deep. Once, when I was a child, there was a brief ceasefire. It seemed like the Republic of Eerin was ready to intervene on our behalf, and that was enough to keep the humans behind their peace walls for a few weeks. It would have been easy for Eerin to overthrow the humans. They are Síofran. They are us. While in Irska, our magic is trapped, but in Eerin . . . all classes of Síofran can thrive. But they abandoned us to the humans, and the humans eventually got tired of waiting. We never knew the price, only that Eerin refused to pay it. So the violence resumed and we continued killing one another.*

*—Lena O'Brien, Síofran Rebel Army*

"Sima," I gasped as she came forward and took my hands, bracing them within her own. She gripped me tight, her fingers still strong despite no longer spending hours of her life kneading bread in the castle kitchens. Despite being dead.

She raked her eyes over my features, while I did the same to hers. Her brown hair was tied back in a neat bun, just like always, though there were no smudges of flour on her cheeks. Her olive skin had more color to it than she'd had in the castle; she must have been spending time outside. While my figure was soft and rounded, Sima was lean and tight, a human servant with access to regular food tempered by hard work.

Except that maybe she was not human at all, not if she was here.

But I did not get to ask any of the dozens of questions that sprang to my lips. She released my hands and turned to the imposing man who stood staring down at us, any hint of that cruel smirk replaced with a frown that could surely make grown men cry.

"Helio," she exhaled, giving me one last look before sighing heavily. "This is not the princess."

He growled. Like a real fecking animal. Wasn't there a class of Síofran who could actually shift into animals? Why hadn't I seen that in my ridiculous dreams?

I couldn't help but laugh. It seemed like a fine alternative to breaking down altogether. Never mind that my laughs had always been counted. What was there to laugh about in a life of desperate servitude in a city-state locked in a deadly guerilla war? About as much as there was in my current situation, but that did not stop the hysterical sound from bubbling out of my chest.

Helio and Sima exchanged a look. He was probably trying to ask if I was insane without actually saying the words aloud.

"I know what she is," he finally said. "We cannot very well call her Aurelle in the streets anyway. Will she answer to Fionna?"

"Of course, it is her name." Sima's eyes darted between me and my captor. "You said you knew who she was—"

"*She* is standing right here," I bit out. I seemed to have left the ability to keep my tongue glued to the bottom of my mouth back in the castle when they'd kidnapped me.

"We do not have time for this," Helio snarled.

Sima took a step back toward the stairwell. I did no such thing.

Helio shoved the remaining pack at Sima. "Get back up with Karine. We'll be along in a minute. Be ready."

Sima spared me one last look, then nodded. She leaned in to say something to Helio—something I could have heard if I were brave enough to take a step or two closer. But despite being unbound, I still lingered by the chair in the center of the room. As if there was any safety to be found in the weakly joined wood.

Helio waited for Sima's footsteps to die away before turning back to me. He kicked my chair out of the way. I did not look back to see if it splintered as it collided with the crates along the rear wall. But I did not flinch, either.

He seemed to note it, his mouth lifting from the deep frown into a severe but flat line. When he reached for me again, it was to settle the cloak back onto my shoulders. It was much too big for me, the ends kissing on the ground. As far as disguises went, it seemed a poor one to me. The garment was clearly not mine. But then again, most of the Síofran in Irska were desperately poor. They couldn't afford to put aside a valuable outer layer just because it was the wrong size.

Unlike the night before, Helio took the time to fasten the cloak beneath my chin. I did not flinch, but I could not stop the gasp as his calloused fingertips scraped across the exposed skin of my throat.

In the hours I'd drifted in and out of sleep, the temperature in the basement had dropped considerably. I'd attributed it to the fire, or lack of one. But the temperature seemed to be rising once more, and there was no blaze in the hearth. Just Helio and me, and the touch of his rough skin against smooth, the towering height of him above me.

I could have lifted my knee and rammed it into his groin. I could have tried to run. My legs were unbound. He'd even given me a weapon of sorts by locking my hands in the heavy iron manacles. They'd do significant damage if I could get them to connect with someone's face or the back of their head.

But I had no illusions about besting Helio.

I did not know who or what he truly was. But I'd seen enough to know that I would not win against him, even without the two females waiting at the top of the stairwell.

His fingers left my skin, sliding the button into place, then the one below it. My hands in their manacles were well concealed beneath the voluminous cloak. But Helio did not release me. His hands lingered, his index finger tracing the thread of the cloak. I had not noticed it in the darkness of night, but I could just see it now. Long, stylized feathers were embroidered along the seam where the edges met, the color of the thread a single shade lighter than the black wool of the cloak itself.

I tried to steady my breath as it came out. But the heat of the room made breathing difficult, and it was a terrible, stuttering sound. It broke whatever hold had come over Helio. He rocked back, putting enough space between us that my next breath came easier, but not enough to remove the threat that his mere existence posed to mine.

"Will she keep your secret?" I asked.

"Our secret," he corrected, tightening the straps of his pack. "I am her superior. She will slit your throat if I tell her to."

That had to be a lie. I'd known Sima for a decade. She'd already been in service in the castle kitchens when Treasa and I arrived. But then she'd died . . . except not, because here she was with the Rebels, and answerable to the worst of them all.

"Charming," I choked out.

"Keep your mouth shut," he said, finding my elbow through the cloak and steering me toward the stairs. The words did not surprise me. The fact that they sounded more like advice than demand, did.

Sima and Karine waited at the top of the stairs. I'd expected another room, maybe a tavern or public space, but the basement opened directly into an alleyway, which accounted for the amount of daylight that had filtered in over the last few minutes and the complete lack of it before.

We moved in a line, Karine and Sima side by side with their heads bent together in real or performative conversation. I knew that Sima was human, but it was jarring to realize there was nothing to distinguish her from Karine. I could not even recall seeing a Síofran. Academically, I knew they dressed differently. Preferred three-strand plaits to the intricate braids popular among the humans in the castle. But in reality, seeing them together, there was no distinguishable difference.

I should have been able to tell, shouldn't I?

But with my bound hands covered by the cloak and Helio a half step behind me, we appeared innocuous. Unremarkable. Or perhaps the people of Irska were so well trained at ignoring the incongruous that we did not even register.

The alley dead-ended into a heavily graffitied concrete wall, where we turned left and started down a wider thoroughfare, though still not an actual road. A few people walked ahead of us; I could hear distant voices behind. I watched the way that only servants know how to do, taking in as many details as possible, while simultaneously drawing no notice to myself. It was no less a game of survival here than it had been in the castle.

The bluish-gray light, paired with the clouds of condensation from our breath, told me it was early morning. From the castle on the hill, I'd only ever seen the citizens of Irska moving as gray and black dots, like ants on the ground. But now that I moved among them I was able to catalog every detail. Their clothes varied from well-made but worn to rough and tattered. But unlike the castle, the quality did not seem to equate to a striation in social class. They all seeped quiet desperation.

I reminded myself to keep my head down as we reached the end of the walkway. The concrete wall still rose to my right, but the buildings on my left fell away to reveal a street already thick with people, despite, or because of, the early hour.

I'd been in crowds before—attended balls and social events at Aurelle's side. They always caused my anxiety to flare, but not like this. The beast in my chest lifted his head as my senses tried to sort out the disparity in the street. It was busy—undeniably busy. Too many people crammed into too small of a space, hemmed in by the wall now at my back and another at the other end of the street. But the most jolting part was not the close quarters. It was the quiet.

Followed immediately by the recognition.

I recoiled, the impact as real as any physical one.

Helio moved with me.

"What is it?" he demanded. The hand that had been at my elbow was now on my waist, gluing me to his side while the other brandished a knife with curved edges and an ominous dried red stain near the hilt.

I shook my head, unable to form words that made any sort of sense.

It was the peace village from my dream. Not just proximally, but literally. There were the shutters hanging at an angle from their hinges, and the line of washing hung out to dry. Ahead was the crater where I'd first seen destruction, and then the building that had been destroyed. And just beyond was the trio of Síofran women. They wore different clothing, their hands were not joined, and the elderly man was nowhere in sight, but they were otherwise exactly as they had been in my dream.

My mind scrambled for explanations.

I must have been conscious when they carried me through this street and into the basement. I did not recall it because of whatever they'd used to incapacitate me, or maybe because of the widowsbloom.

Maybe I had been here in my childhood, in the past when I'd had a family and the illusion of protection. Though that made no sense . . . This was a Síofran peace village, and Síofran and humans did not socialize. Still, I tried to rationalize. My mind could have stored the memory away along with all the others in a desperate bid to protect my sanity in the present. If that was the case, it had given up now.

Captivity was not good for the mind.

Neither was Helio's hand lingering on my waist. Even with the layers of cloth between us, I could feel the heat of every finger.

"I am not going anywhere," I hissed without turning my head. Seeing his sneer would do nothing for my rapidly fraying nerves.

Helio did not remove his hand. "I will make sure of it."

Never mind that I was bound or that we were in a Síofran peace village. There was nowhere for me to run, not with so many Síofran packed into the street. If they realized what I was, they'd probably do Helio's job for him.

We moved down the street slowly, weaving between the crowds with just enough purpose not to draw attention to ourselves. It took nearly ten minutes to reach the end of the street. I kept waiting, expecting the sounds to change. But the only thing that ratcheted upward was my own anxiety.

A few cloaked figures climbed over the wrecked building. Their rags declared them scavengers, searching for any bit of value left among the rubble. A woman knocked into my shoulder. Before I could open my mouth to apologize, she'd ducked her head and disappeared into the crowd. The glimpse I saw of her face was full of fear.

But this was a peace village. Everyone around me was Síofran. Surely they had nothing to fear here . . .

Not from each other, I realized as we turned onto a slightly less busy street. Businesses lined the road, but only half appeared open or occupied. More than one had a shattered front window. A low growl emanated from the darkness of another. A crow cawed plaintively overhead before landing on a dangling storefront sign.

The peace walls had been erected to quell violence, to allow the humans and changelings the peace of their own cloistered communities. I'd been born in a human peace village. There certainly was not abundance, but I remembered laughter. Hunger, but also joy. But this . . .

There might not be outright violence, but no one who walked that street would call it peaceful. It was a ghetto, a prison. A death sentence.

My mind could not process that.

*It would mean that everything I've been taught is a lie.*

The children of Síofra were dangerous. Humans had to protect themselves. We had to separate ourselves to cut down on the fireballs and the attacks.

But had the attacks really decreased? I'd been so preoccupied with mine and Treasa's survival that I'd hardly looked beyond the castle walls in the past decade.

It could not all be wrong. I'd received my education at the side of a princess. It was unlikely she would inherit the throne, though legally it was a possibility. Her tutors would not lie to her. To do so would mean to put all Irska at risk, humans included.

My heart pounded wildly in my chest. A wave of nausea rolled up to join it. I recognized the feeling of the beastly anxiety trying to take control. I could not lose that control, not now. I forced down a breath. That didn't work. My hands were bound. But I could still tap my foot. Three times. If I tapped my foot three times, that would tamp down the intensity. I'd be able to breathe through it.

I lifted my toe. Once. Twice—

I stumbled on the uneven ground, careening sideways into the crowd. Helio grabbed me, the hand on my hip sliding down to cup my bottom, his fingers digging in to keep me in place. My hands pitched forward, colliding with his chest. He did not react to the impact at all, a wall of iron as thick as my manacles.

Helio's other hand braced my upper arm, the knife still in his grip. My heartbeats seemed to slow, the moment stretching out between us. I could feel the people moving around us, the contrast sharp against the solid, unmoving force that was my captor.

My heart threatened to burst from the intensity.

"That's taking the ruse a bit far," Karine barked.

The world around us snapped back into focus. Helio released his physical hold, but his eyes stayed on mine.

I tapped my foot quickly. One, two, three.

On the third tap, I rocked back on my heels, finding them steady enough to hold me. The motion broke apart the last remnants of the hold between us. Helio turned to Karine.

"Who are you?" he snarled.

I blinked, confused, even though her eyes remained clear as she frowned. She opened her mouth, the retort a living thing on her lips. But Sima cut her off.

"We need to move. We're drawing attention," Sima said, one hand on Karine's shoulder. "Come, sister. Let's leave these two alone."

The women were so unalike there could not possibly be family blood between them, even without the difference in their races. But I understood what Sima was trying to do, and Helio's comment as well. We were not meant to appear to be together.

Sima guided Karine away through the crowd. I watched them go, but Helio had already shifted his attention. He was always tense, a block of tight, hard muscle. But now he'd gone completely rigid. I followed his gaze.

Two figures appeared at the top of the street. Male, female. One with close-cropped hair, the other, a long braid. One tall, one short. Gray clothing—a maroon tunic and fitted pants. Their only distinguishing feature was the wide berth of space that the crowd gave them on every side.

Humans.

"Peace Guards wear blue and white," I said before I could think better of it. My heart had taken up residence in my throat now, beating wildly once again.

"Those are Defenders," Helio breathed.

He did not waste time on any more explanation. He returned his hand to my waist, like a man might hold his wife. That was the ruse that Karine had referred to. Karine and Sima played two sisters. Helio and I, a young couple. Not together, just both moving casually through the streets with all the other crowds on an early morning, accomplishing the day's business.

Helio steered me farther down the street, away from the humans.

Defenders—the colloquial name for the Irskan Defense Force. I'd never met a member. Officially, they were not sanctioned by the castle or the king. Unofficially, the Peace Guards looked the other way while the Defenders took care of the extremist Rebels.

Not these people in the crowded street, these normal citizens. There was no place for the Defenders here.

Except the man with an arm around me was a Rebel commander. We were only three or four steps behind two of his subordinates.

The Rebels were everywhere.

The arrival of the Defenders had not made my situation any safer. If anything, my captors were now more on edge and my situation even more precarious.

I forced my gaze down, determined to play my part and make it to the next safe house. The streets of Irska were no place for forming a coherent plan.

I recognized the glow leaking from between Karine's fingers. A fireball.

My anxious mind spun. Reckless, dangerous, suicidal. Who could she possibly be helping by carrying a fireball through a crowded street? She was everything that I'd been warned about, both in my childhood before the castle and my forced adulthood after. Changelings do not care how many people they kill. All they want is vengeance, no matter the cost.

"Feck," Helio cursed under his breath. "They are following us."

My head snapped back, but Helio's hand was already there, cupping the nape of my neck and keeping my face forward. Ahead of us, Karine and Sima reached a crossroads and paused, pretending to look in a window. Helio maneuvered us deftly through the crowd, passing the two women without a sideways glance.

"If you want to live, you will keep your head down and your mouth shut," he breathed into my ear.

"They are humans," I stammered. A stupid fecking statement, and we both knew it.

"You are with children of Síofra in a Síofran peace village," he said. "They will hurt first and ask questions later."

I blinked through to understanding. I'd been concerned about what the Síofran all around us would do to me if I declared myself human. I had not considered what the Defenders might do if they took me for a Síofran myself. There were no physical differences between us, just circumstances. Dormant magic that showed no outward sign. They'd assume I was Síofran because I kept company with other changelings in a Síofran peace village.

But maybe that was wrong, too. I'd seen Karine perform magic. I'd thought Sima was dead. Perhaps there was a way to visually distinguish, and I'd just never been taught.

A stranger, more preposterous possibility took hold.

Was Helio trying to protect me?

*No. He is protecting his treasure.* The Rebels had expended significant energy to kidnap Princess Aurelle, only to get a servant in her place. If something happened to me before they could torture me for information, then it was truly all wasted.

We turned again, this time onto a residential street.

My stuttering heart nearly broke in half.

The devastation was even more apparent here. No fireballs had hit this street, but the houses were half falling down anyway. Lines of washing crisscrossed overhead, the state of the clothing made my stomach turn. Most were little better than rags, and they came in every size, right down to infant. Infants in rags. That was the truth of Irska I'd never seen.

We were halfway down the street before I realized it. I turned to look, to see if we'd been followed . . .

Helio shoved me up against a wall. The wood groaned behind me, but by some miracle it held. He pressed his forehead to mine, one hand sliding inside the recesses of my cloak and latching on to my waist. My head swam. I almost missed the widowsbloom. At least then I had been able to account for the wild tangle of sensations thrumming through my body.

"Just let them pass," Helio said, sliding his nose along my cheekbone and then down my jawline, burying his face in my neck.

I could not have formed a coherent word. The fear of the Defenders, the desperation of the Síofran peace village, the heat of his breath as it slid beneath my clothing . . .

"No rutting in the street!" The male's voice echoed off the buildings. This street was much narrower than the commercial thoroughfares. I swore I felt the wooden structure itself tremble behind me.

A derisive laugh. They were still several yards away.

"I told you, they are little better than animals," the female crowed.

"Do not run," Helio said, his lips brushing the shell of my ear, the words almost disappearing. I knew it was only to keep the words between us, but my stomach flipped. I wanted to tap my foot, just to see if it would make the feeling go away.

His hand moved in the space between us. I gasped as a long, hard shape pressed against my thigh. The knife.

He was going to kill them.

Where the feck were Sima and Karine?

Maybe this was my chance. Surely the two Defenders would listen long enough for me to explain myself. We weren't in a crowd anymore. I could make my case, and they would protect me from . . .

"Learn some fecking manners you animal!" The man bellowed.

Helio spun.

I ripped at my hands, trying to brace myself, only to remember they were bound in front of me. The entire weight of my body fell back into the wall. The wood groaned. I could not help the yelp that escaped my lips.

But at the same moment, a door on the other side of the street crashed open.

Flew open.

By magic.

# Chapter 9

## Fionna

*Changelings will do anything to gain the upper hand. They will sacrifice their elderly, their children. They will kill their own with those fecking fireballs, as long as they take out at least one human in the blast. The magic made them greedy, and even when it was stripped away, they continued to grasp. They try to deceive us. Stir up rumors. My granddad believed that some magic survived the war. But I think it's all a trick to scare the humans. Trick or not, magic is illegal, and the punishment is death.*

*—Petor McConnell, Peace Guard*

Two children tumbled out onto the stoop.

The door could have been explained by anything. A crosswind. An exasperated parent who had promptly disappeared back inside. But the child floating in the air two feet above the stoop could not.

The smaller child squealed as his sibling laughed from the ground, twirling his finger slowly and rotating his brother through the air. In the moment, I did not note that they were thinner than they should be, or the tattered state of their clothing. I just saw children, smiling and laughing and unabashed. Unbroken.

Just like their magic.

It wasn't terrifying to see, not like it had been when Karine wielded it. There was no threat. They were children, being children, and it was beautiful.

It was also a death sentence.

The residential corridor was deserted. Narrow. There was nowhere to hide. And from the expressions of mixed horror and glee on the two Defenders' faces, there was no hope of reprieve.

But there was one notable emotion missing from their faces—surprise. They saw the children's magic, recognizing it for what it was, but they were not surprised by it.

Did everyone know the truth except me?

For once, my heartbeats seemed to slow rather than speed up. The seconds stretched out with painful length as everything happened at once. The Defenders reached for their weapons—batons with spikes at the end. Their charter might be unofficial, but their matched maces were fully legitimate. The child on the ground, the one who held his younger brother aloft, realized he had an audience. His eyes blew wide, his little mouth falling open in an expression of betrayed shock.

And Helio—he transformed.

Gone was the man who'd brushed his body against mine, telling me to hold still and keep up the farce. Neither was he the gruff, commanding presence who had steered me down the street. Nor even the threatening monster who'd so terrified me in the confines of my basement prison.

I realized that until that moment, I'd never seen him truly unleashed.

The barely constrained anger that he'd held in check while demanding to know Vainar's crimes against me burst free in a torrent that shattered the moment. When I saw his face, I thought that rage might be enough to shatter the entire world.

Then the male Defender lunged for the children, and a part of me understood Helio's anger.

Helio did not hesitate. He did not hustle me down the street. He did not look at me at all. He moved with that Defender—faster. Three steps that easily outpaced the man and he was between the human and the child, wicked blade raised.

I would have followed him, but the other Defender stayed with me. She swung her baton, and she did not hesitate, either. She hit me square in the stomach, forcing all the air from my lungs and bringing me straight to my knees. The thick wool cloak protected me from the spikes, but my arms screamed where they took a glancing impact. The wounds from the poisoned rose bushes ripped open anew.

I tasted copper, my chest contracting painfully as I tried to force air back into my lungs. The woman's laugh echoed above me. I lost my balance, couldn't catch myself with my hands bound, fell sideways, landing hard on my shoulder in the dirt.

Maybe I hit my head. I wasn't sure. My whole body was vibrating. But I was barely paying attention to myself. I rolled to the side; I had to see what was happening across the street.

The male Defender swung his mace with wicked brutality. I'd watched enough Peace Guard training to recognize that every attack was meant to kill, not injure. But Helio met every single one. He moved so quickly it almost seemed that he could anticipate the other man's movements. He did not duck away or move out of range. He met each swing of the spiked baton with his own blade.

But they were not one-on-one for long. The female Defender deemed me dealt with and threw herself into the fray. She came at Helio from the side, running at him with force. He met her, grabbed her forearm just below the wrist, and threw her into her male companion.

The woman hit the ground. Her male counterpart did not even pause to check on her before engaging Helio again.

It felt like minutes had passed since the children stumbled out onto the stoop, but it must have only been seconds. Otherwise they would have been back inside already or an adult would have come to fetch them. The floating toddler would have already been safely back on the ground.

But only seconds had passed.

The older child tried to lower his brother down gently, but his entire body quivered. The toddler wobbled in the air and then fell, his shoulder hitting the concrete stoop. His cry split the street, louder than the fighting happening only a few feet away.

Breathing was still hard, but I gasped down air. More people would come. They had to, hearing the child's wails. I couldn't be on the ground, couldn't be a victim. If I was on my feet, I could . . .

I could escape.

Helio had already made his choice when he left me against the wall.

I was bound in iron manacles. All I had to do was run until I found a Peace Guard. I wasn't walking with Síofran Rebels anymore, looking the full part of conspirator. I was clearly a captive. I could get back to the castle, back to Treasa.

The first Defender was fully engaged with Helio.

My elbow cried out as I shoved myself up to my knees, but I ignored it. If pain was the cost of my freedom, I'd pay it a thousand times. I wobbled from side to side, my weight betraying me as I tried to get from my knees back to my feet without being able to use my arms for balance.

Helio slashed the male Defender across the chest. The man screamed, but instead of falling back, he moved forward in a torrent, his swings taking on the wild fervor of a wounded animal. The female Defender knelt, nursing a split lip. She'd be on her feet in a second. This was my one and only chance.

I rose in time with her, ready to sprint. I didn't get much exercise in the castle other than riding with Aurelle. But I could make it. I had to make it.

The Defender lifted her mace. I tensed the muscles of my thighs to run.

But she didn't go for Helio. She lunged for the injured changeling toddler.

I threw my whole body into motion. Not down the street to my freedom. Into the Defender.

We crashed to the ground together, perilously close to where the child had pulled himself up to sit, rocking back and forth, cradling his arm and crying. At least this time I had her body to cushion the force of my impact. Her mace glanced off my cheek. I felt the burn of the spikes, but I let it focus me rather than distract. I drove my weight down into my knee, directly into her chest. She shoved me back, sent me spinning. I rolled and used the momentum to get back to my feet. She was just a breath slower than me. But a breath was all it took. I brought my iron manacles down hard on her head.

For a brief second, I thought it wasn't enough. She blinked. Once. Twice. Then she collapsed sideways.

Instead of triumph, my stomach hollowed out. *What have I done?*

I'd attacked another human. I could have killed her . . . No, her chest was moving. She was alive, just unconscious. Another body hit the ground. I knew without looking who it was.

I couldn't tear my eyes away from the woman's body.

*The woman.* Body implied she wasn't alive, and she was. I had not killed anyone. I was not a killer. I was not one of them.

Who are *they*? My mind whispered.

Footsteps rang from the other end of the street, skidding to a stop when they reached us.

"What the feck happened?" Karine demanded. I kept staring at the ground. A line of blood trickled down from the woman's left temple. It pooled in the dirt.

"Defenders," Helio growled.

My eyes finally broke away from the woman on the ground when he knelt and scooped up the crying child.

A thin woman appeared in the open door, terror twisting her features. How long had passed? What had she been doing that had taken her so long to realize the horror unfolding outside her door?

But part of me knew that while the fighting had felt like a lifetime for me, it must have lasted no more than two or three minutes.

The older child buried his face in his mother's skirts. Both children were safe.

I'd lost my chance to escape. But both children were safe.

Helio shoved the smaller child into the quivering woman's arms. "Two minutes," he told her.

Her eyes blew wide, the tears finally spilling out. But she nodded through them before turning and rushing back inside.

Helio did not wait to watch her go.

"We have to move them now," he said.

Sima and Karine seemed to understand as easily as the mother had. The former fell back into the middle of the street, looking both directions before striding for the end where the Defenders had first appeared.

Karine checked her weapons. I caught sight of several more fireballs strapped to her chest in a kind of crossbody holster. She still held one gripped in her fist. Fecking hell. She was death walking.

"Where?" she asked Helio as she moved on to the blades at her waist.

"Take them to Pearl House. She can sort them out from there," he said.

Karine only nodded. Apparently this was one decision she wasn't inclined to argue with.

The woman reappeared, a carpet bag clutched in one hand, the toddler held on her hip by the other. The older child clung to her leg.

Karine wasted no time in guiding the woman in the opposite direction, down the street. A gate I hadn't noticed before opened and a hand reached out, ushering them in, offering passage without prying eyes.

Eyes. Two mismatched eyes finally came back to me. Helio did not disguise his frown as he looked me over. His gaze lingered on my face, where the scratches from the Defender's mace still burned. But he did not meet my eyes.

"Sima," he called to the end of the street. "Cover our backs. We are going on."

She joined us in a few bounds. "What about them?"

I couldn't look down at the Defenders.

Helio already had a hand on my shoulder, turning me down the street. "Leave them."

# Chapter 10

## Helio

*There is no glory in moderation. There isn't even survival, not since the changelings created the fireballs. No one is safe. Nowhere is safe. Trying to live a normal life is a lie. This is our normal. The sooner that the citizens of Irska accept that and join the fight, the sooner we will win this war.*

*—Ronan Broz, Irska Defense Force*

To the end of the street, around the corner, and into the abandoned haberdashery. The door still locked. I turned the knob behind us. The rear door opened onto an alley that connected to the pie shop near the entrance to the peace village. Peace Guards stood on either side of the gates, monitoring the citizens moving in and out. Humans and Síofran alike came from across Irska to buy Maureen's pies, one of the rare places where we intermingled. Peace Guards marked every human who passed into the Síofran peace village, ensuring they got out safely. They didn't bother giving us the same regard.

In some ways, it was a risky place to pass through. But it would also be the easiest place for us to lose any tails.

We exited through the front with all the other patrons.

Three more turns and we reached the warehouse. This was one of the largest Síofran peace villages in Irska. But that hardly meant it was safe. Not for the occupants, not for the Rebels and Libs who moved in varying levels of secrecy through the streets, and certainly not for my captive.

Fionna kept her eyes down the entire time.

Her name had come as a surprise. An old Irskan name, predating the arrival of the humans all those centuries ago.

It should have given me a clue. Everything about my captive defied expectation. Not the human princess, but a servant. Defiant, but by as many turns, vulnerable. She'd had the chance to escape. She'd saved the Síofran child instead.

Until today, I'd only seen one other human act against the interests of their kind. And that human was currently trailing us a half block back.

My blood had just settled down from boiling when I lifted the heavy beam that sealed the warehouse door. It rolled back on wheels, a familiar face appearing on the other side.

"Where is Link?" I asked. Karine's brother was supposed to be on duty.

"Ate a bad fish pie," Heath answered, sneering down at my prisoner. The urge to punch him in that smug face was even stronger than usual. "Maureen sent me instead."

There was no such thing as a bad pie from Maureen's. It was code. Link had been detained by the Peace Guard. I'd deal with that later.

My current concern was the human at my side and the way her body had gone rigid as soon as Heath appeared. Feck that. I did not know what made me more fecking mad—that Heath had earned that fear by nearly striking her, or that she did not believe my promise of protection.

Or the fact that she was here at all.

Why hadn't she run?

I pushed Fionna over the threshold with a hand on her shoulder. Holding on to her hip was too dangerous. Not only did it cross the one line I'd set for myself as an interrogator but it was also against every belief I'd been raised to value. Síofran did not lower ourselves to consort with humans, even for the purpose of physical gratification.

I'd keep my hands above the waist from now on.

She didn't resist, but she turned her eyes up to me for the first time since she'd knocked out the female Defender in the peace village.

The fear in them reawakened the rage that had only just quieted. I was no stranger to fear. I did not feel it for myself. That was a luxury I'd never been afforded. But fear was as endemic to my people as the dormant magic in their veins. I'd learned to inspire fear as a way to fight back. I'd savored it in the eyes of my victims.

But I was not the cause of Fionna's fear, not this time. And that was fecking unacceptable.

I stepped into the open doorway, filling the entire space with my body, blocking out all the light. Heath was too proud to flinch. Fionna's eyes widened behind me, but she did not turn away and the fear in those dark orbs banked, just enough that I knew I could walk away.

"Remember what I told you," I said.

Heath's brows drew together. The glare of disgust was enough to intimidate most men, but not me. He was descended from wolves. Powerful. But nothing next to what dwelled inside me.

He'd made the same oath as Karine. While my oldest friend wanted to argue with my orders because she believed personal connection entitled her, Heath's entitlement was of a different nature. But the oaths we made were binding and punishable by death.

He jerked his chin down in a nod. Just like I'd known he would.

My eyes were already over his shoulder, on Fionna. The words were not just for Heath.

She didn't give me anything as tangible as a nod. Her eyes had not changed. Like most servants, she was good at hiding her reactions. But her body temperature had cooled slightly, I could sense it even from the doorway.

A stabbing pain in my chest protested as I turned away from her, but I ignored it. The human I needed in that moment had just appeared at the end of the street.

Sima's tight bun had come loose, several strands stuck with sweat to her temples and neck despite the late-winter nip in the air. Like Fionna, she was a servant by training. But a Rebel by choice. Her face gave no hint at what she was thinking or feeling.

"We need to talk," I said without breaking stride.

She huffed out a breath. "We certainly do."

Sima fell into step beside me as I walked the perimeter of the warehouse.

She confirmed Fionna's story with additional color. She was indeed the companion of Princess Aurelle. While Sima had never met or seen the princess herself, confined as she had been to the kitchens, she'd interacted with Fionna on many occasions. She confirmed that Fionna was clever, cautious. She stopped short of calling her calculating, but I kept the word on my own list.

We turned the second corner of the rectangular warehouse. Once it had held imports coming in from the bay. Now Irska was so isolated it had been abandoned.

I shortened my steps so that Sima could keep pace without huffing for breath. "What else can you tell me about her?"

Sima hummed, low and long. She looked past me, to the concrete wall that marked the edge of the peace village, and then through it. As if she could see beyond, even though she possessed none of Síofra's gifts.

We passed the halfway point. Soon I'd be back to dealing with Heath. "Sima, I am your superior. I order you to disclose any information that might be relevant to breaking our captive."

The scope of Sima's gaze tightened. She hummed again, shorter and more pointed this time. Pointed directly at me. But she answered. "She has a younger sister."

She did not deserve a thank-you for following an order. That was the simplest part of the oath she'd taken when she joined the Síofran Rebel Army. But I did nod. A penchant for torture and the dormant magic in my veins were not the only reasons I'd risen through the ranks of the Síofran Rebel Army. I wasn't flattering myself with the belief that I was a good leader of people. I was hard, but I was honest and direct. Those things went further than most people realized. But whatever graces I extended to my own, I reserved none for the humans. I never had.

Sima knew that, because she was the only exception—a human who had proven her allegiance to the Síofran cause beyond any doubt.

"Helio," she said as we turned the fourth corner of the warehouse. "You don't need to break her."

*Please don't break her.* The words she did not say. Could not say, because of the oath she'd taken and the side that she'd chosen in this war. Humans said it was over. The children of Síofra understood the truth.

We reached the door. Heath had closed it.

"I will do whatever I need to do," I said. For the cause. For my people. For freedom.

This time it was Sima who nodded. The motion was a comfort to herself, not to me. I watched her disappear into an alleyway before unbolting the door of the warehouse.

The windows high overhead were either broken or covered entirely with wooden boards. But there was enough scant light for me to locate Fionna, standing near the rear door, and Heath, glaring at her from the dead center of the empty space. The door did not open; it had been nailed shut long before the Rebels had added the warehouse to our network. But I understood the draw it must have on her. She was probably contemplating her missed opportunity. She had to be.

"You are dismissed," I said to Heath, stepping away from the rolling door so he could pass. I had no desire to touch him or talk to him.

"I am on first watch."

I should have known that. I did know it—at least, that Link was supposed to be on first watch and Heath had taken his place.

"You won't see anything useful from in here."

His discontent rumbled out of his chest, an almost wolflike growl, before he stalked out to trace the same path I'd taken with Sima. There may only be one functioning door, but none of us were foolish enough to think it was the only way in or out of the warehouse. Desperate people can do almost anything.

Maybe it was my own desperation that pulled the words from my mouth. It was only power of will that kept my back against the door I'd just bolted shut.

"I told you that no one would lay a hand on you," I said.

She did not turn to face me right away, leaving only her profile for me to consider. "No one except you."

"Was I right?" I knew the answer already. Heath would not dare.

"He did not touch me," Fionna confirmed. As she spoke, she lifted her head to look out a broken window far overhead. The warehouse was easily three stories tall. She wasn't short. Neither was I. Our physical bodies were both dwarfed by the enormity of the cavernous space.

But the questions swirling between us filled it easily.

Her eyes were no longer downcast. That should have felt like victory. But she wasn't looking at me, either. She gazed up at the light from the window. No, her eyes were closed. I watched the soft skin beneath her chin wobble as she took one deep breath and then another and another, carefully spaced and methodical. I could not see whether she was tapping her foot again, not with my cloak dragging on the ground and obscuring most of her luscious body.

Fecking hell.

I needed a woman. I had not struggled with my urges interceding on my thoughts like this since my adolescent years. It was fecking inconvenient. Uncomfortable. I hated it. Just like I hated the tension etched in her body.

I was very good at using my hate.

I pushed off the wall, my steps purposely leaden so they echoed through the empty warehouse. The unstoppable urge for self-protection opened her eyes, brought them straight to me.

I crossed my arms over my chest as I stepped out of the shadows. "Maybe you will finally start trusting me."

"Trusting you?" she breathed, barely loud enough for me to hear. Then she came undone. She spun on the spot, my wool cloak swirling behind her in time with her thick curtain of matching hair. Her pale cheeks colored immediately, the hold she'd kept on herself moments before shattered. "You kidnapped me from my home, threatened to torture me, nearly got me killed in the streets . . ." She trailed off, her dark eyes shifting away but not back down as she recalculated her words. She must have sorted them out, because when she turned that penetrating gaze back to me, her eyes were alight with black fire.

There it was, that spirit she'd shown earlier.

It would loosen her tongue and force her to spill her secrets, I told myself. It was the same tactic I'd used to manipulate countless captives over the years. It wasn't because I wanted to banish her fear.

I wouldn't reveal what I knew about her sister, not yet. I'd save that for a more pressing time. For now I just needed a few details from her, enough to convince my superiors that she was worth keeping around, that her kidnapping had not been a complete feckup.

But she beat me to the next question. "Why didn't you kill the Defenders?" she demanded, a step forward punctuating her words.

*Why did you attack one?* But that wasn't the information I needed, I reminded myself, even if it was the actual answer I wanted. The one that had plagued me with every beat of my blood through my veins over the last hour.

"There would have been too many questions," I said. The clever servant was unwilling to accept that. She rolled her eyes openly. My breath caught in my throat. No one had ever directed such an irreverent condemnation in my direction. Ever.

I didn't like it. But I could not say that I hated it, either. Not coming from her.

For her courage—or recklessness—alone, I gave her a better answer. "They never act alone. Someone in their command structure knew they were in that peace village. If they disappeared, they'd start killing Síofran until we produced them."

She tried to cross her arms. I recognized the motion. But they were still bound with the iron manacles. She frowned down at them, the lines of anger softening in her face as she remembered who and what and where she was.

*Why didn't you run?*

She pursed her lips together as she lifted her gaze back to mine. Her mind was at work again. She took another step forward, joining me in the light.

"I don't believe you," she finally said. "You were willing to let me escape in order to save those children."

I held my stance, but my mind reeled backward. At the accusation. *So much for trust,* I almost said. But this was not about trust. She did not think I'd lied to her; she did not believe the lies I told myself.

*And you gave up your chance of escape for the same reason.*

These were dangerous lines of thought. She was my captive, I, her captor. Human and child of Síofra. Servant and Firebird. Those last two were too close for comfort. I stopped that line of thinking, too.

"Believe what you want," I said, dropping my hands to my side. "But do not make the mistake of letting yourself believe that I am anything other than exactly what I appear to be."

A monster. I'd seen the word in her eyes the first time she fully saw me in the basement. I knew what I looked like. I'd never wanted for female company, but desirable was not the same thing as handsome. Women liked it best when they could avoid my mismatched gaze and take advantage of the hard planes of my body. My scars were not a deterrent; they were badges of honor among the Síofran. But the small magics I performed scared them. No Síofran alive had seen one of our kind at their full power. Let alone a Firebird. And yet even my diminished magics were more than most of them could muster with their entire family in accord and working together.

I was *other*. Even this human could see it.

But she did not retreat. The fear had returned to her eyes. I recognized the glint of it. Still, she stepped forward. That told me more about her than Sima had.

"Mercy is not a weakness," Fionna said. Several of the buttons on the cloak had come undone. On me, they remained taut and reliable. But even though she was buxom and round, she was still no match for my size. They gapped and then slipped free, the wool falling back to reveal the swell of her breasts where her shift had slipped down.

She was shredding my control, thread by thread, without even realizing it.

"Mercy is not in my repertoire," I said truthfully. I had not shown it to the Defenders, no matter how she interpreted the situation. And I could not give her any, either.

She lifted her chin. "But it is in your eyes."

I exhaled, surprised, the knives of her words burying themselves in my chest. Too sharp. A curl of dark hair sprang free from the rest, falling forward over her cheek.

Fionna reached for it by habit only to have it cut off by the thick manacles. She flinched, then sank her teeth into her bottom lip to forestall the sound that tried to sneak out. That's when I saw the chafed red skin beneath the manacles.

I closed the space between us without thinking, catching her hands. Mine were nearly twice the size of hers, but both of our palms were rough. Lives spent in service, though to different causes.

She let the hiss slip through her teeth as I lifted her hands to the light. The dark iron cut into the pale skin of her wrists, leaving behind angry red marks. She wasn't bleeding yet, but it wouldn't take much more to open new wounds on her delicate skin.

I had not closed the manacles this tight. But they were designed to respond to movement, and if the person wearing them tried to break or twist free, they would tighten notch by notch. But Fionna had not tried to run away—

She'd used the manacles to incapacitate the female Defender and protect the Síofran child. And received these wounds as her thanks.

My exhale was more controlled this time. "If you promise not to raise your hand against any of the Síofran, I will remove your restraints."

Wounds were dangerous. They could fester and lead to blood poisoning. Healers were expensive, and finding a Síofran healer willing to treat a human would be difficult. Let alone what it would mean for exposure and endangering the cause. Keeping her from further injury was prudent.

But despite her protestations about my mercy, Fionna pulled her hands back. "I don't want to hurt anyone."

But she had, to protect the child. And she would, to protect the sister Sima had told me about. "That is not a promise."

I wished I could see inside her mind, where she weighed the scales of decision. It would have been easy for her to lie. But the amount of time she took to consider told me she wouldn't.

"I promise not to harm any Síofran," she said at last.

It was the work of a moment to retrieve the key from a hidden inner pocket in my tunic and free her from the manacles. They dropped to the ground. We both let them. She immediately tucked her hands back inside the safety of the cloak.

Did she know that it was my cloak she wore?

Seeing the embroidered feathers, each crafted with meticulous care, so close to her face, the gleaming black blending with her lustrous hair, contrasting with her luminous skin . . . It was too large, yet it suited her.

A gust of cold intruded through the windows. Her hands were free, and she used them to catch the front panels and pull the cloak tighter around her. My cloak.

I refused to be jealous of a garment.

She could have run. She could have backed away or pushed me away. Her hands were free, her legs unbound.

But when I reached down and cupped her face with both hands, the moue of surprise was not scared. It was hungry. And when I took her lips, she opened for me.

It should have stopped there. A flick of my tongue over her lips, a moment of lust-fueled insanity. A thing that should never have happened and could never be allowed to happen again. Except she tasted like dreams.

Bloody fecking hell.

Kissing Fionna suspended me in that moment just before waking, when you knew enough to realize that the dream world where you lingered was not real, but its sweetness was still all consuming.

Heat flooded every sense, the fire inside me kindled to life by our connection. The Firebird awakened not with a screech, but with a song.

I jerked my hands away.

Only Síofran joined in common purpose could awaken magic. Whatever the heat was between Fionna and me, it was not magic. It was far more dangerous.

I retreated into the shadows, where I belonged. Fionna's chest rose up and down rapidly, the cloak falling forward to cover the swell of her breasts. *Síofra be thanked.*

Her eyes glowed with black fire again. The fear was still there, too, though it had changed its shape. She was not afraid of me, not in that moment. But of something bigger. Something more.

She shook it off, rolling her shoulders. My eyes tracked the twitch of her hands beneath the cloak in a steady rhythm. Not just three times, but six and then nine. I still was not sure of the significance.

"Was that what you meant when you said no one would touch me but you?" she asked. Her voice had returned to that careful servant's neutrality.

I curled my hands into fists. "Heath is on first watch. Keep that in mind before you try anything reckless."

But as I stalked out, I had the sense that we both knew those words were as much for myself as for her.

# Chapter 11

## HELIO





The scent of butter and crisp dough filtered up through the floorboards of Maureen's bakery. It was just past midday, the busy shop below our feet covering any sounds we might make. Subterfuge often happens in broad daylight. Especially when you have a little magic to help it along.

But it did not happen by accident. Everything about my life was a practice in intentionality. I did not ignore the way my mind slipped away from the warm attic, back to a brisk warehouse. Even as I shifted my stance, squaring my shoulders, my lips recalled the brush of hers, the firm pressure of her response. The muscles of my abdomen tightened at the memory.

*Acknowledge it.* I'd made a mistake by giving in to my physical desires. *Put it away.* It would not happen again. *Focus on the task at hand.* The council meeting was about to begin.

The six Síofran in the room approached rebellion in six different ways. But our goal was the same, and that gave us power. Enough to lay a trap at the door that would give us a few seconds of warning should any human attempt to broach it.

There was no auspicious dais with superiors sitting behind a table awaiting reports from their captains. This rebellion took place at dinner tables, in market stalls, and in this case, among bags of flour and sugar above a pie shop.

Maureen shoved one such bag of flour aside before climbing atop. She was on her feet all day by necessity; she'd always said she claimed rest by the same. I allowed myself a quick appraisal of her before moving on to the two councillors who'd arrived to hear my report. She looked tired, like usual. We were all tired. Always.

"Captain Forsyth will be here in an hour for his afternoon pie. If you like your heads where they are, I'd better be back behind the counter by then," she said, brushing back a lock of honey and gray hair and leaving behind a line of flour on her cheek.

The Peace Guard captain was stationed on the other side of Irska but made the trek to Maureen's every day he was on duty. Despite his weakness for Maureen's pies, he was as mean as they came. He was also notoriously loose-lipped once he started eating.

I didn't waste her time. Turi and Yelena, the other councillors, appeared as they always did. Karine and Heath were stationed by the two doors, functioning as guards, but they were also my two highest-ranked lieutenants.

"The prisoner was transferred and secured yesterday," I said.

Yelena stabbed her pointed chin into the air. A nod. She didn't smile. I'd never seen her smile. Not that there was ever much of that going around in the Síofran Rebel Army. But she wasn't frowning, which was remarkable in and of itself.

"We have not received any communications from the castle, directly or through proxies. No uptick in violence. No recriminations," Turi said. He was the strategist among the three and the one I would need to convince. Because at that moment, they all still believed we'd kidnapped a princess.

"We knew there was a chance they would try to keep the princess's disappearance a secret," Maureen put in from her flour throne.

"Yes, of course," Turi agreed, stroking his forefinger and thumb over his close-cropped beard.

Except Fionna was not a princess.

Lying was not possible. Not only would it be in direct violation of the oath I'd taken upon induction into the Síofran Rebel Army but it was also wrong. Disloyal to my people and to all the children of Síofra who had died at the hands of the humans. To my parents.

But I had to handle this perfectly.

Failure was not tolerated in our ranks. And this kidnapping could be considered worse than failure; it could be construed as betrayal. What if it had not been an accident? What if someone in the line of intelligence had betrayed us, causing us to take the servant rather than the princess on purpose?

I'd considered as much myself, but dismissed it. I knew my people. But the three councillors above me did not. It was part of how the Rebels structured our cells to keep them separate enough that no one informer could topple the entire rebellion.

"You've interacted with the princess the most," Turi said, turning to me. "Has she given any clue as to how her father might react?"

"No," I said. Truth.

Turi nodded, his mouth moving around unspoken words as he worked out ideas in his mind. Not unlike Fionna, whose mind was constantly turning with thoughts. Fionna, who had forced me into this position to begin with.

Who knew that a princess would have been easier to deal with than her servant?

Yelena scoffed, crossing her arms over her chest. The youngest of the three, she was also the harshest. Her silvery-blond hair was pulled back so tightly that it changed the shape of her eyes. "What does a sheltered princess know of the political machinations of court?"

Fionna knew more, I was certain. She was too clever not to. But they were too busy arguing for me to intercede.

I cleared my throat. They either did not hear or they ignored it.

From the periphery, I caught a flash of movement. By the time I slid my eyes to Karine, she was staring at the floor. Pointedly. While her shoulders twitched with suppressed laughter.

There was nothing funny about any of this, which was one wrong word from spiraling into an unmitigated disaster.

But I was wrong about that.

It took seven words.

"She insists she is not the princess."

The attic went silent. A sack of flour tumbled sideways, knocked loose by the movement of all three councillors spinning to Heath, who guarded the rear door. Who'd dared to raise his voice above not just his direct commander but also those ranked even higher. Who had managed to turn this entire meeting on its head.

I was going to fecking kill him. Maybe not today, maybe not in a month. But someday, I was going to slit Heath's throat. I had no doubt he would one day give me a reason that no one would question. It was only a matter of time.

Turi blinked, his eyed turned owlish and large. Yelena was utterly still.

But it was Maureen who pinned me with her shadowed eyes. She was no longer sitting. "Helio."

Later, I would punish Heath for speaking out of turn. But in that moment in time, I had to answer.

"Sima has confirmed it. The human we kidnapped is not Princess Aurelle, but her closest companion."

The attic erupted in noise. Thank Síofra it was the middle of the day, the packed bakery below covering any ruckus we could make. If it had been night, the Peace Guards would have heard us all the way from the next peace village.

"Fecking hell . . ."

". . . kill her before she learns any more of our secrets . . ." Yelena screeched.

Turi's hands dropped away from his beard, waving wildly in front of him instead. "They will not muster a force to save a servant."

"They won't trade for one, either." Maureen's voice was grimmer, less panicked.

"This makes us look stupid and incapable."

". . . might not even notice she is missing."

*Enough of this.*

The group was too fractured to draw on communal power, but I caught Karine's eye. She inclined her head, and that was enough for me to form the flame in my hand, for the blast of heat that radiated out, flushing the skin of every single person in the attic except my own.

Turi stumbled backward into the wall of sugar sacks. Yelena's face burned brighter still—more than the wave of heat I'd sent out could account for. She was pissed. So was I.

I closed my palm, snuffing out the plume of fire I'd summoned. I let the sweltering heat bank. I had their attention now.

"The Irskans do not know that the princess was the intended target," I said. "We infiltrated the castle and took a highly placed member of the royal household. They know she is missing and they know who took her."

Karine squared her shoulders in my periphery. I clasped my hands behind my back, exposing my chest to them. It was the thinnest act of subordination, but it worked. Turi's shoulders collapsed, his hand going back to his beard. He began muttering to himself again, already contemplating how to turn this change in circumstances to Rebel advantage. Yelena was not so easily appeased. She could manipulate sound.

It was her trap set on the landing. But I had no doubt that if she could have manipulated fire, she'd have burned my balls straight to ash.

"This is a major feckup, Helio," Maureen said. She slid a sideways glance to Yelena. Either an explosion was not as imminent as I thought, or Maureen thought I deserved what was coming.

I bowed my head. "I am aware."

It wasn't quite subservience. It could not be, would never be. Not with the truths we all knew hanging in the flour-fogged air between us. Most of the elders in the Síofran community accepted it. Heath hated me for it.

That could be the only reason for him to lose his head twice in the space of such a small amount of time.

"We should kill her and make an example. Show them that no one is safe," Heath growled. He stepped forward, like he would join the conversation. I did not have to turn to sense it, the shift in the heated air.

Maureen looked vaguely amused. Turi surprised. But Yelena was absolutely livid.

"Your commander has not given you leave to speak," she hissed, the sound no more than a whisper but carrying across the room and directly into each of our ears.

Heath retreated, pressing his back against the door.

A better person would have felt bad for his subordinate taking the anger that might have been directed at him. But I was not a good person. I was a good leader, and in that moment, Heath needed reminding of the order of things.

"My subordinates are entitled to their opinions," I said. Turi flinched from the menace in my voice, so sharply contrasted with the words themselves. "Until I tell them how they are wrong."

I turned away from Heath, dismissing him entirely. He had no place nor power in this conversation. I addressed the councillors, the ones who did.

"She is valuable to them. She has been a servant in the princess's household for a decade. What she lacks in value for ransom, she more than makes up for in intelligence. The princess has been notoriously isolated. Her companion, however, has had free run of the castle. She attends social functions with the princess and fetches her meals from the kitchen. She has the eyes of a servant."

"Which means she could lie to us as easily as help us," Turi pointed out.

But she wouldn't. Not with her sister's safety hanging in the balance. I opened my mouth to say it . . . "Leave her to me. I will ensure she tells the truth."

They all understood what I meant. I would torture the truth out of her.

Somehow that seemed less of a betrayal than telling the council about her sister.

Maureen and Yelena exchanged a look before turning their backs on me. Just as I'd decided that Heath had no place in our discussion, they decided to cut me out of theirs. I could hardly argue. The power structures of the Rebels were finite. Decisions compartmentalized. The good of the cause put above the individual, always. It was how we had survived to fight this long. The only way we had survived, at all.

There were no windows, no daylight for me to track the time. But Maureen began glancing over her shoulder, to the door down to the bakery where Karine stood guard. We were out of time.

And I was out of fecking patience.

"If you want the Firebird, then you will relent on this."

I'd never used it, not once. They all knew it was there. Hell, they'd understood long before I had. I'd been too busy crying about being an orphan, while they moved me from safe house to safe house, ensuring that their most valuable weapon was protected.

But I was not a child any longer. I knew what lurked in my veins better than any of them did. Magic may never be free again. And yet . . . they could not quite let go. They could not quite risk alienating me.

Even so, Yelena's blue eyes looked like they were about to pop out of her head. It was a miracle there was anything left to Turi's beard, given the vigor he'd been rubbing it with. Only Maureen looked at me directly, and her eyes were full of emotions that I was not going anywhere near acknowledging.

"I will stand as his second," Karine said.

Heath's inability to keep his mouth shut had not surprised me, exactly. But Karine's did.

She was a decorated member of the Síofran Rebel Army, but her words had nothing to do with that and everything to do with personal loyalty.

It meant that if I was wrong, if this went to shit, she would take the punishment with me. It was a show of support and belief.

Karine had as little reason as I to vouch for Fionna. We were both orphans; that hardly made us special, neither on the Síofran nor the human side of the conflict in Irska. Maybe it was because her brother was still in Peace Guard custody. She should have known that I'd get him out, regardless of what decisions were made in this flour-dusted attic.

But I could not decipher her expression, and she was looking at the triad, not at me.

"Granted," Maureen said. "Helio, you will take responsibility for the human captive. If the information she gives you is faulty, you and your second will be punished and the prisoner handed over to the council."

They could not punish me, and we all well knew it. But they could get to Karine. That would be the punishment. She would be taken. Those who were taken did not return.

The meeting ended as unceremoniously as it had begun. Yelena threw a hood over her head and ducked out the back door. The rest of us waited to disperse our exits and avoid drawing notice.

Maureen hefted a bag of sugar over her shoulder and made her way downstairs. "Now I have to go feed a pie to that arrogant human bastard before he comes up here looking for me."

# Chapter 12

## Fionna

*We were in constant negotiations with the Irskan government, even from the earliest days after the Fall. They closed the borders, not us. They did not want the children of Síofra in power, but they also did not want them to leave Irska, either. We've had many governments come and go over the years. In Eerin we have elections, not kings. Not a single one of those governments has been willing to abandon our brothers and sisters in Irska. But we weren't willing to save them, either.*

*—Magdulena Byrne, Republic of Eerin*

I stared at the rusted washbasin. Like everything else in the abandoned warehouse where Helio had dumped me, it looked like it had not been used in half a decade. At least.

I'd spent the first night sitting on the floor, contemplating escape, only to conclude that there was none. The only way out was the heavy door that Helio had made a point of demonstrating could be barred from both inside and out. Even if I could get through it, there was at least one Rebel waiting outside, and I'd promised Helio I would not lift a hand against one of his kind.

Apparently injuring one of my own was all it had taken to convince him.

He had no reason to trust me, nor I him. But I'd given him my promise, and I would not break it. Mostly because to do so at that moment in time would have been supremely stupid.

I expected Helio to come back during the day. But he had not reappeared. For a brief moment, I entertained the thought that he might be embarrassed. He'd kissed me. Lost control and given in to his desires. It must have been jarring for a high-ranked Síofran Rebel.

But then reality crashed back in. Maybe he had lost control. Or maybe it was all another tactic to destabilize me. It was hardly the first time a man had tried to use desire or the illusion of affection to manipulate me. I refused to let it work, pinching myself hard on the arm every time my traitorous mind drifted back to the way the heat from his lips spread through me, awakening every part of my body.

I had a bruise on my forearm before midday.

A Rebel I did not recognize brought food. They had not decided to starve me. Yet.

I'd used the hazy light that slipped through the broken windows high overhead to explore every inch of the warehouse that was now my home. Four walls. No bathing rooms in sight. There was, at least, a toilet and washbasin. I'd made use of both out of desperation. Privacy was a complicated proposition at the moment; I was alone but guarded round the clock.

There was a mattress and blanket tucked against one of the towering warehouse walls, as well as a long-abandoned desk. I took the time to shift the papers—the warehouse had once stored textiles—and dust off the wooden surface with the hem of my dress. That gave me a place to eat. The mattress didn't smell too bad, and I'd seen no vermin. So I'd napped there. But after pacing the length of the warehouse for a few hours, reading every scrap of paper left on the desk, and watching the light overhead disappear, I was left alone in the dark. It was time for bed.

Which brought me to the rusty washbasin.

*Calm as a lake. Strong as a tree. I bend but don't break.*

I did not bother telling myself that I was safe. That was too far from the truth for me to convince even my gullible brain.

Every night before bed, I washed my face with water and soap. I brushed my curls out with a comb. I rinsed out my mouth three times, gargling on the last. Then I applied cream to my face, forearms, and hands.

Step by step. Every single night. If I forgot a step, or inverted the order, I started again. It was the reason I always went to sleep after Evie, the maid who shared the bedchamber attached to Aurelle's suite. I did not need anyone to see me going through the entire routine twice just because I'd applied cream to my hands before my forearms.

If I did not complete the ritual with perfect precision, something terrible would befall me or Treasa. That was what my mind told me. I recognized the irony. Something terrible had already befallen me. And yet my anxiety still made its demands.

I was alone in the warehouse. There was no one to see my anxiety-fueled ablutions.

I'd avoided it the night before by not going to bed. My naps during the day did not count. Naps did not have the same rules. But night . . .

I sighed, pressing my hand against my chest, forcing myself to feel my heartbeat.

I would have killed anyone, human or Síofran, for a cup of frost-bloom tea. Anything to calm the beast that roared inside my chest, the anxiety that made demands even in these life-and-death circumstances.

It was so fecking unfair.

Then when had life ever been anything but?

I'd make do with what I had. Surely that would be enough to calm my pounding pulse.

No soap, but I had running water. I splashed some on my face, massaging my cheeks and forehead even though there was no soap to build into a lather. My fingers did the work of untangling my hair in place of a comb.

*Calm as a lake. Strong as a tree. I bend but don't break.*

This was me bending, I told myself. I could not afford to break.

Rinsed my mouth. One, two, three—gargle. Which left applying cream. Nonexistent cream. I looked around my little corner of the warehouse, eyes searching the desk and the mattress with its single blanket, willing something to appear. As if I had not searched every nook and corner multiple times in the daylight.

A shiver of anxiety rolled through my shoulders and then down my spine. My hands flexed, reaching for something that wasn't there. Assurance never was, not really.

I had to get a handle on this. I could feel it spiraling out of control. Losing control was not an option. Not here, not now. No tears and no attacks from the beast that lived ever present in my chest . . .

"You should sleep fully clothed."

I leaped backward, grasping around for something to steady myself and only finding air. Some stupid part of my brain expected him to catch me. But despite whipping my head from side to side, I could not even fecking see him. Nor did the motion help me catch my balance. My bottom hit the concrete floor with an audible *thud*. I had plenty of padding.

I refused to let him see me scramble. Now that I was no longer bound, I was able to climb to my feet with an approximation of grace.

He emerged from the shadows on the opposite end of the warehouse. Despite the cold that leaked through the open windows overhead, he wore no cloak. I'd put the one I'd worn earlier on the mattress along the wall, intending to add it to my blankets for the night. He'd changed his clothing since our jaunt across the city, trading the leather vest for a short, quilted gray surcoat that he belted at the waist. The garment fit him perfectly—too perfectly. It had been tailored to him specifically, there was no doubt. It was a sharp contrast to the garments I'd seen on the Síofran in the streets, wearing whatever they could place their hands on.

*Who was he?*

*A monster,* my mind supplied. For all his well-fitting garments and the way they accentuated the breadth of his shoulders, the man wearing them was still terrifying. His red hair glinted darker in the night, burnished to the color of deep red wine. The moonlight intensified the scar that raked through his brow and curved around his eye. What terrible fight had he incited to earn the vicious scar?

He should have been terrifying—no, he *was* terrifying. I'd just forgotten to be afraid.

"How did you get in here?" I demanded.

I was not so stuck in my own head that I could have missed the heavy warehouse door rolling open.

Helio ignored my question, his mismatched eyes perusing the little setup—washbasin, desk, mattress. It had all been here when I'd arrived. I'd just rearranged it a little. I'd spent enough time in the dark in the last few days. I did not care if he knew that I wanted to see the moonlight. I did want to know how he'd entered so soundlessly.

An unnerving thought formed, half in my mind, half in my stomach. Magic. What if he had used magic?

Even after hours to dissect every moment, from the fire in the cellar to the floating child in the street, I could not make sense of it. Magic still existed. The most fundamental truth of my existence was a lie. And my only source of information was the man determined to torture me.

"You should sleep fully clothed so you are prepared to move at any time," he said, his eyes coming to rest on me. "You are making yourself . . . unnecessarily vulnerable."

Unnecessarily vulnerable to his eyes, which lingered on the neckline of my shift just above my breasts before sliding lower. The garment was loose over my hips, but my nipples pebbled from the cold, pressing out against the whisper-thin fabric.

My hands twitched at my side, the anxious need to replicate an obtuse process temporarily forgotten. Instinct had my muscles asking to move over my body, to cross and cover the vulnerable parts of myself. But something held them at my sides, instead.

"You are the one sneaking up on a woman in the dark."

"I'd have thought you would have learned that lesson by now."

"What lesson is that?"

"I can get to you anywhere, anytime."

The scared, anxious woman he'd abducted and tied to a chair was still there inside me. She quaked at his words, knowing their truth. But everything that I'd learned about Helio up to this point told me he valued strength, not complacency. Keeping my mouth shut would get me nothing; that is what the calculations in my head told me. I'd been with the Rebels too long. Whether I gave them information or not, the humans would assume that I had.

Information was now my only way out. I would have to use it judiciously, and obtain it from him just as skillfully.

I forced my hands to still at my sides. First things first. "Are we leaving now?"

Helio's chest lifted in a soundless chuckle. "No."

I started making a list in my head of what bits I'd offer up and what I wanted in return. Magic. There were a thousand other considerations, including details that might aid my escape. But they all faded to the background, obscured by the pressing need to know.

"Have you come to torture me for information?"

That scarred brow rose. "And if I had?"

"I'd tell you there are other ways of getting information from a prisoner." Like asking. A plan was forming in my mind. One that I would probably regret, but that might just work. Maybe.

"Are you telling me how to do my job, Fionna?"

Not "princess." He'd called me by my name. He had no doubts left, then, about who and what I was. That was a relief, actually. I could not have pretended to be Aurelle, nor would it work with the plan I was tentatively constructing.

His throat slid as he refocused his gaze on my face. I wondered if it was still pink from scrubbing.

"I came to train you," he said.

I blinked. "To do what?"

"To protect yourself the next time you're attacked." He sighed, a long-suffering sound. Like he was speaking to a child.

Maybe I would have taken offense, if the words themselves weren't so far-fetched.

"You want to teach me to defend myself." I laughed, the sensation strange. There was not much to laugh about in the castle. But the suggestion was fecking funny.

"It is the middle of the night," I said. A bit of an exaggeration. It was nowhere near midnight, but it was long since dark.

Never mind that I had slept half the day. My body had claimed what it needed after that restless night fantasizing about futile escape.

Helio was already rolling his shoulders, stretching an arm overhead. "Not all of us get to spend the day lounging about."

How did he know that? The laughter died in my throat. "Open that door and I will happily relinquish my life of leisure."

I did not know where I was, but the castle sat on the hill overlooking the city. I'd find my way eventually. In that moment, I ignored the conclusion I'd come to earlier about the unlikelihood of the castle as a place of refuge. I could figure out another plan.

But Helio was not about to release me, so those thoughts, whipping through my mind all at once, were pointless anyway. I could have stepped back, retreated to my sad little mattress, and tried to go to sleep, knowing I'd have to get up and repeat my blasted ablutions after he left.

Instead, I took a step toward him. I'd left on my laced leather boots, not wanting to soil my stockings on the dirty floor of the warehouse. Damn him. The layers did make me feel less vulnerable.

I already knew the basics from years spent watching the Peace Guards and then practicing in my room with Evie, Aurelle's maid. But there was something to be gained here, by going along with him. There must be. I just was not sure what it was yet. Not his trust; I wasn't that naive. If I could prove myself compliant, show myself to be useful, get him to relax his guard . . . Yes, that would work for my plan. In fact, it was essential.

"Fine. Teach me."

Helio's smile sent a tremor through my chest and into my stomach. I was not as immune to fear as I'd thought.

"Show me your stance," he said, crossing his arms over his chest. I refused to notice how the movement pulled his surcoat away to reveal the muscles of his arms.

His brows rose as I positioned my feet approximately shoulder width apart, my dominant foot slightly back, just as I'd seen the Peace Guards do hundreds of times over the year.

"Do they habitually teach self-defense to servants in the castle?"

I tossed my loose hair back over my shoulder. There wasn't time to tie it back now. "Maybe I am a natural."

"Hmm." He circled me, reaching out to tap a spot on the floor just a few inches from where my foot rested. "Move your back foot here. Your center of gravity is lower than a man's; you need to adjust appropriately."

I did as he instructed, instantly noticing the difference. Helio didn't give me time to appreciate it. He swung immediately, his fist barreling toward my face with devastating speed. I ducked, keeping my balance as I did. I bit down on my tongue to keep the self-satisfied sound inside.

But I wasn't expecting the next blow so fast after the first. Before I'd even fully straightened, Helio cut upward with his other fist—the nondominant one I'd dismissed—catching me in the stomach. I flailed backward. If I hadn't adjusted my stance, I would have fallen. But by some miracle, I kept my feet.

The pride I'd felt a moment before curdled into anger. I swung with my right fist, aiming for his smiling fecking face. How dare he enjoy himself. I didn't get within a foot of him before he grabbed my fist.

My outrage spilled past my lips.

Helio's smile only grew. "Defense first, Fionna."

I tried to rip my hand from his grip. Failed. Resisted the urge to stick out my tongue at a man who I'd surmised was a top commander and experienced torturer within Irska's most notorious rebel group.

He released me suddenly. I only just managed to keep my feet.

When he moved both arms upward, I ducked away, but he wasn't moving to strike me. A low chuckle filled the space between us, then the entire warehouse. It was warm, despite the night air leaking in from the broken windows above. In fact, I had not noticed the cold at all since Helio had appeared. How did that work? Was it related to his magic? It had to be a coincidence, or a side effect of the sparring.

"Protect your face and head first," Helio said, demonstrating by lifting both his forearms in front of his face so they were parallel. "A knife to the arm will hurt, but a knife to the face is fatal."

I blinked. Who, exactly, would be attacking me with a knife?

I refused the image of a particular human prince, even when my mind tried to conjure it.

Instead of asking my question, I lifted my arms, mirroring Helio's stance. He reached out, nudging my elbows an inch higher. His skin seared mine through the loose sleeves of my shift. The heat—it was coming from him.

I gasped. Helio froze.

I almost jerked away—almost. Some instinct, some part of me that recognized what hadn't been said, something stopped me, holding me in place. Maybe it was my anxiety, afraid of doing the wrong thing. In that moment, I could only be thankful.

Helio stood, his fingertips a hairbreadth from touching my arm, utterly unmoving. I was not certain that he was breathing. My chest refused to move, either.

This moment was significant to him. I did not know why or how. But what I did next mattered deeply.

I forced my eyes away from where our bodies had touched. That was hard. The desire to watch, the fascination, the wonder at what might happen next. But meeting his gaze was not difficult at all. I knew what pain looked like. Helio terrified me. His pain did not.

The moment shattered. Helio pulled back and then jabbed. I kept my hands up, successfully blocking my face. He tried a few more attacks, forcing me to pivot and balance while holding the defensive position. Then he proceeded to take me through several more variations to protect different quadrants of my body before graduating me to a forward motion of my arm that was halfway between defensive and offensive.

I gained bruises, but my blocks were getting more effective. Still, I was not used to the intensity of the exercise. I stepped back, wiping sweat from across my brow. The heat in the warehouse had not decreased.

Helio's directions were precise, just like his movements. He offered nothing about himself, nor did he ask me for information. It was not midnight yet, but the night was well on its way. I made a show of rotating my wrist after blocking a particularly brutal blow.

"I am your prisoner. Why teach me skills I might use against your kind?" I said between heaving breaths.

"These are the maneuvers we teach our children," Helio said. I glared at him for the sting, which did not even seem to register with him. "And you promised," he added.

"I'm sure the promises of humans mean a lot to the Síofran." I threw the words out between us, their tone perfectly honed. A blade made of sarcasm.

I saw the moment it hit home.

Helio's eyes crinkled at the corners. Not much, not a true smile. Just enough to let me know he found the comment amusing rather than infuriating.

"You have quite a mouth on you," he said, rubbing a hand over his jaw. "For a servant."

I turned away from him so he could not see my face, crossing back to the washbasin. "Maybe I am tired of biting my tongue," I said before leaning over to splash cold water onto my face.

The force of my own words hit me unexpectedly.

Maybe this was who I truly was. Who I'd always been, beneath the calculation and anxiety and desperate need to make it to the next day.

None of my next days were guaranteed anymore, not as a Rebel captive. Being quiet and subservient would not save me here. But being myself . . . That just might.

Another me would have kept the next thought inside. "Magic is supposed to be gone."

Helio made a low, noncommittal sound. "That is what the king tells us."

"But I saw it." For more than twenty-four hours, I'd been turning over the possibilities in my head. The texts that had formed the backbone of my and Aurelle's education spoke about magic in only the broadest strokes. It had been gone for hundreds of years, so there was not much to dwell upon and few concrete facts to impart. Except that was a lie.

"Ask your question, Fionna." Helio's voice dripped with challenge. Like he saw the person I was beneath the veneer I presented to the world and dared me to shatter the illusion.

I could not resist the invitation. "How?"

Several heartbeats of silence passed. He was not going to answer. Why would he? He owed me nothing. Every choice he made with regard to me was self-serving. I would expect nothing else from a child of Síofra.

"The core of our magic has been suppressed since the Fall. We cannot access our true power. But small magics remain—in some people, in some places," Helio said in a low monotone, devoid of emotion.

"Common purpose," I whispered, a memory emerging from the fog of the past.

I'd read an account, a primary source from around the time of the war. Aurelle had been busy doodling in her notebook, and I'd been tasked with reading aloud.

Behind me, Helio made another sound, this one of assent. I was too petrified to move, afraid that if I did it would shatter the moment before I got confirmation.

"Your magic is based on common purpose. On peace and unity." My mind took the next step. My stomach clenched, my breath deserting my body. "That is why magic fell after the war."

That had not been in my textbooks. Historians suggested that it was Síofra's disfavor or human dominance, a righting of the world, that had caused magic to disappear. But that wasn't it at all. Magic was gone because of the war itself. It was not such a huge leap . . . which meant I was not the first to make it. Which meant that the Crown was deliberately distracting us with lies.

I shook my head from side to side, trying to clear it and anchor myself back to this moment. "But then how is it possible that you can access . . . small magics?" I echoed back Helio's words.

"Only if there are enough of us united in common purpose," he said.

Like the Rebels, committed to my capture and torture. That was how Karine had lit the fire in the cellar. Or the love in a family, like the mother and her two children in the peace village.

My entire world was busy rearranging itself, yet I could not move past the next thought. Helio had just reshaped my reality, but as always, my world narrowed to one thing. One person, and the plan I had to protect her.

He'd trusted me enough to answer my question. Maybe I'd cooperated enough to make executing the second part of my plan possible. There was an intimacy in the air, a feeling that I struggled to describe. Common purpose, that was how he'd phrased it when it applied to the Síofran. But Helio and I did not have common purpose. We wanted separate, diametrically opposed things. And yet . . .

There was something here between us.

I almost regretted exploiting it.

But this was an opportunity I could not let pass. It might be days before Helio returned to the warehouse, and my days were already too few to bother counting.

My hands gripped either side of the washbasin, the knuckles white. I forced the words out before I could lose my nerve. "Let me help."

Nothing.

No laugh of derision. No refusal. Just silence. *Feck me.*

I turned back to face Helio, and this time I did cross my arms over my chest. Maybe it would have been smarter to leave my breasts exposed where they could distract him. But the action was involuntary.

"I will help you," I rephrased.

His dark-red brows lifted. "Me."

"The Rebels. The Síofran Rebel Army. That's who you are, right? I will help you on a mission. Infiltrate the castle, capture a Peace Guard, whatever it is." I sounded desperate. That was not bad, I told myself. I wanted him to think I was desperate, that I was making this offer because I had no other choices, not because I'd carefully calculated that it was my best chance. The less my captor knew about the inner workings of my mind, the better.

Helio crossed his arms, mirroring my stance. "That is a dangerous bargain to make."

I would not kill anyone. I refused to cross that line. But he didn't need to know it, not yet. It was better to get him to agree before I started placing conditions.

"I know the routes used by servants and the rotations of the Peace Guards," I said. Those had to be tantalizing bits of intelligence. The castle was surrounded by thick concrete walls. The Rebels could watch from outside, but only a human would know the inner workings.

Helio tilted his head to the side.

He was considering it.

Fecking hell. He was actually considering it.

"Why?"

I swallowed. I was ready for this question. It had been a part of my careful calculations. The urge to tap the toe of my boot against the ground surged up, nearly overwhelming me. If I tapped three times, it would keep her safe. This would all be okay.

What utter nonsense.

I did it anyway.

Helio's eyes did not shift. He waited for an answer.

I gave it. "My sister is employed in the castle. Liberate her."

Simple terms. Helio slowly straightened his head so he was looking at me directly. His eyes were unfathomable, one a sea of cold blue, the other eerily warm with its streaks of gold settled between the green.

He'd kissed me. That had to mean . . . I had no idea what it meant, really. I'd been kissed by men for all sorts of reasons, ranging from simple lust to attempts to gain an introduction to Princess Aurelle to Vainar . . . no. I shut down that thought immediately. Not only was I not foolish enough to mention his name again in Helio's presence but I also did not want his specter looming in my mind.

"No."

I blinked. My chest threatened to quake at the disappointment, but years of serving Aurelle kept me from letting it show on my face. There was nothing more to say. I was not going to argue with him, not yet. I would give him time to contemplate my offer. Eventually, he would change his mind.

Helio must have agreed that our interaction was at an end. He adjusted his surcoat and then strode to the other end of the warehouse, to the darkness from which he'd appeared.

He stopped just short, turning back, half of his face in shadow. "You gave her up quicker than I thought you would."

My mind scrambled to make sense of his words. "What?"

"Your sister. For someone you're supposedly so determined to protect, you offered up the secret of her existence with hardly any prodding."

He'd already known about Treasa.

The sleeping beast of panic roared to waking, threatening to consume me. If he already knew about Treasa, what else did he know? Just of her existence, or of her position in the castle? Fecking hell, he could know where she slept. He could have set a watch on her already. I'd assumed he did not have another way into the castle, but what did I truly know about it? I was a servant, and he was a powerful leader in the Síofran Rebel Army. I'd offered her as an incentive for my cooperation, but he'd already known about her. He could use her as leverage at any moment. The Rebels did not need to rescue her. All they had to do was threaten to break the status quo, and I would tell them *anything*.

My fingers twitched, but there was no amount of tapping or unhinged compulsions that would quiet this panic.

Helio was not there to teach me how to properly defend myself. As he'd said before, what he taught me was little more than child's play. He'd come for information. Not because he needed it, but because he wanted to see how much I would give up before he even had to start his torture. Or maybe the torture had already begun.

Mercy? What a fecking joke. There was nothing but cruelty in those eyes.

I ground my teeth together, rage subsuming every other emotion. Rage was good. It was the only emotion guaranteed to overwhelm the anxiety. But I would not let him see either.

I stood under his gaze, refusing to let him cow me. Refusing to lose.

"Assume I know all your secrets, Fionna. It will save time for both of us," Helio said. Then he disappeared into the shadows completely.

I waited, trying to hear where he went, how he got in and out without using the door. But there were no clues, and I was not going to blunder about in the dark after him.

I'd been in captivity since that changeling fireball killed our parents. My prison had changed. So had my captors. But this was the same game I'd played for ten years, and Helio had just reminded me of that. I would not let myself forget again.

The Síofran did not care what happened to innocents. Their fireballs had killed my parents, poor humans just trying to carve out a life. Helio was ready to sacrifice my sister to their cause. He hadn't said as much, but the threat was there in his cruel, sadistic words. Fecking monsters, every single one of them.

*He* was a monster. And I hated him.

# Chapter 13

## FIONNA


*There has always been magic in Eerin. This place is ancient, just like the goddess who blessed it. But everything changed when Síofra herself reached down into a cradle and bestowed her gifts upon the first child. The rest of Eerin respects Síofra's gifts. They practice magic freely. Feck, they still have their magic. And what do we have, here in Irska, on the tip of the island that she blessed? We have nothing, and it is all because of the humans.*

*—Tamryn Nowak, Síofran Rebel Army*

Air rushed around me from all sides, cold and crisp as it whipped at my cheeks and filled my lungs. But I was not cold. No, my entire body was suffused with a comforting warmth. It was so easy to sink into, to close my eyes and float. That was what this must be—floating. An otherworldly sensation that I had no right to, that I could not name. Yes, that made sense. I was floating.

But floating was gentle. This—it did not hurt. Not at all. Despite the cold air rushing past me, I knew instinctively that I was safe. The warmth in my limbs was steady, allowing me to appreciate the sensation of floating. No, not floating. The cold air filled my lungs, but it did not burn. It exhilarated. I was not floating.

I was flying.

A current of wind pushed me upward, and I leaned into it, savoring the way it caressed my limbs and tickled my core. The sharp contrast against the warmth of my body heightened the sensation, wiping away all other thoughts . . .

My eyes were closed.

What a travesty, to be flying through the air but not using every single one of my senses to enjoy it. I recognized it as a dream, but dismissed the thought as easily as it came. This dream felt so real that I let myself sink into it, savor it.

I'd spent my entire life caged, but now I was free. Everything was within my power if only I could open my eyes and take it.

So I opened my eyes.

But I did not see clouds or sun or sky, nor a landscape of rolling hills spreading out beneath me. I saw orbs of blue and green, striations of a gold so pure it must have been made of precious metal. They took my breath away.

⁓

I awoke in my bed, the dream of flight still surging through my veins. I refused to open my eyes, determined to hang on to the sensations just a few moments longer. Before, I'd framed my hopes and dreams in terms of escape. Escape from the castle, escape from Irska. I had to get Treasa out; we had to escape. But those thoughts had shifted. Now I dreamed of freedom. Freedom to be, freedom to feel. Freedom not just for my sister but also for myself.

Freedom to savor the hand sliding up over my hip to caress my stomach.

I'd gone to bed in nothing but my linen shift. The garment was well worn, the embroidery my sister had done along the edges earning it special status. The linen was now as soft as butter, as thin as a whisper. So thin that I could feel the scrape of calluses through the fabric as warm fingertips traced the curve of my stomach where it dipped in to join my thigh.

I recognized expert hands even without opening my eyes to look at them. No one could touch with such reverence, linger so perfectly at the juncture of my hip, and be unable to deliver on the promises the searing fingertips made.

The hand moved up, around the curve of my stomach until the knuckles grazed the underside of my breast. My hips rose of their own volition, my shoulder blades digging down into the soft mattress as my core cried out for attention.

There was no cold now, only heat. Such heat unspooling in my stomach, heat in the hands that cupped my breasts, tweaked the nipples. I arched again, searching for something, for someone . . .

⁓

My eyes snapped open. The moonlight accosted my irises. The weight of blankets and cloaks and my own clothing piled on top of me pressed down, pressed me into the thin mattress. A dream. Multiple dreams.

I dragged in a breath, then another, then a third. Always in threes. I tapped my fingers against the mattress. One, two, three. But my racing heart did not slow, because this was not anxiety thrumming through me, but desire.

*Everyone dreams of flying. Everyone dreams of sex.* They must have been two of the most common fantasies in all the world. But they'd never been mine.

Not entirely true. I'd dreamed of sex before.

Yet this had felt oddly prophetic. I'd always seen my partner's face, their body as much a part of the fantasy as whatever I did with it. But the focus of this dream had been my own pleasure. I supposed that made sense, in its own way. Everything in my life had been upended. Why not my dreams?

I was very much alone, still in the warehouse, with the late-winter air seeping in from the broken windows high above. The layers of blankets combined with the wool cloak were enough to keep me from freezing to death, but they did not account for the heat that still burned in my veins. In my stomach. Between my legs.

I was alone.

There was no one to see as I slid my hand up over my thigh, curling my fingers around the soft linen of my shift to pull it to the side. There was no one to see as I arched my hips into my own touch, dragging my middle finger up the length of my seam before circling my clit. There was no one to hear my whimpers as I tweaked my already hard nipple, the combined pressure of both of my hands driving me toward a climax that was already dangerously close.

My eyes flitted closed again.

It was not my hands doing the work, but the hot, capable hands from my dream.

There was no one to know that it was his hands I imagined as I cascaded into delicious oblivion, instead of my own.

# Chapter 14

## Fionna

*I attended three funerals in the space of a year. My uncle was murdered by a fireball they set off on the docks. He was usually back home by supper, but he'd had a particularly lucky day. It took him longer than usual to unload his catch. They left my cousin an orphan. His mother was already dead ten years. Childbirth is dangerous. He joined the Peace Guard. We were all so proud. My father was a Peace Guard. He was always disappointed that I was born a girl. But my cousin did not last a month. A changeling bastard gutted him in an alley one night while he was on patrol. My father's death was slower. Too much scarred tissue from too many wounds over a lifetime fighting the changelings. When he died, I joined the Defenders. Not as good as the Peace Guard. But it is something. There are some who lost more. I suppose I am lucky.*

*—Alexandra Farley, Irska Defense Force*

"Where are you taking me?" I whispered, even though we were alone in the narrow alley.

Sima kept her eyes forward, scanning the street ahead. "You know I cannot answer that."

They'd come for me at noon on the ninth day of my residence in the warehouse. By my count, I'd been in captivity for somewhere around a fortnight. Honestly, I was so fecking bored in that warehouse that I almost welcomed the Síofran who came through the heavy rolling door. Especially because Helio was not with them.

The woman with the golden hair in its tight braid was Karine, the glaring man who'd nearly struck me that first day in the cellar named Heath. I had their names, and that was all I wanted to do with them. Unfortunately, they, along with Sima, made up my escort to wherever I was going and for whatever reason.

Karine had preceded us out onto the street, presumably to look for any rogue Defenders or Peace Guards who might intercept us. Heath was guarding our rear, waiting at the other end of the alley that was barely wide enough for me to walk through. I'd had to angle my body to maneuver around a refuse bin. Of the three of them, Heath was the one I least wanted guarding my back. He seemed most likely to shove a knife into it.

I pulled the cloak tighter around my shoulders and shifted a little closer to Sima. "What if we get separated—"

She shook her head, the ghost of a smile flitting over her face. "There are no Defenders on the street today. There is the signal from Karine." She motioned me into the street with only a light tug on my cloak.

True to Helio's promise, I was not bound.

If I saw an opportunity for escape . . . I would decide in the moment. I hated him. But although I was afraid of the others, excluding Sima, they did not engender the same vitriolic response. I'd had enough time to realize that escape was not necessarily the safer option, given the circumstances. If I stumbled into the wrong human hands, they'd kill me for turning informer before I had a chance to explain myself. There were just too many possibilities to consider them all beforehand. And I'd tried during the nine days I sat by myself in that drafty fecking warehouse.

The street was only mildly busy, lined with a mix of shops, market stalls, and residential doorsteps. I did not recognize it from my earlier excursion. That was probably purposeful, to keep me from becoming familiar enough with the city's layout to engineer an escape.

I walked at Sima's side, as instructed. Karine joined us about half-way to the corner, raising her hand and then leaning in to brush her cheek against Sima's in greeting, two friends meeting by happenstance on the street. But then she fell into step at my side, pressing a little too close.

"Do not try and run," she warned, her voice low enough that even Sima could not hear it.

I kept my gaze straight ahead, not allowing my eyes to stray down to her hand to see if she gripped a fireball. She'd had one every time before, but I did not need to give my anxiety any reason to rear its hideous, debilitating head.

Fingers closed around my arm, the grip tight despite the thick wool cloak. She dragged me against her, even as our feet continued to move.

"Helio has tied his fate to yours," Karine whispered.

I managed not to jerk away from her, but my head whipped to the side. "What do you mean?"

Karine was waiting, her light-brown brows knitted together. Her voice was all menace, but her face . . . She was worried about him.

That was not jealousy that roared to life in my chest. Absolutely not. I could not be jealous that this woman, who was my enemy, cared for a man whom I hated, who was also my enemy. Fecking hell, when had my life become so convoluted?

Probably when I was kidnapped.

"He has staked his life to yours," Karine hissed through her teeth. "So you had better prove to be useful."

I opened my mouth to tell her about the offer I'd made to Helio, that he'd refused my help. But the words refused to come forth. It felt like betrayal, which was ridiculous. I did not owe Helio anything. Every freedom he'd given me—to speak my mind, to move without shackles—was one he'd first taken away.

But the urge to say *something* was visceral. I wanted to demand that Karine tell me what she meant. Force her to explain her connection to Helio. Tell her to keep her hands off.

*Feck. Me.*

Sima's shoulder collided with mine, shoving me sideways through the street and up against the crumbling wall of a boarded-up shop. The impact forced all the air out of my chest. Other bodies collided with mine. Sima, Karine, strangers from the street. Everyone around us had scattered, desperate to avoid the pair of mounted riders thundering across the cobblestones. I'd been too distracted by Karine—

I froze against the wall. My heart beat once—a long, drawn-out tremor as my body tried to decide, then failed. Those calculations I'd promised myself were impossible, not with the terror that lit in my veins.

"Who is it?" Sima whispered. Whether she spoke to me or to Karine or to herself did not matter.

He'd always been a threat. When I'd hidden in the golden apple tree, his brothers had been with him to temper his meaner urges. Trinar would have at least told Aurelle that his sister's favorite plaything was in Vainar's clutches.

But here in the city, in a Síofran peace village, where every single person must bow to him . . . I turned my face into Sima's shoulder.

"Vainar," I rasped, unable to look at him. I believed Helio's promises. One day, he would make the prince pay for his evils. But Helio was not here.

"Feck," Karine said. I had not even realized she was on my other side. She still gripped my arm, but it was less aggressive, more like she was trying to keep us from getting separated in the crowd. "Back this way."

Sima followed the other woman without question. Some corner of my brain that was not percolating with anxiety noted that and wondered whether that made Karine her superior. I still did not know how the Síofran Rebel Army's command structure worked. Not that I thought I'd live long enough to tell anyone about it.

We reached the narrow alley we'd come from, but Heath blocked the way, his body filling up the space.

Karine drew up short. "The prince—"

"I saw. This way." Heath stepped out of the alley only long enough for us to pass him before closing it off again, using his body with all the effect of a door. One with the ability to throw a fireball.

"Into the sewer," he said over his shoulder.

I did not comprehend what he meant at first, but Karine and Sima did. The former was already on her knees, prying open a heavy metal grate from the ground. As soon as she got it open, Sima swung her legs down.

This had to be a jest. Dark basements, abandoned warehouses . . . I thought I'd coped relatively well with being held in fecking captivity. But hiding in a sewer . . .

Karine seemed to read my expression, if not my mind. So much for my servant's disposition.

"Get in," she ordered.

There was, indeed, a glowing fireball in her hand. Part of me wondered if she'd throw it in after me. Sima might be in league with the Rebels, but she was still human.

Hoofbeats echoed from the street. Someone screamed. I climbed down into the stinking pit.

There were a handful of metal rungs set into the stone, but they disappeared well before my feet reached the bottom. I had to jump the last few feet. My heavy cloak billowed around me, scraping against the shit-encrusted walls. Maybe it wasn't shit. Whatever it was, I tried to breathe through my mouth and not look too closely. My eyes moved without thinking upward to the circle of dim gray light that made it between the buildings, into the narrow alleyway, and down. But even that disappeared, Karine no more than a silhouette as she shifted the metal grate back into place and trapped Sima and me underground.

The pace of my heartbeat increased steadily, ticking upward toward panic. I took a deep breath and immediately regretted it.

Regret was all I had.

Seeing Vainar had transported me back to the king's golden apple orchard, where I'd earned the widowsbloom scratches that had made me lose my head, which had allowed the Rebels to take me in the first place. They never would have taken me otherwise. I had to believe that . . . that I had some agency in my own life, some control . . .

Regret morphed into something sharper.

I spun to face Sima, waiting a few steps away where the sewer tunnel opened wider. Footsteps clattered overhead. I told myself it was just Heath and Karine retreating so they would not give away our hiding spot. A horse whinnied in the distance.

"How did you miss that?" I demanded. My steps squelched as I walked, a horrible sound that turned my stomach.

Sima held her ground. Despite our hasty flight, her hair was still tucked neatly into its bun, her close-fitting clothing in place. Unruffled, just like a good servant. Just like I should have been.

Instead, my hair curled around my face in the damp. I shivered, an impulse that had nothing to do with the temperature.

"We swept the route before retrieving you. But the royal family does not ask our permission before riding out."

"You are the Síofran Rebel Army. They watch our every move. You should have known." I was mixing up my yous and ours and theys. Sima was human. I was human. She might know where her allegiance lay, but mine was not so clear.

Treasa.

I pressed my eyes closed, partially from the burning smell. And so Sima would not see the tears I struggled to hold back.

Regret to anger to overwhelm. Anxiety would be next. It always ended in anxiety.

I could not lose control, not in a sewer beneath a city at war, with a human who was also a Síofran rebel, not at all. I curled my arms around myself beneath the cloak.

*Calm as a lake. Strong as a tree. I bend but don't break.*

Dragging in a breath, I tapped my fingers against my opposite forearms three times. Nothing changed. My heart continued to thunder. Again. I must have gotten the rhythm wrong; that's why it was not working. I tapped again, syncing the movement with my breathing. Movement to breathing, that always helped. Except it wasn't helping. My heart was speeding up, tears burned at my eyes.

"Fionna," Sima said softly. My eyes were still closed, but I heard her moving toward me.

"Don't touch me," I snapped preemptively. Backward, away, until my upper back collided with the metal rungs. I welcomed the tremor of pain.

Pain helped sometimes.

It broke through the other sensations. I pressed myself back harder against the metal, anchoring myself in the physical discomfort. My mind grabbed on to the refrain that I'd used so many times over the years.

*Calm as a lake. Strong as a tree. I bend but don't break.* I was able to inhale and exhale.

*Calm as a lake. Strong as a tree. I bend but don't break.* My heartbeat slowed fractionally.

*Calm as a lake. Strong as a tree. I bend but don't break.* I heard the words in my mother's voice instead of my own.

Tears formed at the corners of my eyes, still pressed closed, but my heartbeat continued to slow. The sounds overhead did not abate, but they didn't intensify, either. After a few minutes, I was able to open my eyes.

The cylindrical tunnel we'd climbed down opened up into a bigger chamber. It wasn't particularly wide, maybe the length of my body if I'd lain down end to end. There was a narrow walkway along one edge, where we stood, and then the deeper trench that contained the city's sewage. I tried not to let my eyes drift down that far, though there was plenty of evidence beneath our feet and on the walls around us that the trench tended to overflow. This was a part of Irska I would have happily never seen.

Not that I'd chosen to see any of it.

"How long do we have to stay down here?" I asked, exhaling slowly.

Sima shrugged. "Until they come back for us."

"Do you always follow orders so blindly?" The words were still sharp from residual anger.

"They do not want us dead."

"Speak for yourself," I said through my teeth. By some miracle, I'd begun to adjust to the scent, but my nostrils still burned.

Sima seemed unaffected, her gaze loose and unruffled, just as before. "The Síofran are not what we have been taught to believe," she said. "They are not evil."

"They are not innocent, either."

Sima opened her mouth to argue the point.

"My parents were killed by a changeling fireball."

She cringed at the word. "In the beginning, it was not derogatory. The humans have changed its meaning."

"Children of Síofra. Síofran. Changeling. It all amounts to the same thing. Murderers."

I waited for her to argue with me.

Instead, she turned away from the light, meandering a few steps deeper into the darkness of the sewer. There was no urgency to her steps; there couldn't be, not trapped as we were. But I recognized what she was doing—I'd done it myself enough times. All servants had. We used the pretense of a task—refolding the laundry, fetching tea when we could have sent someone else, checking for another path—to steal a few moments to gather ourselves.

My words had struck at something deep inside Sima.

I refused to feel sorry for them. They were the truth. I was not a brainwashed human; I was an orphan of Síofran violence.

*Síofran.* My mind had corrected itself.

"I understand why you hate them," Sima said.

*I don't hate them.* Not all of them. Not the mother and children I'd seen in the street, or the desperate citizens moving through their daily lives, trying to scratch out a living just like the rest of us. In those ways, humans and Síofran were not so different. But their rebellion against the Irskan king had prolonged a war that should have ended centuries ago. Without the children of Síofra and their fireballs, my parents would still be alive.

I shook my head, unable to make sense of it. "You're human, Sima."

She nodded. "You want to know how I came to align myself with the Síofran."

"You died; they told us that you died."

"I am sure there was a full week of mourning in the castle for a kitchen assistant," she said on a sigh.

"They aren't any better," I argued back. Humans had plenty to answer for, too. But I'd never witnessed the violence of humans against Síofran, just the violence we perpetrated against our own kind.

Sima cocked her head to the side. "You are different than I remember in the kitchens."

I huffed out a breath. "I seem to have left my ability to moderate my tongue back in the castle," I said. At first, I thought it was just Helio who'd destroyed my better judgment and restraint. But apparently they'd both deserted me.

The slight curve of Sima's lips told me she approved. "My mother worked in the castle from the time she was an adolescent. When she got sick, I took her place."

"Your mother was human," I confirmed. I'd never heard of a mixed marriage. It just did not happen. Maybe in Eerin, where there was peace. But in Irska, traitors were treated the same as informers. They were never seen again.

Sima lifted her hand, waving it around in the muddy darkness. "Human. No magic. Not even a little whisper."

Footsteps sounded overhead.

I repeated my refrain. Maybe if I did it three times I'd feel better. Three times always made me feel better.

It didn't.

Sima waited until the only thing overhead was the bit of light that leaked through the sewer grate before continuing her story.

"But like most poor people in Irska who fall ill, my mother did not get better. Her decline was slow, but eventually she needed daily care. I trekked to and from the castle every day so that I could care for her at night. My brother saw to her during the day." She stopped to take a breath, turning away slightly. I almost reached for the wall to steady myself, clenched my hands together instead, knowing already what was coming. "I was late coming to relieve him because the king sent back his supper. He claimed the meat was stringy and demanded we prepare a new meal entirely. By the time I got home, the house was in flames."

It was so shockingly close to my own story. My parents had died in the factory where my father worked. My mother was only there because she'd had a good day selling the knitwear she made and had extra money for lunch. She'd left Treasa with a neighbor because she did not want to rouse her from a nap. I'd been at school.

My story was not special. Neither was Sima's, really. There were thousands of children going back generations who could recite similar ones. We were a city of orphans.

But Sima's story did not explain why she'd faked her own death and aligned herself with the Síofran. It only gave her more reason to hate them.

I frowned, lifting my face to meet hers, to ask her, only to find her ready. Waiting.

"Síofran aren't the only ones who make fireballs," Sima said steadily.

"No." She must have hit her head on the way down into the sewer. Or when we'd careened into the wall to escape Vainar. She could not be saying . . .

"I know what I saw, Fionna. I walked past the Peace Guards every single morning on my way into the kitchens." Sima enunciated every word. "I recognized the two men running away from the fire. They were in plain clothes, not in their uniforms. And they were not running for help."

I shook my head. But Sima did not stop.

"The Peace Guards let my family burn. But you know who did help? The Síofran family that lived on the other side of the peace wall. They dumped buckets of water from their roof onto ours for hours until the fire was out. But it was too late for my mother and brother. By the time the human officials got there, I was already in the next peace village over. I let them assume I'd died there, too. No one ever investigated. They saw fireballs and they assumed it was the Síofran."

I shook my head. Harder. If I stopped, the world would refocus, shift, exist on an entirely new plane.

"They . . . they couldn't, Sima," I whispered. "Humans don't have the magic to create fireballs."

The sharp sound of metal on stone echoed through our dank prison. Light flooded in as the sewer grate was lifted away and Karine appeared overhead.

Sima nudged me away from the rungs. "Haven't you learned by now, Fionna? Nothing in Irska is as it seems." Then she began to climb.

# Chapter 15

## HELIO

*Cultivating contacts is tricky business. Both sides kill informers. It is one of the most basic facts of life in Irska. But people still do it, every day, on both sides. The trick is to keep the information flowing once it starts. Sometimes they get scared once the intel becomes actionable. It is one thing to tell a secret. It is something else to watch people you know die because of it. But there is no going back, not really. One day you might show up to find that your contact turned coat again and gave you up. They never seem to realize that there's no saving themselves. Both sides kill informers. It doesn't matter if they turn back.*

*—Connor Zuric, Peace Guard*

It had to be fecking Pearl House.

I'd given the order to move her, but my superiors had chosen the location. The organization of our cells was particular and deliberate in order to compartmentalize information. Even if an entire cell was taken by the Peace Guard, they knew only about their own operations. Beyond my direct chain of command up and down, no one else in the Síofran Rebel Army knew we'd attempted—and failed—to kidnap the

Irskan princess. The entire scheme had been mine from its inception, and it remained with me now. For better or worse.

My chest protested the destination, even as my feet followed the route by long worn-in memory. For most of the children of Síofra, Pearl House was a rumor. An ideal. A bastion of hope and center for combined magic, should it ever reawaken. Perhaps a dozen of us knew its actual location.

I kept my head down as I moved through the dusk. The streets of Irska had quieted, Síofran and humans alike keeping indoors after Prince Vainar's unannounced foray into the streets. The royals rarely left the castle. But even so, Vainar had a reputation.

*I should have been there.*

I'd had other matters to attend to that afternoon. A new operation to plan with Link, full of updated information after his detention by the Peace Guards. They'd beaten him badly, but they'd only kept him for two days. Most importantly, he had not been alone when they picked him up. He'd been with a Rebel friend from another cell. They were able to verify that the other had never been out of their sight and had not broken or turned. It had saved their lives. And spared me from having to justify myself to Karine.

It had been an act of cowardice to send her in my place to facilitate Fionna's transfer, and Síofra had punished me for it by sending Vainar out into the streets of Irska.

I should have been at Fionna's side. I'd personally promised her that Vainar would never touch her again, yet when she'd next come face-to-face with him, I was nowhere to be seen.

That was what drove me to Pearl House.

There were not many middle-class Síofran families left. We'd never had a nobility, but the most prosperous merchants had fled for Eerin in the early days after the fall of magic. What had once been a burgeoning middle class slowly dwindled away to just a few families. The humans said it was because we'd relied on our magic for an unfair advantage, one of the many justifications for the Fall. But it was the Irskan laws that crippled us. Humans who had once patronized Síofran businesses turned against us. The Síofran themselves became so poor they could not afford to buy anything but the essentials, and often not even those.

I paused on the corner, lingering in the shadows at the end of the street. Both sides were lined with three-story town houses built of pale-gray stone. I knew the occupants of every single residence. Some in passing. Some by the wakes I'd attended. Only five were still occupied by single families. The others had subdivided the building by floor or by room in order to pay the taxes demanded by the Irskans.

The street was empty. I could have walked down the cobbled stones, up the stairs, and through the nondescript door. The original doors, ornately carved, were stored in the basement of Pearl House. Something about anonymity and protecting Síofran heirlooms. I'd just as soon have burned them.

I turned, backtracking nearly two blocks before slipping into a narrow alley full of stacked refuse bins. No one had followed me, not the Libs or the Defenders or another Rebel. But I had no claim to the front steps of Pearl House.

It took longer, but the path was just as familiar. The rear light was extinguished, as usual, but I navigated the small, fenced courtyard by memory. The back door yielded beneath my hand, unlocked.

*What the feck?*

I slipped through, letting my boots scrape across the wooden floorboards. The entire hallway lit up instantly. The narrow stream of light from the window above the door intensified from gray to bright white, lighting every corner and evaporating the shadows that should have existed. It was so bright it burned. My eyes were already closed.

"I expected you to wait for dark."

My eyes remained closed until the light dimmed. Only then did I open them, knowing who waited at the end of the hallway.

"That door should be locked."

Turi had one arm crossed over his chest, the other hand supporting his chin as he considered me. "Better we leave it open than risk them breaking it down."

He'd let the evening light fade back to its natural hue, a cool gray that lit the hallway just enough for me to recognize the familiar details. A long table against the southern wall, two portraits in ornate gold frames opposite, unlit candles in a heavy, engraved candelabra. My eyes snagged on the unexpected—a single small shoe, the sole caked in mud, haphazardly discarded beneath the narrow table.

Turi followed my eyes but did not react, other than to stroke his dark beard. The muted light hid the gray that had appeared over the last few years.

"Nieve will want you to stay for dinner," he said.

"Is she in the kitchen?" I asked. I'd intended to stop there all along.

Turi nodded.

"Then I'll make my excuses to her in person." I did not wait for his response before ducking into the doorway between the two portraits. Less than ten minutes later, I reentered the hall. Turi was no longer there.

I took the stairs slowly, careful with my burden. One level, past the family rooms, up to the top. Her door wasn't locked, either. I took care to make plenty of noise as I approached, to jiggle the door handle so she would not be surprised.

It worked.

She did not twitch a muscle, did not turn to look, did not acknowledge my existence at all. Meanwhile, my entire body lit at the sight of her.

The fire was always close to the surface, my blood always hotter than should have been possible. But Fionna awoke a part of me that I had not even realized was sleeping.

She sat at the small table positioned beside the window, her posture perfectly straight despite my intrusion. The evening light turned her pale skin luminous, sharpening the contrast with her thick black hair.

For the first time since we'd taken her, she'd restrained the curls. An elegant, twisted braid fell over her shoulder, secured with a bit of red velvet ribbon. The curled ends of the plait kissed her collarbone, the way I'd dreamed of doing.

She should have been diminished, without the velvet we'd found her in. But the plain clothes suited her. The homespun fabric of her deep-navy dress highlighted the luxuriousness of her hair and skin, the simple lines of the garment allowing the elegant lines of her face to shine.

But it was the defiant tilt of her chin that truly held me in thrall. The soft lines of her curves and rolls in contrast with the iron will that she hid beneath them. A diligent, biddable servant who nursed a cunning, sharp mind and an even sharper tongue.

I'd seen the anxiety that plagued her. The nervous patterns she tapped out with her hand and foot. But despite those things, she just kept going. It was so fecking admirable, I almost forgot that she was human.

She was the enemy.

My captive.

Any other relationship between us was not only forbidden by Irskan law but also by tradition and hundreds of years of hate.

But I had no interest in a standoff tonight. I set the steaming mug I'd carefully carried up the stairs in front of her, then returned to close the door so we would not be interrupted.

*So I can have her to myself.*

She rewarded my initiative by shifting her gaze away from the window, down to the tea. But she did not look at me, and she did not make any move to touch the offering. "Have you decided to poison me after all?"

I leaned back against the door, hooking one foot over the other.

"If I had, I would not have gone to the trouble of moving you here from the warehouse," I said. Casual, that's what I was attempting here.

Her mouth twitched. That was the only indication she gave that her mind was at work. What would it be like to hear those thoughts spoken aloud? To understand how she came to her decisions, what she weighed? To be part of her calculations, rather than the subject of them?

When she reached a decision, she allowed herself to meet my eyes.

"Why did you move me?" she asked. Her mouth formed the words, but those eyes did the talking.

They were brighter than I'd seen them, thick with tears that she would refuse to shed out of sheer power of will. She'd looked at me with this intensity before. Scanned my features, taking in every detail. But where fear had lined her gaze, now it was replaced with heat. Black fire of her own shone out of her dark eyes, and it had nothing to do with the attraction that raged between us. There was no mistaking the emotion that she directed at me now. Pure, undiluted hate.

My heartbeat stuttered in my chest.

It was better that she hated me. I wanted her to hate me.

It wasn't the reason I'd refused her request to help on a Rebel mission, but it was an effective side effect. She had too much to lose. I'd mocked her for giving up the secret of her sister's existence so quickly, but I understood why she had.

So many of us were orphans. It made us loyal to the cause, not to the individuals within it. Empirically, I could see how twisted that was. But as a leader, I used that fact every day to motivate myself and those within my command.

Fionna would be a dangerous ally for the Rebels. Her focus would always be on her sister, not on the larger stakes.

If I'd had a sister . . . It was impossible. Not just because of my parents' deaths but also because of what I was. There could only be one.

I could use her for information, but I could not allow her any closer than that. Not with her allegiance divided as it was and always would be. She was a sister first, then a human, and then one with morals and beliefs and outside allegiances. I told myself that even if she'd been Síofran, I would have refused her.

But that did not change why I'd come here tonight. The council was getting restless. I needed to prove that Fionna was worth the trouble we'd gone to obtain her.

*And I need to beg her forgiveness for not being there.*

Fecking hell.

I pushed away from the door, crossing to the armchair positioned on the other side of the room by the fireplace. Fully aware of her eyes on me, I dragged it across the room until it was a few feet away from her. She watched as I sat, leaned forward, and braced my forearms on my knees, directing all my attention to her. I still had not answered her, and the accusation behind her words hung in the air between us.

"I will make you a deal, Fionna. A question for a question," I said.

I should not have said her name. The syllables on my lips awoke something in me that was better left sleeping. Or better yet, dead. But I plowed on.

"I will even answer your first one for free. There was Peace Guard activity in the area. They are confiscating unused Síofran property and claiming it for the Crown. We had no idea that Vainar would be in the peace villages today."

She did not flinch at his name. Pride that I had no claim to surged through me.

Her hands were clasped in her lap. But even without shifting my gaze, I caught the movement of her index finger against the back of her hand, tapping out the familiar rhythm, just once. She did not move her chair to face mine, but her posture shifted enough that I knew I had her, at least for now.

"You left me alone in that warehouse for over a week. Was the waiting part of the torture?"

*Yes.* But she had not agreed to my terms. "Is that your first question?"

"Feck you," she snapped.

No one had said that to me since childhood. And I'd walloped the boy so badly he'd had to drink his meals until his adult teeth came in.

In the silence of my surprise, her gaze drifted back out the window. Despite her snipes, she was distracted. I let her have the space, gambling that she'd come back. Fionna did not disappoint me. She might be incapable of it.

Her eyes were clearer, the wetness gone in favor of ire when she turned back. "Fine. I agree," she said. "Tell me about your magic."

"That is not a question," I fired back.

"I fecking hate you," she seethed.

"As you should."

But she had the question ready. "Is your magic related to fire?"

She'd noticed the heat between us, realized it was more than just the flaming attraction.

*Clever girl.*

Fire was the least of my powers. Most Síofran could light a fire, so long as there were two or three of them together who agreed long enough to get it started. Not always a guarantee, by any means. But starting a fire was a small magic, the kind we'd retained after the Fall. In my hands, at my full power . . . the flames would turn into something different altogether. The fire was in my blood. It heated my skin, the room around me. I shaped it in all its forms, not just the flames but also the heat they gave off, the burns they inflicted. In turn, they shaped me. Or they would, if the Síofran ever won this war.

I nodded. "In part, yes."

Her lips pressed together, the lush bow shape thinning into a line of disapproval. The answer dissatisfied her as much as it did me. I wanted to tell her more, to confess the true nature of what lurked inside me. But to do so would betray every generation that had come before, each of my ancestors who had died so I might sit in this room and live to fight this war.

Before I could lose control and do exactly that, I forced myself to ask, "Is the king entertaining emissaries from Eerin?"

Fionna's eyes widened, her mouth forming a delicate circle of surprise. She did not bother to school her features back into neutrality. She let me see the surprise. I'd used the time apart from her to decide which questions I wanted to ask.

*How can someone as clever as you not realize that the humans are brainwashing you? What sacrifices have you made to protect your sister? What would it cost to do something for yourself? Do I plague your thoughts the way you haunt mine?*

"The princess is not invited to political meetings," she said slowly. "But there was an ambassador from Eerin at the last ball we attended."

I nodded. My sources had already reported as much, but it confirmed what I'd known all along. Fionna was not inclined to lie to me.

"Is it possible for humans to make fireballs?"

This time, it was me who could not hide my surprise in time. How had she . . . Sima.

I had not lied to Fionna yet. I would not start now.

I looked her directly in the eyes, challenging her to flinch or to break away. But she held my gaze.

"Yes," I said simply.

Her lower lip began to tremble, but she did not break our stare.

I was torn between frustration and admiration. How could she have lived with the humans for so long, right at the epicenter of their policymaking, and been blind to what they did? Even secluded with the princess, she'd attended feasts and social events. She might not have heard what the politicians and foreign ministers said, but she had noted their presence. She must have been so focused on her one goal, on the deep love she had for her sister, that all other considerations had faded away. I could not pretend to understand love. But duty and loyalty were as endemic to my veins as the creature that screeched inside me.

The urge to reach out and touch her pulsed through my veins. Maybe if I could touch her, I could understand her. If I could feel her pulse thrumming beneath my fingers, I could know whether she was as affected as I was.

*If she is, I should use it to my advantage. She already hates me.*

I curled my hands into fists. "Does the king show favoritism among his sons?"

Her eyes narrowed. She wasn't surprised this time, but contemplative, trying to figure out why I asked the question. Because we wanted to better understand the king's state of mind? Because the king had yet to name an heir? Because we wanted to know which one to assassinate? Yes to all, and I offered none.

"The king does not show affection to his children, but Odinar is the one most often at his side during social engagements," Fionna said.

There were plenty of ways to interpret that information, but she wasn't offering her own views, just facts.

"Do the Síofran have reliable ways to get out of Irska?" she asked.

She was always going to ask this question. Today, tomorrow, in a week . . . I'd been expecting it.

"Yes."

Her hands flattened against the tops of her thighs. I didn't think she was even conscious of her own movements as she leaned forward, shrinking the space between us.

I forced out another question before my throat closed and I lost the ability. "Are there servants in the castle who would be sympathetic to the Síofran cause?"

She nodded her head as she exhaled. "Sympathetic? Yes. Suicidal? Very few."

I found myself nodding along with her, my body syncing itself to hers without conscious thought, just like she'd started mirroring my posture.

"Do you have agents within the castle?" she breathed. I did not know whether she asked for herself, her sister, or because she was desperately trying to reassemble her understanding of the world we lived in.

I shook my head. "Contacts, yes. But no one who would willingly act on our behalf."

Her throat slid. I wanted to know what that motion would feel like beneath my lips. The desire to lean forward and trace the column of her throat from jaw to clavicle was so overwhelming I had to dig my fingernails into my palms to stop myself.

The delicate skin beneath her chin wobbled slightly. She was trembling. I wanted to reach out for her, to steady her, to make her tremble for real, to—

*Bloody fecking hell.*

I forced my gaze up, past her lustrous hair and her intelligent eyes, over her shoulder to the window, to the rack that hung in the corner, draped with an extra shift and a mass of black wool.

"What did you do to my cloak?" I rasped, coming to my feet.

Fionna jumped up as well, lingering at the foot of the bed while I crossed the room.

"Your cloak?" Her voice wasn't quite a squeak; it was too deep for that. But there was surprise and even a little bit of censure in it.

I pinched a fold—one of the only spots that was not covered in muck—and drew the garment out to examine it. There were no tears or damage that I could see, beyond the fact that the thing was filthy. As I inspected it, I waited for the wave of surprise to transform into anger or frustration. The cloak was one of the few bits of my past I'd held on to, the feathers along the front stitched by my own mother before . . .

But the anger did not come. Instead, it was relief. Not that the garment was undamaged, but that the woman who'd worn it was.

"Didn't the other Rebels tell you? We had to hide in a sewer," Fionna said from behind me.

Of course they had. I wanted to turn and look at her face, to see whether she wrinkled her nose in distaste, a motion to match the sour notes in her voice. But I did not. I counted to ten, waiting for the heat in my blood to bank. It didn't. I wasn't surprised.

Fionna moved to the other side of the room, giving me space to pass without touching her. That was for the best, too. We both knew that our discussion was at an end, at least for now. Darkness had fallen outside the window. Nieve would serve supper soon.

I moved toward the door. Fionna drifted across the room behind me, back toward the window and chair where I'd found her.

*Don't look back.*

The door was right there. I reached for the handle . . .

Fionna's gasp ripped through me. I closed the space between us in a second, the blade I kept in my belt already in hand, the creature inside me screeching at the threat.

But there was nothing, no one but the two of us, now dangerously close together, separated only by the space of her hand curled around the mug.

"Frostbloom," Fionna breathed, her dark brows nearly colliding with her hairline.

She did not give herself time to think as her eyes connected with mine. A maelstrom of emotions swirled in those dark depths. I was nearly ready to pitch myself into them, happy to drown.

She wanted to ask how I knew, but not enough to give me another question. She wanted to dash the tea in my face. Less effective now that it had had time to cool, but it would still get her point across. Her lips parted. She wanted to say thank you.

We could not have that between us. Captive and captor. Anything else was too dangerous to fathom. I forced myself away, back to the door.

But Fionna did not let me escape so easily. "You said you did not believe in mercy, yet you let the Defenders live even after they attacked the children."

She didn't phrase it as a question, so it was technically outside the parameters of our agreement. I did not respond. That did not stop her.

"You promised to punish Vainar for everything he's done to me, a lowly human captive."

*Because you are mine.*

"And now you bring me frostbloom tea, which means either you have investigated my background using those contacts in the castle . . ." Her voice had started to shake, but she paused to steady it. "Or you have noticed what plagues me."

"None of that is mercy," I ground out. That was the truth. Mercy was too simple a word to explain what I felt toward Fionna. "They are all tactics to get what I need from you."

Fionna's eyes dipped to the tea again, where a final wisp of steam curled upward. She flattened her palm to catch it.

"Who chose this role for you?" she asked quietly, without looking up. "Did you choose it yourself, or did the Rebels force it upon you?"

With those two sentences, she undid me. As truly as if she'd peeled away my clothes or shoved a blade into my heart. It should not have been possible for her to see. She did not know what I was, what the creature inside me meant to my people. But she saw the effects that living with it for more than thirty years had on me. I wasn't sure that anyone else ever had.

"I am not answering any more questions tonight," I growled as I turned away. The words were gruff and aggressive. *That is for the best.*

"Very well," she said.

"Good night, Fionna," I said over my shoulder.

I made the mistake of glancing back as she took the first sip of her tea. The look of quiet ecstasy on her face would haunt my fantasies for the rest of my life.

# Chapter 16

## FIONNA

*Síofra's gifts pass through family lines and are as varied as the whims of the goddess herself. The high-minded intellectuals try to organize them into classes and orders, but that's all mortals trying to make sense of something bigger than us. No one knows why Síofra bestowed the gifts she did, why she reached down into that first cradle and changed the child that lay there. Some traditions say that the first of our kind truly were Síofra's children, that she gifted her own babes to humanity and took ours into her care. The mothers did not even mourn their taken children, for how could they not wish them an eternal life at the knee of a goddess? My grandmother believed the old stories. I say that if they're true, Síofra must regret it. Humans have not treated her children very well. I hope that someday, she takes her revenge.*

*—Kristofer Gaffney, Síofran Rebel Army*

It was the nicest room I'd ever slept in, and that should have been enough to give me pause. The bedroom I'd shared with Evie off Aurelle's chambers was comfortable enough but built for practicality. Two beds, a dressing table, a washroom with stone fixtures. Of course, I'd spent the last two weeks either tied to a chair or shoved in the dusty corner of an abandoned warehouse, so my basis for comparison might have been skewed.

But I spent hours stroking the silk pillowcase. The room was not extravagant. The bed was made of heavy, unornamented wood. The rug on the floor had been rotated recently so that the worn-out footpath was now under the bed. But there were touches of care in all the right places, intentional choices to make the space more welcoming. The silk pillowcase, the oversize chair by the fireplace, the creams in the washroom.

*The creams.*

My knees had nearly given out when I saw them. Completing my nighttime routine in full had been such a relief that I was ready to . . .

What, precisely?

I'd spent hours turning it over in my mind, and I still could not reconcile Sima's story. She could not have meant that humans had access to magic; that was ridiculous. The only way for humans to obtain magic was to eat one of the King's jealously guarded golden apples. But if everything she'd implied was true, then it implied they had access to someone who did have magic. Children of Síofra who had turned informers and started creating fireballs for the humans. Helio had confirmed it.

But to what end? So that the Peace Guards could use them against our own people? What sense did that make? It might inflame tensions, but those hardly needed help. We were already at war.

Except . . . had I thought of it as a war before?

I'd been aware of the conflict. It was impossible not to be, even removed from the center of it as we were up in the castle. Treasa and I were orphans of a fireball. But as a servant, the world narrowed. I'd occupied such a finite space, serving Aurelle, raising Treasa, staying carefully on my own path to avoid undue notice. For a decade, I'd hardly lifted my head. The war was over. The humans had won. The Síofran rebellion was a heartless and brutal but ultimately doomed insurrection.

And now . . . I felt like my eyes were slowly opening, and I did not particularly like what I could see.

My stomach rumbled, reminding me that it was nearly time to eat. An assortment of clothing had awaited me when I'd arrived at my new, nice prison. Another dress, skirts, a plain but clean shift. Most interestingly, a pair of leather leggings. There was no rule or law prohibiting women from wearing pants. I'd seen plenty of women in them as the Rebels dragged me through the streets of Irska. But in the castle, they were considered too casual. If I'd worn them as a child, I did not remember.

But when I slid them on, I immediately fell in love. The freedom of movement was exhilarating. The fit . . . Whoever had procured the clothing had known about my size and chosen accordingly. The leather hugged my thick thighs but left plenty of room to breathe around my full stomach. The freedom was so heady, I forewent a corset and settled for a loose linen shirt that was probably meant to pair with the skirts. It wasn't as if I would be attending any social functions. I was a prisoner. I might as well be comfortable.

I was halfway through rebraiding my hair when a knock echoed through the room. There was nothing to do but wait. My meals had arrived by the same pattern for the last few days. A knock at the door, then it would open and someone would bring in a tray of food, set it on the table by the window, and leave.

But the door did not open.

Another knock.

I . . . Wasn't the door locked? I had not even thought to try it. I'd assumed . . . which in hindsight, was foolish. I'd taken stock of everything else about the room, including possible egress through the window, but not tried the door? Unacceptable. The comfort had gone to my head. Everything was its own kind of torture. Helio had not explicitly answered when I asked if my isolation in the warehouse had been a technique to get me talking, but . . .

"Hello?" a muffled voice said from the other side of the door.

Was that . . . a child?

The brass doorknob gave under my hand, turning without a single hitch. The door swung open to reveal what I'd suspected—a child—but without what I'd expected—a tray of food.

"Ma sent me to fetch you for dinner," the girl said without preamble.

She rocked forward and backward from her heels to her toes and back again as she spoke, that interminable energy reserved for children coming off her in waves.

I blinked. "I . . . Don't I eat dinner up here?"

A glaring young man had delivered my dinner the past few nights. Though, as I looked closer at the girl, I started to notice the resemblance. They had the same tawny skin and dark-brown hair. But where the young man's had been overgrown curls, the girl's mostly straight hair was pulled back into a tail at the back of her head.

"Ma says it is time for you to join us," the girl said, still rocking. She glanced over her shoulder, then leaned forward to whisper, "Antoni made a fuss about Ma making him bring the tray up every evening."

Antoni must have been the sullen teenager. And Ma . . . Realization took root. A family. The small touches in the bedroom, the delicious meals, the new clothing. This was a family home. And they were inviting me to dinner.

My gaze fell down to my billowing linen shirt, the lack of a corset, the leather leggings. Heat flooded my cheeks. "I . . . I don't think I am dressed appropriately."

The child grinned. "You look better than half the Rebels who come through the door," she said. "Ma says as long as your hands and face are clean, you can eat. Are they?"

I laughed. Actually, truly laughed. The girl could have only been a few years younger than Treasa, perhaps eight or nine years old. But she still had that childlike quality that had deserted my sister around eleven or twelve. It was so pure, so fresh. So at odds with everything that had happened to me over the past several weeks.

"Yes," I admitted.

That was all it took. She darted away down the hall with no further explanation. All that was left was for me to follow.

I retraced the same path I'd taken a few days prior. My door was on the highest floor, along with two others that remained closed. The first stairwell was unadorned, the wallpaper faded but free of any rips or scrapes. The second floor showed more signs of occupation. A well-worn runner covered the wooden floors, old enough that they'd begun to gap. The doors had all been closed when Karine had dragged me past them, but now two were open. I glimpsed an untidy desk through one and a floor strewn with toys through the other.

My little escort waited on the ground floor, hopping from foot to foot in anticipation.

"Ma made roasted quail for dinner. I don't like it, but I'll just sneak down later and have some—"

Her words cut off with a squeal halfway down the hall. I grabbed for the banister, just to keep myself from tumbling down the last few steps. It took me only two more to join her beneath the wide, arched entrance to a comfortably furnished room . . .

I did not understand what I saw. How could I possibly? I had no frame of reference, not even in my wildest fantasies. There was no explanation for what I was seeing . . . except magic.

The curtains along the only window were drawn so that the only source of light should have been the golden firelight from the sconces mounted in the hallway. But those golden rays of light did not even make it past the threshold. They stopped, cut off at an unnatural angle so they would not intrude on the light show taking place in the darkened room.

Striations of turquoise blue, verdant green, and deep pink danced across the darkened wall. Beneath the lights, I was able to make out the shapes of books, but beyond identifying them, they held little interest compared to the glowing array.

As I watched, the colors shifted, the pink fading to a deep violet and the rich green brightening until it perfectly matched the shade of

Helio's eye. The light danced in undulating movements, its colors bleeding upward like lines of paint that had blurred, but inverted, unnatural. Unnatural, and yet my consciousness did not revolt against the sight. The feeling building in my chest was not anxiety, but wonder. Joy.

A small hand brushed against mine. "Da should have been an artist."

I'd forgotten about the child completely, so taken in was I by the beauty of the magic. It was unlike me to completely lose track of my surroundings. Hypervigilance was as natural and necessary as the tapping my anxiety required.

Now that she'd broken the reverie, my mind gobbled up the details. A middle-aged man cross-legged on the floor, a child pressed up against his side in an identical pose. Even at an angle, the resemblance was impossible to miss. Although the man's dark hair was laced with gray and cropped close to his head, it was pin-straight, just like the girl's at his side—and the girl's at my side. My head swiveled back and forth. Twins.

But more remarkable than the resemblance was the movement of their hands. The man's fingers moved through the air like the conductor I'd seen so many times at the king's balls. The light show was his doing. The child—I could not quite make out what she contributed, but she snapped her fingers and then collapsed into giggles, so it must have been something.

The girl at my side clapped her hands in eager amusement, drawing the attention of the pair on the floor. I expected the magic to disappear, for the pair to retreat in the presence of a human. But the man merely lifted a brow in my direction.

"Well done, Nadia," he said to the daughter at my side.

She preened under the praise—that she'd managed to persuade me to come downstairs, I suspected.

"I've never . . ." I breathed, unable to tear my eyes away from the ongoing spectacle. "How?"

The man smiled, one of his hands conducting the parade of lights while the other lifted to stroke the short beard that marked his jaw.

"Síofra gifted my line with the ability to manipulate light," he said.

A fragment of memory. A dream. Not as clear as the ones of the street in the peace village or of flying, but it was there.

Before it could form, someone snapped their fingers and drenched the entire room in darkness, extinguishing the colorful lights and the braziers that burned in the hallway. Twin streams of riotous laughter filled the darkness.

"And my hellion of a daughter with the power to extinguish it," the man said into the darkness. Another snap, and then the lights in the hallway relit, as well as an oil lamp in the book-lined living room. From the position of his hands, I guessed that was the work of the man getting to his feet.

"I am Turi. My daughters, Moira and Nadia," he said, offering a crisp bow. He was several inches shorter than me, square shaped, and unimposing. But there was a certain authority to him even so.

In the castle, a lady of the same station would have curtsied. A servant would not have warranted a greeting. I settled on a strange half-bow head nod that probably looked as uncomfortable as I felt.

We stared at each other—me, heart pounding; him, steady and assured. He was not going to fill the silence. Before being kidnapped, I'd never been expected to. The girl at my side, Nadia, had joined her sister on the floor, deep in whispering that was clearly not meant for us adults.

My eyes lifted to the two bookcases that stood side by side along the opposite wall, where the lights had danced moments before.

"I was taught that magic is dead," I said. Even though I'd seen the evidence since that first day in captivity, and Helio had briefly explained that small magics remained, it still did not feel commonplace.

Turi nodded, hooking his hands behind his back and taking a few steps in my direction.

"Magic can never truly die, so long as there are enough of us united in common purpose. Our magic may have originally come from Síofra, but now it lives within every one of us. So long as two Síofran hearts beat, magic will survive."

My throat thickened with an emotion I struggled to name. He spoke with such conviction, his words so completely at odds with what I'd been taught. They weren't combative, but loving. Like the magic in his veins was not a weapon, but a blessing. How many Síofran thought like him? And how had humans' understanding of them become so twisted?

"Yes, yes, how philosophical and wondrous," a sharp voice said. I turned just in time to avoid being sideswiped by a twirling tornado of a woman entering the room. To Turi, she said, "That is not what she means," before turning to me.

"Small magics survive. This"—she indicated the wall where the light show had taken place—"is a glimmer of what their power should be. My daughter should be able to darken the entire house with the snap of her little fingers, and Turi, he could light up all of Irska."

It was evident that in this woman's estimation, he already did. Her tight curls bounced as she turned to the two girls, directing them to go wash up for dinner.

"My wife, Nieve," Turi said quietly. She waved one hand in acknowledgment, the other full of—

"The cloak," she said. "It took some doing, but I was able to get all the stains out without damaging the embroidery."

I accepted the neatly folded garment, my fingers brushing over the stitching. I'd studied it before, while trapped in the warehouse and trying to avoid expiring of boredom.

"Thank you," I murmured.

Not my cloak, but Helio's. My lower lip caught between my teeth.

"Leave it on the table there for now. No sense in trekking back upstairs when dinner is already on the table," Nieve said, bustling down the hallway.

I did as she instructed. What else was I to do? The entire household followed her with quiet, unquestioning acquiescence. She reminded me of Bela, the woman who'd started as Aurelle's governess and transformed into an overwrought chaperone once the princess came of age.

We proceeded in a line down the hallway and into a dining room adorned with a massive table. Several portraits hung on the walls, each in an ornate gilt frame at odds with the understated elegance of the rest of the house. I didn't recognize any of the faces; they did not match any of the royal likenesses that lined the portrait hall in the castle. *Of course they don't,* I admonished myself. This was a Síofran home; these were likely their revered dead.

I barely had time to marvel at my change in circumstances. I'd gone from eating greasy fried potatoes and fish out of crumpled wax paper to a seated dinner.

"Your home is lovely," I said, taking the chair that Turi pulled out for me.

"We are not the owners of Pearl House, merely its stewards," Turi said, moving to an adjacent chair. The girls were already seated.

"The appropriate response, husband, is 'thank you,'" Nieve interjected.

Plodding footsteps announced the arrival of the young man who'd delivered my meals the few days prior. It took only seeing him in this new context to place him within the parameters of his family. His skin was a few shades darker than Turi's and the girls', favoring his mother's cooler brown complexion. The unruly curls atop his head were hers as well. While I'd thought of him as a man, I adjusted my estimation of his age downward, perhaps fifteen or sixteen years old.

Nieve took her own seat, just to the left of the head of the table, a seat that was left conspicuously unoccupied. "Moira, do not get into those buns. We are still waiting for—"

I recognized the weight of his steps. An instinct born of self-preservation, surely. I was his captive; he, my torturer. Except that he'd never laid a hand on me that I had not welcomed.

*What the feck is wrong with me?*

He filled the space with his presence, sucking all the air out of the room despite the tall ceilings and the wide, arched entryway from the hall. My heart stuttered traitorously in my chest. Not in panic but in anticipation. I ordered it to stop. It did no such thing.

Helio's eyes found mine, just as I'd come to expect. The tangle of emotions between us was quickly escalating into a briar. The first time I'd seen his mismatched eyes, I recoiled in terror. How could I not? Set beneath dark brows, his deep-red hair slicked back and curled around his shoulders, with that scar bisecting his brow and curving around his eye? Fecking terrifying. Still terrifying. But also . . . interesting. Mesmerizing.

His eyes slipped lower, past my face to the front of my shirt. They widened, the effect magnified by the two different colors. I looked down, confused. I'd folded my hands in my lap, inadvertently pulling the soft linen tight against my unrestrained breasts.

"Have you washed your hands and face?" Nadia interrupted, breaking the line of tension that stretched between us with all the physicality of an actual tether.

"I know the rules," Helio said, nodding in the girl's direction before shifting his attention to her mother. "Thank you for the invitation, Nieve."

"You don't need an invitation," Nieve said sharply. "Moira, I swear to Síofra, if you touch that roll again—"

Helio's mouth curved slightly at one corner. "Do not wait on my account."

Moira needed no more encouragement. She whipped the roll she'd been caressing out of its basket and had it in her mouth before her mother could get in another word.

Helio lingered another moment on the threshold before entering the dining room. He walked past the chair at the head of the table, choosing one between Turi and Antoni instead. His eyes did not stray to mine.

Conversation flowed freely between the family. Turi posed several queries about the children's schoolwork, which the girls answered eagerly. Antoni gave little more than grunts, a typical teenage boy. Helio ate quietly, speaking occasionally with Antoni in low exchanges that did not invite the rest of the table to join in. I spoke only when asked a direct question.

This could be another strategy of Helio's, another means of torture to extract information from me without realizing it. Using the family was clever. They were very disarming. And if I had to pick an ally to help me turn someone to my side, Nieve would have been high on my list.

Or it could just be dinner.

When the meal finished, the three children helped clear the plates, and then the family retired to the living room, where they'd gathered before. I drifted along behind them, unsure of what to do with myself, unnerved by the casual warmth of the entire evening.

Of course, I knew that Síofran families existed. The sullen teenager did what all teenagers do—lingered on the periphery while still paying rapt attention and secretly hoping for attention and validation. The twins curled up on either side of their father, one resting her head on his knee, the other twirling a bit of ribbon around and around her finger as Turi read to them aloud. It was so domestic. So pure.

Beyond the mere logic of it, I'd seen the reality with my own eyes both times I'd been escorted through the streets of Irska. But I had never thought of them like this.

Why not? Hadn't I had a childhood like this, before the fireball that stole my parents from me? There had been less food, and we'd certainly never had our own bedrooms. But there had always been plenty of love. My parents had created moments of peace and security while a guerilla war waged in the streets. Just like Turi and his wife did for their children here at Pearl House.

I had not thought of anyone but myself and Treasa, not for years. I'd been singular in my pursuit of escape. I did not have friends in the castle. Plenty of acquaintances, like Evie and Sima before her, the tea master who provided my frostbloom tea, and the master gardener who'd bred the roses that had led to my downfall. But I had never allowed myself to become close to anyone. I'd closed myself off in a prison of my own creation in order to protect myself and my sister. Mostly, it had worked.

Surely, had I grown up with my parents, I would have noticed the complexity of the conflict that colored every single moment in Irska, touching every person and every place. Wouldn't I?

I could not give myself an honest answer.

"You can join them." A shiver snaked down my spine as Helio's breath caressed the exposed skin at the nape of my neck.

How had he gotten so close without my noticing? I'd been transfixed, watching Turi and Nieve's family. I looked over my shoulder, expecting to find Helio's eyes waiting for mine. But he watched them, too, with the same wistfulness that I felt in my own soul.

Outsiders, both of us.

For me it made unequivocal sense. But Helio was Síofran. He clearly knew the family, was friendly—as much as he had the capacity for—with all its members. What set him apart?

Over his shoulder, I caught sight of the neatly folded and laundered cloak. The feathers embroidered along the collar and front edges, so lovingly wrought . . . What did they mean? Was Helio one of the Síofran that could shift into an animal form? A literal changeling? But he'd said his power was related to fire. That accounted for the heat that seemed to flow from his very presence.

At least, some of it.

The other heat—the one that came from an unexplainable and inexcusable part of me—rose and twisted in my stomach.

"I should go back upstairs," I heard myself say.

Helio did not move to block me. He did not say or do anything at all, which convinced me retreat was the right thing. If he wanted to keep distance between us, so did I. We were aligned, for once. It was so much easier to hate him from a distance.

"Do you knit, Fionna?"

I stiffened, Nieve's question freezing my intention to slip away. I cleared my throat. The thickness did not budge. My voice came out raspy as I answered. "Passably. I'm better with a needle and thread." There were others in the castle responsible for providing Aurelle with her knit goods, but it fell to me to repair her gowns and to reshape them for myself once she discarded them.

"I have those, too," Nieve said, nudging a thick bag at her feet.

I swallowed, hands curling to fists at my side.

Nieve had not even looked up, her eyes focused on a complex series of stitches in the garment she was knitting. "You don't have to," she said. "I find it soothing, but my girls would rather stick the needles in their eyeballs than help me. To each their own, and may it keep their hands from trouble."

My hands uncurled.

There was no malice in her voice. No expectation. Just an offering.

I still might have retreated, if not for the growing heat at my back. Helio's presence set my nerves burning, but I could not quite rally myself to extinguish the flame. I was not sure I should feed it, either. I dug around in Nieve's sewing bag until I found a half-constructed garment held together by pins, settling on the thick carpet before the fireplace. Helio remained standing just inside the threshold. I did not look his way, but I felt his gaze on me.

As I crossed my legs, the leather leggings pulling against my thighs and calves, I thought I felt the heat rise a few degrees. It was probably just my proximity to the hearth.

Setting the stitches soothed the jagged edges of my mind. It allowed my mind to relax, to unfurl, for me to center my breathing and sync it with the motions of my hand. Syncing my breath to my movements was one of dozens of strategies I'd developed to manage my anxiety.

From the periphery of my vision, I noticed one of the twins' heads twitching in my direction. I'd lost track of which was which when they'd transitioned out of the dining room. I kept my attention focused on the garment in my hands, a pleated skirt that looked about the right size for the girls. But the movement continued, a persistent wiggle until Nieve cut it off with a heavy sigh.

"What is it, Nadia?" Nieve asked, her hands never pausing over her knitting.

"I want to ask about the castle," the closer twin said.

"Me too!"

Turi sighed, quieter than his wife but still so characteristically parental it made my heart tighten. He closed the book in his lap.

Had Helio put them up to it? I did not let myself look over my shoulder, though I knew he still leaned just inside the living room. I was painfully, acutely, annoyingly aware of his every movement.

"You can ask, but Fionna does not have to answer. She is our guest," Turi said.

So maybe Helio had not orchestrated the whole interaction.

"Helio kidnapped her," Nadia or Moira said. "She's not allowed to leave."

Nieve flicked a knitting needle in the girl's direction. "And you will find yourself similarly confined, but to the walls of your bedroom, if you continue to sass me."

Neither girl looked particularly worried about their mother's threat. They both turned to me, eyes shining with excitement.

"Do you get to wear beautiful dresses . . ."

"Does the princess ever let you borrow her crowns?" they asked, words toppling over each other.

I bit my tongue to keep from laughing. There was absolutely no chance Helio had planned this.

"I alter Princess Aurelle's dresses to fit me once she is tired of them, and no, she does not share her jewels. She hoards them like a dragon."

That earned a round of delighted giggles from the twins. After that, they were utterly unleashed. They peppered me with questions, not even one of which could have been used to help the Rebels in any meaningful way. Answering them was almost as soothing as sewing the lines of neat, even stitches.

"Have you ever eaten one of the King's golden apples?" one of them asked.

My finger stilled over my stitches. I forced in a breath, another stitch, then an exhale. "I have not eaten one myself," I said carefully, already anticipating the follow-up question . . . and seeing the opportunity the girls had given me. The chance to be useful, to gain trust while sacrificing little.

"I have retrieved one for Aurelle"—I held up a finger to forestall the next question—"but I did not get a chance to see her use the elemental magic they promise before I . . . departed the castle."

I lifted my eyes to Helio.

His gaze seared into mine, understanding passing between us in a current so strong I felt I could have curled my fingers around it.

"Widowsbloom," he said, his voice audible to the others but directed straight at me. "You had cuts on your arms and legs. You were poisoned with widowsbloom. That is why you passed out instantly when we put the valerianroot hood over your head."

I could see why the Rebels had shaped him into their primary interrogator. His mind was miraculous, able to find the threads and make the logical leaps that others might miss. He saw things that others could not. He saw me.

Suddenly, the intensity of our connected gazes was more than I could take.

I turned back to the twins, forcing a conspiratorial smile to my face. "The master gardener created dastardly hybrids, roses with thorns coated in widowsbloom poison to keep monsters from stealing his precious golden apples." I infused the words with drama, earning little gasps of appreciation from the girls.

"Ask her something useful."

It took me a moment to place the voice. I'd barely heard him use it. Antoni, the not-quite man, had tucked himself into a wingback chair in the darkest corner of the living room. Moira and Nadia went wide eyed at his words. Turi frowned. Nieve finally paused the stabbing of her needles.

Behind us, Antoni pushed to his feet. "Isn't that why you brought her here?"

This was directed at Helio, who had crossed his arms over his chest. Whether it was an intentional move to make himself look more imposing, it succeeded in that effect.

My heart beat loudly into the silence. I was shocked that no one but me seemed to be able to hear it.

Nieve dropped her hands into her lap and pinned her son with a look that would have cowed many a Peace Guard. "Interrogations will not take place in my living room. If Helio can respect that, then I'd think my own son could as well."

The youth's dark brows knit together. "Ma—"

"Good night, Antoni."

He did not dare glare at his mother, so he glared at me instead before stomping out of the room. His step faltered almost imperceptibly as he passed Helio in the doorway, looking for an ally and finding only cool impassivity.

Antoni's steps echoed on the stairs.

Nieve sighed. "You too, girls. Go upstairs and get ready for bed. We'll be along in a few minutes to tuck you in."

There was a bit of arguing, but after their brother's display the twins seemed disinclined to push their mother. They said good night to me, then to Helio, accompanied with lots of giggles, then disappeared up the stairs with their heads bent together.

I waited until I heard doors close on the next floor, tied off the row of stitches, and then moved so that I sat up on my knees, bottom resting on my heels. It did not quite bring me face-to-face with Turi and Nieve, sitting in actual chairs, but it lessened the height discrepancy.

"Let me help," I said.

Helio's reaction was instantaneous. He pushed away from the wall, closing the space between us until he loomed over me. "Fionna."

A single word. I refused to be cowed by it. I pushed up to stand. He was still taller than me, but I was not afraid of him anymore.

The tension in the air between us solidified. It weighed on my chest, made my limbs feel like I was pushing through water. This was a calculated betrayal. Helio had already said no to my requests to aid the Rebels. By going around him and addressing Turi directly, I violated the tentative trust we'd built.

But the pulsing in my stomach told me that he'd forgive. That he'd understand. I might not share his conviction for the Síofran cause, but I knew what unfailing loyalty was. It was another thing that joined us, an unexpected parallel in otherwise disparate lives. Both Helio and I were wholly committed to our causes.

Still, heat crept up the back of my neck.

"This is not a council meeting, Helio," Turi said. Whatever that meant. And then, "Let her speak."

Helio, to my complete and utter shock, closed his mouth. He did not stop scowling. No, that was a full-fledged glare, which he divided indiscriminately between me and Turi. But he made no further audible protest.

"I have had plenty of time on my own to think," I began. Helio's eyes narrowed, the green and gold one catching the firelight. I shifted my stance ever so slightly, so that it was harder to see him, and addressed Turi instead. "However you got me out of the castle, the Peace Guards will have figured it out by now and removed that as an option. You need another way in. I can provide that."

Turi's hand was on his beard again, an affectation that he seemed to take up when thinking. Nieve was more difficult to read. Not because she wasn't expressive, but because I did not know her well enough to recognize the expressions. The tilt of her lips and narrowing of her eyes could have been suspicion or consideration or even derision.

I swallowed, tapped my fingers against my thigh three times as inconspicuously as I could manage, and continued. "You said you had no one in the castle you could count upon to act."

The expression on Turi's face confirmed the truth of what Helio had told me during our stilted exchange of questions. If he regretted sharing that with me, too damn bad.

"It is a tempting offer," Turi said. "And exactly the argument that Helio made when he advocated for your usefulness."

For my life. That was what Turi did not say. My heart sped up until I was certain that if I looked down, I'd see my chest vibrating from the force of its beating.

"But the fact remains that not only are you a captive but you are also a human. You've likely already deduced that your long-term survival is unlikely. What incentive do you have to tell us the truth?"

Other than doing what is right?

Since when had I started to believe that the Síofran cause was valid?

"My sister."

Helio already knew, which meant the rest of them did, too. Didn't it? I could not pause now. Helio had rejected my proposal. But I suspected that Turi was, if not his superior, at least his equal within the ranks of the Síofran Rebel Army. I could wake up in the middle of the night and be moved to a new prison tomorrow. This was a chance I might not be afforded again.

"You are right. I have plenty of reasons to sabotage your cause. My parents were killed by a Síofran fireball. I have spent the last decade of my life in service in the castle, subject to the whims of the princess, scraping out a minimal existence so I could save every coin for the possibility of an escape from Irska. And I still have it better than most humans orphaned by this violence.

"But one reason supersedes all of those. My sister." I turned to look at Helio. "Her name is Treasa. She is a firestoker in the castle. If your contacts in the castle will not act on your behalf, they can at least confirm that I speak the truth." Then back to Turi and Nieve. "Get her out of the castle, get us out of Irska, and I will give you the keys to the castle." Figuratively. Though if I'd had them physically, I'd have held them out at that moment to reinforce my sincerity.

Turi's fingers paused in his beard as he leaned forward, his eyes glinting. "What is to stop us from taking your sister for ourselves and using her as leverage? Perhaps you would be more useful as an informer within the castle walls, passing us secrets."

He said it with such mildness, I almost thought I'd misheard him. Turi, the doting father, casually threatening my sister's life.

I was human. I had no magic. If I had, it would have burst from me then. It should have scared me, to realize what it might mean if the children of Síofra ever truly regained their powers.

"I could lead them here," I whispered. "I could reveal your secrets."

Turi did not flinch. "And risk losing your sister."

"I am risking her just by offering to help you," I managed to get out through the shrinking passageway of air in my throat.

Safety was as much of an illusion as luck. Neither truly existed. Other servants called me lucky. But if I was lucky, I'd never have been taken. If we were actually safe, we would not have needed to wish for luck.

Turi and Nieve exchanged a look I couldn't hope to decipher, the privilege of a shared life.

"We will not expend our resources to infiltrate the castle again to retrieve your sister just to use her against you. You are valuable, Fionna, but not that valuable. Your offer of help is heard. I do not have the power to decide, not on my own," Turi finally said. "But I will take your proposal to council."

My breath whooshed out of me. I lifted my hand to my chest, pushing on the burning sensation between my breasts. I grappled for the word . . . hope. That was hope in my chest.

The temperature of the room dropped several degrees. I turned, words I didn't plan coming to life on my tongue.

But Helio was already gone.

# Chapter 17

## Helio

*Fireballs changed the course of the war. There was conflict before that, of course. But the changelings showed what they were truly capable of by creating the fireballs. Their magic wasn't a gift. Their magic was rooted in violence. Humans had to take over, or they would have eliminated us entirely. We are fighting for survival. That is what it comes down to. We are all just fighting for survival, even all these years later.*

*—Rian Bar, Peace Guard*

She was going to get herself killed. Which should not have rankled me, considering that from the inception of the plan to kidnap the princess, I'd been the one tapped to do it. Except that Fionna was not the Irskan princess. She was more, and she'd managed to crawl beneath my skin.

Like a fecking tick.

I rolled my shoulders. Unnecessary. My body was plenty loose from the hours I'd spent walking the streets of Irska. I told myself it was a patrol. A way to get a sense of the city. The night was just as telling as the day. Who braved the streets, who lurked on them, who had nowhere else to go.

Keeping my people safe meant always being hyperaware of the city's pulses and tremors. If I worked out some of my own pulses and tremors as I walked, then it was twice as useful.

I'd never doubted my purpose. Feck. My parents had died for it. What right did I have to question the fate I'd been handed, that had been handed down for generations? But Fionna, born within my city yet insulated from its nature, saw it differently. She saw me differently.

Naivete or wisdom. Maybe something of both.

Only when I neared the edge of the city, a city wall on one side and a concrete peace wall on the other, did I realize I had a destination. It was one of only a few unique sites in the city, chosen for their obscurity and their remoteness. I was aware of every member of my cell's duty schedule. I knew who would be inside.

I entered the forge with just enough noise to prevent surprising the person working within. Making fireballs was dangerous fecking business.

"I expected you'd be guarding your treasure," Karine said, sparing me no more than a glance to confirm my identity.

Even if I'd been a Peace Guard, she would not have flinched in that moment. Not with her metal poker deep in the vat of molten fire. A single abrupt movement was all it would take to ignite the mass.

I'd seen the forge at work a thousand times. I was the one who lit its flame. But the heat of it still called to the primal beast inside me. That had drawn me as much as the desire to speak to my friend. It was counterevidence to Fionna's claims about my nature, that I was drawn here to this place of violence.

"She is safely settled in Pearl House," I said, taking a position between Karine and the door. I was here. I might as well stand guard, even though I knew I'd passed half a dozen Rebels hiding in the shadows on my way here. The forge was too valuable to leave undefended. The humans had already managed to steal at least one over the past century.

"I know. I am the one who delivered her there," Karine said, completing another smooth, stirring pass.

I did not speak as she lifted a casting mold with her other hand. The next step was the most dangerous of the process. She had to lower it into the vat at precisely the right angle to fill the circular indentations while disturbing only the very topmost layer of the fiery miasma. An inch too low, and the liquid would react with the mold and create sparks. If even a single captive spark got free, the entire building would burn to ashes.

But Karine did not let her task keep her words in check.

"She is a prisoner, Helio. You should not be worried about her feeling settled. In fact, you should be working to ensure the opposite." She lowered the mold into place.

Whatever had drawn me here, it was not a desire to discuss Fionna. Talking about how she made me feel, the conflict she'd awakened within me, felt like more than a betrayal. It felt dangerous.

I matched Karine's tone. Serious but unemotional. "Every prisoner is different. Some require physical torture. Others can be convinced in more subtle ways."

The red-orange liquid rushed in to fill the mold, its color darkening and hardening seconds later.

"You care for her," she said. Nonchalant. Like she was cooking a meal instead of making fireballs. Like she was not making a serious accusation.

I waited until she withdrew the mold before speaking. I pretended not to hear the screeching beast within me.

"I care for the cause," I said. "Only for the cause. You of all people should know better than to question that."

My birth had killed my mother. My father perished close enough thereafter that there was no use distinguishing the timeline. My father's parents had cared for me briefly, but when they died, I'd ended up in Pearl House. I had no memories before my arrival there at the age of five.

All I had was the Síofran cause.

*Until Fionna.*

Karine's gaze flicked my way as she lifted the next set of molds. Whatever she saw, she did not like it. Neither did I. She turned her face down to the burning mixture, but the sound of displeasure from her throat was too familiar.

She hated Fionna; I knew that. Karine hated all humans. A feeling I shared and that we were both entitled to. But it begged the question . . .

"Do you regret standing as my second before the council?"

She huffed a laugh, but without the movement that should have accompanied it because of her task. It was strange enough that my beastly instincts took note, watching her closer.

"No," she said. "Believe it or not, I do not actually resent you your command. I have never been interested in leadership."

That came as a surprise. I'd thought she, like Heath . . . It did not matter. Not to this moment. What did was understanding what *had* pissed her off so thoroughly.

Karine's written reports had been shorter than usual. Factual, but clipped. If Turi took Fionna's suggestion to council and they approved it, and we went into the castle . . . I needed my lieutenant to get whatever the feck this was out of her system.

"Then what was that sound?" I pressed.

Karine grabbed the next mold with a little too much force.

Fecking hell. If she'd had that reaction while holding a full mold . . .

"Didn't your mother teach you not to feck with the woman making the fireballs?" she snapped.

But she took a moment to breathe. Inhale, exhale, avert her eyes from me. I did not trust myself to maintain that same control. I waited until her hands were empty again.

"My mother did not live long enough to teach me anything." A fact she knew. Why was she baiting me?

She was supposed to be my oldest friend.

Karine did not reach for the next mold. Judging from the amount left in the vat, she could fill at least two more. She'd stopped stirring when she began filling. If she left the forge untended another two minutes, the mixture would become inert and unusable, wasting the resources and magic that had been pooled to create it in the first place.

But she faced me instead. Her dark-blond brows lifted in challenge. Why had I come here, truly?

It was not about getting Karine in line. Unlike Heath, who balked at every order, Karine would follow them. She might disagree, but she would follow.

For counsel? Comfort? Karine had often provided the first. She was my lieutenant within the cell. But the second? It was not in her nature. She was too hard, just as I was. Being orphaned from a young age had that effect.

"I do not understand you," she finally said.

It was a fair assessment. I did not understand myself at the moment. But I was not about to let her see that. We were friends, yes, as only those who had grown up together could be. But she was also my subordinate. She could not see everything.

"You have known me longer than anyone living," I said. Not technically true. Karine, Link, and I had come to our guardians at Pearl House at the same time. But if I'd ever come close to showing myself to anyone—willingly—it was Karine.

Fionna had taken her pieces without asking for my permission.

Karine narrowed her eyes, her face glowing from the heat of the forge and emotion. "Which means that I understand better than most the roots of your anger and what you suppress beneath your skin. I saw what it was like for you, growing up. Feck, I was there when you got that wicked scar."

She did not mention the part she had played in the fight that landed me with it. "Your point?"

She exhaled heavily, her cheeks ruddy now. "Our people need you, Helio."

I waited for the anger that should have come at her words, the accusation in them. But after what Fionna had said, what she'd claimed to see in me . . . it was not just anger there in my chest anymore.

"I have spent my entire life in service to our people, Karine. Our people are why I am a fecking orphan," I said.

My mother had died for the Síofran. Just like every Firebird before her. Just like I eventually would. Karine should understand *that*.

She met my eyes, holding them for several heartbeats. Then she picked up the next mold. I watched in silence as she finished her task, the rows of new fireballs laid out on the rack to her left. They were only slightly less dangerous in this state than they had been in the vat of molten death.

Karine stood watch over the dregs of the mixture. Ensuring that it went inert was one of the many steps in the process that had been drilled into everyone entrusted with running a forge.

"Thank you for getting Link out," she said after a while.

As we watched, the fiery red-orange color of the liquid began to dull.

"You can repay me by getting him to talk to Heath."

She inhaled sharply through her nose. "You are the leader of our cell. Link is a child of Síofra. I should not have to repay you at all."

I matched her with an exhaled sigh. "And Link should be more careful. The only reason he was allowed to live is because the Peace Guards who captured him were eliminated before they could pass along any information."

She crossed her arms over her chest. "Fine."

That was nearly as bad as her scoff of displeasure.

"Karine."

"I said I would do it," she barked. She reached for the pitcher of water behind her, dumping its contents into the now completely darkened vat. "You should go now. I need to cure them."

It involved a flash of light. If she did it at night, the unnatural flash would draw too much attention. But wait too long into the dawn, and the streets would begin to fill. If something went wrong, she'd blow up not only herself but Síofran citizens as well. Her window of time was small, and I was intruding upon it.

She'd already turned away from me, giving her attention to the racks of fireballs awaiting the final step that would turn them into wieldable weapons.

"Karine," I said her name again. This time, it was an order. She heard it. She turned.

I waited for her to meet my gaze before speaking.

"I understand my role," I said.

Despite the questions Fionna raised, I knew what my people expected from me. I let that knowledge shine out, as unflinching as I'd ever been. The tension eased from Karine's shoulders, just enough that I felt comfortable walking away.

She nodded. "Then I am proud to be your second."

I left her to finish her work. I had not lied to her. I knew what the council and all the others expected. What I was beginning to question was whether that was what they truly needed.

# Chapter 18

## Fionna

*My ma was a Rebel, my da a Lib. She tried to bring him over, always saying she could get him in, but he never had any interest. He said there were too many rules with the Rebels, too much structure. Feck, you might be sitting next to one in the pub and not even realize it because they were so damn secretive. That's what he'd say. But really, my da couldn't keep his tongue when he drank, and the Rebels never would have taken him for that alone. I'm a lot like my da. Everyone always said so. My brother chose the Rebels. I chose the Libs. I guess we're still a family divided. Not that Ma or Da are alive to argue anymore.*

*—Sorcha Melnyk, Síofran Liberation Corps*

Most people believed that midnight was the hour of subterfuge, but they were wrong. Too many people were still awake at midnight. Mothers rocked their colicky children, staring aimlessly out their windows as they swayed to and fro. Young people were still stumbling home from trysts, middle-aged men from a night at the pub. The best hour for subterfuge was two hours before dawn.

An hour before and the merchants and factory workers were awake, preparing to emerge and start the day with the sun. But an hour before that, all of Irska was sleeping. That was the hour I moved through the city.

By that hour, most of the lamps burning outside of shops had run out of oil. Any light was a luxury I did not need. I knew Irska like my own body. I'd spent every moment of my life here, from infant to adulthood. I had never stepped beyond the city walls, never swum beyond the bounds of the bay. My whole life was spent fighting for Irska, even in the witching hour. Even now.

I left the Síofran peace village not by passing through the gates, but through a hole in the peace walls. Most of them were patched up before they could become well known, but I'd found a few over the years and done my best to disguise them. It was not a perfect plan. I'd lost some to industrious citizens on both sides. But they did not fail me tonight as I ducked down, climbing on hands and knees through the waist-high passage of crumbling concrete. Rebar pulled at my clothes, but I wiggled free without tearing anything. I did not have a cloak to get caught.

My teeth bit into the flesh of my cheek to keep the growl of revulsion in as I emerged into the human peace village. The houses here had space around them, a few even had flowers growing in the yard. The Irskan nobles made no pretense of impartiality when they drew the lines designating the peace villages. Though we outnumbered them, the Síofran were shoved into tighter spaces, given less access to the harbor for trade, and forced to exit the city along the northern edge, farthest from Eerin, the mainland, and the more lucrative trade routes.

Logic demanded that I acknowledge not all humans lived in comfort. There were plenty of poor and destitute humans in Irska, too. Which made their unfailing allegiance to the Irskan king even more impossible to fathom.

But it would not last, not much longer. Soon this war would end. Magic would be freed. I would tear down those peace walls with my own two hands.

Which brought me back to my purpose. I chose the street over the alley. There was nothing about my physical appearance that announced me as a child of Síofra. Sneaking in through the rear door would only draw suspicion.

The pub had closed hours ago, but the door opened freely under my hand. The only light came from an oil lamp on the bar top, where two wide-shouldered human males waited, looking anything but casual. I fought the urge to roll my eyes. Fecking humans.

They'd shucked their blue and gold uniforms, but the weapons at their waist were standard Peace Guard issue. All our contact thus far had been through proxies. This was the moment where everything could go to shit—or I could change the entire tide of the war.

"Dagda?" One of them said, loud enough that a bystander could have heard it from the fecking street.

"Moccus and Sucellus." I knew by each of their reactions which false name belonged to each. Moccus's mouth quirked with pride. They hadn't done any research, then.

If they had, they'd have realized that I'd saddled them with the names of two minor, trickster demigods of Síofran lore. Demigods who, legend held, were put to death by Síofra herself. Fecking humans. Síofran legends were Irskan legends. They originated in this land. The incompetent guards did not even know their own history.

"You promised real information this time," Sucellus said, bustling to his feet. He kept one hand on his weapon. Not entirely stupid.

"In exchange for gold," I countered. Holding my ground did not require thought; I could slaughter these two where they stood. But the blood would draw attention I didn't need. "I want to be long out of this feck-hole before you blow it up."

That was a lie.

But the humans needed a believable reason for me to betray my own kind. Money was as good as any.

"We have your gold," Moccus growled, tossing a sack onto the ground between us. He could have slid it down the bar top. Or set it on one of the scarred, empty pub tables. But he wanted me to bend down and expose my neck.

I'd do it. For the rebellion. For freedom. So that one day, no Síofran would have to bow before a human ever again.

They snickered as I straightened.

Maybe I'd find them once things were underway. Butcher them slowly, so they could contemplate how they'd underestimated me and all of Síofra's children.

They were still grinning those disgusting, malicious grins as I stepped forward, holding out a rolled scroll of paper. Writing things down was dangerous, but I did not trust these imbeciles not to feck up the intel I gave them. We were so close now. I did not have time for mistakes. I'd disguised my handwriting. By the time it could be traced, this would all be over.

Moccus unrolled the paper and began to read. His eyes blew wide. Mine remained steady. Sucellus had not stopped watching me, his gaze darkening with the desire to kill and maim.

I lifted my hand, allowing the glowing embers to peek from between my fingers. The texture of the fireball, rough and warm, was as familiar as the fabric of my well-worn garments against my skin.

Sucellus's face shifted as he recalculated his chances against me. Moccus finished reading the scroll, saw the interplay between us, nudged his companion to the side.

"This is enough," Moccus said. "Let's go."

Sucellus wanted to argue. He was torn between fear of my fireball and desire to prove his superiority. Let him fecking try.

Not now. Not tonight. Every human would pay for what they had done to my people. Very soon, I'd shove us over the precipice. Very soon.

Moccus and Sucellus disappeared out the rear door of the pub. I went to the keg behind the bar and pulled myself an ale. I drank it alone while the sun rose over Irska.

⁓

177

I jerked awake, my heart pounding wildly in my chest, already halfway in the clutches of that beastly anxiety that lived inside me.

It felt so real. The anger, the satisfaction, the anticipation—I'd felt them in my own stomach, fierce and all consuming. My brows had lifted. My hands twitched around the fireball. Except that I was not holding a fireball. I was in my bed—*the bed*—in Pearl House. Through the parted curtains, I could see the now-familiar outline of town houses.

Could it be magic? Had the week I'd spent in Pearl House with Turi and Nieve's family, surrounded by their love and community, allowed me to access some untouched depth within myself?

Was I a changeling?

I dismissed the thought as quickly as it came. It was ridiculous. But the idea of magic . . . Helio had said that it was possible for humans to make fireballs. Sima had seen Peace Guards wielding them. I'd assumed that meant that there were children of Síofra aiding the humans. But was that wrong, too?

My understanding of Irska had been shifting since the moment I woke up strapped to a chair. And it had yet to crystallize into something understandable.

I was not a child of Síofra. I was a human. An orphan. A servant. A sister. And yet.

I'd seen the street from the peace village in my dreams. The light magic that Turi and his daughter wielded had echoed with familiarity through my consciousness, even if I could not remember an exact dream.

Someone within the Síofran Rebel Army was passing information to the Peace Guards. I'd seen it, felt it, lived it. It was as clear in my memory as the details of the dinner I'd shared with the family in Pearl House, or the last time I'd hugged Treasa.

Guilt—that's what this was. I felt guilty for betraying my own kind. That's what I was doing by helping Helio and the other Rebels get into the castle. Or would be doing, if they agreed. No one had sent word, Helio had not come back to Pearl House, and Turi and Nieve had kept to lighter topics since my proposal.

Guilt. Regret. Fear.

The pounding of my heart intensified until it was not just the organ in my chest moving but my hands and legs, too. My entire body began to shake. Nausea rolled up through my stomach and into my chest. A wave of heat suffused my entire body. Not a heat that lit, like Helio's, but a heat that burned away bits of myself. It burned away logic and left only feelings. Feelings that I could not control, feelings that choked me and made breathing nearly impossible.

My fingers curled around the bedspread. I tried to anchor myself, tried to force down a breath.

*Calm as a lake. Strong as a tree. I bend but don't break.*

But I was breaking. I was breaking in half, torn between two realities that I could not reconcile.

*I am safe. I am safe. I am safe.*

My breathing slowed. Slightly, almost imperceptibly. But it was enough to break the cycle. I dragged in a breath, counted to five, then exhaled it. Again. Three more times. Always sets of three. Slowly, ever so slowly, I started to regain control of myself. My body stopped shaking.

I felt safe at Pearl House, in the custody of a Síofran family, at the mercy of a powerful Síofran Rebel with scars to match his menace.

A man who'd kissed me. Teased me. Tortured me. But never with pain. Only with words. With his body.

I felt safe.

And while somehow that calmed me enough to fall back asleep, there was nothing peaceful about my dreams.

# Chapter 19

## Helio

*It takes a certain kind of person to climb the Rebel ranks. Killing isn't a pre-requisite. Following orders is. From the moment you take the oath, your life belongs to the Rebels. Induction is for life. Even if you go inactive, you are held to the oaths. If a superior shows up at your door twenty years later and gives an order, you obey it or you die. Those who make it to leadership are either lucky or vicious. Or both. Which is the most fecking dangerous of all.*

*—Maeve Volkova, Siofran Rebel Army*

"It is too fecking dangerous," I argued, again. The words were beginning to wear tracks into my vocal cords. But if that was what it took to get it through their thick fecking heads, then so be it.

"She is a human prisoner," Yelena sniffed. "Her only value is the information she can give us."

Maureen's mediating voice was nowhere to be heard. She couldn't get away from the bakery. Which left Turi on one end, Yelena on the other, and the council member they'd brought along so they'd have a quorum to take a vote. I'd never interacted much with Val, but from the last hour of circular conversation, she appeared to still be undecided.

I did not get a vote.

"Indeed," Turi agreed. "Which means that if she dies too soon, we squander the opportunity for more."

I'd promised Fionna that no one would touch her but me. Which meant that if the council ordered her death, that would fall to me, too. The beast inside me screeched in visceral, unheard protest.

"If they do go in, it should be Xena's cell. It is imprudent to send in faces that might be recognized," Val reasoned.

Not fecking likely.

Turi stroked his beard, the telltale sign of his sharp mind at work. "But Helio's cell is already familiar with the castle, which could get them in and out faster."

"I go where she goes."

They continued as if I had not spoken. Yelena was ready to launch an operation tomorrow. That same day, if she could have managed it. The revulsion in her voice filled in the spaces; she wanted Fionna dead.

They weren't ready to pay that price.

The heat in my blood rose, the temperature of the room with it. This time it wasn't intentional. The Firebird was getting stronger. I'd felt it closer to the surface, rearing its head, demanding my attention more and more in the past weeks. It shouldn't have been possible; all but small magics were bound. And this thing inside me was not small.

They would hear me this time. "The prisoner is not going anywhere without me."

Fionna. I kept her name to myself, even though they knew it. Saying it to them felt . . . wrong. A violation of the intimacy I had no right to.

I had their attention now. "I have taken responsibility for her. Karine stands as my second. Taking the prisoner out of my custody is a violation."

Not just of Rebel rules, but of Síofran custom. Even Yelena could not argue with that.

But it was Val whose gaze held the most intensity. Her distinctive violet eyes lingered on my face, meeting mine and holding them without any hesitation. I always won this sort of interaction. Whether it was the two differently colored eyes, the scar that ran through my brow, or the beast lurking within me, everyone eventually turned away.

Val was no exception. But when she did turn to Turi, speaking in a voice low enough that I knew it was not meant for me—nor could I strain hard enough to hear it—a chill countered the heat in my heart.

Yelena joined the hushed conversation. I knew when Turi's hand dropped away from his beard that they'd made their decision.

"Go ahead with the operation," Val said, the unexpected spokesperson for the trio. She caught my gaze again, as unflinching as before. "Make sure you get the human out alive, Helio. We are not done with her yet."

I'd never accessed my full magic. The fall had come generations before my birth. But in that moment I was certain that if it had been free, talons would have burst from my knuckles. I walked away from the council without awaiting further instructions. I'd do this my way.

But a persistent thought slid into my mind, burrowing into my consciousness.

What power had Síofra gifted to Val?

# Chapter 20

## Fionna

*There is a phrase emblazoned on the walls of the barracks. No one really knows who carved it there. It predates all of us currently serving, and that is saying something. There are old fecks in their seventh decade who have been here since birth, handed over by their parents before they were even off the teat. Every action ties back to those words. Transgressions can be contested if the guard is wily enough to justify himself using those words. Most guards end up with it tattooed somewhere on their body, sometimes in the old language, though I prefer the words in the common tongue. I have them right here, over my heart. "He who dares will conquer."*

*—Casimir Loughlin, Peace Guard*

"Time to get out of bed, Princess."

Karine's sharp voice jolted me to wakefulness. I blinked up at the ceiling, heartbeat ratcheting up as I quickly became aware of not just one intruder in the room, but two. Too dark to see. No weapons to grab. Overmatched even if I'd had one.

By the time I sat up, Karine was already throwing clothing onto the bed. The oil lamp in the corner flared to life, illuminating Heath and the menacing glare that he always wore.

"What is happening?" I asked as I pulled a dress over my shift and shoved my stockinged feet into boots.

They were moving me to another prison, of course. I did not really need to ask. Helio had warned me about sleeping fully clothed. But I'd allowed myself to become too comfortable at Pearl House.

My mind shifted to practicalities. I did not have a satchel or bag, but I could use the loose linen shirt to bundle everything up. I started for the washroom, determined to bring at least the night cream, but Heath stepped into my path.

"It's time to make yourself useful," he sneered.

I did not cower from him, not this time. I wasn't to be afforded time to pack. Fine. But I was not leaving without the cloak.

"Leave it," he ordered, brushing my hand aside.

"No." I reached around him.

Before he could lay a finger on me, heat blasted over my shoulder, and a larger, stronger hand closed around his arm.

"If she can't follow orders, she has no place on an operation," Heath said between his teeth.

"She'll follow my orders," Helio said, a wall of heat at my back. "Leave the cloak, Fionna. You are coming back here." *I promise.*

His unspoken words competed for attention in my mind with Heath's last—"operation." I was not relocating to a new prison cell. The Rebels had decided to make good on my offer.

Heath maneuvered around me, careful not to touch either Helio or I.

My hand fell away from the cloak. "You decided to use me."

Helio stepped back, putting enough space between us for me to turn, but the heat remained, my body acutely aware of his presence.

"The council decided to see if you're worth all the trouble you've caused," he said.

He held up a fitted jacket, made from a dark wool similar to the cloak, with leather reinforcements at the collar, shoulder, and elbows. I took it without thinking, my mind already racing ahead.

"We are going to the castle," I said as I slipped my arms into the narrow sleeves. I waited for resistance, expecting the cut to be too slim. But they fit my arms perfectly.

I lifted my arms, experimenting with the movement, wondering at how well the garment was tailored to my body. The curves told me it was made for a woman—a woman who was exactly my size.

It was hard to discern in the darkness, but I thought Helio's mouth twitched. "Yes."

Yes. We were going to the castle. "Where? Why?"

That was most definitely a twitch. Almost a smile. Only because it was dark.

Karine and Heath had already exited the bedroom, their quick steps moving down the stairs.

"You'll see when we get there," Helio said.

I did not even feel the need to argue.

Nieve and Turi stood in the kitchen, each holding a steaming mug. Between them, a nearly empty bottle of amber liquor stood sentinel. Maybe they'd share a portion with me if I made it back.

*When I come back.* Helio's promise was still fresh in my ears. What choice did I have but to believe him? The Rebels would only give me one chance to prove myself. This had to go well. It might be my one and only chance to rescue my sister. Whatever else I might say about Helio, he'd never lied to me. He'd kept his word. I could not pretend that he had my best interests at heart. But I could trust that if he told me I would return to Pearl House, then that was the truth.

Outside, we joined up with a fourth Rebel. This one I did not recognize. Of average height and build, her one distinguishing feature was her red-gold hair. She kept it tied in a tight knot at the back of her head, but it was still undeniably beautiful.

Karine jogged past, scouting a block ahead. The new woman fell into place just ahead of me and Helio, who remained at my side. Which meant that Heath had to be in the rear, watching for attacks from the back and ensuring that we were not followed.

I wasn't certain of the hour, but every street and alley we turned down was deserted. A few establishments still had lamps burning out front. We turned into alleys to avoid those. I did my best to regulate my breathing, but by the fifth block I was not moving as quickly as the first.

The Rebel in front of us paused in the middle of the next street, looking back over her shoulder to scowl at me as I increased my brisk walk to a jog to reach her.

"Keep up," she bit out.

"You do not need to concern yourself with me." I hated how winded I sounded, but I planted my hands on my hips for defiant effect. The range of movement in the fitted jacket really was amazing.

Her dark-blue eyes narrowed. "The last time I saw you, Helio had you slung over his shoulder like a sack of grain."

She'd been a party to my kidnapping, then. I hated that she recognized me when I could not say the same. The power differential was infuriating. I should have been used to it after a decade in service, and weeks in fecking captivity. But what I really wanted was to use one of those defensive hooks Helio had shown me and punch her in the jaw.

"I've got her," Helio said, wrapping a hand around my elbow. I felt the warmth of every finger, even through the leather and reinforced wool. "Mendara, fall back and replace Heath."

A punishment for the woman, Mendara, or an indication of how little he trusted Heath to watch our backs? From the disgruntled twist of her brows, I guessed the former. But she followed Helio's orders without question.

I fit another piece into my understanding of the function and structure of the Síofran Rebel Army. Sima, Karine, Heath, and this new woman, Mendara, all reported to Helio. They all answered directly to him. Turi was his superior, though maybe not directly. Turi and Helio had both spoken of a council but not revealed who comprised it. My guess was that Turi must have been a member, to be given stewardship of Pearl House, which was at the very least an unofficial center for Rebel operations.

My thoughts distracted me enough that by the time we stopped again, I did not even notice the frigid breath knifing in and out of my lungs. But I could not miss the sound of metal scraping over concrete, or the fetid scent that leaked into the narrow alley.

We were going back into the sewers.

"No wonder you told me to leave the cloak," I said. Though it was a shame that I'd soil the marvelous new jacket. I quickly did up the clasps along the front so it fit as close to my body as possible.

Helio rewarded me with a slash of a smile before he disappeared down the tunnel. He would never be considered handsome by Irskan court standards. He was too rough—shoulders too broad, hair too long. The scar that he wore as a mark of honor would have been considered disfiguring. But to me . . .

"Faster," Karine urged. I managed to get my hands off the rungs just before her boots squished my fingers against the metal.

It was a different tunnel, but just as before the rungs ended several feet above the concrete floor. I jumped, tensing my muscles and praying that I'd keep my balance and not careen into the refuse-soaked walls.

But I needn't have worried. Helio caught me against his body, arms encircling my waist to steady me. Heat flamed through my body, and whether it belonged to Helio or to me, I couldn't quite distinguish. Karine was fast behind me. Helio and I needed to move to make space for her.

Even so, his hands lingered a little longer than necessary on the small of my back.

Then Karine jumped to the ground, Mendara moved the sewer grate back into place above us, and we started moving again.

I tried to keep track, but the series of turns and loops was too complex. This was not the time to run. I had not even considered it. But if they took the winding route specifically to disorient me, they were plenty successful.

I began to question why they'd brought me at all. If they planned to access the castle from the sewers, I was not sure I would be much help. But before I could work up a way to ask or decide whether doing so was even wise, we reached another juncture and set of metal rungs leading up. Helio gave me a boost, and then I was emerging onto the smooth stones of a well-maintained courtyard.

The Mountain Gate.

I recognized it even shrouded in darkness. How many times had I knelt behind the crenulations overhead to watch the Peace Guards training? I'd walked across these stones on the morning of my kidnapping on my way back from the golden apple orchard.

But even though every arch and door was familiar, the emptiness was not.

The guard stations were unmanned. We were not the first to arrive.

Sima waited beneath the portcullis. We did not pause long enough for words, but she offered me a small smile before turning to speak to Karine, who fell into place at her side. I did not want to think about what Sima had done to ensure the Mountain Gate was unguarded when we arrived.

Helio left the two women without a word, steering me into the same corridor where I'd entered after retrieving Aurelle's golden apple. I did not look to the side to see if the ruined cloak I'd left hanging was still there, nearly a month later. But I could not stop my eyes from lifting, scanning the shadows for any sight of a soot-covered imp.

Treasa was safe in her bed, where she belonged, I told myself.

But the pressure in my chest increased, the anxiety threatening to rise up. What if she was not in her bed? What if I was caught here with the Rebels? Both sides knew my affiliation with Treasa. Was I dooming us both?

I tried to force it down, focusing on where Helio's hand still cradled my elbow.

"Why leave them there?" I asked, purposefully keeping my voice quiet enough that neither Mendara nor Heath could hear us. They kept pace a few steps behind.

"Sima has the second-best knowledge of the castle, after you. She and Karine will secure an alternate escape route, if this one becomes inaccessible," he said, his voice equally soft. His breath caressed the thin strip of skin exposed above the leather neck of my jacket.

We reached the end of the hall. Helio's hand fell away. I understood—we'd gone as far as he could reliably navigate.

"I think it is time for you to tell me where we are going," I said around my thundering heart.

I thought I heard a hiss from behind us, but I ignored it. Karine and Heath were not my concern. Helio was here. Helio was the one I trusted. Now was the moment to find out whether he returned the sentiment.

Oil lamps lined the hallway. They warmed the ice of Helio's blue eye to a soft violet and enhanced the gold striations in the green.

He held my gaze as he spoke. "The dungeons. We are extracting three Síofran prisoners."

I nodded. "And what about the guards? The hallways will be quiet, but they won't leave prisoners unattended."

"That is why we are here," a new voice said, this one belonging to a broad-chested, blond man.

Heath, Mendara, and the man from that first night in the basement. Having spent more time in Karine's presence, I was confident now that he was a brother or cousin. The resemblance was not outrageous, but it was there for the observant, which I had always been. Which would serve me now.

The pounding beast of anxiety in my chest demanded the next words. "What about my sister?"

Another hiss from behind us. But Helio's gaze was steady, unflinching from mine. "If this operation is successful, and the information you give us tonight is good, the council will officially sanction your sister's extraction. I cannot say when." He paused, his eyes fixed on my own. "They will only send another cell back in when they have a compelling reason—a mission worth the risk. But when they do, they will get her out as well."

I wished that he still held my arm, because the relief threatened to take me out at the knees. I wished that we were alone, so I could reach up and thread my fingers into the dark-red curls at the nape of his neck. But mostly I wished I could kiss him.

Feck.

"Thank you," I managed instead, the words thick with emotion I did not try to hide behind a stoic servant's facade. For two brief heartbeats, I thought I saw that same intensity reflected in Helio's eyes.

Then his face hardened. "Show us the way."

My stomach tightened, but though my heart still thundered, it did not crack. Helio was right to focus. I must do the same. The next few minutes might determine the rest of my life.

"I've never been into the dungeons themselves," I explained ten minutes later. "Aurelle would probably have been allowed, but she never had a reason."

Just as deftly as the Rebels had navigated the sewers beneath Irska, I'd led them through the royal castle. Instead of ducking between streets and alleyways, I cut through deserted ballrooms, tip-toed down servant stairwells, and motioned for them to avoid the creaking board in the presentation chamber.

They should have spoken to me before planning our entrance; I could have told them that the Mountain Gate was almost as far away as one could get from the entrance to the lower levels the dungeons occupied. But it did not matter now.

"Around the next corner there is a wooden door," I whispered to Helio. "It will be guarded."

Helio nodded, then stepped back to confer with the other three Rebels. They all had various weapons in hand. I was relieved not to see the glow of a fireball.

Then his hand was at my elbow again, this time guiding me back. "You are on watch. Can you sing?"

I blinked at him, not comprehending. "Of course I can sing."

Helio nodded like this was a completely normal conversation to have before breaking into a dungeon. "Once you hear us break through the door, start singing. Only stop if someone—not one of us—comes down here."

Understanding dawned upon me. "Like a songbird in a mine."

It was also protection. If a Peace Guard or other member of the household found me, I might be able explain away the singing long enough for Helio to come to my aid. If I just yelled for him, I'd give myself away.

The brow with the scar in it crinkled. "Except that you are not allowed to die." Helio leaned in close to me as the others passed us by, moving into position. Another hairbreadth, and our foreheads would touch. "Promise me, Fionna."

"I promise." I would survive. For Treasa. For Helio. And for myself.

# Chapter 21

## HELIO

*There is only one rule you need to remember if you are captured by the Irskans. Keep your mouth shut. Most Rebels end up serving time in the Irskan Penal Colony outside of the city. That's where they take you for the minor offenses, when they suspect you but can't actually connect you to something. At one point, I was there with my mother, sister, and cousin. I think we overlapped with my great-uncle, but they keep the men and women separated, so I'm not sure. We've all been in and out so many times that it is hard to remember. But the castle dungeons . . . those are different. When you go in, you don't come out. Ever. The best you can hope for is not to disgrace yourself in death.*

*—Kira Balfour, Síofran Rebel Army*

My instincts screamed at me for leaving her. But my duty was to the Síofran Rebels trapped in the cells below, and the three comrades at my side. Their lives were in my hands as well.

The hope shining in Fionna's dark eyes when she thanked me for something I hadn't done—I took it like the selfish bastard I was. If it had been up to me, she would be safe in her bed at Pearl House. But now that I'd brought her back into the castle, I had a duty to her, too. Her sister's freedom hinged on the successful completion of this operation.

Did Fionna realize that she had not yet bargained for her own freedom?

She was so focused on saving her sister, she had not realized that the council had not agreed to let her go free. Not yet.

But I would ensure it. If it meant supplicating myself at the feet of the council, I would get her out of this—out of the castle, and out of Irska. For her good, and for my own.

Link went first, taking the stairs with soundless steps that belied his girth and breadth. Mendara was next, her shortsword in hand. I adjusted the throwing knives in my hands, brushing the heel of my hand over two more sheathed in a bandolier across my chest.

The moment Link's foot had touched the top step, the clock began. He didn't need to look back over his shoulder to make sure we were ready. The count hit twenty, and he threw his entire body weight into the door.

The thick wood quaked under the force but didn't give. Voices sprang to attention on the other side. Link retreated two steps and leaped, colliding with the door. Still, it held. Feck.

One more hit, and then I would rally the meager magic between the three of us and set the door aflame. It would exhaust us for later, but we could not afford to waste any more time or give the guards on the other side time to prepare.

But the wooden slats of the door splintered under Link's third smash.

The next series of actions were carefully choreographed. Mendara hit the ground, making way for my daggers. I threw the two in my hands, snagging the remaining two on the backward flick and sending those as well. I caught one Peace Guard in the throat. Another in the shoulder and belly. He hit his knees. The third dodged to the side.

Before the second guard could rock forward from knees to hands, I extinguished the torches, blanketing the chamber before us in darkness. That was Mendara's signal to move forward. She could not shift into the creature of the night that the gift beneath her skin promised, but she could see as well in the dark as in daylight.

I tracked the sounds of carnage. I'd counted five Peace Guards in those brief moments of light. I'd taken down two. I heard Link snap the neck of a third. Which left two for Mendara. She was more than capable of managing.

From the top of the stairs, Fionna's voice quivered around the words of a vaguely familiar lullaby.

"Helio, lights!" Mendara yelled.

I relit the lamps with a snap of my fingers, my hatchet already in the other hand. But it was too late to counter the scene in front of me.

One Peace Guard remained standing. And he had his arm around the shoulders of one of the Síofran prisoners we'd come to save. His eyes gleamed with malice as they slid over the three of us—all armed, but too far away to do anything.

Whether he'd used the time it took for Link to bring down the door or the darkness to retrieve the prisoner, he'd used it well.

He did not try to barter or wait to see if we'd pause. He slit the woman's throat without hesitation.

It was a mistake. He now faced down three enraged children of Síofra, and we'd already lost one third of the reason we'd come.

Link had the guard's head in his grip before my foot hit the last stair. Whether he snapped his neck or squished his skull, I did not much care. But he waited for my word to do it.

"Are there any other guards on duty down here?" I demanded.

"Feck you." He opened his mouth to spit, but he was dead before he could rally the muscles.

I was too focused on surveying the layout of the dungeons to hear the sound of his body hitting the stone floor. We appeared to be in an antechamber. Another set of stairs, directly opposite the one we'd come down, descended into darkness. But the room only had three walls. The fourth was lined with a waist-high railing.

My feet carried me toward the edge, slower than the situation called for. Below me, there was only cavernous darkness. Until I snapped my fingers.

Torches flared to light. Some set into the walls, others on poles sunk into the ground so they could line the walkways that wound between the prison cells. Rage obscured my ability to count, but there were dozens of cells. Maybe more than a hundred. And every one I could see was occupied, some with multiple prisoners. Children of Síofra. My people.

"We could free them all," Mendara said from my side.

But we couldn't. That was what ratcheted the rage up even higher, until my body felt like a living flame.

"No. We'd be caught on the way out," I said, hating the words even as they left my mouth. "Just the three we came for."

She did not correct me—that there were only two. She could have argued that we take another, save another, in the dead Síofran woman's place. But even the ones we took were not guaranteed life. They would be interrogated, and if the other Rebels determined they'd given up secrets, they would be put to death. But it would be a kinder end than any they would receive here at the hands of the Irskans.

Mendara and Link's footsteps pounded down the stairs, the need for silence dead on the floor around me. They moved quickly, but already we'd been in the castle too long. When we'd taken Fionna, we'd been inside the castle grounds for less than a half hour. I didn't have a watch at hand—they encumbered my movement—but I estimated we'd already overshot that.

I fought the urge to yell down to Mendara and Link. It would only distract them. A single, melodious thread kept me in check. I let the sound rise in my consciousness, superseding everything else in the way that only she could.

But the sound did not soothe the way it should. It awoke the beast sleeping within me.

Fionna's voice had changed. She still sang, but the notes were weaker, shakier. I had to get back to her.

"Keep going," I yelled into the cavern. Mendara and Link did not need me watching to complete their task. They did not need me at all, not truly. But Fionna did.

I sprinted up the stairs, my mind conjuring a barrage of hellish scenarios in the brief space of a few heartbeats. She was captive. A blade to her throat. A Peace Guard forcing her to keep singing.

But when I turned the corner, she was alone in the dark hallway.

"Fionna." Another heartbeat, and I was in front of her, scanning her up and down for any sign—she was whole, uninjured. "What is it?"

She kept singing, the notes wobbling.

The subtle changes emerged. Her pale skin was fully ivory now. Her eyes were unfocused, despite the mere inches that separated us. Fionna had never hesitated to meet my eyes, not even that first night in the basement when she'd been terrified. Whatever this was, it was deeper than terror. For the first time in memory, *I* was terrified.

"Fionna," I said again, grasping her hands. I couldn't recall sheathing my hatchet. I didn't fecking care where it was now. "You can fight this."

Her fingers were ice cold in my grasp. The contrast of my heat should have been painful, but she did not react. Her hands shook—her entire body shook. She began to vibrate so violently, I worried that her legs would give out on her. I eased myself closer, into her space, waiting for some reaction, for that spiral of heat that always kindled to life when we touched. But nothing. Only the wobbling notes of her voice around a song that I no longer recognized.

Panic took over the anger I'd felt minutes before . . . *Panic*. That's what this was.

The continuous tapping, always in sets of three. The way her heartbeat increased erratically at moments I couldn't explain. I'd seen this disorientation in her before, in those first moments of consciousness when she'd awoken in captivity. Then, she'd been able to pull herself out. Maybe given enough time, she would have managed again. But the anxiety held her fully in its thrall.

A wave of something I did not dare to name crested in my chest. We were the same. Born on different sides of a deadly conflict. Destined to always be at odds. Yet we both fought a beast that lived inside us, always trying to take control.

I guided her back using my body until we were flush against the wall, the stone at her back and my own hard planes caging her in from the front. I'd never fought this particular monster, but I knew plenty about trusting my own instincts. They'd led me to her.

Using my body, I applied pressure to hers. Not enough to be painful, but hopefully enough to break through the panic. I'd used similar tactics on gravely injured Rebels, squeezing their hand so tight they could refocus their mind. I disentangled our hands, sliding hers into the pockets of my own pants. The fit was tight, but that seemed right. In any other moment, my cock would have risen to excited attention at the proximity of her graceful fingers. But lust was nowhere in my mind.

No, what swirled through me was much more dangerous.

"Fionna," I said, cupping her cold cheeks. I throttled the heat seeping from my skin, an effort that should have been gargantuan, given the surging emotions, but was surprisingly easy. Because it was for *her*.

"Fionna." Again. Every time I uttered her name it was a prayer to Síofra. "I am here. You are safe. No one will touch you. I promise."

Her song paused.

I repeated myself, each sentence punctuated with a swipe of my thumbs over her cheekbones and the gradual increase of heat from my body into hers. "You are safe."

Her eyes snapped to mine.

"Calm as a lake. Strong as a tree. I bend but don't break," she whispered.

I pressed my forehead to hers, bone-deep relief coursing through me. "You are safe."

Fionna's exhale shook her entire body, but I held us steady. Through that one, and several more, until she was soft in my arms again.

Footsteps echoed behind us. Link and Mendara burst into the hall, two haggard Síofran prisoners in tow. Fionna blinked at them, her eyes still shining but able to focus and take in details.

"Where . . . I thought there were three?" she stammered.

"Two, now. There's no use carrying a body." Mendara left the prisoners to Link, striding past us down the hall. No one commented on Fionna and me, still pressed tightly together.

"We have to go now," I said as gently as I could. I disentangled our bodies, slipping her hands free of my pockets. But I kept one in mine, threading our fingers together. "Do not let go."

She nodded, the motion jerky, but at least she was no longer violently shaking.

We were halfway down the hall when all hell broke loose.

Mendara's battle cry was the only warning. A troop of Peace Guards burst around the corner, cutting off our exit.

Link put weapons into the hands of the rescued Rebels. I did not need to worry about them. My only concern was getting Fionna out. I'd made her two promises—that she would return to Pearl House, and that no one would touch her but me. I would keep them both.

A troop of Peace Guards was eight. With the liberated Rebels, we were five. I refused to count Fionna. She could defend herself passably, but she was minutes out of a panic attack, her hand still clammy in mine. I was not about to test her limits. Not when I was a perfectly tuned instrument of death.

I met the guard that moved to engage us with my hatchet. I'd returned my throwing knives to the bandolier, but the quarters were too close to trust a throw. His hair was laced with gray, a veteran Peace Guard, but a shit fighter. I had him on his knees in two parries and one thrust. I could have used the shaft of my axe to knock him unconscious. I buried the blade in his chest instead. We could not leave behind a guard to identify us later.

Fionna's fingers slackened in mine.

*Hold on, my love.*

The next guard was upon us before I could make the mistake of saying the words aloud. Or recognizing them for myself.

This one was younger, greener, but smarter. He went for Fionna.

Fire blinded my vision. Inside me, the Firebird screeched, an unholy sound of vengeance from a creature of hope and peace. My hatchet sliced through his throat, severing arteries beneath his lightly stubbled skin, cutting through the sinew and muscle like they were a single silken thread.

Blood spurted from his jugular, the droplets sizzling against my heated skin. I did not close my mouth or my eyes. He'd lost all right to live by swinging his weapon at Fionna. I let his dying blood sustain me. The monster inside me savored the flavor.

Mendara cried out again, but this time it was a sound of pain, not warning.

Fionna released me as I lunged. Fecking hell—I'd thank her or admonish her later. I was too late to save Mendara's leg. The crunch echoed against the unadorned stone walls. But when the Peace Guard swung his barbed mace down for the killing blow, I met him with my hatchet. The thick carpet on the stone floor muffled the sound of his body hitting the ground.

For one brief moment, there was stillness, the only sound our breaths coming in heavy gasps. The entire troop of Peace Guards lay around us in various states of bloody death. One of the prisoners held a hand to their side, staunching a seeping wound.

Behind me, Fionna was still. At least she was not shaking. I remembered the way out. I had only to jerk my head, and the others fell into formation around us.

I wiped the blood away before reaching for her hand, my body craving the closeness—

"Do not touch me," she cried, jerking away so violently that her shoulder collided with the wall. I reacted to catch her, to steady her by reflex, my body moving in answer to hers. But she plastered herself flat against the wall, determined to remain beyond my reach.

She did not flinch away from meeting my gaze. Not Fionna.

But there was none of the soft emotion I'd seen before. The hate was back, flavored with revulsion and betrayal. For a heartbeat, I struggled to process why. Then I saw the blood coating her skin.

We did not have time for an explanation. I did not want to owe her one.

I was a commander in the Síofran Rebel Army. She'd been foolish to think or expect anything different from me.

That was what I told myself, again and again, as we ran through the halls, retracing Fionna's path, not bothering to cover the sounds of our footsteps. We did not encounter another soul until we reached the courtyard. Karine levered the sewer grate loose, we climbed down, and we were away.

But in more than thirty years, I'd never felt so fecking lost.

# Chapter 22

## FIONNA

*Hostage exchanges are a perennial discussion. The Irskans want their Peace Guards back. They don't negotiate as hard for the members of the Irskan Defense Force who get themselves captured. There are no official communications with the Síofran Rebel Army or the Síofran Liberation Corps. They are terrorist groups. We can only talk to the Síofran Children, and they have political influence but no way to enforce it. But it doesn't really matter. The negotiations always fall apart in the end, and not for the reasons you think. It is always our moderators who back out, once they hear the likely fate of any returned prisoners. If they've spent even a minute alone with the other side, they are at risk of turning informer. And both sides kill informers.*

*—Mila Sheridan, Republic of Eerin*

Sleeping was nearly as terrible as waking. The hours passed quicker when I slept, but my dreams were torturous. I saw the light leaving their eyes, felt the warmth of their blood as it sprayed across my skin. It was not my blade that felled them, but the witness I bore to their deaths felt just as damaging.

But then I woke suddenly, my stomach twisting with nausea and heart beating out of my chest, the panic already in control of my body.

I lay in bed shaking for five minutes, ten, until I had no sense of time. I ate from trays left on the table by the window and then returned to the blankets. There was no comfort to be found there, but at least I did not have to put in the energy required to keep my body upright.

Rare early-spring sun leaked through the window when I opened my eyes on the fourth day since the castle.

Someone had come while I slept and piled the bed with heavy blankets. The first breath was difficult to draw, but the second . . . inhale, exhale. Inhale, exhale. By the third, it was easier. The combined weight of the quilts kept my limbs from shaking. They pushed me down with just enough pressure to force my body to yield, but not to inflict pain.

I had used pain to cut through anxiety before, but this was gentler. I wondered vaguely if someone had done it on purpose. Maybe they'd noticed my shaking and mistaken it for shivering.

Nieve had laundered and folded all my clothes, leaving them in a neat pile. Maybe she had been the one to pile on all the blankets as well. I needed to thank her. She'd cooked every meal. Put fresh toiletries in the washroom.

I would venture downstairs long enough to find her and thank her, then I could return to my nest. I could do that. *I can do that.*

I tugged on the leather leggings and loose linen shirt because they were closest. My hair caught in the button meant to close the throat of the shirt, jilting me off balance, my hip banging into the bedpost.

I hissed through my teeth, ripped the curl loose, and twisted the disastrous mass up into a knot on top of my head. Aurelle and the other ladies of the Irskan court would have been appalled. But what did I fecking care anymore? I was the next thing to a murderer.

And Treasa? I'd failed her.

The council—whoever they were within the Síofran Rebel Army hierarchy—would not reward me for what had happened in the castle. One of the Síofran we were supposed to rescue was dead, another injured. If Mendara's leg was broken, it would take months to fully heal.

My eyes snagged on the coat-tree in the corner. Helio's thick black cloak hung from it, untouched. I did not know whether I would ever be able to bring myself to don it again. But it no longer hung alone. The lush black wool kissed the leather-accented jacket that Helio had slipped onto my shoulders on the night of the operation. I could see even from where I stood at the foot of the bed that it was no longer caked with blood and sewer grime. Nieve had been hard at work while I slept. But I doubted I'd be able to put that garment to use again, either.

Even if he'd had it made specifically for me, the perfect fit a testament to how closely he'd watched me these past weeks. Not just watched, but talked. Listened. Without meaning to, I'd allowed Helio too close. He'd slipped past my defenses and into the long-neglected corners of my soul. Denying him had been impossible. Forcing him out would be worse.

*Stop being so dramatic,* an internal voice admonished. I gave it enough rein to slip into the mental calculations that had served me so well, that I'd abandoned in favor of feelings and instinct.

Even in early spring, Irska was cold. I'd need a covering when Treasa and I escaped this place. Practicality must reign. I'd decide which one I loathed less later, cloak or jacket.

But none of that was immediate. I needed to find Nieve, thank her, and eat something. Then I would be able to think clearly. My situation may have shifted since the operation in the castle, and I needed to understand exactly how much in order to plan.

I walked slowly down the stairs, holding tight to the rail to soften my steps. I saw no sign of Moira, Nadia, or Antoni. From the light leaking through the windows, I guessed it was still before midday. They must have been at school.

There was a good chance Nieve and I were the only ones in the house. In the time I'd spent here, Pearl House followed a predictable cadence. There was a bustle in the morning that I usually slept through. Then things quieted until the hour before dinnertime, when the children returned and a parade of Síofran visitors entered through the front and rear doors. Some seemed to appear from nowhere at all. Magic or hidden entrances, I was not sure.

It was harder to remain silent once I reached the ground floor. I'd slipped on my boots, lacing and tying them loosely. I needed to be ready at any moment. No more sleeping in just a shift. No more waiting for things to happen.

But that was exactly what I did.

I did not even make it three full steps before I froze, waiting. Voices leaked from the living room where Turi and his daughters had performed their light show. They twisted and melded, slightly overlapping one another.

The stairs were behind me. I could retreat a few steps and slip back upstairs to wait for the house to empty. My stomach rumbled at that thought. From now on, I'd begin to save some food from every meal tray delivered to my door. Another act of preparedness.

But that determination did nothing for my current predicament. The minute the group assembled in the living room saw me, they'd stop talking. Maybe they would leave. Maybe they would voice opinions on what should be done with me. Retreat was the safest choice. But I was done retreating.

They'd only stop talking if they saw me. So I made sure they did not.

"They've both been cleared, thank Síofra," a female voice said. There was a slight rasp to her voice. Not harsh or unpleasant, but like she perpetually needed a sip of water.

"But they will not be of use to us anytime soon. The Irskans broke their spirits." The second voice was also female, but sharper. Despite coming from farther away—the owner must have been seated deeper in the living room—her words felt like the edge of a razor.

A low growl rolled over me. "Your methods of interrogation did not help matters."

Helio.

I'd felt his warmth the moment my foot touched the landing. Having it confirmed—and my unnatural sense for him verified—was not a comfort I wanted, even as the tightness in my shoulders softened, my stomach twisting with anticipation.

The second female huffed a sharp, dismissive sound. "I did what was necessary. Torture is supposed to be your specialty, Helio. I don't know why you have suddenly gone soft."

I heard it for the insult that it was. Helio had never hesitated in his cruelty when he thought it would get him what he wanted. I'd been the recipient of it. The night in the warehouse, when he'd taunted me about my sister, lived in a dark corner of my heart. But he'd also wielded mercy, though he insisted he was a stranger to it.

He did what he had to do for his people. I no longer resented him for that manipulation. But for what he'd done in the castle, slaughtering the Peace Guards . . .

*How is it different?*

My mind thrashed as the claws of reason and emotion tore at its fibers.

The Peace Guards were anything but peaceful. I'd always known it, but now I'd seen it. The Síofran weren't any better. Helio and his companions killed just as indiscriminately. But the lines of right and wrong were no longer so clearly drawn within my mind.

Slow, steady steps sounded. I recognized Helio's tread. He was standing, and as he spoke he moved across the room, stopping somewhere near the fireplace. I could picture him, clad in tight leather and cleverly disguised weapons. His dark-red hair was slicked back, like always, the strands just starting to curl behind his ears.

"There is more than one way of extracting information. A good interrogator knows when to apply pressure and when to soften it," he growled.

I flinched, not because of him, but in empathy for the person on the receiving end of that snarl.

I counted two heartbeats of stilted silence. "Are you questioning a member of the council?" the sharp-tongued woman asked.

The council. Both Helio and Turi had referred to them and their decision-making capacity within the Síofran Rebel Army. I suspected that Turi was a member, and that Helio reported directly to them. This was the moment that might confirm it all; the thorny woman who owned that voice was a member.

I fought the urge to step closer as their voices dropped. Or maybe they were just facing away. It was hard to catch every word. There was a male voice—Turi was there. Another member of the council.

Had I actually stumbled across a council meeting? And if so . . . why was Helio there, if not an actual member?

"My cell is motivated and ready to move," Helio said, his voice cutting through the rest.

"What about Mendara's leg?" the first woman said, her voice still raspy. She was either ill or it was a permanent affectation. After the second woman's grating threats, even the rasped words felt like honey.

"Broken," Helio confirmed. "She's out for at least six weeks."

I pressed my eyes together, regret burning in my chest. The woman held little to no regard for me, but I did not want to see her hurt. I did not want *anyone* hurt. Maybe that was the real reason I was so out of place in the war for Irska.

"This could all be over by then," Turi said.

I flailed for the wall, surprise threatening to send me stumbling forward.

*What . . . How?*

"We have never implemented an offensive of this scale," the more measured female said. "I worry that a week is not long enough."

Only to be countered by the other. "Any longer and we risk exposure."

"But with the information Simon and Genna provided"—Turi must have been referring to the two prisoners we'd liberated from the castle dungeons—"we could take out more than half of the Peace Guard. If we are careful, the initial explosions will pull in enough Defenders that the second round of detonations will decimate their numbers as well. Then we are poised to take the castle."

They were planning another operation. Except unlike our infiltration into the castle, what they discussed was a siege. More than half the Peace Guard . . . That had to be at least a hundred humans. Maybe two.

My heart beat wildly in my chest. I closed my eyes, forcing in several silent but moderated breaths. Thankfully, the anxiety quelled this time, worn out from what had come before.

A female sigh. "We have to consider the civilian death toll."

Finally, someone was speaking sense. I might not be able to parse where the fault truly lay within the human and Síofran conflict, but I could say unequivocally that the everyday citizens of Irska—on both sides—were innocent.

"They fecking deserve every death." I had not seen the owner of the voice, but I was quickly constructing an image in my head. Gnashing her teeth, leaning forward, scowling. Pretty. Intimidating women often were.

"It will not just be humans. The peace villages closest to the castle draw a more mixed crowd, especially on a day like that," the reasoned female voice said.

Helio was conspicuously silent.

*A day like that.* Market day? Was one of the princes' birthdays near? That would not give the Síofran cause to celebrate . . .

Equinox.

I was not sure how many days I'd lingered in bed, but assuming it was no more than four . . . the vernal equinox was a week away. There would be celebrations in the castle, ambassadors welcomed from the Republic of Eerin, Irskan nobles traveling in from their country estates. In the city itself . . . thousands would fill the streets to celebrate. The four solar holidays were kept by all Irskans, though celebrated differently by humans and children of Síofra.

"The children of Síofra will sacrifice themselves for our freedom," the sharp one said.

"Citizens have not taken oaths," the other countered. "I am not against it. But we must make these plans in full cognizance of the cost."

I could picture Turi's index finger and thumb, sliding down his jawline to meet at the apex of his chin. "Indeed."

My heart dropped out of my chest and into my stomach.

"We have quorum and agreement!" A quick, sharp sound, like someone stomping their foot. The female councillor was excited. Excited to kill my people. To kill her own people. Nausea replaced hunger in my stomach. "I will begin contacting the cells—"

I heard Helio's voice, his deep timber commanding the room with its resonance. But I was already on the move. "What will you do—"

"You cannot!" I exclaimed, storming into the room.

This time, I did not pause on the threshold. I crossed it without a second thought, without calculation. So much for not allowing myself to be ruled by my emotions; that had not lasted a quarter of an hour.

The sharp female voice belonged to a blond woman, her platinum locks braided back in the Síofran style so tightly that it made my head ache just to look at her. She shot to her feet at the sight of me, standing on the far side of the room. Helio was a few feet closer, leaning against the mantel. He alone seemed unsurprised to see me. Had he sensed my presence, the same way I'd felt his?

That was impossible. He had fire magic. And I had none at all.

Still seated on the sofa was a middle-aged woman, dark-gold hair threaded with gray, dressed for practicality in a loose dove-gray skirt and fitted ivory blouse, complete with an apron that had already seen a busy morning of use.

Turi occupied the chair he had every night after dinner. Nieve's was conspicuously empty.

"Helio, your pet has slipped from her cage," the farther councilwoman snarled.

"Yelena," the woman on the sofa warned.

I assigned the name to the blond harpy glaring at me with so much hate I would not have been surprised to look down and see claws instead of fingers. But whatever her gift from Síofra, it did not manifest.

Helio's eyes settled on me with a physical weight, like the blankets piled on the bed or the press of his body that he'd used to calm me when I lost control in the castle. No matter what he'd done or how I felt about it, he'd demonstrated that he understood me at a level no one else ever had. He saw me, when I'd spent my entire life trying to stay invisible. I couldn't shrug that off, not when my body and soul ignited in response. But I was angry enough to coexist with it.

"What have the human civilians done to deserve death?" I demanded, glaring right back at Yelena. If I was not afraid of Helio, I was certainly not afraid of her.

She barked out a harsh laugh. "They have not risen up against their king. They offer their sons to the Peace Guard, give shelter to the Defenders. I could go on, but I do not consort with humans."

Yelena broke the stare. Victory surged in my veins. I pressed it. "Because if you did, you'd realize that we are no different from you. That you are not superior."

I was done bowing before my betters.

*Because they aren't my fecking betters.*

I had failed spectacularly at my one goal—keeping Treasa safe long enough to get us out of Irska. Walking this careful, reticent line had not served me. Not in the castle, and not since my kidnapping. I would get my sister back in my own way. But until that moment presented itself, I could not just sit up in a comfortable room. I was so sick of death. If I could play even a small part in stopping the violence, I would not waver.

"Civilians on both sides have paid your price, again and again and again. All we want is to live in peace with our families," I said, my breathing more labored than I expected. There was my heart, racing to account for it.

"There can be no peace while some of us are oppressed," the other woman said. She kept her hands neatly folded in her lap. A faint aroma of sugar wafted from her general direction. If she was a council member, that was certainly not all she was. "Maintaining the status quo might keep more civilians alive longer, in the short term. But it will prolong this war. What you call peace is only perpetuating violence."

And her point was valid.

I nodded, willing my chin not to shake. "We are culpable. I am culpable," I said, and meant it. I'd been so concerned with Treasa and my safety, I had closed my eyes to the injustices in Irska. Now my eyes were open. "But that does not absolve you, either. We must forge a new path forward. A new peace."

Even as the words came out of my mouth, I felt their power. It felt obvious, even though I could cognitively recognize that it was anything but. We'd been entrenched in our hate for so long . . . but I didn't hate the children of Síofra. There hadn't been time for personal vices like hatred or vengeance when I was busy raising Treasa and attending Princess Aurelle. And when I'd been captured, and I finally had the luxury and reason to hate my captors . . . I'd discovered that I didn't. Couldn't. Not when they wanted the same things I always had. Safety. A future.

The woman's eyes flickered with emotion, the barest hint of a smile turning the corners of her mouth. Then her eyes narrowed. "The king will never give up his advantage. The laws of Irska favor the humans. They would have to be rewritten entirely," she said.

"Now you are speaking treason, Maureen," Yelena hissed, "to the oath you took."

That confirmed they were all members of the Síofran Rebel Army, obvious though it was. But it felt like another piece of a puzzle slipping into place, the picture slowly getting clearer, fragment by fragment, since I'd awoken in a darkened basement.

Helio pushed away from the mantel, taking two steps in my direction, putting himself within lunging distance—and between me and Yelena.

"We have never pursued true peace," he said.

He'd read her correctly.

Yelena sprang forward, her eyes full of fury. "You are the fecking—"

"I know what I am," Helio cut her off.

He did not even lift a hand, but she broke against the air like it was solid. Her face flushed, skin turning pink instantly.

Was it . . . Had she come up against a wall . . . of heat?

What exactly was the nature of Helio's magic?

He'd said, and Turi had confirmed, that there must be common purpose in order for a Síofran to wield smaller magics. Yet this did not look like smaller magic. This heat was something else, something tied to Helio's suppressed power. Not fully suppressed. And who in this room was creating the common purpose that allowed him to access it?

None of my questions would get answers today.

Yelena took another step back. The flush remained. Her eyes bored into Helio, but I could not see what expression he gave in return because he was a few steps in front of me. I hoped whatever it was, it fucking melted her where she stood.

Feck. So much for my stance against violence.

I took another silent series of breaths. The room lingered in tense stasis until Yelena retreated another step, the backs of her calves hitting the sofa. She did not sit, but the flush in her cheeks began to fade.

"Too many of us have died. Humans and Síofran," I said, keeping my voice low and nonthreatening. "You could at least consider a peaceful demonstration instead of a violent one. It would not change everything. But it would be a start."

Yelena clenched her jaw so tightly, I expected to hear a crack. But the other woman, Maureen, nodded. Not a nod of agreement, I recognized, but of contemplation. Turi paused stroking his beard long enough to nod over my shoulder.

"I believe Nieve is in the kitchen. She'll want to see you now that you're up and about," he said.

"Of course." I did not dip my head. I did not bow. I held each of their gazes for three heartbeats. Even Yelena. I counted every one. Then I left them to argue.

Helio followed me, his heat enveloping me a second before his words. "Fionna."

Gods above, my name in his deep, rough timbre did things to me. Unconscionable things, after what I'd seen him do. Torture. Kill. That was who Helio was. And yet I paused short of the kitchen, turning to face him. I did not jerk away when he reached for me.

His fingers closed around mine. "This could go to shit very quickly."

This thing growing between us? It already had. The proposition I'd just made? Surely. Whatever operation the Rebels planned? My heart twisted.

"I know," I said softly.

Heat spread from Helio's fingers into mine, through my bloodstream, until I felt him in every corner of my being. How did he do that? It had to be his magic, powerful even though it was suppressed. It could not be . . .

I squeezed his hand tighter.

Helio inhaled sharply. "But you're still asking me."

"I am still asking you." I inhaled, the scent of him, of me, mingling together as we shared breath. "And I know I have no right to ask such a thing, but—"

"Fionna," he interrupted me, my name almost painful as it ripped from his chest. He pressed his forehead against mine. "Haven't you realized by now that you have every right?"

My mind grappled with his words, struggling to understand. Refusing to.

There was only one explanation for how quickly my defenses had crumbled around him, even after everything that happened in the castle.

Helio drew back first. My heart screamed in protest.

"I will do this, I will go in there and fight for this, on one condition," he said.

It was always an exchange between us. It should not have surprised me, now. In some ways, it was a comfort. It simplified the otherwise intractable tangle of decisions and emotions between us.

"What is it?"

"You answer the question you owe me."

Truth. That was his condition. I nodded.

"Why did you pull away from me in the castle?"

I could see it in his eyes. They were so different, both in color and the way they showed his emotions. The blue darkened when he was angry, while the green and gold of the other melded into citrine. But I saw the knowledge reflected back at me in the icy contours of blue and the glimmering gold striations in their field of green. Helio already knew the answer to his question. But for a reason I was just short of comprehending, he needed to hear me say it.

"You killed them. Indiscriminately. Some of those guards . . ." My voice faltered. "They were barely adults."

I waited for his eyes to harden, for him to shut me out. But they remained open—open and unrepentant.

"They were old enough to kill you. That was not an acceptable outcome." He did not pull away, not exactly. But the air shifted around us, still warm but not welcoming. He was about to draw a line, one I would not like. "I have never pretended to be anything but what I am, Fionna."

There it was. "I know, but—"

"No," he stopped me. Our hands were still joined, but I could feel a cavern opening between us. "You don't know."

"Then tell me." I could stand it.

"You have to decide. This is a war, and you cannot waver between two sides and hope to survive. Even if you choose, this conflict claims lives every single day."

Was that what I was doing by seeking peace? Delaying an inevitable choice? Maybe. But I was not convinced that a choice *was* inevitable. I could love my sister, want my people to survive, *and* see the Síofran plight. I was complex enough to hold all those nuances inside me. So were Helio and the council, and every fecking person in Irska—if they were willing to try.

"On both sides," I echoed back. "What if I can't?"

"That is also a choice."

He leaned forward again, pressing his forehead to mine. But that was all he gave before turning back and leaving me alone to unscramble my thoughts.

# Chapter 23

## FIONNA

*The Firebird is our most sacred legend. A symbol of peace and a harbinger of hope. The children of Síofra claim it for ourselves as our sacred symbol, but that is a misremembering of the Firebird's legend. The Firebird predates Síofra's foray into our world. It existed long before she blessed that first child in their cradle. The story says that as she turned away, having gifted the first human with magic and changed us forever, a flash of golden light caught her eye. High in the sky, a firebird crossed the sun, its wings of scarlet and gold blocking out all other light. Mesmerized by its beauty, Síofra returned to the cradle and made the child in its image. The Firebird was never meant for some, but all. The Firebird is a gift from Síofra herself. May we one day live to see it rise again.*

*—Deidre Dvornick, Síofran Children*

There were some dreams that I wished would never end.

Eating a meal with my parents. Sitting in a nook in the castle library, teaching Treasa to read. I held them close to my heart, little jewels of peace and happiness from whatever gods took responsibility for the humans.

But I suspected this one was sent from Síofra herself.

It started in the middle, with my skin already burning. I tried to form a curse on my lips, angry at being deprived of the buildup. Even in dreams, the moments with Helio were stolen. Captor and captive. Síofran and human. Leader and servant. Every detail should have conspired to keep us apart, and yet we were drawn together by our similarities. Our unfailing loyalty. Our ability to analyze and calculate and plan. The shared pain neither of us could quite acknowledge.

Whoever had sent me this dream, I opened my mouth to demand more. Pleasure stole the words before I could speak them.

He pressed open-mouthed kisses to my throat, nipping at the sensitive skin with his teeth and then teasing the tingling hurt with a flourish of his tongue. I sank my teeth into my bottom lip, trying to hold back the feral sounds that bubbled out of me.

But his finger was there, forcing my lips apart. I twirled my tongue around the tip by reflex, mimicking what I wanted to do to the hard length pressed into my leg. He rewarded me with a deep groan that vibrated against the soft fold of skin where my inner arm met my body.

Gods, how could every part of me suddenly be transformed into a pleasure point?

His finger tugged at the seam of my lip, urging them apart once more. His tongue swirled around a nipple, and I arched, my body desperate and needy and completely unrestrained. I couldn't hold in the sound, and his growl of approval told me what he thought clearly enough.

"Fionna," he growled, the syllables scraping across my lust-addled mind in time with the stubble on his jaw over my breasts. "So fecking perfect."

Whether he meant my body or the dream, I did not care. I was inclined to agree with him. I'd never been particularly self-conscious about my body, except when it got in the way of otherwise easy tasks. When I had to alter one of Aurelle's dresses, or when the arms of a chair dug into my wide hips. But he worshiped those same curves with such reverence . . . I'd never bemoan my soft curves again. Not if this was the response they earned from the one man whose esteem I craved.

I'd never cared about others' approval, because I only allowed them to see the fractions of my being that were necessary. But I'd let Helio see my true self. I'd discovered that self at his side, at his urging. To see him look at me, not with revulsion but with adoration . . . broke and remade something vital inside me.

I slid my fingers into his hair, finding it every bit as silky as I'd imagined. How had I gone so long without touching him? This was my dream. And in my dreams, nothing could keep me from exploring his body.

I let one hand linger in his hair while the other slid down over his neck, then his shoulder. His head bent in thorough, tantalizing homage to my breasts. I explored the taut tendons where his neck met his shoulder, the bulging muscles I could trace with my fingernails.

He caught my nipple between his teeth, and I gasped, digging my nails into his flesh. I jerked my hand back, but he caught it. Returned it. Bit me again for emphasis.

The heat built steadily between us—literal heat, his skin searing mine, a sheen of sweat coating our bodies. I was a breath from bursting into a living flame as he relentlessly drove me higher, hotter, brighter.

I whimpered when he pulled away from my breasts, bereft at the loss. His low chuckle slid over my skin, across my stomach, and up my breasts until it caressed my consciousness in time with his mouth and hands.

He traced his tongue along the sensitive juncture where my leg joined my body, the seam of my hip, a place I'd never imagined could conjure such . . .

*Oh, gods, yes.*

His finger circled my clit, the knowing twirl of his hand a sharp contrast to the mockingly chaste kiss he pressed to the top of my mound.

This was how I would die. Gladly, gratefully sacrificed on the altar of a burning passion that consumed me like wildfire. For the first time in my life, I was completely unrestrained. I was free, and he was there to help me claim my freedom. That was what Helio meant to me—freedom. Here, in this moment, neither of us was bound to family or faction. With every kiss, every touch, we chose each other. It was the first and only selfish choice I'd made in my entire life.

It was a dream.

His mouth circled lower, planting a ring of kisses on the insides of my thighs, against my seam, and then directly on my clit as he slid one broad finger inside me. I lifted my hips greedily, aching for more. He withdrew his hand slowly, methodically, curling his fingertips to stroke me from the inside. I felt the flood of wetness, my desire made real as it soaked his hand.

A deep, appreciative growl rumbled through him, reverberating against my abdomen and intensifying the need between my legs. He withdrew until just the tip of his finger remained inside me, while his thumb skated over my clit in a teasing, repetitive motion.

It was too much. The heat on my skin, in my stomach, burning in my chest. His touch was not just physical. His flame reached inside me. It had awakened a part of me that I'd left sleeping, dormant, afraid. Here, I was unbound.

With him, I was free.

He slid a second finger inside me, and I ceased to exist at all. I was a creature of pleasure, as much a part of him as myself as he slowly worked his fingers in and out of me. The fullness was exquisite, but the connection . . . the connection was everything.

The syllables of his name played across my lips, desperate to get out.

"Hush, my love, just enjoy it," he murmured against the inside of my thigh.

Before my mind could wrap around his words and what they meant, the heat and desire reached a peak. I dug my nails into my palms, desperate to hold on, desperate to extend the ecstasy. But there was no stopping this moment between us, and when he dragged me over the edge, his hand was in mine.

I came awake with my climax still in pieces around me, sweat drenching my skin. I'd awoken with a frenzied heartbeat hundreds of times in my life, but never like this, desperate for it to continue. Longing for the touch of hands that I could not quite place—

*No.*

I knew those hands, and I was through pretending that I did not want them on me. I wanted every piece of Helio that he was willing to give, and I wanted to hand over pieces of myself in return.

Maybe it was because it was forbidden—an impossibility. Helio and I could never be together, even if we consummated the physical fantasies that haunted my dreams.

Impossible.

That was what Helio had been from the beginning.

The cool night air chilled the sweat on my skin. I burrowed beneath the coverlet, determined to hold on to those fragments of fantasy. That was all Helio and I would ever be . . . a fantasy.

My heart slowed, and then it began to break.

# Chapter 24

## FIONNA

*The Rebels think they are better than us because they are more disciplined. But the truth is that they are cowards. They get so caught up in their plans, they never fully execute. They choke. We are the ones driving the conflict forward. There is a reason that humans are more scared of Libs than Rebels. We fecking earned it in the only way that counts—with blood.*

*—Casey Koval, Síofran Liberation Corps*

Three sharp raps on the door sent my hand skittering across the paper, leaving behind a jagged line of charcoal.

I looked up, trying to assess the time of day by the light of the window. It had been early afternoon when I sat down at the table, but I knew I'd been so engrossed in my work that hours could have passed.

Sure enough, what I could see of the sun through the clouds hung lower over the western edge of Irska. At this time of year . . . dinner would be soon. Maybe it was Antoni, arriving with a tray. I ate with Turi's family most nights, but there were some where a tray was delivered to my room instead, with no explanation. Not that I was owed any. Despite everything, I was still a prisoner.

I tucked the paper away quickly, sliding it between the pages of one of the books in the stack that Turi had loaned to me. Even as I stood to open the door, the lines of charcoal I'd sketched out remained bright in my mind. It was far from complete, but I'd spent hours constructing the map of Irska, using the view I remembered looking down from the castle, the three forays I'd made through the city since, and every possible look I could get from the third-floor windows of Pearl House.

Incomplete, but hopefully enough.

I smoothed my hands over the deep-green skirt I wore, wiping away any remnant traces of charcoal. Antoni was already suspicious of me. I supposed he had good instincts.

But it wasn't Turi's sullen teenage son on the other side of the door.

My heart lodged itself in my throat with one mighty leap.

Karine was a few inches shorter than me, but her presence filled the doorway and seeped from the hallway behind her. There was only one reason for her to be here. I was moving again.

My mind spun into action. I already wore my boots and a complete outfit. I'd been ready for a sudden flight since returning from the castle. But I'd need to distract Karine long enough to rescue my map. Everything else was already tied up in a spare shirt, an easy-to-grab parcel stashed beneath the bed.

Karine folded her arms over her chest. "Are you going to stand there gaping at me, or are you going to invite me in?"

I blinked at her, confusion front and center and unhidden. "I was not aware I retained that right."

"Turi and Nieve insist that while you are in their house, you are treated as a guest," Karine said, her eyes scanning the room over my shoulder.

I wondered at her description. Turi had been clear that Pearl House did not belong to them. He'd made a point of the distinction.

No matter what Turi and Nieve said, there was a power dynamic at play here. From what I could tell, Karine was the closest thing to a second-in-command that Helio had. She was involved in every opera-tion, every transfer.

I stepped back, allowing her entrance to the room I still could not quite claim as my own, even within my mind.

She'd braided her golden hair across her head in a coronet that I couldn't help but admire. My fingers twitched at the memory of all the elegant coiffures I'd learned over the years at Aurelle's behest. My own dark curls hung loose around my shoulders, untamed.

Karine continued her unhurried perusal of the room. I melted backward, bracing my bottom against the table by the window, doing my best to obscure the stack of books without drawing undue attention to them. My fingers rested against my hip. I had to keep them still, had to remain composed . . .

*Tap. Tap. Tap. One. Two. Three.*

At least my fingers against the woven fibers of my skirt were soundless.

But the books did not catch Karine's interest. She looked over the neat stack of clothes on a chair in the corner; there was no chest of drawers in the room. Her eyes lingered on the silk pillowcase. She did not go into the washroom. What was she looking for? Why the long, drawn-out silence?

"You are not here to relocate me," I exhaled, realization crash-ing into me.

Over the past month, I'd been treated to an array of expressions from Karine. They'd ranged from outright hate to undisguised distaste. This was the first time I saw her smile, and I did not like it. Not at all. There was a cruel tilt to her mouth that my mind said should remind me of Helio but felt instinctively different. Her eyes lingered on my hand, my fingers now still, but . . . she'd noticed my anxiety, my dis-comfort. She enjoyed drawing out the moment of uncertainty.

Fecking bitch.

She sat on the edge of my bed without invitation. That was where her consideration for Turi and Nieve's instructions ended.

"He has done as you asked," she said, looking over my shoulder to the slice of the city visible through the window. "The Síofran Rebel Army has planned a peaceful march through the streets of Irska, to terminate at the castle gates. They've gotten hundreds of citizens to pledge to join as part of the equinox celebrations."

To hide their identities. As fodder?

No. If the Síofran could remain peaceful, the humans could, too. I had to believe it, otherwise . . . what was the point of any of it?

But the anxiety gave way to something else, a feeling more powerful . . . one I'd had precious little of in my life—hope.

I exhaled, trying to moderate the shakiness of my breath and failing utterly. I could feel Karine watching me, even as she faced the window. She was not as subtle as she thought. Or I was better at reading the clues she tried to hide.

"No one has ever had this sort of power over him."

The disdain was there in her voice, unmistakable. But that wasn't the totality of it. Was that . . . jealousy?

I refocused my attention, trying to wipe away my preconceptions of the Rebel who stood closest to Helio.

"I did not choose this. I was kidnapped and dragged into your fight," I said slowly, watching her for reactions, for the subtle changes in her body language that would tell me more than words ever could.

Her eyes flared wide, a single crinkle appearing above her brow. My words made her angry, but she tried to moderate her reaction, keeping her palms flat on her thighs. But she tried so hard I could see the cracks.

"Is that really what you think? That just because you choose not to see, you are not culpable?" she bit out.

"I used to. Not now," I answered honestly.

Just like that, a portion of the fight and tension relaxed. Her brow smoothed, but the corners of her mouth dipped.

"That is something," she said.

What was her relationship to Helio? Why had she come up here, if not to relocate me? To heckle me? Maybe she was having a bad day and thought she'd get in a little torture to raise her spirits.

But the cruelty I'd noted a few minutes before . . . I might have judged it wrong. It might have been a front for vulnerability. That I could understand. I'd used my calm, quiet, subservient servant's mask to protect Treasa and me for a decade. Karine was a rebel. Her life had not been easy, either.

Like everything about this bloody fecking conflict, there was nuance to the woman sitting across from me. I'd just never allowed myself to see it.

"Why did you come up here? Did Helio send you?" I asked, my voice gentler than I'd heard it in ages, the sound akin to how I'd spoken to Treasa when she would fall and scrape her knee. Or when she had nightmares about fireballs.

For once, Karine did not have one in her hand.

"No. I haven't seen him in a few days," she said. I watched as her gaze shifted. She no longer stared over my shoulder, but met my eyes. I was waiting. She sighed. "Everything is going to change."

I pushed to my feet. "I hope it does. The people of Irska deserve a chance at peace."

Karine mirrored the motion, curving her hand around the bedpost. "I meant because of Helio."

That fast, she'd averted her gaze again, examining the wooden bedpost. It was a simple design, no decorations. She avoided my eyes purposefully. Which meant . . . what?

"I don't understand," I admitted, suspecting that was what she wanted.

She lifted a golden brow but still stared at the bedpost like it was the most ornate piece of furniture she'd ever examined. "He hasn't told you what he is?"

Oh, she was a clever thing.

In the space of the time she'd been in the room, she'd shown more emotions than most people did in an entire day. If she meant to set me off kilter, she was failing. Every twitch of her face gave me more information. Helio was much better at this game than she was. I never quite knew what he was thinking. But Karine? She wanted to destabilize me, make me question myself and the understanding I'd been shifting into place since opening my eyes in that dark cellar. The piece I had not quite figured out was *why*. So I'd indulge her a little longer.

"What, is he some sort of Síofran prince?" I asked, sending my brows upward into my hairline. "The leader of the whole fecking rebellion? A murderer? What?"

"We do not have royalty," Karine said, dragging her finger along the coverlet, slowly moving to the other side of the bed. "I'm not jealous of you, or anything as trite as that. Be careful with him, Fionna. That is all I ask. I have known him since we were children, plucked from an orphanage. We grew up in this house—me, Helio, and Link."

I'd never even suspected. Not so observant, after all.

*No. Do not question yourself.*

Karine wanted me to know about her connection to Helio. She wanted to reinforce its strength, their primal alignment. Maybe she was jealous, after all.

Trite. She had no fecking idea.

I would tear her apart before I let her put a hand on Helio.

Below us, a rush of footsteps pounded down the stairs. Voices did not carry up to the third floor, but I recognized the meaning.

"That's Nieve calling for dinner," I said, crossing my arms over my chest.

Karine smiled. Soft. Gentle. Pitying. "I'd better get going before she realizes I'm here and forces me to stay and eat."

I rewarded her with a smile of my own. A placid human smile. "Thank you for coming, Karine."

The moment the door closed behind her, I went to the book and retrieved my map. I folded it carefully and slid it into the space between my corset and my skin. From now on, I would carry it on my person at all times.

I knew what Karine wanted, her purpose for visiting me in my cozy prison. She needn't have bothered. I already knew there was no future for me and Helio. But I could still save my sister.

# Chapter 25

## FIONNA

*The Síofran Rebel Army has one goal. It is not to kill humans or to overthrow the Irskan king. It is not to rule Irska. Those things are all in service of what we truly want. What we vow to do when we take the oath and swear to obey our superiors without question. We want one thing—freedom. If we free the children of Síofra, we free magic.*

*—Zofia Murphy, Síofran Rebel Army*

I was halfway through my dessert, a delicious apple torte, and determined to keep my mouth shut. Sides had been taken. Votes cast. Then the yelling began. By the time the back door of Pearl House opened, I was ready to welcome whoever entered to break up the fighting, even if it was Karine or Yelena.

After everything that had happened in Irska over the last thousand years, I doubted that Síofra had much regard left for humans. But one of the gods must have had me on their mind, because the person I really wanted to see appeared on the threshold to the dining room a moment later.

"Helio! You can settle the debate!" Nadia cried, springing from her seat. "If you could have the power to manipulate light, or the power to—"

"I am quite certain that Helio did not come to Pearl House to mediate an internal family debate," Turi said, catching his daughter's arm as she passed.

"Especially not one that is destined to continue until the end of time," Nieve added, dropping her fingers from where they'd been busy massaging her temples.

I was still frozen, a bite of apple torte halfway to my mouth, my heart doing ridiculous somersaults inside my chest that would have made swallowing that last bite of torte impossible.

"Nadia, clear the table. Moira, wipe it down. Antoni, you're on dishes tonight." Just that quickly, Nieve cleared the room of children. She waited for the huffing teenager to disappear through the swinging door to the kitchen before crossing her arms over her chest. "I presume you timed your arrival so you would not have to join us for dinner."

Helio inclined his head, the dark-red curls at the nape of his head bobbing. Whatever he used to slick back his hair at the start of the day started to give up by this time of the evening, letting his curls loose.

"I need to speak with Fionna about tomorrow," he said, addressing Turi.

I used the break in intensity to set down my fork before I accidentally stabbed myself with it or dropped torte in my lap. Thus far, the only information I had about the march planned for the equinox were the tidbits that Karine had given me. If I had a role to play, no one had said anything to me. Though I supposed that it made sense to wait as long as possible to let the human in on the plan. I may sit at the dinner table with Turi's family, but I was not one of them.

"You may use the living room," Turi offered.

"No," I said, shaking my head as I rose. "Thank you. We will not impose on your evening." And somehow, I sensed that this conversation was better had away from any curious ears.

Helio followed me silently up the two flights of stairs to the bedroom on the third floor. The door was open. I'd taken to leaving it that way so I could hear anyone approaching. Every member of the house sounded different. And I did not want to be surprised by Karine again.

But as we entered, Helio closed the door behind us.

My heart thrummed in my chest, but the anxiety did not threaten to overwhelm me. My other emotions were doing a more than adequate job at that.

Helio stood just inside the closed door. He did not lean back on it in a false repose. He did not cross his arms over his chest. Nothing to soften the tension between us or to feign a casualness that had ceased to exist.

We'd been in this room together before. At night. Alone. But everything about this moment felt different.

Karine had been right about that; everything was about to change. For me as much as anyone. If this was my last moment, then I would seize it.

"A peaceful march," I said, tapping my fingers against my thigh out of habit, rather than a need to calm myself. There was no calming the fire that raged between me and Helio. I'd realized that already.

He didn't ask how I knew. Maybe Karine had told him about her visit. Maybe he assumed that Turi had informed me. Amid a million things that did, that one detail did not feel important.

"How did you manage to convince them?" I asked.

"You did most of the convincing." He shook his head from side to side, a slight smile ghosting over his lips. But it was the way the curls at the nape of his neck moved that held me transfixed.

"They were far from convinced when I left the room," I countered. How could talking to someone feel this good? It should not have been possible for mere words to feel like a caress.

"I finished what you began," he said.

I expected him to take a step closer, but he held the distance between us. The need to close it built inside me, a physical ache in my stomach and my limbs and deep in my chest.

But he held my gaze in that steady, unflinching way of his. Even from across the room, I could feel the power in his mismatched eyes. No, not mismatched. That was wrong and wholly inadequate. They were complementary. A jarringly beautiful juxtaposition.

And behind that fire, or maybe because of it, Helio burned. His power was more than flame and fire. Greater. Bigger. Important.

*He hasn't told you what he is.* I'd dismissed Karine's words as a taunt, a clever little twist of phrase meant to haunt me and make me question the fragile trust between me and Helio. But then he turned away from me and . . . Could there be more?

I opened my mouth to ask, even though I had no right.

Except I did. Helio had told me—I had every right. The enormity of what that meant . . .

He cut me off without meaning to, breaking our gaze, striding away from me to face the window. It didn't feel like an admonition, exactly. Not a fracture, but an easing. The intensity between us was all consuming, and he needed to temper it momentarily or risk losing control. I managed to keep myself from reaching out for him as he passed.

I let the silence stretch between us, knowing inside me that he needed it. The same depths told me that the distance was only temporary.

He exhaled, the motion moving his shoulders. They fell and stayed there as he began to speak. "Pearl House is mine. It belonged to my parents, my grandparents, my great-grandparents. It has been in my family since before the Fall."

My mind spun from emotion to calculation and back again until I realized I could no longer separate the two. One informed the other, and I'd been naive to ever think otherwise.

There was not a single calculation that could ease the ache in my chest.

Helio was important to the children of Síofra. I did not know how, precisely; I was not privy to that information yet.

But it did not matter. Because he was important to me.

I reached for him.

For a brief second, I thought he would jerk away. His muscles tensed beneath my fingers. But then he covered my hand with his own, spun around, and in the next breath I was in his arms.

"Fionna," he said softly into the space between us. I felt his breath on my lips, smelled the brimstone in his pores, savored his heat.

"Helio," I breathed, giving him those parts of me, as well.

There was no future for us, and there never could be. Never had been. Helio would not abandon the Síofran cause, and I would never ask him to. His dedication and duty to his people were what had originally swayed me to trust him. Nor could I give up on what I'd promised myself, promised to my parents, all those years ago. I had to get Treasa out of Irska.

His hands slid from the small of my back to bracket my waist. I wore the thin linen shirt and leather leggings, though this time I had the corset on underneath so that I could tuck my little map inside. But the lower edge of the corset sat just above my hipbones, giving Helio access to an inch of delicate skin above the waistline of my leggings. The linen of my shirt was so thin, so insignificant under the heat of his hands, it might as well have not been there at all.

But then he stroked his hands upward, along my collarbone, and up to cup my face.

I thought the linen made no difference? I was an arrogant human fool. Helio's hands on my actual skin, with no barriers between us, was as close as I'd ever come to heaven.

"This house will be empty tomorrow."

My mouth fell open. Helio pressed his thumb to the center of my lower lip.

Did he know about my plan to slip away and retrieve Treasa? Was it possible that some strange tangent of his fire magic gave him the power to read my mind?

I dismissed the thought as soon as it formed. If Helio could have read my mind, he'd never have bothered with the stilted exchanges of information. He would not have gone to all the trouble of knowing me, just to extract what he needed.

But as his thumb stroked over my cheekbone . . . maybe it hadn't been trouble at all.

"I do not want you here alone," he continued. "Too many people know you are here. Without Turi and Nieve to dissuade them, someone might take it upon themselves to dispose of you."

I swallowed, Helio's words doing nothing to quell the fire burning in my chest. Threats of death were so commonplace between us that they hardly registered.

I fought with my emotions, struggling to see past them to where reason waited. If Pearl House was empty, I'd be able to slip out without any fuss at all. Even if they locked the doors, I'd break a window. Fight the urge to leave an apologetic note for Nieve and make my run for the castle.

"I can manage myself," I said, not having to fake the lump in my throat. It hurt to lie to Helio, even if it was only by omission. He'd chosen peace for me, and I was using it to escape.

We were both being exactly who we were. Who we'd been since the beginning. He'd reminded me of that after the operation in the castle.

He stepped closer, so that our bodies were flush against one another. Even with my corset on, the heat of him leaked through, pebbling my nipples. Both of us wore fitted leather on the lower halves of our bodies. There was nowhere to hide the need he felt, his cock hard and reaching for my center.

But even with my hips rocking forward to answer that need, gladly and willingly, his focus remained on my safety.

"I want you at my side."

The crack in my heart that had slowly grown over the past week spread, spiderwebbing out so that no part of me was safe.

*It is where I belong.*

I almost said the words. The ones that would have changed everything between us. Declared my allegiance. Externalized the mess of nuance that lived within me. Tethered me to him.

But there was one thing I needed more. And I could not have both.

Helio waited, brushing his fingertips over my face. First along my temple and down to my jaw, then over the bridge of my nose to trace the shapes of my eyebrows. He waited to see if I could give . . . but we both knew I could not. It was as close as he'd come to asking.

He reached my lips last, tracing their shape, lower and then upper and then lower again. He replaced his fingers with his mouth. A single, gentle kiss that contrasted sharply with the one that lived in my fantasies. There was still heat, but it was warm, soothing, bittersweet. A goodbye.

When he pulled back, it felt like he took all the air from my lungs with him.

"Sima will come for you in the morning," he said, his breathing as labored as mine.

I nodded. What else could I do?

We'd been brought together by a twist of fate. The Síofran commander and the fake princess. Captor and captive. Though what held us prisoner now was entirely different from the shackles Helio had put on me weeks ago.

It was better that I would not be at Helio's side tomorrow. Getting away from him would be impossible. But Sima . . . I could not hurt her, both because of the vow I'd made to Helio and my own conflicted feelings. But it was lucky, really, that she was to be my guardian for the equinox. If anyone would look the other way while I slipped away to rescue Treasa, it would be her. Maybe luck did actually exist. Or maybe on some level, Helio knew what I was about to try and had decided to allow it. And luck was still just a figment of desperate imaginations.

If I was successful in rescuing Treasa, I would never see Helio again. If I died in the attempt . . . the outcome was the same. This was the only night we'd get.

He turned to leave. Toward the door. Out of my life forever.

I rushed forward, letting emotions overpower calculations. I grabbed his hand. "Helio."

The connection sizzled through me, a living flame that raced from my heart out into my veins and back again. It pulled us together, the snap of a flame that split and then rejoined. That's all we'd ever been— two halves destined to come back together.

Our mouths collided, gentleness gone. This was desperation, the two of us reaching for a single incandescent moment in time.

Helio swept his tongue into my mouth, but I was focused on his hair. I was done imagining what those strands felt like. I allowed my thumbs one brief moment to caress his cheeks, to appreciate the day's stubble, before sliding my fingers past his ears and into his hair. It was as thick as I'd imagined and so impossibly soft. Whatever oils he used to tame it turned it silkier than the pillow I slept on or any of the gowns I'd mended for Aurelle. It threaded between my fingers, slid over the backs of my hands, brushed my wrists.

I groaned into his mouth, unable to hold in my appreciation for the absolute beauty of him.

I was so lost in exploring his hair, rubbing the strands between my fingers to enjoy the texture, tugging on the ends, that I did not notice his hands until they tugged my linen shirt out of my leggings and slid beneath the taut leather to cup my bottom.

"These leggings," he groaned. "The first time I saw you in them, I thought I might die on the spot. The way they fit you . . . I see you even in my dreams."

I dreamed of him, too. Nearly every night. But I was too raw to admit it. My mind latched on to something else. I jerked back.

"The leather jacket," I said, already panting.

"I fecking love seeing you in my cloak," he admitted without a second's hesitation. "But I wanted you to have options."

He'd commissioned the jacket. He'd known my body well enough to have it cut to exactly the correct dimensions. No one had ever cared about me like that. Not since my parents. Treasa loved me, but she was a child, I, her caretaker. It was inherently different.

But Helio . . . he saw my mind. My body. The nuances of both.

It put me over the edge.

I hooked a leg around his hip. It was easy, with his hands already around my bottom. He lifted me the rest of the way, carrying me easily to the edge of the table and setting me there. One hand slid up from where I'd linked them at his nape to grab on to the curls. The other hand I pulled forward, unbuttoning his shirt. Heat poured off him with such intensity, I expected it to burn when I laid my palm flat against his chest. But his heat was mine. It only felt right.

I leaned forward and pressed a kiss to his chest, right over his heart.

"Feck, Fionna." He captured my face again, one hand on either side, holding me in place while he ravaged my mouth.

He left no corner unexplored, every dip and crevice claimed by his tongue. Then he dragged it out, along my jawline, to nip at the base of my ear. And his hands . . . gods, his fecking hands. They were unlacing my leggings, sliding them down so I was entirely bare from the waist down.

I did not even protest. Not so long as he . . .

"Helio," I moaned, throwing back my head as he plunged a finger inside me. He did not circle my entrance to see if I was ready. He knew I was.

The sounds tearing from my throat only intensified as he pumped his finger inside me once, twice, three times. He covered my mouth with a searing kiss, devouring every moan. They all belonged to him anyway.

But even as he worked me slowly wider, his fingertips trailing along the sensitive inside of my channel, I wanted more. I could feel how badly he wanted me—I'd felt it for weeks, now.

The outline of him pressed against my bare thigh was no longer enough. If Helio was a flame, then that was his burning center, and I wanted to experience it for myself.

I kept my hand on his chest. The steady pounding of his heartbeat beneath my palm anchored me. If I let go, I might float away from Irska and reality entirely. Sliding my other hand from his silken hair was a loss. But I promised myself an even greater reward in return.

I forced myself to savor the downward journey, tracing his muscles, first his pectorals and then his abdominals, all carved with a Síofra-gifted knife. But I did not linger. His own pants gave easily beneath my fingers, and then I had him.

Gods spare me. My head was thrown back, eyes closed, Helio making love to my throat with his mouth while he stroked me languorously. But I did not need to see him to realize that he was perfection. The length of him stretched beyond my combined fingers and palm, but the girth . . . I wanted him inside me.

I encircled him and stroked from base to tip. This time, it was him groaning, and me catching his mouth to feed on his pleasure.

"The bed," I moaned against him. "I need you inside me." Not his tongue or his capable fingers. I wanted to feel him stretching me, filling me so completely that all the other worries and duties we owed to others melted away.

I waited for the world to go vertical. For Helio to sweep me up into his arms, lay me on the bed, cover me with his delicious weight and warmth.

Instead, he jerked away.

I could still see the evidence of my desire—and his need to fulfill it—glistening on his fingers. Gods, I could feel the heat of his cock where it had pressed against my leg, then my hand. But this distance . . . it felt fecking final.

"Please," I heard myself say, my voice strained. Not weak, but broken. That was what was happening. I was breaking. Shattering.

"Fionna." Helio reached for me instinctively, freezing halfway, his gaze dropping to his hand with a mix of confusion and accusation.

I shook my head. "You do not owe me an explanation."

"I want to give you one."

But I shook my head again. I might have the right to his words, but I did not need them. There were only three I wanted, to give and receive, and neither of us was ready for that exchange and the world those words would remake.

He dragged a hand through his hair. Maybe he meant to smooth it. Or it was a nervous habit. This time, at least, I knew it was not to torture me. This time, I was fairly certain that Helio was torturing himself.

He almost changed his mind. I saw that in his eyes, those glorious eyes. Then he thought better. Regained control. Turned for the door and left without saying goodbye. We'd already said it in the ways that mattered.

I closed the door behind him and prayed to Síofra herself that I'd have the strength to close my heart as well.

# Chapter 26

## FIONNA

*In the three hundredth year since the fall of magic, the King of Irska decreed that all citizens take to the streets to celebrate the vernal equinox. We received our orders in the mess hall on the eve of the equinox. Following orders is what we do, and these were clear, passed down from the king himself. Whatever the changelings had planned, we'd be ready for them. They'd surprised us for the last time.*

*—Garen Adamova, Peace Guard*

The equinox dawned bright and clear. A rare blue sky looked down on Irska, the bright-white sun lighting the rolling green hills beyond the city walls.

I'd slept in my clothing. Risen with the dawn. There was no more use lying in bed, staring at the ceiling. My plans were made. I went into the washroom, repeating my routine with Nieve's luxurious little jars of cream for the last time.

I combed out my curls and then twisted them into a knot atop my head. If I could not have it loose, I wanted it completely out of the way. No pretty braids or castle coiffures. Just me.

I was sad to leave the lovingly fitted jacket, but the cloak hid the parcel I'd packed. If Sima questioned me about it, I'd say I was taking Helio's advice to be ready for things to unravel at any moment. It was not even a lie.

The morning dragged on. Nadia delivered my breakfast on a tray, Moira behind her with a steaming mug of frostbloom tea. It felt like Nieve's final goodbye.

Even though my stomach rebelled, I forced myself to sit at the table and eat while the household bustled around below me. Mornings were always hectic at Pearl House, and this one was no different. There was no school today, the equinox honored by both sides, but Helio had said the house would be empty.

An hour slipped by. Then another. They passed faster than they had any right to. The house quieted. That did not mean it was empty. I stayed in my room. Despite Helio's warning, I was not afraid of anyone inside Pearl House. At least, not what they could do to my body. My resolve felt much less sturdy.

Footsteps on the stairwell announced Sima's arrival. I did not know her tread yet, but I knew it did not belong to any of the residents of Pearl House. Or to Helio.

She nudged the cracked door the rest of the way open, hovering in the hall. Had Nieve given her the same instructions as Karine? It would not have been necessary. Sima understood what privacy and autonomy meant to someone who'd had very little.

"Ready?" she asked, her eyes doing a quick scan of the room. Unlike Karine's gaze, there was no calculation in it. I recognized hypervigilance born of a life of trauma.

"Has everyone else left?" I asked, standing from my chair by the window and straightening the cloak around me. Beneath it, I'd chosen my leather leggings, covered with a simple dress. Serviceable garments that would do their jobs even beyond Irska.

"Nieve took the children to her mother's house in the country this morning," Sima confirmed.

No word on Turi's whereabouts. I could only assume that as a member of the council, he had duties to attend to today. So did I. The less either of us thought of the other, the better.

The same went for Helio . . . but with a thousand times more importance. And difficulty.

But for Nieve to flee the city . . . "She has so little faith in the Rebels to keep the peace that she fled."

"This was your idea. Do you have faith in it?"

"I have faith in Irska." I did. I had to. Because I could not stay to see what happened.

Sima frowned. She seemed poised to ask another question but dismissed the impulse with a little shake of her head. "Let's go. We need to be in place before the march begins."

The noise was audible before we even left Pearl House.

To my relief, there was no yelling or angry chanting. A few people sang. But at least on the residential street where Pearl House sat, the crowd was peaceful.

*Maybe this would work. Maybe this was the moment that everything in Irska changed.*

*And I will not be here to see it. But Treasa will be safe.*

I'd never seen so many people on the streets. From the castle, people appeared as little more than dots. But I'd watched them for so many years, I felt comfortable in the observation. And thankful. The crowds would provide the cover I needed to slip away.

The other benefit was that we could not move quickly without disturbing the tenor of the crowd. Sima did not need to tell me; I could sense it as we wove through the streets. The Síofran around us were peaceful—for now. They were willing to try this new way, but they were poised to defend themselves. To defend themselves if needed and attack if it came to it. I prayed that my own people could exercise the same restraint.

Our moderated speed meant that I was not short of breath, and able to track our progress through the city. My mind conjured the map tucked safely into my corset, imagining Sima and myself as small dots moving along the corridors I'd drawn. Twice we turned onto streets I did not know. But both times, we reemerged onto main thoroughfares that I did. And always, the castle loomed above us.

We were getting closer to it . . . though Karine had told me that the march was to terminate at the castle gates, not begin there. But Helio and Sima had not really told me anything about where I was bound. Only that I would remain with Sima. Feck. I should have asked more questions. If we met up with more of Helio's Rebels, slipping away would be next to impossible. Which meant I needed to go *now*.

But that plan soured in my throat as we turned the next corner.

We were near the eastern wall of the city. On one side of the street, the row of businesses had shuttered their doors and windows for the day. On the other, a steep, grassy embankment sloped up from the street to meet the three-foot-thick concrete wall. Lining that embankment, stretching as far as I could see, were Peace Guards.

Their deep-blue and shining white uniforms created a jarring contrast with the muddy gray of the city wall behind them.

Walls. Irska was all about walls. The city walls that separated us from the country that existed only to feed the metropolis. The peace walls that supposedly kept us safe. The castle walls, encircling the grounds so thoroughly that the citizens of Irska did not even recognize their princess.

I wanted to tear down the walls of Irska with my bare hands. I wanted to scream up at the Peace Guards, whose faces I would surely recognize if I allowed myself to look closer. Begging—I would beg the people of Irska, human and Síofran both, to keep the peace. To find another way.

It was impossible to ignore the shift in the crowd. The children of Síofra continued to walk down the street in a singular direction, presumably toward the march the Rebels had organized. Above them, the Peace Guards stood in silent threat. They glared but did not speak. Everyone bore a weapon, and most of them were already freed from sheaths or belts. They feigned idleness in the way they held the weapons, but violence lurked just beneath the veneer.

*Maybe this was a mistake.*

"Is it like this everywhere?" I whispered to Sima.

"Along many sections of the route we mapped out for the march," she sighed. "We expected them to come out for the equinox, but not in this force."

And yet here they were, not just patrolling the city in their units of eight, but lined up to a purpose. Which meant . . . "Someone leaked the route."

"Someone leaked the route," she confirmed.

Sima guided me down the street, though even her posture had tightened at the appearance of the Peace Guards. The farther we moved, the composition of the humans perched on the embankment became more mixed. There were ununiformed humans as well. Rogue Defenders. They had to be. The normal, everyday human citizens of Irska did not want this. I did not want this.

We reached an intersection where two other thoroughfares joined with the road we'd walked along the edge of the city. I could tell instantly where the march was meant to go—only one of them was lined with Peace Guards and Defenders. There was no grass embankment to give them an advantage, so they stood on doorsteps and overturned crates. The businesses here were closed, as well.

This was a Síofran peace village. The business owners would not have willingly ceded their storefronts to the Peace Guard. This was an occupation.

"Do not give up on them yet," Sima said from my side.

I turned to look at her, realizing I'd stopped in the middle of the intersection. For once, neither of us wore the servant's mask of complacency. I let all of my worry shine through and saw it reflected back by Sima. Validated. But I also saw something in the slight crinkle of her eyes, the quirk of her lips, that was missing from my own.

Hope.

"The Peace Guards have been out here since dawn," Sima said. "Thus far, not a single incursion has been reported by either side. Not in the entirety of Irska."

It blazed to life, flames licking through my body with a heat that I normally attributed to . . .

"Helio," I breathed, each sound a beat of my heart as it threatened to burst out of my chest. I was not supposed to see him again. I did not want to see him again. My composure would crack and I would lose control.

But it didn't. I didn't. The anxiety was still present, but so was the warmth. I worried for what his presence meant, but I was still glad he was there.

He maintained a careful distance, a difficult feat as the crowd thickened around us by the second.

"I am sorry that I cannot take you myself," he said.

I blinked up at him, confused.

He sighed, head dipping both directions before he stepped closer so that he could keep his voice low. Still, he did not touch me. "Sima and Heath will get you in and out of the castle, but you must find her quickly once you are inside. The king has deployed almost all of the Peace Guards into the city, so you should have an easy time of it."

*Her.* My sister. Treasa.

Emotion swelled in my chest, more powerful than panic or anxiety. This dwarfed anger and even hope. I'd never felt it for a man.

The council be damned. That was what Helio did not say. *He* had done this—he was doing this. He had not told me my role in the march because I did not have one. He'd planned for me to be elsewhere. Emotion surged inside me, the intensity so strong it threatened to force out the words that would upend everything. I could feel them, but I did not dare acknowledge them or speak them.

I tried for humor instead. "An easy time infiltrating the castle and kidnapping my sister?"

Helio rewarded me with a rare smile that reached his remarkable eyes. "An easier time than I had with you."

I laughed. Because what else was there to do, in that moment where my entire life coalesced into something I still could not entirely understand.

There was one other thing to do.

I swung an arm around Helio's shoulder and stood on my tiptoes, pressing my whole body into his. It still would not have been enough, if he had not leaned down those last few inches to meet me.

There was no time for gentleness and nothing gentle about what I felt for him. The feeling inside me burned at the same time that it caressed, flowing through my veins and my chest, demanding a physical manifestation even if I could not form the words.

I took his lips like they were mine, because they were. My tongue surged into his mouth, meeting his in a grasping, delirious dance to music that only the two of us could hear. It was the kind of kiss I'd read about while secreted alone in the castle library. A melding of hearts and souls as well as bodies. I did not think of the future, only lived in that one moment. That beautiful moment where I could not tell where Helio started and I began. Where the only duty was to the love between us.

And then we broke apart.

I did not know who was responsible. My head was too busy spinning, my world tilting with what I'd admitted to myself without meaning to.

"Go. Every moment matters now," Helio said.

"Thank you," I murmured. If they were my last words to him, they were honest and pure and real.

If he had any for me, I could not stay to hear them. Sima caught my hand and tugged me through the crowd toward the castle.

# Chapter 27

## HELIO

*The Síofran would never admit to it, but some bloodlines are considered more valuable and venerable than others. It shouldn't mean anything now, with magic suppressed since the Fall. We all have such limited use the difference is negligible. But as someone born to a shifter line, I always knew where I stood. We were considered the most rudimentary, our magic the least nuanced, even though we are truly changelings. Since we cannot practice our magic while in our human-formed bodies, we are often considered a liability. We cannot hide as easily in plain sight. But none of that should matter. It is hypocritical mind-feckery that we rage at the humans for setting themselves above us, and then create our own stratifications.*

*—Heath Kolas, Síofran Rebel Army*

Watching her go was like seeing my heart outside my body, weaving away from me through the crowd.

Mendara was laid up in a safe house. With Heath and Sima escorting Fionna, that left Link and Karine. Our cell had been assigned the northeast quadrant of the city. It was a lot of space to cover, but it also abutted the castle, which made the operation to retrieve Fionna's sister possible.

*I would have found a way.*

I could not name when my priorities shifted. For more than thirty years, I'd never taken an action for my own sake. Every single one had been in service to the Síofran cause. Taking the oath to join the Síofran Rebel Army had been nothing, because I'd already committed the ideals to heart. How could I not, given what I was? My entire bloodline had sacrificed and died for the Síofran cause. We were her first children. It was expected.

But I had not expected Fionna.

When she'd first told me that she was not the Irskan princess, but a servant, I'd thought her a cruel joke from Síofra herself. A reprimand for not pushing myself hard enough, not fighting for my people. I'd tried to harden myself accordingly.

Until Fionna began kicking down the walls I'd erected over a lifetime. She was not a curse from Síofra, but a gift.

She was the only person who had ever asked me what I wanted from my life. The first who had looked at me and seen something other than violence. I still did not see the kindness and mercy she noted. But she had awoken something in me that I did not think I had the capacity for—love. I loved Fionna. A human. My captive. My life.

Once I realized I loved her, every decision had been easy. Painful to execute, but easy to make. I was deeply loyal to my kind and my cause. I understood my place in our rebellion. But the love I had for Fionna was different. It was pure.

I was not naive enough to think that peace would be easy; one march would not solve everything. It would not free magic, and it could not erase three hundred years of conflict. Magic needed harmony to thrive, and even if peace was achieved today, harmony was still a vague, distant hope.

For the first time in more than three decades, the flame inside me was not just rage.

This march would never have happened without Fionna. Whether the council believed she deserved it or not, I did not fecking care. Her sister would not spend another night in the castle. As for what happened after . . .

It would all depend on how this day progressed.

I had a role to play. I forced Fionna from my mind—with only mild success—and scanned the intersection. The road extended in four directions, but only two of them were crowded. The ones that were on the direct march route, and lined with Peace Guards.

We'd been betrayed.

Logically, we all knew there were informers within the Rebels. Within all the organizations. It was the entire reasoning behind the structure of the cells. Isolate information, isolate the damage any one individual could do. But an undertaking of this scale required multiple cells coordinating together, and even with careful parceling of information, enough had gotten through to cause problems.

Even if the route had not been leaked in its entirety, someone—or multiple someones—had passed enough information to the Peace Guards for them to make reasonable guesses about the gaps.

I found the sun overhead, noting the time. The march had only just begun. The people in the street around me shuffled around, stagnant, waiting for the main thrust of demonstrators to arrive so they could join in. But stagnation could too easily lead to malaise, and with the Peace Guards lining the streets, violence was only one bad decision away.

A familiar face appeared in the crowd. If I'd believed in luck, I might have thought him summoned by my own misgivings. But there were plenty of other shitty explanations for all the things that happened in Irska. Luck did not even enter the equation.

"What is it?" I said as Link arrived at my side, slightly winded from his half walk, half jog.

His fingers danced around the hilt of the dagger tucked into his belt. All Rebels were under strict orders to keep their weapons sheathed unless directly attacked. But I felt that same draw to arm myself.

"They've started throwing rocks," he said.

"Fecking Peace Guards."

We turned down one of the less busy streets. We could move faster here.

"It isn't Peace Guards or Defenders. From what I can tell, they are civilians."

My head whipped his way. "Human civilians are throwing rocks at Síofran civilians?"

It was not unheard of, but it was a problem I had not fecking anticipated. The equinox always riled people up, but for celebration. The fights did not usually break out until the evening, when both sides had had plenty of time to get drunk.

Keeping the Rebels and Libs in line was an impossible task. Civilians? Feck. Feck. Feck.

I broke into a jog. Link kept pace at my side.

I knew without Link telling me where we were going.

The northeastern quadrant covered three peace villages, two Síofran and one human. I'd spent hours with Turi planning the route for the march. If the demonstration was to remain peaceful, nothing could be left to chance. But there was no way to avoid the human peace villages entirely. There were two places where the march would have to briefly pass through them, one in the northeastern quadrant, and one in the northwest.

It took too long to get there even at a jog. Any faster, and we'd risk setting off a cascading sequence of our own. All it would take was one accidental bump into an already primed human or Síofran, and a fight could break loose.

By the time we turned the corner, through the wrought-iron gates that separated the peace villages, one already had.

"Stop!" I caught the man's arm as he swung it back, a kitchen knife gripped in his fingers. I twisted to avoid the blade sinking into my own arm. The blade was caked with old food. The bastard had not even bothered to clean it before bringing it into the street.

I squeezed his wrist until he released the knife, catching it with my one hand and shoving him away with the other.

"This is a peaceful demonstration," I seethed. We were in a human peace village, but the man I'd disarmed was Síofran. Which I knew because the man he'd been about to stab stood with his back to the row of Peace Guards that lined the embankment. A child of Síofra would never have willingly shown a Peace Guard his back.

He had a rock in his hand, just like Link said. There were several already spread across the ground near my feet—evidence that he'd already launched more than one projectile.

Fecking hell.

The disarmed Síofran snarled in my face, actually saw my face, stumbled back a few steps. I did not even have time to enjoy the effects of my menace.

"They are the ones throwing rocks," he bit out, straightening his filthy lapels. He already smelled of liquor. It was not even noon.

I wanted to snarl back. Mediated myself to the tone I used with Antoni, Turi's eldest. "You sound like a petulant child." He opened his mouth to argue. "And children don't get to play with knives."

Unlike Antoni, who respected me by default, I was no one to this man. We were both Síofran, but he did not know what lurked beneath my skin, dormant and dangerous. He was not a member of my cell, bound by oath to follow my orders without question. I grabbed his shoulders and shoved him into Link's waiting grasp.

"Take him," I ordered.

Link *was* bound to follow my directions. "Where?"

"I don't fecking care." An honest answer. Link could knock him unconscious and drop him next to a refuse bin. "As long as he does not cause any more trouble."

The man protested, but Link slung his arm around the other man's shoulders and said something that quieted him as he led the man away.

I turned back to the human—only to find empty space. It wasn't difficult to locate him, given my height, and the way he scurried through the crowd. The Síofran parted to give him a wide berth. But no one reached out to harm him. I exhaled slowly, trying to calm the flames.

But the stretch of rocky grass did not remain empty. A Peace Guard stepped out of line. His blue-and-white uniform was immaculate. Unlike many of his peers, he had not drawn his weapon. It did not lessen the threat in his smooth movements as he knelt and picked up one of the stones that littered the ground.

As he stepped back into line, he held my gaze.

I sensed Link back at my side, his clipped footsteps easy to pick out from the shuffling gaits of the other civilians in the street.

"Trouble?" Link said.

"Not yet." I dismissed the Peace Guard. He was one of a thousand. I'd sooner kill them all, one by one, then let them threaten my people. But the peace must hold. "Is he taken care of?"

Link nodded. "He wouldn't have lasted much longer before passing out. He had an empty bottle of liquor down his pants."

The last thing this tinderbox needed was alcohol. But with the two brawlers gone, the tenor of the crowd quieted. Not peaceful. If that had existed at all, it was long gone now. But there was no outright violence at the moment.

I had to hold this together long enough for Fionna to get out of the castle. If the city erupted into chaos, the Peace Guards would close ranks around the castle walls, and it would be impossible for her to get out.

I would not lose her, not like that.

A life without her was inevitable. But I would only accept that if she was free.

"This won't be the last skirmish," Link said. He settled a hand around the dagger in his belt, remembered himself, and crossed his arms over his chest instead. He was trying. My own Rebels were trying. If we could keep the peace, so could the citizens.

He was right, though. This was the first of dozens of altercations that would break out over the next few hours. Our job was to isolate and de-escalate them before they spread and turned the tide of the march.

I scanned the street one last time, looking for any other signs of unrest to be put down before I backtracked. "No, but . . ."

My eyes caught on the row of blue and white. "That Peace Guard, the one who was kneeling down—where did he go?"

Link turned, scanning the row of guards along the embankment. "He's not there."

"He was the instigator." Feck. And now he was gone.

Link frowned. "I don't know about that, Helio. Any of them could be responsible."

Link could be right. But every instinct in me screamed . . . he could have chosen to stay in line. But he'd picked up that rock, and he made sure I saw it. Now he was gone.

"We have to find him, now."

# Chapter 28

## FIONNA

*My ma died when I was barely weaned. My pa was already long dead. That just left my elder sister and my gran. Gran worked in the castle. She gave up her place to Ma when her arthritis got too bad to take the stairs down to the laundry. When my ma died, it was my sister's turn to go. She worked in the castle for almost twenty years. When I came of age, I joined the Peace Guard so I could be near her. Gran was gone by then, too. I thought . . . at least we would be together. But my sister cried and cried and cried when I showed up in my uniform. She said she'd washed too much blood out of uniforms just like that, and she would not wash blood from mine. Things were never okay again, after that.*

*—Kyle Rybka, Peace Guard*

Sima had already done most of the work to get us to the castle. Only a few more breathless turns, and we were there, across from the gates that led to the castle grounds. For a terrifying heartbeat, I thought that she meant to walk right through them. Relief flooded through me when she steered me into a small café instead.

All the peace villages that abutted the castle walls were human. Like the one we'd seen earlier, this business was closed. But the door remained unlocked.

"I still have a few human contacts," Sima said, ushering me through and locking the door behind us. She lingered at the door for a few seconds, watching the street from behind the window shade.

The café was well kept and clean, but truly tiny. There was one table for two and a counter along one wall with three stools. The case was clear of food, the oil lamps all doused. The lack of dust was the only sign that it wasn't abandoned.

Until a door slammed in the back.

I dropped to the ground, ducking beneath the singular table. Sima crouched at my side, a comically small knife in her hand. There'd be nothing funny about it if that was what she used to defend us.

Just as I was about to start tapping, a half laugh whooshed out of her and she stood.

Too late. I'd already tapped twice.

Once more, then I stood, too.

"Today is bound to be dramatic enough without you helping it along," Sima admonished Heath.

"The back door sticks," he said from the other side of the counter. "There's an attic to stash your weapons and your clothes," he added before stepping aside.

Sima moved past him without offering me an explanation, and leaving me alone with Heath for the first time.

I'd never seen Heath without a weapon. Outside the confines of Pearl House, I'd never seen any of the Rebels without at least two or three strapped to them, Karine with a fireball perpetually in hand.

But what I found more startling were the dark circles under his eyes. Like Helio, he had his own rough handsomeness, his dark-brown hair a complement to his tawny skin and dark eyes. He'd only ever looked at me with hate and malice. Now he just looked tired.

The exhaustion did not stop him from looking me over, nor his tired eyes from snagging on the embroidery on the collar of my cloak.

"That fecking cloak," he muttered under his breath.

My fingers lifted to the clasps by reflex.

Sima emerged a second later, interrupting the disconcerting exchange. She'd traded her surcoat for a worn leather vest over a wool shirt that buttoned all the way to her throat. She had not been gone long enough to change out of her pants, so I guessed she'd just put the skirt right over the top, like me.

"You look fine," Sima said, raking her eyes over me critically. "Leave that pack, though, and put on this satchel; it has food in it. We are extra kitchen helpers being called in on our day off to assist with the feast. That's your dinner."

So much for the pack I'd made myself being inconspicuous beneath the cloak.

"They don't serve you dinner? Even if you work in the kitchens?" I asked, trading her for the satchel and settling it onto my hip.

Heath groaned. "It is that sort of naivete that is going to get us all killed."

"I'll let Sima speak on all kitchen-related matters," I bit back.

I was not the same cowering victim he'd tried to strike in the basement below Irska a month ago. It was more than just Helio's promise, which still burned bright in my mind. The change was soul deep. I'd been blinded before. Maybe sleeping was a better metaphor. But the last month had opened my eyes. Rescuing Treasa would require me to keep them open wide.

Heath lifted one brow. "Good."

An alliance. Sort of. Temporarily.

But Sima was not as easily convinced. She turned on Heath, planting a hand on each hip. "Heath, tell me right now. Can you pretend to be human?"

"I have orders."

"Our orders are to retrieve Fionna's sister and get the feck out of the castle. If you cannot play along convincingly enough to achieve that, then your orders are best served by staying here."

Heath glared at her. Sima did not waver an inch. As we watched, Heath reached inside the front of his shirt, pulling out a penknife that had been stashed . . . I did not even know where. He slammed it down onto the countertop. "Feck you."

I finally understood. None of us could carry weapons—it would out us immediately. And if we were searched or suspected . . . we could not have a single one on us. The dinners packed in our bags were further support for our story.

Sima smiled at Heath and winked at me as she turned for the door. Heath waved me forward, scowling. There was no way we were going to get into the castle.

Outside the café, we fell into a line. I kept pace with Sima on one side, Heath on the other. I waited for one of them to veer to the side, perhaps toward the sewer once again. Or one of the ancillary gates that were used only for deliveries. Or anywhere but straight toward the main fecking castle gate.

"Start talking," Sima said.

While I'd been busy gaping at the gate, Heath was busy glaring at me.

*What the feck about?* "I wanted her to study Old Irskan. It isn't standard instruction in schools anymore, but the roots underlie so many of our words that it does serve you even if you never have occasion to speak it."

Heath looked like I'd physically struck him rather than just assaulted him with verbal babble. We were too fecking close to the gate for that expression. I pinched his arm.

"My mother spoke Old Irskan," he said, swallowing his yelp.

Sima snorted on my other side but didn't contribute otherwise, so I kept going.

"Did she teach you any?" I asked, leaning in as if I were actually interested. Which I was not.

"Mostly just sayings that don't make much sense when you translate them. She'd yell them at me and my brother, sometimes at my gran when she got annoyed," Heath said.

I sank my teeth into my lower lip, biting off a genuine chuckle. "You grew up with your family. It sounds lovely. And loud."

"It was," he said. "Until it wasn't."

His face shuttered. I did not want to ask.

There was no more time anyway. We'd reached the gate. Sima handed over three rectangular papers the size of my hand to the Peace Guard on duty. City passes. I recognized the pale-gold paper. I might have obtained one for myself, if I ever wanted to try. But everything I'd cared about was inside the castle, not down in the city.

Maybe if I'd ever ventured beyond the castle walls, I would have realized. I would not have remained complacent and complicit for so long.

The guard shuffled through each one, handed them back to Sima, and, just that easy, we were through.

I grabbed Heath's arm to steady myself. Sima snorted again, quieter this time. But we managed to keep walking up the wide cobbled path that led up the hill to the castle.

"I don't understand," I whispered once we were twice as far as the Peace Guards at the gate could reasonably hear. "If it was that easy to get into the castle, why haven't you kidnapped anyone before?"

Sima pocketed the passes, looking around us before responding. The grounds were mostly just expanses of green lawn, except for the golden apple orchard. But that was on the other side of the castle entirely.

"Because it has never been that easy before," she said. "The Peace Guard who checked the passes is a sympathizer. An informant."

My heart began to race. "Helio said there was no one in the castle who would help us."

"There wasn't." Sima's gaze flicked in my direction. "Until they heard about the plan for a peaceful march."

And then the informant turned coconspirator. Not because of a bribe or an offer of escape from Irska or a threat. But because of hope.

I could not . . . no. I could not claim responsibility for that. Helio had fought for my proposal. The Síofran Rebel Army's council had agreed to it. The Síofran civilians had agreed to march with the Rebels. Thousands of people had brought this change into being. And I had every single one of them to thank. Because of them, I had a chance to save my sister.

The weight of it was almost enough to drown me.

I could not let it. My fingers curled against my thigh beneath the cloak. I tapped them three times. But the real difference came from the fire that burned low in my belly. I took deep, drawn-out breaths, not to quell it but to fuel it. While that flame burned, Helio was with me.

# Chapter 29

## Fionna

*When I was young, I used to ask about my father every day. My mother was patient. I was a child. I did not understand why he was missing. Plenty of my friends were fatherless, but they were the children of martyrs. They could tell you exactly where the fireball that killed their father had exploded. As I got older, I noticed the expression on her face. I asked less. It was my great-uncle who finally told me. My mother worked in the castle as a maid. She was attacked by a Peace Guard. Not very fecking peaceful. I never mentioned that bastard again. I joined up with the Defenders to protect my mother. I don't care much one way or the other for the humans or the changelings. Bad people are bad whether they have magic or not. But I knew if I became a Defender, if people knew that her son was a Defender, they'd leave her alone. And it's mostly worked. I'm still alive. So is she. That's enough.*

*—Maxim McConville, Irska Defense Force*

Every step up the path felt dangerous. One of the other guards from the gate would realize our passes were fake. Someone up in the castle would look out a window and recognize me or Sima. There was not a single more precipitous moment in my life. If I failed to rescue Treasa, then . . .

Then I would try again. And again and again. I was not the same scared young woman who'd been kidnapped from the castle. Nor even the frightened, anxiety-ridden one who'd been here less than a fortnight before.

I still had plenty of anxiety. But I also had strength. Perseverance. I'd learned it at the side of the Síofran Rebels.

The conviction didn't do much for my racing heart as we sighted the Sea Gate. In the distance, I could just make out the golden apple orchard, where I'd hidden, overlooking the city, more than a month ago. If I climbed one of those trees today, I knew that I would see a completely different city spread out below. Irska itself had not changed. But I had.

Everyone entered through the main archway of one of the gates, nobles and servants alike. But from there, several entrances split off into the castle itself. The Sea Gate was the least used, and the one I was least familiar with because it was the farthest from Aurelle's apartments. But I knew enough to navigate once we were inside the castle. Sima could fill in any gaps.

Except Sima stepped to the side a few yards before the arched entrance to the courtyard. "You two go on ahead now."

I gaped at her. "What?"

This could not possibly be part of the plan they'd arranged with Helio. I cut a look to Heath, who appeared just as nonplussed as me.

"We are posing as kitchen helpers. There's no reason for all three of us to be out of the kitchen. If you two are questioned, pretend you are sneaking away for a moment of privacy," Sima said, her tone even and countenance unfaltering. Fecking hell, she was good at that servant's mask.

Heath made a sound of utter disgust.

"More than reciprocated," I hissed.

But I was more worried about what Sima hadn't said—where she would be. A thought had occurred to me as she spoke.

"Sima, you're dead," I said gently. "They think you are dead. You cannot go into the kitchen. Maybe you should not be here at all." It was dangerous to bring her into the castle in the middle of the day. Another servant might recognize her.

Feck. We shouldn't have brought her. Why hadn't Helio thought of that? He had to have. He was too thorough for such an omission. Which begged the question, Why had he decided to risk it? Maybe Sima waiting outside *had* been the plan all along.

But if so, neither of them had apprised Heath of it. And unlike Sima, he had no talent for disguising his emotions. His mouth and eyebrows cooperated to form an intimidating scowl. Of course, Sima was unfazed.

"I am ready for that," she said. She pulled a pair of garden shears from inside her bag. "I'll rub a bit of dirt on the knees of my dress, and suddenly I'm not a kitchen helper, but a gardener."

It was thin, and we all knew it. I wondered whether this was truly part of Helio's plan, or whether Sima could not bring herself to cross that threshold in daylight. If that was it . . . I would not be the one to make her. Plenty of my own demons dwelled in the castle, but so did someone more important than any fear.

We reached for each other at the same time, our hands clasping together so tight fingers crunched.

"Stay safe," I said to Sima.

She smiled. "Go get your sister."

Just like that, three had become two.

Not looking over my shoulder took continuous effort. I didn't allow myself a glance, not even once we entered the protection of the courtyard.

Protection. That was a fecking lie. We might be less physically exposed, but there were more eyes here. With most of the Peace Guards deployed into the city and the servants all hard at work at their posts, preparing for the equinox festivities, there were fewer familiar faces for us to run into. But we could still get unlucky.

I wished Sima was still at my side.

"Where are we going?" Heath said as I guided him through a portico along the western wall of the courtyard.

The layout was the same as the courtyard of the Mountain Gate, where the Peace Guards trained, which was also closest to Aurelle's chambers. We were on the other side of the castle now.

"What time is it?" I had not paid attention while we were outside. All I remembered was the sea of blue overhead and the watered warmth of the spring sun on the back of my neck. That must mean something, if it was on my neck when I was facing . . .

"It is almost midday," Heath supplied.

He came to a stop at my side, just inside the thick wooden door that separated the courtyard from the castle itself. Servants used the small space as a mudroom, stashing jackets, parcels, and other paraphernalia out of the way of nobles for easy retrieval later.

Two paths lay in front of us. One lined with plush carpets and expensive tapestries. The main arteries of the castle that I'd walked as Aurelle's companion. Those hallways were likely deserted, the nobles in residence all resting up for a long evening of celebrations. But there was no way to explain our presence there if we did encounter anyone. I was dressed as a kitchen helper, not a princess's companion.

"All the fires are usually lit by now," I mused aloud.

Whether someone had told Heath that my sister was a firestoker did not matter. He was about to find out. *And he is helping me rescue her*. I had to trust him now, impossible as it felt.

"What about the holiday? It's equinox." As he spoke, he took another few steps into the antechamber, peering into the castle itself.

Just to the left there was a gilt golden door, decorated with old Irskan symbology I'd never gotten to in my studies. Behind it lay our second path, the unadorned green walls and uncarpeted wooden floors of the servant corridors.

"Servants do not get to celebrate. Even human ones." The words came out sharper than I'd intended. I expected Heath to bite back. I still remembered his hand flying toward me through the air while I was bound to a chair, powerless to protect myself.

But he said nothing. No counter. He hung up his cloak like any other servant reporting to the castle for duty. I was loath to abandon Helio's cloak, but I mimicked the action. Yet I kept the satchel.

"It is possible she could still be finishing her rounds if any of the nobles decided to sleep late in preparation for the festivities tonight," I said.

"You are supposed to be the castle expert." There it was.

I glared at him. "After her morning rounds she bathes and has lessons until the evening rounds, which will be later tonight because of the feast. But there won't be lessons today, so it is possible she is with the other firestokers."

"Which means?"

I cringed. "She could be anywhere."

"Fecking hell. We don't have time for this."

No. We absolutely did not. I made my decision, and I did not wait to discuss it with Heath. I opened the door to the servant corridor and ushered him through. We'd keep our heads down and pray that none of the servants we passed recognized me.

"Her quarters. I might be able to tell where she's gone by what is there—or what isn't."

Soot-covered clothes meant she'd bathed and was somewhere within the castle. No sign of her dirty garments, and she'd gone outside onto the grounds. That would be better, in some ways. There were fewer recreational spaces that servants could make use of outside. In the castle, there were a thousand nooks and crannies where the preteens might ensconce themselves.

I motioned Heath in front of me, keeping my head down and a half step behind him. I whispered directions. It was not a perfect system, but at least it made it harder for the other servants we encountered to get a good look at my face. Twice, I trod on Heath's heels. At least he did not try to hit me back.

When we reached the corridor where my sister lodged, I nearly collapsed with relief. It might also have had to do with the three flights of stairs and the punishing pace that Heath had set running up them.

"Her room is just down there," I said between puffs of breath.

Heath stepped to the side, positioning himself so he had a view of the narrow corridor as well as the stairwells we'd just climbed. "Go quickly. I'll stand watch."

"You don't have any weapons." Not a world-altering observation. But what would he do if someone did come along? They'd assume he was human by default, but . . .

Heath lifted one finger and pointed down the corridor.

"Fine."

The skirts caught annoyingly on the leather leggings I wore underneath. I supposed that was why the garments weren't usually paired. Silken stockings did better beneath linen shifts. I tugged the garments loose, cursing beneath my breath. When I got back to Pearl House . . .

No more time for distractions.

My mind had tried to avoid it. But now here I was, at her door. *Please, gods, let her be safe. Let me keep her safe.*

Servants were not allowed locks. The door gave way freely under my hand. I swept my eyes over the room, past each of the four narrow beds, trying to temper my disappointment with expectation. It was the wrong time of day to find her here, or any of her roommates. It was good that I did not have to try to explain myself.

A dark head popped up from the side of the farthest bed. The last one.

"Fi," she whispered.

I had all of one heartbeat to take her in, clad in clean but slightly wrinkled clothes from where she'd been sitting on the floor against the bed, a book dangling from her left hand. Then she leaped—right over the bed and into my arms. The book went flying.

"Treasa," I sobbed into her hair, inhaling the familiar, smoky scent of her. No matter how many times she washed it, the scent of fire clung to her silky dark tresses. She'd forever begged me to borrow scented oils from Aurelle. But I'd never smelled anything so perfect in my entire life.

"I knew you weren't dead!" Treasa said against my chest.

"I am not dead," I confirmed. Only a few tears slipped down my cheeks, despite the rapid heaving movements of my chest. I pulled her in a little tighter, blinking away the tears, the room coming back into focus—including the book now on the floor.

"What are you doing . . . Were you studying?" I gasped, pulling back with a hand on each of Treasa's shoulders to get a better look at her and ensure I had not mistaken one of the other firestokers for my sister.

Treasa shrugged. "I figured you would be mad at me if you came home and found I'd fallen behind."

I tugged her tight against me again, still not quite able to believe that she was actually in my arms. But this was not the time to savor it.

I forced myself to pull back again. "This is not our home."

Treasa frowned. "Fionna . . ."

"Do you have the money I saved?"

She nodded, eyes darting back over her shoulder. She must have stashed it somewhere near her bed. "Yes. Evie gave it to me after you disappeared."

And I'd classified Evie as an acquaintance. I moved her firmly into the category of friend.

"Good. Get it, and anything you want to bring that you can shove into your pockets. But we cannot carry any bags." Her eyes widened with every word I said, but I kept going. "We are leaving the castle."

Her eyes were huge now, but after a few fishlike dips of her mouth, open and closed, she nodded. Bringing anything was a risk. But Treasa was a child and less likely to be searched. I did not add anything to my satchel. Still, my heart trembled in my chest.

It took her only a few moments to return from her bedside, pockets hardly showing any difference. I settled her one and only coat over her shoulders. Today might be warm, but I did not know what waited for us on the mainland. That was where we were going. Maybe not today. Maybe not even this week. But I would get her out of Irska. I'd stood over my parents' graves and promised them. Now I would finally make good.

I gave her one last squeeze and steered her toward the door.

Footsteps—heavy. Too heavy for Heath.

I'd left the door open. Stupid fecking mistake. I shoved Treasa away and opened my mouth to order her under the bed, but the door swung inward the rest of the way. It was too late. He'd seen us both.

Blue and white assaulted my vision. A Peace Guard. What the feck was he doing up here?

I dipped my chin by rote. The muscle memory came back with such startling speed, I almost jerked it right back up in reaction. With my head tilted down, I could see the toes of Treasa's boots a few feet behind me to the right.

I lifted my gaze slower than was necessary, but I wanted every advantage I could get, even if it was only a second. First his stubbly double chin, then his mouth and nose, and finally his rheumy brown eyes. A brick of anxiety disintegrated in my chest. I did not know him. Plenty others remained in place. I waited another tense heartbeat. He did not recognize me, either. Thank the fecking gods.

He must have been very junior, new to the ranks of the Peace Guard. The more experienced guards were deployed in the city. He looked me up and down, then lifted his head to see over my shoulder to Treasa. I moved without thinking, trying to shield her from view.

It regained me his attention—and a snarl. "This hallway should be clear."

What did that mean? I'd never heard such a thing in a decade of service in the castle. I'd never even seen a Peace Guard in these hallways before. Their barracks were in a different wing of the castle entirely, and there was no need to patrol servants' quarters.

Until now.

"We heard there was unrest in the city. I came to check on my friend." If he did not know she was my sister, he did not know the potential for leverage.

Where the feck was Heath?

Cold realization froze the blood in my veins, killed the vestiges of warmth that Helio had left behind. Heath was the turncoat I'd seen in my dreams. Had he been the one to pass the plan for the march to the Peace Guards as well? He'd hated me from the beginning. Helio had intervened on my behalf. Oh gods, this was my fault. If Helio had turned me over to the Rebels in the beginning instead of fighting to keep me alive, Heath might never have turned—

"I am not on duty until dark," Treasa said, stepping out from behind me. "I can go where I please."

Gods spare me.

"Treasa." My fingers closed around her arm, but she could still twist away from me if she tried.

"You will do whatever the feck I say." The guard puffed up his chest. He couldn't be much older than Treasa. Sixteen years old, maybe. The minimum age to join the Peace Guard.

They were both children, and acting like children.

I could use that.

"I am expected back in the kitchen. She is coming down with me to provide an extra set of hands. You know what tonight will be like. We cannot afford to lose time to burned cakes."

He did not know what tonight would be like, and that was what I banked on. He was so young and new to the Peace Guard that it was likely he'd never witnessed a celebration of this scale. It was risky, to position myself as the knowledge holder in the dynamic, but if I reminded him enough of his mother, maybe he'd let us pass.

For half a heartbeat, I tasted victory. Then he reached for Treasa.

"You can go. She stays."

I shoved his arm away. "No fecking way . . ."

He swung. But he'd barely begun his Peace Guard training. Helio had been my teacher. His nose crunched brutally beneath the heel of my palm. But before he could spurt blood all over us, he collapsed forward . . .

To reveal Heath, standing behind him with a heavy iron candelabra in his hand.

"I'd have been here sooner, but I had to check three rooms before I found something heavy enough to knock him out." He kicked him in the side for good measure. I wasn't inclined to stop him.

My sister stared up at me like I'd grown a second head. No, I'd just set the one I already had back on correctly.

"Treasa, this is Heath," I said around my wildly beating heart.

"Is he . . . a changeling?" She didn't flinch as she said it. I squeezed her arm.

"Síofran or child of Síofra," Heath corrected. It was missing all the malice he usually directed at me. I started to comment, but he leaned down and dragged the Peace Guard deeper into the room so that the door could close freely. "We don't have time for this."

"No," I agreed, following him into the corridor. I put Treasa's hand in mine and squeezed tight. "We are getting out. Don't let go of my hand."

Helio gave me that exact command the last time I was in the castle. He'd seeped into my consciousness even when I was determined not to think of him.

We retraced our steps. We passed by seven servants in the corridors as we made our way back to the Sea Gate. I counted every one, as well as the beats my heart skipped as they walked away without revealing us.

We were going to do it.

The dreams were just that—dreams. My mind working out the intricacies of what it meant to be human in this never-ending conflict, especially a human helping the Síofran. Of course there were themes of betrayal in my dreams. I'd been grappling with the meaning of the word since my kidnapping.

We paused so that Heath and I could reclaim our cloaks in the antechamber before the courtyard. I flinched at Heath's suggestion that we switch cloaks. Parting with Helio's thick black wool for even a few minutes felt outrageous. But it made sense. The less recognizable we were, the better, and the black cloak was distinctive. A guard noticing a man wearing it instead of a woman might give us the minute we needed to escape into the city.

"You are going to see someone you might remember. But you cannot show your surprise," I whispered to Treasa as I fastened the buttons of the elbow-length scarlet cloak that Heath gave me.

I expected to see confusion in her eyes. They were the dark mirrors of my own. But what I saw instead . . . was hope.

My heart fractured. She did not remember either of them. She'd been a toddler when they died. But there was only one—or rather two—people who could have ignited a spark that bright.

"Not Mother or Father," I said gently, squeezing her shoulder. "I should have said that."

"I am not a child, Fionna," she insisted. But she buried her face in my chest.

Heath gave me a long look over her head. I did not need him to repeat himself. We had no time for emotional breakdowns.

I squeezed my sister back. "Calm face. Just like when you go to stoke a fire and find one of the court ladies doing something ridiculous."

When I pulled away, she wasn't crying. That was enough for now.

On the other side of the courtyard, a bumbling young man chased an escaped chicken. A chambermaid beat a rug against the crenulations that overlooked the courtyard, and a few older men stacked firewood against the wall beneath an overhang where it would stay dry. None of them paid us any attention. We were three first-shift servants, leaving a few minutes early.

Never mind that all shifts worked on feast days. And you were only dismissed early for dire circumstances, usually involving death.

We exited the Sea Gate through the archway, and all that stood between us and freedom was the long, cobbled road and a few Peace Guards, one of whom had already given us aid.

But even now that we were three, we were missing one.

"Where is she?" I asked aloud, whipping my head from side to side in search of Sima's familiar frame.

Heath stepped in front of us, providing cover but also inhibiting my sight. I leaned around him, scanning . . .

"There," he said. I followed the direction of his gaze.

The hedge maze was only knee height, despite more than two years of the master gardener's diligent attention. Only a small section of it was visible from this side of the castle, but it was easy to pick out Sima—and the Peace Guard she spoke to.

"Feck. Where are they coming from? They are all supposed to be deployed in the city," Heath cursed.

I exhaled slowly, counting as I did to try and calm the anxiety lying in wait. "They left behind the junior guards. The newly initiated." In some ways, the most dangerous. Too much power and too little training on how to wield it.

Sima was not speaking to the Peace Guard. She was arguing with him. Yelling. I could see her chest moving.

"We have to intervene," I heard myself say. It didn't feel like I was quite in my body as the words left my lips.

"She knows better than this. Feck," Heath swore again. "Our orders are to get you and Treasa out. Maybe she's causing a distraction so that—"

She swung at him.

I gasped. Or maybe it was Treasa. Heath swore, again.

The Peace Guard didn't bother with any of those responses. He unsheathed his sword and drove it into Sima's gut in one fluid motion. Maybe an initiate guard, but already a skilled one.

She hit her knees. Mine gave out.

Even at a distance, I was certain I saw the light leave her eyes.

Sima was dead.

# Chapter 30

## HELIO

*Taking my oath to the Rebels was the proudest day of my life. No one is there to witness it but you and your commander. You can spend your whole life in the Síofran Rebel Army and never meet a member of the council. But I knew from that moment that I was a part of something important. I sat at dinner that night, my ma on one side, my pa on the other. Paps was upstairs, sleeping. A fireball had wrecked his hearing decades ago. I didn't say anything to my parents. Pa was an oathbound member himself. But we were in different cells. After dinner, I went up to Paps's room and told him all about it. He did not react at all. He couldn't hear a word. But I swear, when I leaned down to kiss him good night, there was pride in his eyes.*

*—Cara Muldoon, Síofran Rebel Army*

The marching route. He had to be moving along the marching route because it was the only thing that made sense. Starting conflicts in other parts of the city would cause distraction and danger. But the fastest way to ensure violence was to concentrate conflict where there were the most people.

But why . . .

Because Peace Guards were the lowest fecking rung of humanity. Most people thought the Defenders were more dangerous. They were certainly wilder. But the Peace Guards were trained to systematically kill my people. They were more successful at it. Defenders mostly got themselves killed.

We'd followed the disappearing Peace Guard for almost an hour before he slipped away again. In that time, he had only stopped to speak to a few fellow guards, all standing menacingly over the marching route. There was lots of shoulder slapping and raucous laughing that belied the tension that permeated the streets. But thus far, no more incidents of violence.

No violence, but the tenor of the crowd had begun to shift the closer we got to the march. There'd never been an event like this in Irska in my lifetime. Maybe there never had been at all. But the march had started over an hour ago, and we were about a third of the way along the route. The marchers would arrive soon. The streets were half full of Síofran, shuffling around, waiting to join the peaceful protest.

I was proud. So fecking proud of my people. Their discontent was palpable. Many had weapons tucked into their belts. But there had been no violence. Even with the Peace Guards lining the route. Maybe Fionna was right. Maybe all the people of Irska truly needed was a chance. If the Síofran could hold the peace, then maybe the humans could, too.

So long as we could figure out what that fecking rogue Peace Guard was up to.

Karine hadn't found us or sent a messenger. She had to be managing her quadrant just fine, then. My focus had to remain here.

A crown of blond hair wove through the crowd ahead of me. Link, returning. We'd parted ways at the last intersection to try to follow the instigator. That had to be his play; otherwise, why was he moving through the city instead of standing in line with his peers?

The sooner we located him—and covertly knocked him out— the better.

Link stumbled to a stop in front of me, his usual grace stolen by the fact that he had to dodge around so many civilians.

He did not waste time on a greeting. "The road is blocked."

"What does that fecking mean?"

"There are too many people. I cannot get through. No one can." He lifted his hands, palms up, in a gesture of defeat. Utterly unacceptable.

How far ahead was the blockage, what was blocking it, who was involved—they were all questions that would take time to answer. Time was the one thing I didn't fecking have.

I stepped free of the crowd, approaching one of the dozens of closed-down businesses that lined the street. I gripped the doorknob until it liquified, the metal melting down the door, taking the locking mechanism with it.

Link's footsteps pounded behind me as I threw open the door and took the stairs two at a time. I cursed the fact that I had to waste time crossing the length of the building to the stairwell at the rear. One flight. Two. There had to be a way up onto the roof.

That took too long to locate, too. But I found the descending staircase where it latched into the ceiling and yanked it down. Less than a minute and we were on the roof, looking out across Irska. The castle was behind me. Fionna was there somewhere. *Safe, she is safe.*

I had to keep the streets quiet so she could make it back to Pearl House. She'd be safe there with Sima and Heath. Heath hated Fionna, and he'd disobeyed orders before. But with Sima there to keep him honest, he would do his part. I had to do mine.

Link saw the barrier before I did.

"They've put down sandbags to stop the march," he said, cursing under his breath. There weren't enough curses in any Irskan language, old or new, to describe the anger that flamed to life inside me.

"And to stop help from getting through," I said through gritted teeth. There were Peace Guards lining the streets beyond the barrier as well. "They are driving us into a dead end."

All the Peace Guards from this side of the barrier to the castle gates were either a distraction or a force meant to dispose of any Síofran who tried to come to the protesters' aid.

Link shook his head slowly. "Why?"

There was only one answer. "To make us easier to kill."

—⁓—

Down to the ground floor, out the back door, and into the alley. The alleys were still deserted. But they wouldn't be for long; not once people started fleeing for their lives in every direction.

We crossed into a Síofran peace village. I knew the layout better here. We could move faster. The blockade was in the next peace village. There were no holes in the walls. The Peace Guard patched them too fast for them to be of any use. But there were ways.

The sewers were too slow. Rooftops it was.

I lost track of Link. He couldn't make the jumps. He didn't have the Firebird lifting his steps. But he'd keep pushing to get through. I'd see him on the other side of whatever awaited us.

I only descended when I reached the other side of the barrier. Up close, it was exactly as Link said. Sandbags, stacked high enough that it would take one man lifting another to his shoulders to climb over. They reached all the way from the city wall to the business on the other side of the street.

My instinct was to pause in the alleyway and take stock of the situation, but there was no time for that.

A line of humans separated the Síofran in the street. It was impossible to tell Defenders from citizens, but they were all yelling.

"Bastard children of Síofra! Where is your blessed goddess now?"

"Go back to your hovels!"

Filth. They spewed filth. And the Peace Guards looked on from atop the embankment, smirking, laughing, weapons in hand. Doing nothing to keep the peace. Any pretenses had fallen away.

"This is our land! You are the invaders!" a Síofran woman yelled. I vaguely recognized her. I thought she might be a Rebel from a different cell.

The street filled quickly, even as I darted to her side. The march was almost here.

"Do not engage with them!" I yelled, not to the humans, but to my own people. "This is a peaceful protest!"

Someone collided with my back. There were too many people. I took a step toward the barrier.

"Disperse! This demonstration is illegal!"

Someone yelled back—many someones. Tracking the voices through the crowd was nearly impossible. Then I saw him.

The Peace Guard I'd chased all over the fecking city.

I would drag him down by the front of that blue-and-white uniform. Use what was left of my accessible magic to force flames down his throat until he burned from the inside out.

But I could not do one fecking thing.

*Yes, you can.*

Her voice echoed in my head. Danced on the flames that rippled inside me.

"Do not fight them!" I yelled.

One of the humans advanced. Then another.

"This is our city, too!" someone at my back yelled. We were retreating without meaning to, to avoid colliding with the line of humans advancing down the embankment.

The Peace Guards stood in place, watching, unmoving. Still brandishing weapons.

A human leaned down and picked up a rock.

Maybe they threw it. Or maybe it was someone else. There was no telling where the first rock came from. Who drew the first blade.

"Stop!" I yelled, but the sound was lost.

A battle cry ripped from the humans. The Síofran woman behind me started to sing, then to scream.

The rest of the marchers were arriving. One person shoved into another. But who had done the shoving? It did not matter. Rocks flew. The man at my shoulder fell to the ground, blood leaking from his temple.

The barrage intensified. Rocks and dirt and then fists and feet. Around me, my people fell. Those that could drew their weapons. The screaming. So much fecking screaming. It was not a protest. This was a riot.

Above it all, the Peace Guards stood in their line. They did not need to intervene. The citizens of Irska were more than willing to tear each other apart.

I was too late. Fionna's hopes, my promises, they dissolved into puddles of blood beneath Irska's sunny skies.

Heath and Sima would get Fionna and her sister out of the castle. Karine had orders—if I did not return, she was to put them on a boat. I'd already paid the captain in the bay for the human passengers. Fleeing Irska wasn't explicitly illegal; it was just expensive as hell. But it was a worthy use of the untouched financial resources my parents had left to me.

Karine would hate my orders, but she'd follow them, even unto my death. We'd all taken our oaths. Now was the time to make good on them.

A rock collided with my head. I drew a dagger from within my leather vest. There would be no more peace in Irska today.

# Chapter 31

## FIONNA

*There are core tenets to our manifesto. In order to be invited to court and recognized as a political entity, we had to codify them. They are fancy words finagled into terms the Irskan king could accept. But they boil down to one essential principle—self-determination. We all want the right to self-determination. That is what the fight is about, as much as magic or its absence. The ability to choose is everything.*

*—Patro Blackburn, Síofran Children*

I was on fire. The flames moved in an undulating dance to the beat of my heart. Each beat, a new color. Red and orange and yellow and then black. Black. Black like death.

Sima was dead.

*Tap. One. Tap. Two. Tap. Three.*

Sima was still dead.

*Tap. Tap. Tap.*

"Fionna, we have to move now."

*Now.*

Now Treasa's hand trembled in mine. She'd never seen anyone die, let alone be senselessly murdered. Her fingers were icicles in my hand.

Now the sun shone down on my face, inexplicably hot for early spring. My fair skin would wear the burns to prove it come tomorrow.

I could not think about tomorrow. First, I had to live through the now.

*Now I have to live.*

I snapped the bindings. Not forever, but for long enough.

My heartbeat slowed, just enough that I could recognize it *was* my heart beating.

"Now," Heath repeated.

Nausea rolled through me, then a spell of dizziness and a sickening twist of both together. It was always like this after the beast of my anxiety attacked. But I didn't have time to linger in it.

Heath started running in the other direction, away from Sima and the Peace Guard who stood over her, watching her die. He trusted I would follow, and he was right. There was one thing more powerful than my anxiety. My love.

I held Treasa's hand as we ran, not for the gate where we'd entered, but to another. Farther. I squeezed her fingers between mine to hold us together as we slowed to a walk so as not to draw attention to ourselves. We walked through first. Heath behind. We left the castle grounds with no trouble. No notice. No Sima.

My heartbeat slowed . . . only to increase again.

The tension on the streets of Irska had changed in the hour we were in the castle. The hopeful anticipation had shifted into something darker. Still anticipation, but darker. Sharper.

"What happened?" I asked Heath.

We'd started at a walk, but the deeper we got into the city the faster his pace. We'd been walking forever. We had to be close to wherever he was taking us.

"Something bad," Heath said.

I knew that. I'd hoped I was wrong.

The next street was familiar. We were only two blocks from Pearl House. Treasa squeaked at the pressure of my hand around hers. I forced myself to loosen it, even as my heart lodged itself in my throat. We were so close, but it took so little for things to go wrong.

There were no Peace Guards here, we weren't along the route of the march. But something was wrong . . .

A distant scream rent the air. Treasa and I both turned, but Heath shoved us forward, hands in the centers of our backs.

"Keep going!" he yelled.

Why was he yelling?

It was the only way to make himself heard. An explosion shook the ground beneath our feet. A fireball. That meant . . .

The march had failed.

The scent of smoke reached us on a spring breeze, a cloud of marring gray carried across the crystalline blue sky. The sky was the same color as Helio's eye. Helio was out in this—wherever that screaming was coming from. Helio was there.

We turned the corner and there was Pearl House, a silent sentinel, waiting inconspicuously in a line of other townhomes. I did not need Heath to tell me what to do now. I ran those last few yards, dragging Treasa with me.

Up the stairs, through the door, expecting Turi, waiting for Nieve, only to find . . .

Silence.

I stumbled over the entryway rug, falling to my knees. Treasa managed to catch herself on the banister at the foot of the stairs. The only sound was our ragged breaths. My own blood pounding in my ears.

Slowly, I spread out my fingers, the texture of the well-worn rug soft beneath them. Even so, I could feel each individual fiber. I inhaled the warm, welcoming scent of Helio's ancestral home. Exhaled. *One. Two. Three.*

I pushed up from my hands, through my knees to stand. Treasa still had her hand on the banister, her eyes wide as she took in the details around her. She had not stepped foot outside of the castle grounds since she was old enough to walk.

Heath lingered by the doors, already locked. They were thick, solid wood. But he stood with his head at the seam where they met, like they might burst open at any moment.

"Is she safe here?" I asked.

Heath turned slowly, blinked slowly. Looked at me like I'd left my mind somewhere out on the street. "It's Pearl House," he said, then added, "It cannot burn."

Helio's power was based in fire and heat. He'd told me. I'd felt it. This was his ancestral home. It made sense that it was impervious to flame. It also meant that it would not burn beneath a fireball explosion, no matter who threw it. Human or Síofran.

But also not the answer to the question I'd asked.

"Helio did not want to leave me here alone. He was afraid that some enterprising Rebel would come and dispose of me." My heart threatened to burst out of my throat. But I kept it inside. "Is she safe here?"

Heath straightened fully. But he did not look at me. His gaze traveled over my shoulder, to where Treasa stood at the foot of the stairs. It softened. So slightly.

It had never occurred to me to ask Heath about his background. Did he have a family . . . a sister or even a daughter close to Treasa's age? His coloring was similar to Turi's. Was he related to Nadia and Moira?

Had he lost that family to Irskan violence?

If I survived—when we survived—I would ask him.

His gaze returned to mine, his chin dipping in acknowledgment. "I will not leave her side."

I bit my lower lip to keep it from trembling as I nodded back. Once slowly, then a second time sharply. I did not let myself nod a third time. This was not the moment to add to my litany of compulsions.

Treasa watched the whole exchange with wide-eyed confusion. But by the time I reached for her, there was understanding in her eyes. And worry. Her head moved from side to side in silent negation.

"The kitchen is in the back. Get food and then go upstairs to the third floor. The room with the table facing the window. That is my room. Go there." The words thickened in my throat. "Heath will stay with you. Do not let him leave your side. Do you understand?"

She wanted to argue. I could see it in her dark eyes, the mirror of my own. But I'd been both mother and sister to her for the past ten years. And after what she'd been through today, she did not have the words. I would pay the price for leaving her here. But my life was a series of calculations. I'd learned to weigh them with emotions.

The guilt I would feel if I did not go to Helio would cripple me forever.

"Where are you going?" Heath asked, even as he moved away from the door to allow me to pass.

"Thank you," I said instead of answering him. "Now give me my cloak."

His eyes rolled skyward, but he unfastened the thick black garment and returned it to me. I passed him back his own.

"He'll kill me for letting you go out there alone," Heath said, shifting a little closer to Treasa. I appreciated the gesture of protection.

"For letting me escape?" I settled the cloak across my shoulders.

"For letting you walk into danger."

"Well, then at least that means he's alive." I slid the final clasp into place. Stroked my fingertips over the embroidered feathers. *Inhale. Exhale.* "I love you, Treasa."

Her knuckles were white where they grasped the banister. "I love you, too."

"I am coming back," I declared. "We are both coming back."

# Chapter 32

## Helio

*There can only be one Firebird. I used to think this thing that slept inside me was a curse. I'd wake in the night, my entire body burning from the heat of it. We talk so often of the absence of our magic, but never about the ways it is still present. Am I the only one who feels it there, waiting? Suppressed, but strong. These gifts from Síofra . . . I know they will one day be free. I know that my son, or daughter, or their child, someday, they will know what it feels like to have those tethers unbound. It wasn't me. It did not happen in my time. I have made my peace with that and with the future. I have no regrets, only a few wishes left unfulfilled. I wish I'd had the chance to fly.*

*—Svetlana Egan, Síofran Rebel Army*

My daggers were gone. Throwing them had been a mistake. Saving the young Síofran woman's life had not. I felt nothing for the human I'd killed. Nor the middle-aged man who'd tried to slit my throat. Or the Defender who came at me with his spiked club.

The shortsword was my least favorite weapon. But it was effective and I was effective with it. I lost count of how many humans I felled. Did not pause long enough to sort the dead from the wounded. I just kept moving. Every blow I endured was one that did not land on my people, too many of whom littered the ground around me.

Link never appeared. I vaguely hoped he was alive. Karine would be devastated by his loss. She'd been nearly out of her mind during his brief stint in Peace Guard custody.

But their names lived in the back of my mind. My heart was full of *her*.

I stabbed another Defender. I saw Fionna leaning against the wall outside the dungeons, shaking, lost in the throes of her anxiety.

I ducked to avoid a rock flying through the air. She was there, her lips pressed against the hollow of my throat while her hands tugged my head back, her fingers tangled in my hair.

Another step back, blocking off an alleyway so that Síofran protesters could run for their lives, run to fight another day. The scent of her skin, warm with a mixture of jasmine and spice, lingered in my senses.

Stab. Duck. Step.

Again and again, for as long as it took.

She appeared so suddenly, I thought my mind had conjured her. I'd swallowed too much blood, taken too many blows to the head. But she strode toward me, kicking aside an attacker, all flesh and blood and ire.

"Karine!"

She knelt down, clasping her hand with mine and pulling me up to stand. I did not even remember how I'd ended up on the ground.

"Helio," she exhaled, pulling me into a tight hug I would not have accepted from many others. "You're here. You're alive."

I pulled away first, checking her for wounds. Blood matted her golden braid, but she appeared unhurt. "How did you end up here? What is happening in the northeastern quadrant?"

Her eyes were hard. "This—this is happening. It's happening everywhere." She paused, both of us moving to defend against an attack. Fighting back to back, like we had many times before. Our attackers hit the ground. She spun back to face me. "Peace is a lie. A foolish dream."

Maybe.

But what would have happened if the Peace Guards had not instigated the violence? Encouraged the Defenders? Blocked the road?

It was not a debate to have here, now, fighting for our lives.

"Karine, you have to go," I said over my shoulder, both of us engaged again. "You have to get Fionna out of the city."

She yelled something back, but I could not hear it over the roar in my ears. I thrust my knee up into the groin of the man I fought. He dropped to the ground, my boot connected with his face. He rolled away, leaving the way clear.

"Now you'll join the fight, you fecking coward?" I snarled.

There was not a single drop of blood on his pristine blue-and-white uniform. He'd watched the people of Irska tear each other apart from safety. I would let myself savor these next few minutes.

I lost myself in the tearing of flesh and the spraying of blood. One of his teeth came away in my knuckles when I punched him. Where he was going, there was no need for chewing. He was well trained, all Peace Guards were. But they were unimaginative. I didn't know what they did in their barracks, but I'd spent more than thirty years lying awake at night imagining new ways to punish the humans for what they'd done to my people.

I loved a human.

But this man had betrayed the cause she believed in. He would fecking die for it.

There she was again. Her scent, her voice, her face. How strange that she kept appearing to me, a creature of peace amid all this violence.

"Helio!" She grabbed my arm.

My entire body reacted, the creature inside me screeching. Not in protest, in satisfaction. But my mind did not agree.

"Fionna—you cannot be here." I shook her away without thinking, my body reacting viscerally to her presence.

Her gaze collided with mine, her attention narrowed on me to the exclusion of all else. "I got my sister out already."

I gripped her arm with the same intensity as the terror sinking its claws into my chest. "You are supposed to get out. Both of you. Out of Irska."

She blinked as the understanding took hold. I hadn't told her that before, when I'd sent her to retrieve her sister. I'd foolishly hoped for the chance to say goodbye. But now . . . Fionna blinked, her head slowly turning to take in the rest of the scene around us.

We were pressed up against an alley—where she'd come from, I realized. She'd seen Síofran running for their lives, and instead of joining them, she'd run to me.

Fecking hell.

She stumbled back a few steps, her eyes blowing wide as she took in the carnage in the street.

"Helio . . ." She said my name again, this time a whisper that I felt even if I could barely hear it. A prayer for salvation from this hell.

I had no answer for her. No defense for the violence. I would not apologize for defending my people. But there was no hate in her eyes, and I knew its contours well. The fighting raged around us, but for a few heartbeats, everyone was engaged and Irska forgot about us.

Fionna took a step forward. Toward the fighting. Unacceptable—

"I know him."

My blade drooped. "Him?" I pointed the tip at the Peace Guard, half conscious on the ground.

Fionna's pale skin was whiter than I'd ever seen it, even when in the grips of panic. I expected her to start shaking, but her body was still, even as her words quivered.

"I . . . I saw him in my dreams," she said. "He was meeting with . . . you."

Oh, Síofra, what had happened to her in the castle? Had she taken a blow to the head as well? Was she even seeing clearly? Then how had she managed to find me?

But Fionna was not looking at me. She stared past me, to my oldest friend. The orphan who'd grown up at my side, played hide-and-seek in my parents' house.

"Why would Karine meet with a Peace Guard?"

My hand tightened around the shortsword, the rest of my muscles rising to taut attention, protesting the absurdity of it. Fionna had never lied to me.

Fionna shook her head like she was trying to clear it.

"She was passing them information. You told them about the march. You . . ." Her words trailed off, eyes getting wider by the second. I fought the urge to reach for her, worried it would break her stream of thought as she sorted things out. "She told me everything was about to change. This—she meant this."

This. The peaceful march turned riot. The carnage. The bodies of Síofran and humans that littered the street.

Fionna's dark eyes were hard as onyx. There was more than hatred there. Rage and betrayal kept grim company.

"You saw her giving information to the Peace Guards in your dreams," I repeated. I could not have heard her right. My ears were still ringing from a blow to my head sometime in the last hour.

"Yes." There was no tremor in her voice. No uncertainty.

For Fionna to see something in her dreams, but to know that it was not imagination, that it was true, with that much certainty . . . there was only one explanation. Magic.

She was human. It was impossible.

But the hate in her eyes was more visceral that any she'd ever pointed at me. For once, she was the one emanating heat, and I was the one drawn to it.

My feet remained rooted to the spot, my mind and heart unable to reconcile. The demands of the moment, my aching limbs, the ever-present danger now too close to the woman I loved . . . Those demands pushed my denials about magic to the back of my consciousness.

"Karine." My voice did not sound like my own. It was too vulnerable to belong to me.

She did not look at Fionna, not even to return her hate. She appealed directly to me.

"This does change everything," Karine said, rocking forward. "Now that we know peace is not a way forward, we can focus on obliterating the humans, as we should have done centuries ago."

That wasn't an admission.

"You conspired with humans," a voice that could not have belonged to me said.

I waited for her to refute it.

"Oh, stop blubbering," she spat at the Peace Guard at our feet. She knelt down long enough to slit his throat.

His blood was on her hands as she straightened. "I did what was necessary for our people, Helio. For the cause. We took oaths to fight for the children of Síofra. To free magic. We cannot do that while there are still humans in Irska."

We had taken oaths. But part of that oath was obeying superiors, acting as part of a cell. Karine had betrayed that oath. Did it matter what her reasons were?

Fionna stood frozen just outside the entrance to the narrow alley. Karine had her back to the street. But who would attack her? She was a Síofran. She'd made a deal with the humans.

I could see Fionna's mind at work. But she did not open her mouth to argue, to justify or eviscerate. She could have done either with that razor-sharp mind of hers. But I understood why she kept her own counsel. This was my decision. My moment to sort out. My personal definition of right and wrong.

"You disrupted a peaceful Síofran demonstration. Aligned yourself with Peace Guards. Caused the deaths of . . . I don't know yet how many of our own people. For what, Karine?"

The conviction in her face cracked for the first time. "To motivate you and the rest of the council. You are the fecking—"

"I know what I am." I stepped away from her. I stepped to Fionna's side. "But you clearly do not."

My hand found Fionna's, drawn by a current of heat, our fingers sliding together. The answer to a question that my soul had been asking since the moment I was born.

Sudden warmth flooded my veins. My entire body burst into flames. I stared down at my hands, expecting to see fire.

I was not disappointed.

Golden flames encircled my fingers, wreathed my wrists, danced up my arms. It burned, but not to sear or to melt. It burned with magic. And Fionna's fingers, still entangled with mine, did not burn at all.

Blinding pain seared up my back. Not pain—more heat, now a thousand times more intense. I dropped Fionna's hand, determined not to burn her with whatever this was. Even as I knew. I knew what this was.

Children of Síofra could access small magics if there was enough of us united in common purpose. Fionna was not human, and this was not small magic.

But what united us went beyond common purpose. It was forged in our souls, deeper than an agreement about war or peace. There was no greater unity than love.

Wings of flame ripped from my back, illuminating the entire street in an unearthly glow. But the transformation did not end there. The creature inside me ripped loose from three hundred years of bindings. Talons speared from my knuckles, my neck elongated, the shape of my body shifted.

I was no longer a Síofran man. I was a child of Síofra. The first child of Síofra.

The Rebels had honed me into a weapon, but Fionna saw me for what I was. She saw the truth beneath my skin that I'd spent a lifetime trying to deny.

The last thing I saw with my own eyes was Fionna. My last thought was that maybe now she would understand.

For the first time in three hundred years, a child of Síofra had accessed their full power. The love of the woman at my side had awoken what three hundred years of oppression had kept sleeping.

The Firebird was free.

# Chapter 33

## FIONNA

*Magic fell and we had nothing, no way to defend ourselves against the humans. Some of us had small magics. More gained them, as time went on and our souls began to heal. We began experimenting with fire. The saying goes that so long as two Síofran hearts beat, magic will never truly be gone. But that is a mistranslation of the original Old Irskan text. The words are close, and the verb order is variable in the old language. Mistakes are more common than accurate translations, these days. There are so few of us who can read Old Irskan anymore. But I taught the phrase to my grandchildren—correctly. When two hearts beat as one, then magic shall truly be freed. At least someone in this generation will know it.*

*—Madja Zolkov, Síofran Rebel Army*

He shot into the sky, a creature of such majesty and terrible beauty that watching him almost hurt. But it had always been that way with Helio. The feelings growing between us were painful and beautiful and inescapable. Just like this moment.

A moment that would change everything, but not in the way that Karine had thought.

Helio was not just important to the Síofran rebellion. He was the heart of it. The symbol of peace, the harbinger of hope as old as Irska itself.

The Firebird had returned.

Wings had ripped from his back, iridescent red that alternated gold and dusky orange as he arced overhead . . . The feathers now covered his entire body. His entire form was different, molded into the shape of the legendary Firebird.

It was impossible. They only existed in drawings, paintings, Old Irskan texts, and children's bedtime stories. Yet there he was. He'd held my hand, wreathed it in flame, and yet all I'd felt was pleasant warmth.

His magic was more than fire. Just like Helio. I almost laughed at the absurdity of the question I'd asked him all those weeks ago.

He was so much more than I'd ever imagined.

Far above, a screech echoed through the sky. I must have been able to hear it because of . . . because it was silent.

I could not tear my eyes from him. But around me . . . not a single body moved. Not a single word was spoken. All the fighting had stopped.

For one too-brief heartbeat, he blocked out the sun entirely. The sky darkened from crystalline to deep, royal blue. Bright golden light outlined every feather, the rippling flames that emanated from him leaving streaks of luminous fire in the darkened sky.

As one, Irska inhaled. Every breath caught in its throat, every heart given pause.

No one could raise a weapon in the presence of the Firebird, the emissary of peace and hope sent to our world by Síofra herself.

A warm breeze wrapped around me as he circled, lower and lower with each pass. His flames brushed the rooftops, but no fire started. There were gasps of awe. I thought I heard the sound of someone nearby quietly weeping.

He shifted in the air, the feathers burning away to reveal the familiar lines of his body as he swept down into the street. The crowd parted, giving him plenty of room. But there was no fear on their faces. Only shock and reverence. The Firebird was nothing short of a holy visitation, and Irska was suddenly a city of believers.

I had not doubted him, not from the first day when he promised to keep me from harm at all hands but his own.

He landed in a blaze befitting the Firebird, the wings of flame still intact. I did not recall taking the steps or whether he closed the distance. Only that I was in his arms the instant he touched the ground, my fingers splaying up over his back, suddenly smooth again, the glorious wings of flame gone as suddenly as they'd appeared.

Warmth engulfed me, heat spreading through my chest and into my limbs until they were nothing but extensions of my beating heart. Helio's hands encircled my waist, tugging me in tighter against him—

"Fionna!"

Cold everywhere. The heat of Helio was ripped from my body, leaving behind an ache and a rush of feelings just as intense.

Frigid fingers gripped my upper arm, dragged me backward. I twisted, determined to get myself free.

"Fionna, stop fighting! It's me! It is Garen! You know me!"

The words made no sense, but the voice was vaguely familiar. I stopped fighting long enough to get a clear view, blinking rapidly, not believing what I saw.

A uniform of blue and white. A familiar face, a too-familiar hand closing around my upper arm, the other gripping my shoulder.

"Fionna," he said for the third time, shaking me a little too hard.

I recognized his face. Once, he'd been my friend. Then, briefly, my lover. And finally a Peace Guard. My stomach turned.

Garen tugged me against him, hugging me tight. I did not fight him.

"I cannot believe I am the one who rescued you," he said into my hair.

A shiver snaked down my spine. Unpleasant and unwelcome. How could this go on for so long, how had Helio allowed—

Our eyes met over Garen's shoulder. One as blue as the sky over-head. The other the color of citrine, striated with gold that perfectly matched the flames that had encircled our joined hands.

We only had a second, but a second was all it took. I did not flinch away from the intensity of his gaze, nor from the choices I saw there. I'd kept my silence while Karine showed the depths of her betrayal and let Helio make his own judgment.

This decision was mine.

One word, one look, and I would be back in Helio's arms. I would be free—not just of Garen's hold. Treasa waited at Pearl House. We had the money I'd saved. Helio had planned our escape. The Rebels could not ignore the request of the Firebird. A word was all it would take, and Treasa and I would be free of Irska forever. My sister would be safe.

Or I could choose to stay. Turi's suggestion at Pearl House had ter-rified me. But the world was different. I was different. Treasa would be safe with Helio. The Rebel council was right—Irska could not continue as it had for the last three centuries, especially now that the Firebird had been freed. True peace would require work . . . and sacrifice.

I could allow Garen to rescue me, return me to the castle. And I could tear down the human regime that had oppressed the Síofran for three hundred years from the inside. I could find out the names of every Peace Guard who had conspired with Karine. I could fight.

I held Helio's gaze, losing myself in it. There were no calculations to make. This decision came from my heart.

And I had no doubts as I made it.

# GLOSSARY

## *HUMANS*

***The Irskan***–The ruling class of Irska, including the King of Irska, the royal family, and human nobles

***Peace Guard***–The Crown-sanctioned force tasked with controlling the changelings and keeping peace in Irska

***Irska Defense Force: "Defenders"***–Human paramilitary group that works outside of the Crown but are rarely punished for violating Irskan law

## *CHILDREN OF SÍOFRA—"CHANGELINGS"*

***Síofran Rebel Army: "Rebels"***–Highly organized and most active Síofran paramilitary group operating in Irska

***Síofran Liberation Corps: "Libs"***–More violent and erratic Síofran paramilitary group operating in Irska

***Síofran Children***–Nonviolent Síofran political group with presence in the Irskan court

***Republic of Eerin***–Neighboring Síofran free territory that occupies the majority of the Isle of Eerin

# ACKNOWLEDGMENTS

More than two years ago, I sat down before vacation and started loading up my Kindle with e-books. After downloading a slew of beach reads, I texted my long-time best friend Nicole for nonfiction recommendations (she insists that she does not read nonfiction, and yet she is responsible for my two favorite nonfiction reads of the last decade). At her urging, I added Patrick Radden Keefe's *Say Nothing* to my vacation TBR. If you've read it, you know what I mean when I say I was *obsessed*. If you haven't, you have a new directive. I ate up the chilling recounting of the Irish Troubles and spent many late nights googling news articles and researching. And through it all, I kept thinking, What if this was fantasy? So my dearest college-roommate-turned-bridesmaid, best friend, and found family, thank you for the book recommendation.

This story would not have come to page so soon if not for the work and encouragement of my agent, Amanda Jain. Thank you for taking a chance on me and for championing my work so fully. Also, thank you for challenging my creativity and pushing me to write something other than fae. You were right.

Thank you to Elizabeth Agyemang at 47North, for immediately "getting" this story. You understood the vision for Fionna and Helio's world and your feedback only made it better. Your communication, support, and vision for this book have been monumental.

Thank you to Lindsey Faber for the pages of thoughtful feedback and encouragement. The romance and banter in this book are so much stronger because of your insights and gentle pushes.

A most heartfelt thank-you to the readers who have come along with me on this author journey, and most especially to those of you who've been with me since *Crown of Earth and Sky*. Your reviews and posts encouraged me to keep going in a new genre that demanded but also gave me more than I ever expected.

Finally, thank you to my husband, Bryan. Thank you for seamlessly taking over our life when I disappear into my writing cave. Thank you for not only listening to me talk about my dream to write a book on that winding road trip in Hawai'i nearly a decade ago but also for pushing me to actually publish that book (and twenty more). Thank you for being mine.

And always, thank you to E. You are my motivation. You made me brave enough to chase my dreams.

# ABOUT THE AUTHOR

*Photo © 2021 Stacey Feasel*

Emberly Ash is the author of the Secrets of the Faerie Crown series and The Covenants of Velora series. She stole her first romance novel off her mom's bookshelf at the age of ten and never looked back. The author of eighteen romance books under her first pen name, Emberly craved something darker and steamier—enter the world of fantasy romance. Her books are dark, twisty, and not for the faint of heart. In the real world, she manages a fire-breathing seven-year-old and a grumpy mage of a husband. But you'll most often find her in her hot-pink writing cave, dreaming up your next book boyfriend. Spoiler alert: He's fae. For more information, visit www.emberlyash.com.